# skeleton lake

## also by mike doogan

*Lost Angel*

*Capitol Offense*

G. P. PUTNAM'S SONS

*New York*

# skeleton lake

a nik kane alaska mystery

MIKE DOOGAN

G. P. PUTNAM'S SONS
*Publishers Since 1838*
Published by the Penguin Group
Penguin Group (USA) Inc., 375 Hudson Street, New York, New York 10014, USA • Penguin Group
(Canada), 90 Eglinton Avenue East, Suite 700, Toronto, Ontario M4P 2Y3, Canada (a division of
Pearson Canada Inc.) • Penguin Books Ltd, 80 Strand, London WC2R 0RL, England • Penguin
Ireland, 25 St Stephen's Green, Dublin 2, Ireland (a division of Penguin Books Ltd) • Penguin
Group (Australia), 250 Camberwell Road, Camberwell, Victoria 3124, Australia (a division
of Pearson Australia Group Pty Ltd) • Penguin Books India Pvt Ltd, 11 Community Centre,
Panchsheel Park, New Delhi–110 017, India • Penguin Group (NZ), 67 Apollo Drive, Rosedale,
North Shore 0632, New Zealand (a division of Pearson New Zealand Ltd) • Penguin Books
(South Africa) (Pty) Ltd, 24 Sturdee Avenue, Rosebank, Johannesburg 2196, South Africa

Penguin Books Ltd, Registered Offices:
80 Strand, London WC2R 0RL, England

Library of Congress Cataloging-in-Publication Data

Doogan, Mike.
Skeleton Lake : a Nik Kane Alaska mystery / Mike Doogan.
p.      cm.
ISBN-13: 978-0-399-15492-8
1. Kane, Nik (Fictitious character)—Fiction.   2. Private investigators—Alaska—Fiction.
3. Alaska—Fiction.   4. Police—Crimes against—Fiction.   I. Title.
PS3604.O5675S58      2008                    2008018589
813'.6—dc22

Printed in the United States of America
1   3   5   7   9   10   8   6   4   2

BOOK DESIGN BY MEIGHAN CAVANAUGH

This is a work of fiction. Names, characters, places, and incidents either are the product of the author's imagination or are used fictitiously, and any resemblance to actual persons, living or dead, businesses, companies, events, or locales is entirely coincidental.

While the author has made every effort to provide accurate telephone numbers and Internet addresses at the time of publication, neither the publisher nor the author assumes any responsibility for errors, or for changes that occur after publication. Further, the publisher does not have any control over and does not assume any responsibility for author or third-party websites or their content.

*To Peggy, Pat, Reenie, Dan, and Kathy,*
*who taught me everything I know*
*about brothers and sisters*

# acknowledgments

As always, I want to acknowledge the assistance of my wife, Kathy; my agent, Marcy Posner; and my editor, Tom Colgan. To Marcy, in particular, I can honestly say, I'd never have written this book without you.

skeleton lake

one

Listen: Billy Pilgrim has come unstuck in time.

—KURT VONNEGUT

## MARCH 2007

*Lights. Siren. Voices.*

Christ, I can't find a vein. He's too shocky. They've all taken a dive.

Drill harder. If we don't get fluids into him, he's not going to make it.

*Sharp pain.*

Damn, I lucked into one.

"What's happened to Danny? Is Danny okay?"

God, he's a mess. How can he still be talking?

Is he going to make it?

I don't know. Maybe God knows. Maybe nobody knows.

*The last words stretch and bend into the silence.*

Noobooodyyyy knooowwwwssssss.

two

Life is all memory, except for the one present moment that
goes by you so quickly you hardly catch it going.

—TENNESSEE WILLIAMS

## SEPTEMBER 1985

"Nobody knows what he was doing up here," Jackie Dee said, taking
a long drag on his cigarette. "When the kids found him, there was no
one else in sight."

Kane looked at the crime scene. The little clearing on the shore
of the lake was crawling with cops, maybe a dozen uniforms milling
around like some Little League team at its first practice, a clutch of
suits getting wetter and wetter. Parked cars pointed in every direction, and some of their headlights lit up the wet, slick ground around
the body, where Kane could see a regiment's worth of footprints rap-
idly filling with rain.

"Jesus, Jackie, did every one of these fucking idiots have to check
for vitals?" he said. "This circus isn't going to leave enough evidence
to stick in your eye."

Detective Sergeant Giuseppe Donatello DiSanto—"Call me Jackie

Dee, everybody does"—nodded and flicked his cigarette butt away into the night, away from where the body lay.

"Too right, kid," he said, "but Fireball there broadcast an 'officer down' and every unit in town came screaming out here. Plus those yahoos"—he pointed at the suits—"who were getting loaded at the Roadhouse. What can you do?"

Not a goddamn thing, Kane thought. Bad enough to get a dead cop as my first murder case, but this is a cluster fuck, pure and simple.

"Better save what we can," Jackie Dee said. He walked over to the nearest unit and flipped its mic to PA.

"Listen up," he said, his booming, metallic voice knifing through the hubbub. "Everybody who is not investigating this homicide will immediately vacate the area, taking care to disturb the crime scene as little as possible. Not that that will make any difference now."

The cops all stopped moving and turned to look at Jackie Dee.

"Wait a minute," one of the suits said, "I'm the ranking officer here…"

Jackie Dee's amplified voice cut him off.

"This is a crime scene," he said. "My partner and I are the investigating officers. If you guys don't beat it, I'm going to start taking names, and you can explain to the chief why you were out past midnight fucking up the investigation of a slain police officer. I need Fireball to stay, and whoever was next on the scene. And Harry and Larry, stick around and help with the crime scene. Everybody else, get lost."

The crowd began to break up, the uniforms tiptoeing to their units like mice trying to creep past a sleeping cat, being careful way too late. Kane walked over to where Jackie Dee was talking with a slightly unsteady bald guy in a black raincoat.

"Honest to God, Lieutenant," Jackie Dee was saying, "if we need anything at all from admin, I'll call you personally."

A couple of the bald man's buddies led him off.

"Christ," Jackie Dee said, "the admin lieutenant. Do you know how you get to be admin lieutenant, kid?"

Kane shook his head. He had an idea, but Jackie Dee wasn't a guy who liked to be interrupted.

"Admin lieutenant requires two—count 'em, two—qualifications," he said, holding up two fingers. "First"—he folded down his index finger, leaving his middle finger sticking up—"first, you got to be a Grade A brownnoser. That's how you get to be a lieutenant. Second"—he folded his middle finger to make a fist—"you got to fuck up every other assignment so bad they won't trust you with nothing but paper until you get your gold watch."

Jackie Dee shook his fist at the admin lieutenant's back.

"And Barnes there has those qualifications, in spades," he said.

Kane didn't say anything. For one thing, he supposed Jackie Dee was right. He hadn't seen anything in ten years on the force to prove him wrong, anyway. For another, Jackie Dee had more than a decade's seniority, which made him the senior partner on their two-man team. For a third, Jackie Dee was as wide as he was tall, and he probably went six foot four. He was fat, it was true, but not that fat. All in all, not a guy Kane wanted to be contradicting.

"Okay," Jackie Dee said, "they teach you anything about what we do now?"

Kane laughed.

"Teach me anything?" he said. "This is Anchorage, remember?"

Jackie Dee nodded. The Anchorage Police Department was modernizing, but the process was slow, and the department was still dominated by men who'd been chosen for their size and availability rather than their skill or intelligence.

"But I did do some reading," Kane said. "I know a guy with the FBI, and he gave me some manuals."

Jackie Dee looked at Kane with mock respect.

"Reading, huh?" he said. "Maybe I should try that."

"Hey," Kane said, but Jackie Dee held up a hand.

"Don't take it personal, kid," he said. "I'm not at my best after midnight. Or at cop killings." He stopped and took a couple of breaths. "So what do the manuals tell you?"

"They say to keep the crime scene intact," Kane said. "Little late for that. Anyway, photograph everything. Medical examiner. Transport. Divide into quadrants. Search for clues. Witness interviews."

Jackie Dee was nodding by the time he finished.

"That's the stuff," he said. "I don't suppose those manuals told you that on cold, wet nights, the new guy does all the crime scene stuff and the senior detective gets into a warm unit that damn-sure better have some hot coffee in it and does the initial interviews. Did they?"

"No," Kane said with a laugh, "but I'm not surprised to hear it."

Jackie Dee walked to where a cop in a black rain slicker stood.

"Where're the kids found the body?" he asked.

The cop pointed at a police cruiser. Jackie Dee walked over and climbed in.

Kane pulled his raincoat tighter around him as the police photographer worked his way around the body, his strobe throwing harsh light over the mortal remains of Danny Shirtleff.

"Hey, careful not to step on anything," Kane called.

The crime scene photographer, a skinny, long-haired, bearded number named Murphy, stopped shooting long enough to give Kane a disgusted look.

"Who do y'spose has been to the most scenes, pal?" he called back, and returned to taking photographs.

Well, Kane thought, that's one of the reasons I became a detective. Respect.

The body lay just outside the open door of a fire-engine-red Corvette Stingray, just off the muddy road that ran halfway around the small lake. The clearing appeared to be a long-abandoned homesite. The ground was littered with rotting twine tied to pegs that had fallen over, and a pile of lumber nearly overgrown with brush sat to one side. There didn't seem to be any homes nearby.

Development probably stopped dead in its tracks by the housing slump that had followed a big drop in oil prices, Kane thought. Oil was what kept the Alaska economy going, and the fortunes of Alaskans rose and fell with every shift in its value.

Kane could see two or three lights from inhabited houses, none of them close. He'd have to knock on those doors, but he didn't expect much.

"All done," the photographer called.

Kane nodded.

"Can you print those PDQ?" he asked.

"I know the drill," Murphy said. "The prints'll be on your desk in the ay em."

"Thanks," Kane said. He walked to a nearby car, extracted the medical examiner, and walked him forward. The ME was a crotchety old GP named Owens whose humor wasn't improved by the rain, the cold, or the late hour. Kane did his best to keep the old man from further wrecking the crime scene, if that was possible.

Danny Shirtleff lay on his back, large, dark eyes staring up into the rain, one expensive-looking brown loafer nearly twisted off by the turning of his body under the impact of bullets. His dark, curly hair was speckled with mud, as was the right side of his face. The ME knelt next to the body and placed two fingers on Shirtleff's neck. Then he shifted them to hover beneath Shirtleff's nose. After a moment, he said, "No pulse. No respiration. I'm pronouncing him at"—he looked at the gold watch on his wrist—"twelve thirty-seven a.m., September—what is it now, the twelfth?—September the twelfth." He looked up at Kane. "You getting this, kid?"

Kane took a small leather notebook out of his shirt pocket. The notebook was a gift from Laurie to mark his transfer to the detective squad. It came with a little gold pen that fit through a loop in the leather and several replacement pads of paper. Kane could tell the moment he saw it how impractical it was, but it was a gift from his wife after a pretty rough patch in their marriage and he was going to use it. He wrote the date at the head of the page, then the ME's name and the time of death, ignoring the drops of rain that tried to wash away the ink.

"Gonna give me a cause?" Kane asked the ME, who had unbuttoned Shirtleff's blood-soaked shirt.

"Looks like three in the pump," the ME said, "but I won't say for sure until I get him on the table. Nice tight pattern, though."

"Hey, Doc, it's a fellow officer," Kane said.

"Maybe to you," the ME said, "but it's just another body to me. That way, I don't lose my perspective. You'll be smart to do the same, kid."

That was one "kid" too many for Kane.

"I'm thirty-six fucking years old," he said. "I'm no kid."

The ME gave a snort.

"Whatever you say, kid," he said. "You going to accompany the body?"

"We'll send a uniform," Kane said. "I've got work to do here."

"Your call," the ME said. "I'll get right to him. I know how you guys are when it's one of yours."

The "officer down" call had brought out the paramedics from the nearest firehouse, and Kane watched as they wrestled Shirtleff's body onto a stretcher and carted it back to their vehicle. He followed the stretcher as far as the unit Jackie Dee sat in and knocked on the window. Jackie Dee rolled it down, and a blast of heated air rolled out. He stuck a hand out, palm up.

"Still raining, eh?" he said with a grin. "And cold, too."

"I need a uniform to ride with the body and observe the autopsy," Kane said, "unless you want to do it, or shift your fat ass out here and secure the scene while I do it."

Jackie Dee laughed.

"So," he said, "you do have an attitude. That'll work for you. Give me a minute to talk to Buck there, and we'll send him with the body. If you two don't mind waiting a little longer?"

The boy and girl sitting in the back of the cruiser shook their heads. They looked to be high schoolers and excited about the story they'd have to tell their friends. Jackie Dee shut off a portable tape recorder that lay on the front seat, got out of the unit, and walked over to a cop in a slicker, who leaned against the front of another blue-and-white. They talked for a few moments, and the cop in the slicker walked over and got into the paramedics' truck. The cop, Buck Adams, was a big, blocky, sandy-haired youngster, a newbie, and Kane couldn't tell if sending him back with the corpse was just Jackie Dee hazing the kid. But somebody had to go, and if you didn't develop a thick skin you didn't last very long as a cop.

"Roust Harry and Larry out of their cars and work the scene," Jackie Dee said, "for all the good that's going to do us. The stuff's in my trunk. Here're the keys."

Kane opened the trunk of Jackie Dee's car, a tricked-out Trans Am that must have been hairy to drive in the winter. He removed the crime scene kit, then went and knocked on the window of a brand-new black Ford Taurus that sat pumping gray exhaust into the air.

"I'll need some help," he said when Detective Harry Callaghan rolled down the window. Callaghan and his partner, Larry Camp-bell, had been the first full-time detectives the department had ever had and, in Jackie Dee's estimation, delivered that morning in the cubicle he and Kane shared, weren't competent "to investigate their own dicks."

"C'n you an' me do it?" Callaghan asked. "Larry's sleepin'."

Kane could hear the booze in the other detective's voice.

"You sober enough to help?" he asked.

"Fuck you, kid," Callaghan said.

"Look," Kane said, "no offense. But this scene's already a mess, and I don't need you to make it worse."

Callaghan threw his door open, forcing Kane to jump back, and got out of the car. He stood there weaving for a moment, then took a deep breath and seemed to get himself under control.

"I'm a better detective drunk than you are sober, you little prick," he said.

Kane let that go and walked over to what was left of his crime scene. He took pegs and twine from the kit, and he and Callaghan laid out a grid that ran the length of the Corvette and to about ten feet out from it. Kane drew the grid on a sheet of his notebook and numbered the squares, starting at the front of the sports car and working down, then out. He took a flashlight out of the kit and started on square A-1.

"Hey, I ain't getting down in that muck," Callaghan said. "I got good clothes on."

Kane waved him away. He had good clothes on, too. When Jackie Dee told him on the telephone that the call out was an officer down, he'd thought the brass might show up, so he'd chosen a suit over the jeans and sweater that would have been much more practical. He wouldn't make that mistake again.

The phone had awakened him from a sound sleep. He'd tried to get it before it woke Laurie, who was, as usual during one of her pregnancies, moody as a movie star. He didn't blame her, really, but he never knew exactly what he'd be dealing with. That's why he'd come right home from work to give the girls their baths rather than going out to celebrate his first day as a detective.

"Who the hell is that at this hour?" she snarled as he put the phone back and swung his legs out of the bed. "Some of your friends at a bar want you to come out and play?"

"No," he said with a patience he didn't really feel. He took a clean shirt from a hanger and swung his arms into it. "That's my new partner. There's been a shooting of some sort, and we've got the duty."

Laurie sat up in the bed, struggling to do so despite her already-sizeable belly.

"Fine," she said, "you're just going to leave me in the middle of the night? You said you'd change your ways."

Kane did up his belt and reached for his suit coat.

"I have changed my ways," Kane said, adding a silent "somewhat." "But this is work, Laurie."

He shoved his wallet into his back pocket, slipped his new gold shield in an inside coat pocket, and clipped his service .38 to his belt. "It's the job."

She lay down and turned her back to him, and he left without another word.

Had she seemed more irritable than usual? Kane couldn't tell. He shook his head to drive the thoughts from his mind so he could concentrate on the scene. What he really wanted to do was stop for a smoke, but he didn't want another cigarette butt polluting the scene. Besides, if Laurie smelled it on him he might get another lecture about quitting. As her pregnancy had progressed, the lectures about his bad habits had gotten more frequent.

At some point he heard a car door close, some voices, and the sound of several cars leaving. But he stuck to his examination. He'd already marked the location of the discarded gun and the shell casings, duck-walking for a while, then dropping to his knees to give his thighs a rest.

"Which one's this?" Jackie Dee asked, pointing at the top, outside square.

"A-10," Kane said, and the big man got down on his knees and began examining the square with a flashlight.

Kane's watch read three a.m. when they finished. The knees of his pants were soaked through, and rivulets of rainwater ran from his hair and down his back inside his shirt. He got wearily to his feet, and Jackie Dee did the same. They took evidence bags from the crime scene kit and put in their haul: a semiautomatic handgun, seven shell casings, a soggy cigarette butt, pieces of broken beer bottles and what looked like a roach from a marijuana joint, a candy bar wrapper, a well-chewed pencil stub, and two used condoms.

"Not much," Jackie Dee said when they finished labeling the bags. "Footprints won't do us any good. Neither will tire treads. We'll have the car towed to the shop and have it gone over, but unless we get really lucky, or the shooter was really careless, the physical evidence won't do us much good. Especially since the top's down and it's been raining all over the interior for hours."

Kane made a note to check when the rain had started.

The sound of an engine gave way to headlights.

"That'll be the tow truck," Jackie Dee said. "I'll wait until he gets it on the hook and follow him in to the shop. You go dry out and get a few hours' sleep. We'll meet at Leroy's at, say, ten a.m.? Go over our notes and try to figure out what to do next. I told Fireball to come into the shop for his statement about eleven-thirty. I already took one from the kids who found the body. I'll type it up and get them to sign it tomorrow."

Kane nodded and trudged to his car, trying without success to keep his legs from rubbing against the cold, slimy legs of his trousers. Unlike every other idiot on the force who'd come sightseeing, he'd parked well back from the scene. He got into the Chevy Monte Carlo he was driving that year, opened the glove box, and extracted a pack of Marlboro reds. He lit one and sucked the smoke into his lungs. When the cigarette was half smoked, he backed carefully around and headed down the hill. The crime scene was way the hell and gone up in the foothills of the Chugach south of downtown, an area that had been moose browse until the past decade, when the growing city finally reached it.

What the hell was Danny Shirtleff doing out here? he thought as he bounced along the gravel road. Kane had only gotten an hour's sleep before the phone rang, so he decided to concentrate on his driving and leave speculation until he was better rested.

It took him a careful half hour, and three more cigarettes, to navigate the web of rain-slick roads and pull in at his house. He left his car in the driveway; the garage door opening and closing was too likely to wake the household. He slid through the front door and shed his coat and shoes in the entry, then crept up the stairs to the bedroom. He shucked his clothes, not bothering to hang anything up since the suit was headed to the cleaner, anyway.

"Is that you, Nik?" Laurie asked, sitting up in the bed. "What time is it?"

"Going on four," he said, getting beneath the covers. "Come on, go back to sleep."

Laurie shook her head.

"Four?" she said sleepily. "In the morning? Where have you been?"

He reached up and put an arm on her shoulder, pulling her gently down flat.

"I got called out, remember?" he said. "Work."

"Oh, yeah," she said. "What was it?"

"We'll talk about it later," Kane said, then winced. Treating Laurie like a child wasn't smart.

"Fuck that," she said, snapping on her bedside lamp and flooding the bed with light. Her face looked puffy and soft, but her voice was anything but. "Tell me now."

Kane shrugged, and raised himself on an elbow so he could see her.

"If you insist," he said. "It was Danny Shirtleff. Sometime last night, somebody shot him dead."

Kane could see the information sink in, and Laurie gave a little grunt like she'd been struck. Then she began to cry.

"Oh, Jesus, Nik," she said. "Danny? Danny Shirtleff? We know him."

Damn those hormones, Kane thought as he reached for her. She pushed his arm away.

"Oh, poor Danny," she said, her voice nearly strangled with tears. "Oh, oh, oh."

three

Time is an illusion. Lunchtime doubly so.

—Douglas Adams

## MARCH 2007

*Lights. Hissing. Voices.*

Motherfucker! What happened, a bomb go off in here? Bleeders everywhere. Start feeding me clamps.

"Daddy? Is that you? Dad?"

Is this guy talking? Christ, I haven't seen anything like this since Desert Storm.

"Dad. Dad. Where's my dad?"

Shit, he is trying to talk. Will somebody just knock him the fuck out?

*Louder hissing.*

Are you going to be able to save him?

Shit! Come back here, you little bastard. Ask me again in a couple hours. Right now, I just don't know.

*Again, the words shift and swirl.*

I jjuusstt dooonnnn'ttt knnnnooooowwwww.

four

It doesn't matter who my father was;
it matters who I remember he was.

—ANNE SEXTON

## AUGUST 1962

"I don't know where your father is, Nik," Cecelia Kane said. "Will you just leave me alone?"

Nik could tell his mother was losing patience, but he didn't care. He didn't like mysteries, didn't really believe in them, in fact. Somebody knew where Teddy Kane was. All Nik had to do was find that person and he'd find his father.

"Somebody's got to know," he said. "People don't just vanish into thin air."

Cecelia Kane's lips settled into a thin line, and her eyes glowed with a dangerous light that usually foretold a beating. Just turned thirteen years old, Nik was nearly her size and could have resisted, but the idea of fighting with his mother was too shocking to contemplate. He shifted his stance slightly to give himself a better start toward the door. But the light went out as quickly as it had ignited, and his mother's shoulders slumped.

"Cee Cee," she called, "come and get your brother. He's giving me a headache."

They were living in a trailer that year, nine of them, parents and seven kids, Nik the youngest, crammed into seven hundred square feet, plus another couple hundred worth of uninsulated plywood wanigan. The four boys slept in that, the three girls in the single bedroom, and their parents on a foldout in the trailer's main room. An outhouse supplemented the tiny bathroom.

"If this isn't the bottom, you can see it from here," Cee Cee had said when they moved in.

She was the oldest of the Kane children, just nineteen, and seemed to have accepted with good grace her mother's transfer of responsibility for the rest of the kids. She was good at stretching a dollar, an inventive cook, skilled with a darning needle, patient and plain as homemade bread. Fourteen-year-old Aurora had gotten the good looks in the family; all Cee Cee had gotten was her mother's name, abbreviated to lessen the confusion in a family that was already deeply confused.

Cee Cee stuck her head out of the girls' room.

"Nik, why don't you go outside and play, honey?" she asked.

Nik didn't reply. Cee Cee was the only one in the family who seemed to care about him, and he returned her affection with a fierce loyalty that made defying her painful. But this was his father.

"Nik?" his sister said again.

"Aw, Ceese," he replied, "I'm just trying to get her to tell me what happened to Dad."

His sister came into the room and took his hand.

"Let's go outside and talk, Nik," she said, and he let her lead him through the wanigan and into a steady rain. The two of them scampered over to the little gazebo that served the trailer court as a community gathering spot and sat at the single picnic table it covered. As far as Nik knew, no one had ever picnicked here, but he'd seen couples necking and toughs drinking out of paper bags.

"What is it, Nikky?" his sister asked. "What's wrong?"

Nik dug his chin into his chest and mumbled.

"Don't mumble like that, Nik," Cee Cee said. "Speak up."

Nik sighed. He could feel a stinging in his eyes that he knew to be tears trying to get out. But he was too old to cry now, so he squeezed hard with his stomach muscles until the urge to cry retreated.

"I said what isn't wrong," he said. "We don't have a pot to piss in or a window to throw it out of."

Cee Cee reached out and ruffled his hair. He shrank from her touch instinctively. Hands coming his way weren't usually gentle.

"Don't talk like that, Nik," she chided. "It's vulgar."

"It's what Mom says," Nik said hotly. "She says it to Dad all the time, when she's complaining about how this isn't the life he promised her. And now he's gone."

His sister let her hand rest on his shoulder.

"Dad's gone off before," she said. "You know that, Nik. He always comes back."

She was right. Their father wandered off for a day or a week and always came back, looking sheepish and smelling of cigarette smoke and alcohol. The last time, several months before, he'd returned with a spectacular set of bruises. But this time didn't feel like any of the others to Nik. His father had been gone a long time, weeks, and Nik had heard Cee Cee and Michael, his oldest brother, talking about the possibility that they'd seen the last of Teddy Kane.

"Who cares?" Michael had said. "He's just a drunk and a bum."

I care, Nik had thought then, and he still felt the same way. Or did he? Maybe he didn't want his father back so much as he wanted to know why Teddy Kane left.

"I don't know, Cee Cee," Nik said. "I just don't think he's coming back this time. Neither does Mom. I can tell."

"How can you tell, Nik?" his sister asked.

"I just can, Cee Cee," he said, and that was the truth. He didn't know why he thought Teddy Kane was gone. He just did. And he knew, somehow, that Cecelia Kane did, too. "What will happen to us if he's gone for good?"

The question hung between them for a long time, and when his sister answered she sounded, for once, like the girl she was.

"Only God knows that, Nikky," she said.

"God?" Nik said. "Where is God? What's he done for us, anyway? What good is God if he won't help?"

Cee Cee ran her hand back up to the top of his head.

"It's not for us to know God's ways," she said, sighing. "Although there are times I wonder, too."

She straightened up on the bench.

"What we'll do is stay together as a family," she said, determination overlaying fear like a thin skin of ice on a bottomless lake. "We'll all work, and the parish will help us."

"The parish," Nik said, his voice thick with disgust. "Charity. That's just a way for people to look down on us."

"That's enough, Nik," his sister said, the girl gone from her voice, replaced by the woman who expected to be obeyed. "Shouldn't you be getting downtown for your papers?"

Nik was feeling so low he almost complained. But he knew that Michael was working out of the back door of the laborers' hall and Barry cleaned rooms at a hotel and Kevin was busing tables at a restaurant and Oregon and Aurora were babysitting and Cee Cee would soon put on her uniform and go check groceries. Every child in the Kane family worked and no child complained about it.

That wasn't just a point of pride; it was what really made the Kanes a family. Without that pact among the children, the family would have flown apart the last time their father got fired and wandered off. Or the time before. Or the time before that. For all the devotion Cecelia Kane showed to her children in public, inside her, where real love should have been, was just a cold place. Nik was convinced that if she woke up one morning to a house empty of children she'd go on as if nothing had happened.

No, what kept them together wasn't Teddy Kane or his wife. It was Cee Cee and the example she set for her brothers and sisters, an example that could be resented but never ignored, and never, ever challenged out loud.

"You're right," Nik said, getting to his feet. "I should get going."

He and his sister ran back to the trailer. When they were indoors, he said in a low voice, "I'm sorry, Ceese. I don't mean to make trouble. But I have to know what's happened to Dad. Why won't Mom try to find out?"

Cee Cee leaned down so that her lips were next to her brother's ear.

"Mom can't do that, Nik," she said. "She can't ask about him. She has her pride."

Pride, Nik thought as he put on the raincoat that fit him. Adults got to have pride. Kids—poor kids, anyway—couldn't afford it. They did what they were told to do, like wearing a girl's purple raincoat when that's all there was.

The city was small, not much more than sixty thousand people. Some of them were far-flung, on homesteads and little, pioneerlike clusters of dwellings in the spruce and birch forest, but most lived in a close-fitting collection of houses centered on the original town site laid out by the Corps of Engineers in 1915. The Kanes' trailer huddled with a couple of dozen others on a dirt road off a gravel road on the eastern edge of that collection. Nik had a distance to walk. Even with the raincoat he got wet, and it didn't help that a brand-new Chevy Impala full of teenagers hit a big puddle just as he was walking past it, sending a wall of water to break over him like a wave. The boys laughed and the girls smiled, and, in that moment, Nik would gladly have killed them all. By the time he got to the newspaper office his Keds, raggedy from having passed through two kids before him, were soaked, and very little of him was truly dry.

"Nicholas Kane," Obie Lyons said when he walked up on the loading dock at the rear of the newspaper building. "Don't you owe me money for yesterday's newspapers, Nicholas Kane?"

Nik shook his head.

"No, Obie, I don't. Check your list," he said. "And my name is Nik, not Nicholas."

Obie Lyons was a moonfaced adult who talked and acted more like a kid. He sat, as usual, in a little wooden kiosk on one side of the loading dock, a line of empty green Coca-Cola bottles at his elbow. The boys who sold papers on the street swore Obie drank twenty bottles of Coca-Cola a day. He pushed his thick eyeglasses up on his nose and made a show of checking the list he kept on a clipboard.

"I'm not sure, not-Nicholas Kane," he said. "I was a dollar short yesterday. I think you still owe me a dollar."

Obie Lyons did this to a kid every once in a while. Some of the paperboys thought he just got confused because he was simple. But Nik, with three older brothers, recognized a demonstration of power when he saw one.

"I don't owe you anything," Nik said. "I have a receipt."

That was a bluff. He'd gotten a receipt just like always—Obie insisted on filling out a receipt for each purchase no matter how big a hurry a kid was in—but he had no idea where it was.

Obie nodded several times, as if Nik's invocation of the receipt was a sign of submission.

"Now, then, not-Nicholas Kane," he said, pushing his glasses up on his nose, "how many newspapers would you like to purchase today?"

"Twenty, please," Nik said, thrusting a dollar bill at Obie. The company charged five cents for each newspaper. The boys, in turn, sold them for a dime. If you were lucky, you could start with a dollar and, by selling and buying and selling, end the day with five dollars.

Of course, if the newspapers didn't sell you lost your money. So it paid to be first in line, as Nik was that day.

Obie counted out the newspapers carefully and filled the receipt form, with its duplicate copy, with neat, square printing. As he was filling it out, Nik took a piece of plastic from under his raincoat and wrapped it around his newspapers. Rain turned the cheap newsprint into a soggy mess.

Obie was handing the receipt to Nik when Billy Crocker and his gang showed up.

"Hey, punk," Billy said, giving Nik a shove, "get out of the way. And don't let me catch you trying to sell in any of my spots."

"Stop that, William Crocker," Obie said, "or you will receive no newspapers today."

Nik picked up his papers and left the two of them arguing. He crossed the street and went into the first bar. The lights were dim and the air was thick and gray with cigarette smoke. A line of people sat at the bar with their backs to him. Men mostly, but a couple of women skinny as plucked chickens. Probably not much action here, but you never could tell.

"Paper!" he called. "Get your *Anchorage Times* newspaper here!"

The bartender, a man with a beaten-up face and a strip of white hair on either side of his bald head, looked up from taking the caps off a couple of bottles of Pabst Blue Ribbon.

"Beat it, kid," he called. "You're too young to be in here."

Nik shrugged and walked across the bar and through the connecting door into another just like it. Much of this block of Fourth Avenue, and the next and the next, right on down the street, were bars.

Working the bars had its dangers. A drunk might take three or four papers from you for his dime or not pay you at all. The bartender might be in a bad mood and throw you out, like this one had. You might run into a cop and get a lecture. And there was always Billy Crocker and his gang. Billy was a couple of years older than Nik and the other boys who sold papers and he thought that gave him some special claim on selling in the bars. His response to competition was a flurry of punches.

But the returns were worth the risks. People in bars had time on their hands and, usually, money. Throw in a few drinks and they were willing customers. Nik sold out his papers quickly, then went through the routine with Obie Lyons to get forty more papers. He had to hustle to stay ahead of Crocker's crew, but he had no trouble selling that bunch, too. As he sold the papers, he listened to snatches of conversation. Most of the talk was about the Russians, the Kennedys, and the shocking suicide of the actress Marilyn Monroe.

Nik was running out of time and bars, so he bought just twenty papers on the third go-round. He was working his way through them when he ducked into a place called the South Seas. It was late enough that an after-work crowd was gathering; businessmen and government workers and secretaries were overwhelming the regulars. Nik wove through the crowd doing a brisk business, and he was down to his last paper when he reached the bar.

"Paper?" he asked each of the customers who lined the bar.

The last guy in the row was a burly, black-haired fellow with a dark mustache. He was dressed in a dark suit, a blue-and-white-striped shirt, and a big, bright bow tie.

"What did you say, kid?" he asked.

"Do you want to buy a newspaper?" Nik asked politely.

The bartender walked down to where the man sat.

"Sorry about this, Mr. McCanta," he said. "Get out of here, kid. Don't be bothering the customers."

"Gosh, mister," Nik said, "I'm just selling newspapers. What's wrong with that?"

"Don't sass me, kid," the bartender said. "Get moving."

Nik turned to leave.

"Wait a minute," one of the other regulars said. "Isn't that Teddy Kane's kid? Aren't you Teddy's kid?"

Nik didn't get a chance to reply.

"Teddy Kane?" the bartender said. "That son of a bitch owes me money."

He looked hard at Nik.

"Now you'd really better beat it, kid, unless you're here to pay your old man's bar bill."

"Don't be like that, Billy," one of the women said. "He's just a baby. Besides, Teddy's a gentleman. And a nice dresser."

The bartender's laugh wasn't pleasant.

"A bum in a blue blazer is still a bum," he said.

He scowled at Nik.

"You see your old man, you tell him to come in here and settle up. Now beat it."

Nik turned to go.

"Give me the paper, young fella," the dark-haired man said.

Nik handed the man his last newspaper.

"Say hello to your mother for me," the man said, and dropped a Liberty silver dollar into Nik's palm.

A big grin split Nik's face. This was the payoff for working the bars, all right. He slid out the door before anyone could intervene. He turned to run for home and ran instead into Billy Crocker and his gang. The other boys quickly formed a circle around him.

"Well, look who's here, boys," Billy said, giving Nik a shove. "It's that little creep-o Nik Kane. I thought I told you to stay out of my territory, creep-o. We didn't sell hardly no papers today because of you."

Nik said nothing. The other members of Billy Crocker's gang weren't much, but Billy had several inches and several pounds on him.

"I tell you what, creep-o," Billy said, giving him another shove. "You just hand over, say, half your profits, and we'll call it even."

Nik gripped the silver dollar more tightly and shook his head.

"That's not smart," Billy said, giving Nik a shrewd look. "But I'll be fair. Just give me what you've got in your hand, and we'll call it square."

Nik gripped the coin more tightly, jumped forward, and hit Billy Crocker as hard as he could on the nose.

"Yow," Billy said, and stumbled backward.

Nik ducked through the hole that left in the circle and sprinted down the street.

"Hey, this is blood," Billy Crocker screamed. "You made me bleed. I'll kill you, creep-o."

But his voice was fading in the distance, and the kids who had chased Nik weren't trying very hard to catch him. After a few blocks, he slowed to a walk and opened his hand. The beveling on the dollar's edge had left a red welt in his palm, but he still had the dollar, and all the other money he'd earned that day. Cee Cee would be happy when he handed it over to her.

All except the dollar, he thought as he walked on through the rain. I'm going to keep that. I need to start saving so that, when I get older, I can find my dad.

five

The only reason for time is so that everything
doesn't happen at once.

—ALBERT EINSTEIN

## MARCH 2007

*Soft noises. Low voices.*

This patient is named Nikiski Kane. He came in through the emergency room and spent four hours in the OR. We're monitoring him closely for temp, BP, any signs of post-op distress.

Nikiski, that's an interesting name. Four hours in surgery? Car accident?

Gunshot. He was part of that mess up at the Capitol Building earlier today.

I heard something about that on the news. Hand me his chart, would you?

Hmmm. His vitals don't look all that good. Have we notified next of kin?

*The words bleed and run.*

Neexxtt ooofff kkkkiiiinnnn.

six

Memory is a complicated thing,
a relative to truth, but not its twin.

—Barbara Kingsolver

## SEPTEMBER 1985

"Next of kin?" Jackie Dee said. "I don't know if they've been notified. Danny's from Seattle or somewhere, ain't he? So some other poor bastard is going to have to break the news."

They were sitting in Leroy's Pancake House, an L-shaped collection of spavined red vinyl benches and chipped beige Formica tables with the initials of several generations of punks and lovers gouged into them. Leroy's customers matched the décor: unkempt young men in flannel and denim sitting with unwashed young women with tattoos, a skinny, twitchy guy who looked like a speed freak in a booth with a couple of tired-looking hookers, and a big, round corner table full of what looked like very wide-awake real estate salesmen. The odor of sweaty people mixed with the smell of fried foods and smoldering cigarettes to give Leroy's a funkiness unmatched outside of whorehouses and locker rooms.

Jackie Dee loved Leroy's, and said so at every opportunity.

"I'd work out of the place if the pencil pushers'd let me," he said whenever the subject came up. "Hell, I'd live there if I could get Jackie DeeTwo to move with me."

Jacqueline DiSanto, known throughout the department as Jackie DeeTwo, was his wife. She was beautiful, brunette, and as tall and wide as the front end of a White Freightliner. Unlike Jackie Dee, she didn't look to have an ounce of misplaced fat on her. But then, she didn't eat four or five meals a day at Leroy's.

That morning Jackie Dee was sitting behind his usual breakfast: coffee, milk, orange juice, a stack of pancakes topped with fried eggs, a hubcap-sized sweet roll, and a plate of bacon. He poured maple syrup over everything, including the bacon, and started eating.

"Dig in, kid," he said around a mouthful. "It takes a lot of fuel to keep the Jackie Dee machine operating at peak efficiency."

Kane pushed a forkful of eggs around his plate and said nothing.

"Whatsa matter, kid, no appetite?" Jackie Dee asked. He leaned across the table to get a closer look at Kane, dropping his tie into a pool of maple syrup.

"Aw, fuck," he said, rearing back and mopping at his tie with a napkin. When he'd finished spreading syrup the length of the tie, he said, "You don't look too good this morning. Hard time sleeping?"

Kane nodded.

"Laurie pretty much freaked out when I told her about Danny Shirtleff," he said. "I had a hell of a time getting her calmed down. Then, this morning, when she's driving me over here, she gives me the silent treatment."

Jackie Dee held up a finger while he swallowed another gargantuan bite.

"Women," he said, wiping his mouth with the back of his hand. "Jackie DeeTwo went a little bananas when I told her, too. Every cop who gets killed is a reminder to the wives what kind of jobs we got. And for some reason that seems to upset 'em. I imagine there'll be tears and yelling in most of the married households in the department."

He swallowed some coffee.

"Plus, yours is knocked up, right?" he continued.

Kane nodded.

"Well, there you go," Jackie Dee said. "Pregnant women get moody."

Kane nodded again. His partner was right. But he didn't need trouble on the home front while he was breaking in a new job. The hell with it. He'd try to get home at a reasonable hour and bring flowers, and maybe everything would be better.

He picked up his fork and made serious inroads into his breakfast. While they ate, they talked about the case.

"Those kids—Mike and Berta, I think their names are—said they drove up there to Skeleton Lake just to talk," Jackie Dee snorted. "Just to talk, my ass."

Kane knew about Skeleton Lake. It had been called Skellings Lake back when he was in high school, named for the homesteader whose land it sat on. It'd always been a party spot for teenagers. Then, about the time he'd gone onto the force, somebody'd been digging a basement somewhere in the area and found bones. When they were identified as human, the kids all started calling it "Skeleton Lake," and the name had stuck.

"So I know right off these kids are liars, right?" Jackie Dee said. "But the rest of their story seemed straight enough. They saw the scene as they pulled in. All the guy saw at first was the car, but the girl spotted Shirtleff's body right off. They turned around and got right out of there. The guy was all for not telling anybody. Didn't want the girl's parents to know what they were up to, apparently. But she insisted they had to tell somebody. They were just about to the Seward Highway when they spotted Fireball's unit and pulled him over. He had them drive back up behind him, so they were there when the cavalry and the Marines and the Three Stooges showed up and fucked up the crime scene. But they didn't really have much to add."

Jackie Dee ate for a while, then said the rest of his preliminary interviews had given him "diddly-squat." The two of them swapped impressions for the rest of the meal, and Kane got another lecture on the worthlessness of police brass who didn't work the streets anymore. When they were finished, Jackie Dee said, "Now we go down to the shop. You walk Fireball through his statement, and I'll go talk to that prick Jeffords, who's getting his ticket punched at narcotics. Shirtleff was working undercover for him, so maybe he knows something, the worthless paper pusher."

They left the restaurant and got into Jackie Dee's muscle car. Kane pulled the Marlboros from his pocket and offered Jackie Dee one, lighting both of them with a battered stainless steel Zippo with a military insignia on it.

They were supposed to be driving a department sedan, but Jackie Dee refused.

"One of them baby carriages don't fit the Jackie Dee image," he said whenever the lieutenant in charge brought the subject up. Jackie Dee had a big personality and a hell of an arrest record, so the lieutenant never pushed.

He spread gravel over the parking lot as he fishtailed onto C Street. He made a couple of lefts and pointed the Trans Am's nose toward downtown.

"Why do you call Jeffords a prick?" Kane asked as they rolled through Chester Creek Valley. "I worked under him on swings, and he seemed okay."

Jackie shifted a toothpick from one side of his mouth to the other.

"There's lots worse," he said. "But Jeffords is more interested in power than police work, and Jackie Dee is all about police work. I suppose if he plays his cards right, and don't get knifed in the back by some other ladder climber, Tom Jeffords'll be chief someday. But if Shirtleff's dead because of some fuckup on his squad, he'll do everything he can to keep us from finding out. Doesn't want any black marks on his jacket."

They rode in silence the rest of the way to the police station, a low concrete building with a bunch of cars parked behind a high, barbed-wire-topped Cyclone fence. Jackie Dee pulled in through the open gate and tucked his car between a couple of blue-and-whites.

"Okay," he said. "I'll talk to Jeffords and then come find you. Go easy on Fireball. He seemed pretty shook last night. Just get him to tell his story into a tape machine and let him go home. But do it by the numbers."

Kane nodded, and got out of the car to follow Jackie Dee into the building. They shook out their raincoats and slid their badge cases into their top breast pockets so their shields showed. They walked past the front desk and split up, Jackie Dee climbing the stairs and Kane continuing to the back. He walked down a hall and entered a fair-sized room that had been cut up into cubicles by metal dividers. Fireball Roberts sat in a chair beside Kane's desk, waiting for him. Kane sat and swiveled to look Fireball over. He wasn't a pleasant sight. Red whiskers stuck out of his pale, freckled jaw, and his thick shock of red hair hadn't been visited by a comb. His eyes were bloodshot and had hound dog–sized bags under them.

"Officer Roberts," Kane said. "Thank you for coming down. Are you ready to give your statement?"

Red crept up Roberts's neck and into his face.

"'Officer Roberts'?" he said in his squeaky voice. "What is that shit, Nik? 'Officer Roberts.' We rode together."

They had. Anchorage Police officers usually rode solo in their blue-and-whites, but when Kane joined the force they'd put him with Fireball for a week to learn the ropes. It was all they had in the way of training, and the duty wasn't much sought after by the veterans. Fire-

ball, who had been on the force for fifteen years by then, had been
pleasant and conscientious, and indulged in the minimum amount
of hazing newbies were expected to undergo. But Fireball had shown
how he'd gotten the nickname a time or two during Kane's training,
and Kane wanted no demonstration in the shop, for Fireball's sake
more than his.

"Sorry, Fireball," Kane said, "but you know how it is. In any
officer-down, we do things by the numbers. So just stay calm, and
we'll get this finished and get you home to Jamie. How is she, by
the way?"

Fireball bristled again.

"Whaddya mean, how is she?" he demanded. "How should she be?"

Must be tough going through life with that big a hard-on, Kane
thought. But Fireball had extra reason to be touchy about his wife.
The rumor was he'd taken her out of one of Molly Wren's houses
when she was fourteen and married her the day she turned sixteen.
They made an odd couple. He was in his late forties. She was in her
early twenties, as dark as he was fair. She was a head taller than he
was, and as gorgeous as he was ugly. So if Fireball was overly protec-
tive, well, look what he was protecting.

"Calm down, Fireball," Kane said. "It's just that both Laurie and
Jackie DeeTwo pitched fits when they heard about Danny."

Fireball nodded, and the red left his face.

"Yeah, Jamie did, too," he said. "I didn't get much sleep. I don't
know how much you know about Danny, but the wives liked him.
Maybe because he has—had—good manners. God knows we don't,
most of us. And I kind of took him under my wing when he first got
here, like I did you when you were a newbie, so Jamie probably knew
him better than most of the wives. And the women really don't like it
when one of us goes down."

He sighed.

"So how about we do this so I can go home to her?"

Kane pulled a big, square portable tape recorder out of a desk drawer, plugged it in, and set the little microphone on its stand between the two of them. He loaded in a cassette tape and punched "Record." Everything seemed to be working.

"Interview with Officer James Roberts on September—what is it?—September 12, 1985, at eleven-seventeen a.m," he said. "Interviewer is Detective Nikiski Kane. I will now do a tape check."

He stopped the tape, rewound it, and played it back. Sound was fine. He hit "Record" again and said, "Back on record with Officer James Roberts. Officer Roberts, would you please tell me in your own words how you came to find Officer Daniel Shirtleff?"

Fireball gave him a sour look as he dug out his notebook. Kane knew what he was thinking: Whose words would he tell the story in if not his own? But like so many things in police work, Kane's question had been part of a formula.

"On September 11, I was working the swing shift in a marked police vehicle in southeast Anchorage," Fireball said, his voice taking on a mechanical lack of inflection. "The night was rainy and, because of the cloud cover, dark for late summer here. At approximately eleven-thirty p.m. I was exiting the Seward Highway onto O'Malley Road when I was flagged down by two young people named"—he flipped the page in his notebook—"named Michael Lewis and Roberta Haines. They told me that they'd seen a body in the vicinity of what they called Skeleton Lake. I had them lead me to the body."

Kane held up a hand and Fireball stopped.

"You didn't call in at that point?" he said.

Fireball shook his head.

"There was nothing to call in at that point," he said. "They could have been mistaken. It might have been a prank. Teenagers often use the area, for illegal drinking, drug use, fights, and, uh, amorous activities, so they might have seen something much different and simply misunderstood what they'd seen."

"Thank you, Officer Roberts," Kane said. "Please continue."

"When we reached the area, I saw the car and what appeared to be a body lying near it," Fireball said, his voice reverting to its mechanical cadence. "I exited my vehicle and approached and found Officer Shirtleff lying there. I used my portable radio to contact the dispatcher and call for backup and medical assistance. I searched for vital signs and, finding none, attempted to administer CPR. After some minutes—I don't know how many—it was clear that my efforts would not revive Officer Shirtleff. I then searched the surrounding area in case the perpetrator might still be nearby but found nothing. At about that time, the first of the responding units arrived. I returned to my vehicle and waited for the detectives to arrive. After some time, I was interviewed by Detective Sergeant Giuseppe DiSanto. At the end of the interview, he told me to go home. I did, remaining there until this morning, when I came to police headquarters to give this statement."

Fireball quit talking.

"Thank you, Officer Roberts," Kane said. "If you wouldn't mind answering a few additional questions?"

"Sure," Fireball said. "Ask away."

"When you first saw Officer Shirtleff's vehicle, were his car headlights on or off?" Kane asked.

"On," Fireball said, "although the car was pointed away from me so what I saw first were its taillights."

"And the driver's door was open?" Kane asked.

"Yes," Fireball replied. "The passenger's door was shut, but the driver's door was open. As I recall, the way the body lay it looked as if Officer Shirtleff was exiting the vehicle when he was shot."

Kane nodded.

"Did you see anything on or near the body that might be significant?" he asked.

Fireball closed his eyes.

"There was a firearm lying in the mud to one side of the body, an automatic of some sort, and what might have been shell casings in the mud a little farther away," he said. "That's all I can remember."

"Keys still in the ignition? Motor running?" Kane asked.

"Yes and no, I think," Fireball said. "I'm not sure. I didn't change anything, so the way you found it was the way it was. Why you asking, anyway?"

"I didn't find it, Officer Roberts," Kane said, as much for the record as for Fireball. "Several people had been through the scene before I got there. The keys were in the ignition but the engine wasn't running. I don't know if it ran out of gas or if Officer Shirtleff had turned it off. So I'm asking you."

Fireball nodded.

"I understand, Detective," he said, nodding toward the tape recorder. "It's just that it was a hell of a shock to find a fellow officer lying in the mud and not knowing why he'd been shot or if I would be next. So some of the details are a little blurry."

"Okay," Kane said. "Is there anything else you can tell me that might be germane to the investigation?"

"I don't think so," Fireball said.

"Thank you, Officer Roberts," Kane said. "This is Detective Nikiski Kane ending the interview with Officer James Roberts at eleven twenty-eight a.m."

He reached over and switched off the recorder.

"Okay, Fireball, that's the official part," he said. "Now tell me what you know about Danny that might have gotten him killed."

Fireball shrugged.

"I don't know that much about him these days," he said. "When he first got here, we had him over for dinner, went out, that kind of thing. Jamie tried to fix him up with some of her single friends, but nothing took. And then, well, you know how it is with undercovers.

He'd disappear for weeks at a time, and I'd only see him around the shop here, or maybe at a party. I don't know where he was living or who he was seeing or what he was working on. So I'm not going to be much good to you."

"Might your wife know more?" Kane asked.

Instead of bristling, Fireball ran his hand over his face, then shook his head.

"I don't think so, Nik," he said. "Question her if you want, but give her a day or two, would you?"

Kane nodded. He couldn't actually see getting much out of talking to the woman, so she wouldn't be his first stop, anyway. Or his second. Or probably his tenth.

Fireball got slowly to his feet and shuffled out of the cubicle. The situation seemed to have taken a lot out of him, but then Kane didn't know how he'd react to finding somebody he knew dead in the mud. Probably worse.

He sat at his desk, smoking and making notes, until Jackie Dee came into the cubicle, moving like a pissed-off rhinoceros. He slammed himself into the chair at his desk, which sat nose to nose with Kane's.

"No-good ass-covering chain-of-command motherfucker," Jackie Dee said loudly, pulling out a cigarette and lighting it. "Lying needle-dicked I'm-more-important-than-you-are asshole."

"Tell it like it is, Jackie Dee," a voice called from the next cubicle.

"Meeting with Jeffords didn't go so well?" Kane asked.

"If you like being shuck-and-jived, it was fine," Jackie Dee said, blowing smoke out his nose.

"Did he tell you anything?"

"Sure. He said that Shirtleff had no large-scale cases going at the moment, so he loaned him out to the troopers to make a case in Kodiak. Coke going to the crab fishery. Said Shirtleff'd been working it six weeks, and had been back two or three times during the case. A couple days ago, they busted the whole distribution network, here and in Kodiak. Said there were probably people in Seattle and points south involved, too, but none of them had been made. Guess the D.A. figures somebody they got'll roll over on 'em."

Jackie Dee stopped and rummaged around in a drawer until he came up with a Reese's Peanut Butter Cup. Jackie Dee ate a dozen or so a day, maybe two dozen on a bad day. He peeled off the orange wrapper and popped one of the cups into his mouth, following it quickly with the other.

"These fuckers are supposed to help me stop smoking," he said.

He got up from his desk and carried his coffee cup out of the cubicle, returning in a moment with a full cup. He sat down again and drank, then went on:

"Shirtleff spent some time debriefing and doing paperwork, then caught a flight back here. Got in last night about eight o'clock. Was supposed to report here right away and write a report for our files. And that's all Sergeant My-Shit-Don't-Stink had to say. Said it all with his current butt boy, Charlie Simms, sitting there taking notes."

When Kane was sure Jackie Dee had finished, he asked quietly, "How much of it do you believe?"

Jackie Dee gave Kane an appraising look.

"You might be better at this than I thought," Jackie Dee said. "Don't get me wrong, it takes balls to do what you did to get this promotion. But balls and brains don't always go together."

He sat, apparently lost in thought, for a minute or two.

"I don't know how much I believe," he said. "I believe that Shirtleff was doing some undercover work in Kodiak, and that should mean he was working with the troopers. But I wouldn't put it past Jeffords to run something on his own hook, territory or no. There's something bothering him, that's for sure. Even a Grade A prick like him wouldn't be behaving like this in a cop killing if he didn't have something at stake. Something big, too. So maybe he tried to run something over there and it went wrong and got Shirtleff killed."

He ran his hand through his hair.

"I'll ask around," he said. "I've got sources of my own. And if you've got any, work 'em. Now, what did Fireball have to say?"

Ticking off Fireball's story only took a couple of minutes.

"Not much to go on there," Jackie Dee said.

Kane nodded.

"Why do you suppose Jeffords didn't show up at the scene last night?" he asked.

"I asked," Jackie Dee said, lighting another cigarette. "He gave me some song and dance about being at a charity dinner. Said he didn't hear about Shirtleff until he got in this morning. Said he was going to make trouble for whoever had the duty last night because he wasn't informed. The prick."

Jackie Dee's phone rang. He picked it up and listened.

"No, goddamn it, Willie," he said. "If you do that, I'll have to spend all my time sitting on my ass here coordinating things."

He listened some more.

"Well, no, we don't have any real leads," he said, "but I don't see how putting more bodies on it is going to help."

He listened some more.

"Look," he said, "give me and the kid another couple of days, and if we don't have anything then we can gangbang it."

He listened some more, said "Uh-huh" a couple of times, and hung up.

"That was our loot, Willie Tolliver," Jackie Dee said. "Brass is already feeling the heat, wants to form a task force. You heard my end of it. We better shake something loose or else we'll have every cop with time on his hands mucking around in our investigation."

He took a couple of tape cassettes from his pocket and handed them to Kane.

"Take these and Fireball's statement and find a steno to type 'em up," he said. "I'll scan the autopsy report, then we'll head out and look at the crime scene in daylight. Unless we want every deadbeat in the department on our hands, we'd better find something."

seven

Time flies like an arrow; fruit flies like a banana.

—GROUCHO MARX

## MARCH 2007

*Hissing. Beeps. Floating.*

He was floating. The back side of his body was lighter than the front and held him up. His surroundings were a blue blur. The skin of his cheeks and lips and chin buzzed with numbness. He reached up to touch them but he could not feel his arm move. He forgot what he was doing.

I have a name, he thought. I should know my name. But he didn't. His lack of identity didn't bother him. It, too, was wrapped in a blue blur.

He tried to speak. The buzzing in his cheeks and lips moved but no noise emerged. He could feel cold air blowing in his nostrils, blowing him up, helping him float. He could smell something. He knew the smell.

Somewhere close he heard a thrumming. Something warm spread up his arm. His eyes closed. Good-bye buzzing blue blur, he thought.

The smell. The ssmmeellll-el. It's foooddd.

eight

Memory is a crazy woman that hoards
colored rags and throws away food.

—Austin O'Malley

## AUGUST 1963

Nik scraped the remains of a slice of German chocolate cake into
the garbage can, following it with what was left of the short-rib special. The plate was thick with orange grease. Not the most appetizing
sight, but in the past couple of months Nik had become pretty much
immune to the sights and smells of the restaurant.

The heat was another matter. The open flame, the griddles, the hot
water the dish washers used were all contributors, as were the active
bodies crammed into the small space. Despite the fans blowing from
every direction, the kitchen of the Harbor House was as hot as the
hinges of Hell. The cooks and dish washers were all pouring with
sweat, and even waitresses and table flunkies like Nik who were in
and out were more than damp.

The scraps of a Porterhouse steak with baked potato were next into
the garbage can, then the remnants of a couple of baked halibuts,
a variety of desserts, and, last, an almost untouched kid's plate of

mac and cheese. By the time he was finished, Nik reckoned that he'd thrown away more food than his family had eaten that day.

Then again, maybe not lately. For some reason Nik couldn't understand, from the time his father had gone for what looked like for good the Kane family's material condition had actually improved. Part of it was that the three oldest Kane children had gone off one at a time; Cee Cee to a convent, Michael to college on an engineering scholarship, and Barry to sea to work on an ocean liner. Three less mouths to feed. Part of it was that there was more help from the parish. But much of the assistance came from what his mother described as "friends of your father." Nik hadn't known that his father had had so many friends. But, then, he didn't know much about his father at all.

As always, when Nik thought of his father he felt a pang of guilt. What had he done lately to figure out what happened to Teddy Kane?

Nik deposited the pile of dirty dishes next to a sudsy sink manned by a skinny, white-haired guy named Hackett, whose cigarette cough gave him the nickname "the Hacker."

"Here you go," Nik said. The Hacker nodded without saying anything, as usual. Nobody'd heard the Hacker say more than three words together since Nik had gotten the job.

That hadn't been easy. The day Nik turned fourteen, he showed up at the back door of the restaurant looking for a busboy job. The manager had been nice enough, and the head chef had accepted him with a grunt and a nod. But when Nik showed up that night to go to work, the manager greeted him with a grim face and a ten-dollar bill.

"Sorry, young man," the manager said, "I made a mistake. There's no job for you."

She thrust the ten at Nik, who reached for it instinctively. The Kane family could always use ten dollars. But at the last moment, he turned his palm down and shook his head.

"I don't take money I haven't earned," he said. "Just tell me what happened. Please."

The manager, a stocky woman with a kind face and lots of brown hair, looked at Nik closely.

"I probably shouldn't tell you this," she said finally, "but when I told the owner about you he put his foot down. 'That fellow is not going to work here,' he said. When I asked him why, he just shook his head. What did you do?"

Nik searched his memory.

"I didn't do anything," he said at last. He thought some more. "Who is the owner?"

The woman shook her head.

"If I tell you that and something happens, it'll cost me my job," she said. "And I need this job."

Nik didn't press it. He knew all about needing a job. He needed one now. He was getting too old to sell newspapers on the street. The buyers favored younger, cuter—and maybe less threatening—guys. Nik was starting to get some size on him and he didn't smile much, and the combination seemed to put the hackles up on a lot of men. He was maturing without any of the cracking voice or ravaged skin that afflicted many of his classmates, so women had a different reaction, but not one that sold many newspapers. He needed a job in which age and size would be a benefit instead of a problem.

The next day, ignoring a cold rain, he went to the back door of the newspaper office and asked to see one of the reporters, a rumpled cube of a man named Al, who he sometimes saw in the bars.

"Whaddya want, kid?" Al asked when he finally arrived at the door, flicking cigarette ash in Nik's direction

"You know me, Al," Nik said. "I need to know who owns the Harbor House."

"Whafor?" Al asked suspiciously. "You get the ptomaine at 'is place or sumpin'?"

So Nik had no choice but to tell Al the whole story. When he was done, Al said, "God-curst capitalists. Wait here, kid, an'll find out whatchu wanna know."

Nik waited another ten minutes, and Al returned with an envelope.

"He's a goddamn kraut," Al said, handing Nik the envelope. "Got'is name an' address here, even a pitcher. You get in trouble, yo'don know me, right, kid?"

Nik nodded and took the envelope. Instead of buying papers to sell, he sat in a corner of the loading dock out of the rain and looked at what Al had given him. When he was satisfied he'd know the man by sight, he went and stood where he could see the restaurant entrance. Going to the man's home struck Nik as a recipe for trouble, but accosting him at his business seemed safe enough.

He waited every afternoon for three days, until he saw a well-preserved, gray-haired man get out of a black Mercedes 220SE and start for the door.

"Hey, wait, wait," Nik called, running across the street. The man stopped, turned, and greeted Nik with a scowl.

"Why are you shouting like that in the street?" he demanded. "You young people have no respect for your elders."

Sure enough, Nik could hear a slight accent.

"I, I mean, my name is Nik Kane," Nik said, "and I want to know why you won't hire me to work in your restaurant."

The man's scowl deepened.

"Bah!" he said, and turned to go.

"Please," Nik said. He could hear a pleading note in his voice and he hated it. But he had to know. "Really, sir, I just want to know the reason."

The man turned back and said, "If you must know, young man, it is your brother who is the reason."

"My brother?" Nik said. "Which brother?"

"It rains out here," the man said. "If you must know about this, step inside with me."

Nik followed the man into the restaurant. The manager stood at the cash register, talking with a deliveryman, and gave Nik a worried look as he passed. He followed the owner through the restaurant and into an office in the back, just opposite the kitchen.

The man removed an expensive-looking raincoat and hung it on a coatrack and took a seat behind a big desk piled high with papers. He motioned to a chair and Nik sat. The man dug around in a desk drawer and came up with a manila folder.

"Your brother is named Kevin Kane?" he asked.

Nik nodded. His stomach felt suddenly hollow. He knew that Kevin had been busing tables somewhere and had been fired, but he never knew the name of the restaurant or why he'd lost the job. It was just one of many problems Kevin had had in the past year. He was always angry, and had been cutting school, getting into fights, and generally behaving in a way that made his mother say he was headed for real trouble.

"This Kevin Kane, he once worked for me," the man said. "He was at first a good worker, but he changed. He began reporting to work late and, perhaps, stealing liquor. I had the manager speak to him. Then, one night, he becomes enraged at a table of religious who are here for dinner. Nuns and priests; he is screaming at them the most obscene things. What else was there to do but fire him? And when that is done, he accosts me on the street, just as you have done, and says the most vile things about the religious. I tell him to go before I call the police, and that is the last I see of him."

The man stopped to look at Nik, as if trying to gauge if the boy understood what he was being told.

"When I hear your name, I remember that boy and his trouble," the man continued, "and I decide that I will hire no more of the Kane family. I run a good business, but there are other restaurants to which people can go. I want no trouble."

Nik thought for a moment.

"Do you have any brothers?" he asked.

The man seemed surprised by the question but finally nodded.

"I have brothers," he said. "Two of them. So?"

"Are you responsible for everything they do?" Nik asked.

Again, the man reacted with surprise. He sat thinking for a moment, then smiled and shook his head.

"Indeed I am not," the man said, "just as you are not responsible for your brother's behavior."

He got to his feet.

"One moment, please," he said, and left the office, returning a minute later with a worried-looking manager.

"Mrs. Thompson," he said, "this young man has given me a lesson. And, in return, I believe we shall give him an opportunity. Please engage his services as a busboy. But show him no favor because I have interceded on his behalf. If he does not perform in a satisfactory manner, treat him as you would any other."

He turned to Nik.

"Now, young man, go with Mrs. Thompson and fill out your paperwork," he said.

He waved off Nik's thanks and pointed at the piles on his desk.

"As you can see," he said, "I have some paperwork of my own to deal with."

Nik let the memory go, picked up his plastic tub, and headed back into the dining room, a large rectangle filled with tables, noise, and tobacco smoke. The smoke made Nik's eyes water and nose itch, but he dove right in, finding a littered eight-top lined with hard-looking men and flashy women. From the looks of the table, they'd been concentrating more on drinking than eating.

"Are you finished?" he asked each of the diners politely before whisking away the plates, silverware, and glasses. He made a kitchen run with half the debris, returning quickly for the rest. As he cleared the last place, the woman sitting there, a big bleached blonde with a spectacular bust, ran a hand up the inside of his thigh. Nik practically jumped out of the building.

"Ooh, he's cute," the blonde said, "but he sure is ticklish."

Everybody laughed. Nik scowled. He thought about saying something, but that would only lead to trouble. Better finish fast. He dropped a water glass into his tub, and it tipped, sending a piece of ice down the front of the woman's dress.

The woman gave a little shriek, wiggled a moment, and sighed. Again, everyone laughed.

"I don't suppose you'd reach in and find that ice?" the woman said.

Nik could feel his face turning red.

"No, ma'am," he said. "I'm really sorry. It was an accident."

"It's all right, sonny," the woman said, putting her hand on his thigh again. "I need some cooling off."

More laughter.

"That's enough, Isabelle," one of the men said. Nik recognized him by his mustache and bright bow tie. He was the same man who had given him a silver dollar once, and Nik had seen him around town since.

The blonde smiled, gave Nik's thigh a squeeze, and let her hand drop. Nik quickly jammed the rest of the table's contents into his tub, barely remembering to leave the coffee cups and spoons.

"Over here, boy," the man in the bow tie said. Nik hefted the tub and walked around the table. The man stuffed a bill into his shirt pocket.

"For your trouble," he said.

"Thank you," Nik said, and made his escape.

The rest of his shift went quickly, with a rush just before the kitchen closed at ten p.m. Even though business seemed to be flattening out, Friday nights were still like that. It was nearly midnight when they finished clearing away and setting up for the next day. Nik was tenting the last napkin in his section when the head cook called, "Come and get it, kid, before I feed it to the pigs."

One of the good things about working at the restaurant was the free food. Nik had had dinner at the start of his shift, but the whole crew—cooks, waitresses, dish washers, busers, even the manager— got a crack at what was left at the end of the night. Nik snagged a chicken dinner and sat, pretending to eat it. He always took the end-of-shift food home for someone else. Every little bit helped. The rest of the crew pretended not to notice, but the waitresses always made sure there was a foil-lined doggie bag near at hand.

Nik sat listening to the crew wind down, chattering and laughing. As he moved his fork around on his plate, he could feel the bill the man had slipped him crinkle. He reached inside his shirt pocket and took a careful look. It was a hundred-dollar bill.

"Holy cow," he said, bringing the bill out. "I guess this needs to go into the tip pool."

"Nice," the cook sitting across from Nik said. "Where'd you get that?"

"Guy gave it to me," Nik said. "The one who seemed to be running things at that eight-top earlier."

The other front-of-the-house personnel knew which eight-top he meant.

"The one with the blonde who was all over you?" one of the waitresses said. She was a slim, dark-haired young woman named Carrie, a senior in high school. Nik had trouble speaking to her, so he nodded.

"'Course she was," another waitress, a leather-faced redhead named Norma, said. "She was drunk. Even a woman like that wouldn't be mauling a boy his age if she was sober. At least, I don't think so. That's a bad crowd travels with that gambler, that Pat McCanta. We shouldn't serve these people so much alcohol after they've already had enough."

Several heads nodded, but the manager said, "That's easy for you to say. But the bar brings in a lot of money. And the tips seem to be pretty good, too."

"Why would he give me such a big tip?" Nik asked.

"Probably just trying to make up for the way his girlfriend was behaving," Norma said.

"Were you scared?" Carrie asked with a smile. Nik realized she was teasing him and the thought gave him courage.

"Terrified," he said. "I thought she was going to start tearing my clothes off."

"In your dreams," another of the busers said, and everybody laughed.

"Tearing your clothes off," Carrie said, with an altogether different kind of smile. "That's an interesting thought."

The smile more than the words broke Nik's nerve. He could feel a blush creeping up his neck. He shoved the food into the doggie bag, pocketed his share of the tips, mumbled his good-byes, and bolted. As he went out the door, he could hear Norma say, "You shouldn't tease that boy."

"Who's teasing?" Carrie said.

The closing door cut off the crew's laughter. Nik was sure they were laughing at him. He dropped the doggie bag into the basket of his bike, unlocked the bike as fast as he could, swung onto it, and practically ran over the Hacker, who was standing near the door with a cigarette in his hand. The Hacker saw him at the last moment and shrank back against the wall. Nik swerved to miss him and slammed on his brakes.

"Oh, sorry," he said.

The Hacker nodded, and Nik got ready to set off again.

"You're Teddy Kane's kid, ain't you?" the Hacker said.

The question made Nik wary. He had been asked the same thing several times since he'd last seen his father. If a man asked it, the questioner would quickly launch a story about how Nik's father owed him money. If a woman asked, it was usually a prelude to saying what a gentleman Teddy was, followed by a gentle inquiry as to his whereabouts. Nik was both keyed up and tired, and would just as soon have avoided a conversation. But what could he do? He couldn't dodge the Hacker. They worked together.

"I am," he said carefully. "One of them, anyway."

The Hacker nodded, took a drag on his cigarette, and cut loose with a rough, painful-sounding cough that went on and on.

Jeez, Nik thought. What'll I do if he just drops dead?

After what seemed like a long time, the Hacker quit coughing.

"You all right?" Nik asked.

The Hacker nodded and drew a long breath.

"Yeah," he said, "although these things will kill me soon enough."

He drew another long breath, made a last hacking noise, and spat into the gutter.

"I know your dad," the Hacker said. "Me and him worked together when he first got here, out at the base."

When he didn't continue, Nik said, "Which base? I never knew he worked out there."

"Elmendorf, Fort Richardson," the Hacker said. "We started about the same time, just before the war ended. We worked civilian construction. They was building Fort Rich and fixing up Elmendorf, taking out a lot of temporary buildings they'd thrown up for the war, putting up permanent. It was good work and lots of it, and we was young and tough and making good money, for them days."

The Hacker's voice had gotten softer as he talked, younger somehow, full of a warmth that Nik was too young to recognize.

"Your dad was odd for our group," the Hacker went on. "Oh, he worked as hard as anybody and liked a joke and so on. But when the workday ended, he went right home. Same on payday. The rest of us would go out to the bars on Fourth Avenue, have a few drinks, look for women. Weren't that many women here then. But Teddy Kane went home. 'Cecelia will kill me, if I don't,' he'd say, but you could tell he wanted to go home. He'd take your mom out from time to time, I'd see them in this place or that, but Teddy never went out by himself. I guess that was the advantage of having a woman of your own."

There was a long pause. The Hacker took a pull on his cigarette and flicked it into the street. The orange coal arced through the summer twilight and hit the wet pavement with a hiss.

"Gotta go," the Hacker said.

"Hey, wait," Nik said. "Is that the end of the story?"

The Hacker laughed, coughed, spat.

"That's the end of the story as I'm telling it to Teddy Kane's boy," he said, and turned to reenter the restaurant. Nik put his hand on the Hacker's arm.

"Please, Mr. Hackett," he said. "I have to know more. My father has been gone for more than a year now, and nobody knows where. Anything you could tell me might help me find him."

The Hacker looked at Nik in the dim light. Nik wondered what he saw. A younger Teddy Kane? A stupid kid? Somebody his information gave him power over?

"Okay, kid," the Hacker said at last. "If you gotta know." He paused as if to arrange his thoughts. "Must have been '49, the fall there, that Teddy changed. Don't know what happened. One day, he was the same as usual, working and laughing and going right home. The next, he was following along to the bars. After a while, he was leading the pack to get there. Then he started getting to work late. The rest of us covered for him, but the bosses noticed. Our foreman spoke to him more than once."

The Hacker paused again, thinking.

"Then one day, musta been in the fall that year, there's a big to-do at work," he went on. "Some sort of war surplus is missing. There's questions, and threats, and, at the end of the day, they fire the lot of us. Me and your dad and a few others get on at a job out at Fort Rich, but in less than a year there's another theft, and we all get run off again."

Again the Hacker paused to think. Then he shrugged, and said, "Might as well tell you all of it. I decided then that I wasn't going on any more jobs with your dad or any of the others were on that second job. So I didn't. I heard your dad kept having trouble of one sort or another. I'd see him down in the bars once in a while, and we'd talk. Then he started borrowing money off me, and, after some of that, I started making it a point to avoid him."

The Hacker gave a big sigh.

"And that's all I can tell you about your dad," he said. "But I can give you a piece of advice. Let him go. A grown man who disappears most likely don't want to be found. And the direction Teddy Kane was headed, you'll just be disappointed if you do find him."

Nik wanted to argue with the Hacker about that, but he didn't know what to say. He wanted to find his father for his own reasons, reasons he barely understood. Not so he could have a father again or anything like that. Just...just because. He thought about just leaving, but now that the Hacker had gotten the hard part off his chest he didn't seem to be in any hurry to leave.

"How's your mom?" he asked. "A fine woman. And a hell of a dancer. The two of them together, your dad and mom, could really cut a rug. Your dad told me that dancing was one of two things they did well together."

The Hacker giggled then, and Nik realized that smoking wasn't all he'd been doing since the shift ended. Must have a pint on him. That explained his sudden bout of talkativeness.

"Yes, a fine woman," he said. "Not a great face, but that body..."

The Hacker seemed to realize who he was talking to then because he cleared his throat and said, "Sorry, son. I shouldn't be talking that way about your mother. Forget I said anything."

Nik let the silence grow, then said, "I have to be going."

The Hacker lit another cigarette.

"You do that," he said. "Tell your mom I said hello."

"I will," Nik said. "And thanks for talking to me."

"Sure thing, kid," the Hacker said.

Nik remounted his bike.

"Wait, kid," the Hacker said. "I did see your dad around, though. The last time I seen him was a year or more ago. I ran into him in some joint. He seemed to be flush. Bought me a couple drinks. But that's all I remember. I got pretty drunk that night, I expect."

When he was sure the Hacker had finished, Nik said thanks again, pushed off, and rode along the dimly lit streets. They were living that year in a sprawling construct of logs and plywood, with low ceilings and many tiny rooms. The heat was uneven and the plumbing balky, but he'd heard his mother say that the rent was right.

He thought about his promise to himself that he'd find his father. He'd meant that when he said it, but so many things had happened since then. Sister and brothers leaving. School and work and trying to get enough to eat and finding the money for medicine for the baby, Deidre, who had been born sickly. Nik hadn't even known his mother was pregnant again when his father left, and now there were five kids at home. With all that, and thinking about Carrie and trying to find the time to make some friends, he'd let his determination flag.

I'm going to find him, he thought fiercely. It might take a while, but I'm going to find him. Then, for the first time, he thought, or find out what happened to him.

nine

The past is never dead. It's not even past.

—WILLIAM FAULKNER

## MARCH 2007

Kane made the long climb to wakefulness like a man fighting his way
out of a silo full of spiderwebs. He was sweating, his breath coming in
short gasps, worn out from the effort of opening his eyes. His vision
was blurry, but when he tried to wipe his eyes he couldn't move his
arm. Either arm. He tried to open his mouth to call out but his lips
seemed to be sewn shut.

What's going on? he thought.

"Be at ease, Mr. Kane," a voice said. "Just lie still."

Drops fell into his eyes, and, as he blinked them away, the face of
his benefactor swam into focus. The face was round and black and
cheerful and female.

When is this? he thought but couldn't open his mouth to ask the
question.

Something cool and wet touched his lips, and he sucked on it greedily, trying to pump out the moisture like some single-celled organism.

"Do not struggle, Mr. Kane," the round, black, female face said, showing even, white teeth as it talked. "This is a safe, calm place."

She took the cool thing away, and Kane found that he could open his mouth.

"Wha?" he said. He sounded like a frog. "Wha? What am I?"

No, he thought. That didn't come out right. I meant to ask something else.

"Do not try to talk, Mr. Kane," the woman said. She laid something cool on his forehead. "Just rest. You have been hurt. You will be all right, but you have been hurt."

Hurt? Kane thought. How did I get hurt?

"Your sister has been sitting with you," the woman said, "but she is resting now. And you have had another visitor, a big man named Mr. Jeffords. He is your friend?"

Jeffords? Does he want to talk about Danny?

"When am I?" he said. Or did he? There was no reply. Maybe I didn't ask that out loud. Maybe I never woke up.

ten

The memory represents to us not what
we choose but what it pleases.

—MICHEL DE MONTAIGNE

## SEPTEMBER 1985

"I tell ya, that rat bastard knows somethin' and he ain't sharin'," Jackie Dee said, banging his glass on the faux-wood tabletop. The Keyboard Lounge was full of cops unwinding after a hard day's work. A couple of them looked at Jackie Dee out of the corners of their eyes, but nobody said anything. An angry Jackie Dee was a sight to make strong men quiver. Pour some booze on that and anything could happen.

Or maybe they couldn't hear him. Some joker had put a couple of bucks' worth of quarters in the jukebox, and it was blaring "Take Me Home Tonight" over and over again.

Jackie Dee looked at his glass owlishly.

"Empty," he said, "just like that dickhead Jeffords's soul."

He waved the glass over his head to get the waitress's attention. The waitress was an overfed bleached blonde who'd stuffed herself into a black-and-white costume with a short skirt and a plunging neckline.

She wiggled over to the table, and Jackie Dee handed her his empty glass. The waitress smiled and rubbed an ample hip against Jackie Dee's shoulder. Jackie Dee put a hand on her butt, and she giggled.

"This here's Ronnie, kid," he said to Kane. "You met Ronnie? She likes cops. Any cop. All cops. And, if the stories are true, more than one at a time."

Ronnie giggled again and slapped Jackie Dee on the top of the head. Her hand connected with a solid *thwok*.

"Oh, you," she said.

Jackie Dee scowled and rubbed the top of his head. He looked to Kane like he was going to say something nasty, but instead he smiled and said, "What say, Ronnie? You and me in the back room?"

Ronnie gave Kane a smile and winked.

"Sure thing, Jackie Dee," she said. "Think your wife would like to watch?"

From her tone, and his, Kane knew they were performing a well-worn routine.

"Jackie DeeTwo would kill the both of us," Jackie Dee said, feigning sadness.

Ronnie nodded.

"That she would," she said. "So how about I bring you another Seven and Seven instead? And how about you, young man? Still nursing that beer?"

Kane nodded, and Ronnie wiggled off.

"How come you ain't drinking, kid?" Jackie Dee asked. "We're off duty for the night."

Kane nodded and lit a cigarette. He was trying to quit. Laurie didn't like him smoking around the kids. Said it was bad for their development. He wanted to do what she asked, but between the stress of the job and the way a cigarette tasted with a drink he couldn't quite kick the habit. Despite his best efforts, he smoked. Hell, they all smoked. That's why the air in the Keyboard was thick enough to carve off chunks.

"Yeah," he said. "It's been a rough forty-eight. But the way Laurie's behaving, no way I'm going home plastered. She threw my ass out of the house once already for doing that, seven, eight months ago. Wouldn't let me see the girls until I promised to cut down on my drinking. Spent goddamn near two months in a motel room until she called and told me I could come back. So now I'm more careful when I drink. Especially since she's pregnant. She's always been a Tartar when she's pregnant."

Kane had seen his wife exactly once more in the past two days, when he'd dropped in to change clothes. She was worn and red-eyed and started crying the minute he walked in the door. He tried to comfort her, but she shrugged off his attempted embrace and his soft words and began railing against him, his job, his mother, her pregnancy, and everything else she could lay her tongue to. The mention of his mother was troubling. He wanted to ask Laurie what Cecelia Kane had done now, but his wife wasn't interested in conveying information. She was interested in lashing out. Kane bit back several hot retorts, took a quick shower, changed clothes, and left the house, moving as fast as a felon breaking jail. He'd done what sleeping he'd managed since then in an empty holding cell at the police station.

When he told Jackie Dee about Laurie's behavior, the big man held up his hand and said, "Hey, kid, what do you expect? You knocked her up. Deal with it."

Jackie Dee wasn't in a very good mood, either. Two days of dead ends meant the case would be a lot harder to solve. As the senior detective, he had every reporter, politician, and police brass hat in town breathing down his neck. And the more lines of inquiry that petered out, the surer he became that Tom Jeffords was hiding information.

"He knows something," Jackie Dee said for about the hundredth time, lighting a cigarette. "I can tell. He knows something."

Ronnie came wiggling back and set the big man's drink in front of him. Jackie Dee pawed at her halfheartedly, and she fended him off, giggling, then went on her way.

Kane finished his last swallow of beer and set his glass down.

"Have another, kid," Jackie Dee said. "One for the road."

Kane shook his head. One he could handle, but he knew from experience where two would lead.

"I'm going home to get some sleep," he said. "You should, too. Want a lift?"

Jackie Dee shook his head.

"Naw, I'm fine to drive," he said.

"Okay," Kane said. "Tomorrow, I'll go talk to Jeffords. I know him a little. Maybe he'll tell me something he won't tell you."

Jackie Dee straightened up at that.

"Why's that?" he asked. "Why would he tell you somethin' he wouldn't tell me?"

Kane got to his feet and stood, smiling at his partner.

"Maybe because you're a big, loudmouthed asshole," he said, "who hates his guts."

Jackie Dee guffawed at that.

"You got that right, kid," he said. "All of it. Wanna meet me at Leroy's about eight?"

Kane nodded and left the bar. On his way out, he practically ran over Murphy, the police photographer.

"Hey," Murphy said, "watch out, would you?"

"Sorry," Kane said, then, "Thanks for getting those photos to me so fast."

"The Shirtleff scene photos?" Murphy said. "You bet. Getting anywhere?"

"Not so's you'd notice," Kane said.

"Too bad about that," Murphy said. "I liked that Shirtleff. The rest of you guys treat me like I'm some sort of appliance with arms and legs, but he always took time to chat."

"No kidding?" Kane said. "What did you two talk about?"

"Photography, mostly," Murphy said. "He was a pretty serious amateur photographer. He showed me some animal photos he'd taken, and they were quite good."

Kane nodded. He knew that Danny had liked to take pictures. He'd tell stories about it at parties.

"Well, I hope you catch whoever did it," Murphy said.

That seemed to exhaust the subject they shared, so Murphy nodded and continued into the bar. Kane jaywalked over to his car. The rain that fell was cold. Not cold enough to be snow yet, probably not for another month, but headed that way. Kane was glad he didn't have to sweep snow and scrape windows yet. Winter would be there soon enough, and, tonight, he was tired.

He lit a cigarette, started the car, flipped on the lights, and pulled out for home. Even this older, more settled part of downtown was vastly different than it had been when he was a kid. High-rises had sprouted up all over, sometimes overshadowing the older, smaller buildings and sometimes replacing them. And places like the spot they'd found Danny's body? They'd just been woodland back then. Things happened fast here, or at least they had until this year, when the bottom fell out of the economy. Guys were putting their tools in the backs of their pickups and their families, if they had any, in the fronts and pointing the trucks south, pausing only to hand their house keys to the banks. Kane was sure that he should be worried about his future, about all their futures, but he was just too busy right now. Maybe later.

The stoplight gods smiled on him, and he pulled into his drive-way in less than ten minutes. The house was dark. He entered qui-etly, hung up his wet overcoat, and left his shoes in the entryway. He padded up the stairs and looked in the girls' room. Amy, as usual, had fought sleep until she was overcome. Evidence of the wrestling match was everywhere: blankets on the floor, pillow at her feet, sheet twisted into a rope. He knelt and rearranged everything, covering her gently. Her older sister, Emily, slept neat as a pin, lying just the way Laurie had tucked her in. Kane kissed them both and walked quietly into the master bedroom.

Laurie had fallen asleep with her reading lamp on. The light left one side of her face in darkness. The side he could see was soft and youthful, reminding Kane of the young and hopeful woman he had married.

What happened to that woman? he asked himself. Is it living with me that's made her so snappish and difficult?

He took off his clothes, hanging some and dropping the rest into the big wicker laundry hamper. He belted a bathrobe around his body and tiptoed into the bathroom. Pulling the door quietly closed, he clicked on the light and did what needed doing. He ignored his reflection in the mirror as he brushed his teeth. In his mid-thirties, a sleepless night or two was starting to take a toll. He looked like hell, and he knew it.

He clicked off the light and tiptoed back into the bedroom, took off his robe, hung it on the bedpost, and crawled into bed. He lay with his hip and shoulder touching Laurie, listening to her even breathing. For some reason, he was sure she was awake. If she was, pretending to sleep was a sure sign she wanted to be left alone. As Kane lay there thinking about that, Laurie sighed and rolled over to put her back to him. When she was settled, their bodies were no longer touching. Kane turned to put his back to her.

I just don't have the energy to get mad, he thought. And the next thing he knew, the girls were jumping on him, laughing and yelling for him to get up.

Crap, he thought, I forgot to set the alarm. But when he looked at the clock radio, it read seven a.m., so he had time. He wrestled with his daughters for a minute, then put on his robe, shuffled to the bathroom, and climbed into the shower. A few minutes later, Laurie stuck her head in.

"You want breakfast?" she asked in a tone that suggested the best answer was no.

"I'm meeting Jackie Dee at Leroy's," he said. "I'll eat there."

Laurie closed the door again without saying anything. Kane finished showering, climbed out, toweled off, and wiped the steam from the mirror. He needed a shave, so he gave himself one, then returned to the bedroom and got dressed. When he got downstairs, he found Laurie putting coats on the girls.

"There's coffee in the kitchen," Laurie said. "I've got to deliver these two."

She seemed better this morning, composed but distant.

"You okay?" Kane asked.

She nodded and finished putting Amy's coat on. Like anything involving Amy, it was a struggle.

"Did you find out who shot... Officer Shirtleff?" she asked.

"No," Kane said. "We're getting nowhere."

Laurie nodded and put on her own coat.

"No clues?" she asked.

"No clues," he said.

Laurie nodded again, her head bobbing like a child's toy.

"Okay," she said. "Well, I have to get the girls where they're going."

Emily and Amy went to day care three days a week, some place Laurie had found that was trying to actually teach them things. Laurie gathered up their lunch boxes and Pee Chees and herded them toward the garage.

"Laurie," Kane said.

She stopped and turned to look at him.

"Things will slow down some on this case soon, and I'll be able to spend more time at home," he said.

Laurie looked at him like he was speaking some particularly obscure foreign language. Finally, she said, "That will be good, Nik."

She turned and resumed moving the girls toward the garage.

Kane walked into the kitchen and poured himself a cup of coffee. He listened to the garage door open and close and the sound of Laurie's station wagon pulling out. He walked out into the garage and sat in a lawn chair he'd set up there, lit a cigarette, and sat for a while, drinking coffee and smoking. When he was finished, he put the cigarette out in an ashtray that sat on his workbench and walked back into the house. He dumped his cup into the sink, put his coat on, and drove to Leroy's. The sight of Jackie Dee in the booth made him laugh.

"What's so goddamn funny?" Jackie Dee asked belligerently.

"You are," Kane said, sliding into the booth opposite his partner. "You look like something that fell out of a tall cow's ass."

Jackie Dee laughed, then winced.

"You think I look bad from out there," he said, "you should see what I look like from in here."

The waitress arrived with Jackie Dee's order and took Kane's. During breakfast, they went over what they had, an exercise that brought another "diddly-squat" from Jackie Dee.

"We don't find something soon, we're gonna be completely high-centered," Jackie Dee said, "and that's gonna be an uncomfortable thing to have to explain all the way up the chain of command."

Kane nodded. He was just the junior guy, but failure would rub off on him, too.

"Anything about people he put away, maybe?" he asked. "Current cases?"

"If there is, Jeffords isn't saying," Jackie Dee said. "The last time I talked to him, I said we needed files on Danny's current cases, and he gave me the smile the python gave the pig and said he'd cleared it with the chief that his people would handle that. 'We have some sensitive operations running, Giuseppe,' he said to me. 'We don't need you rampaging through our operation.' I really, really wanted to pinch his head off then."

Jackie Dee rummaged in his pockets, came out with a handful of pills, popped them into his mouth, and washed them down with coffee.

"This goddamn war on drugs," he said. "Waste of time and manpower. Junkies are gonna be junkies no matter what you do. But the feds are putting big money behind it, so we gotta have an antidrug operation to get our share of Uncle Sam's coin. Jeffords has figured out every angle of that, and the chief loves him because he doesn't have to bother the mayor with a bigger budget request. The tail's wagging the dog, but that's politics."

Kane had heard all this before, and not just from Jackie Dee, at drunken bull sessions. He didn't really disagree with it, either, but his job was serving and protecting, not politicking. He downed the last of his coffee and stood up.

"I'll go see if I can do better with Jeffords," he said. "See you at the shop."

He thought about how to approach the issue on his drive downtown, but nothing brilliant offered itself. So he just walked into Jeffords's office and sat down. The fact that Jeffords had an office all to himself was proof of his standing in the department.

Jeffords was reading some report and kept doing that, making a show of ignoring Kane. Finally, the phone rang, and Jeffords reached for it.

"If you pick up that receiver, Sergeant," Kane said, "I'll be forced to draw my service revolver and blow your telephone away."

Jeffords looked at Kane for the first time, the hint of a smile running across his lips. Even sitting he was an imposing figure: big,

blond, and, to all appearances, bursting with health. Despite spending more and more of his time behind a desk, Jeffords didn't seem to
be developing the gut that many of his contemporaries had.

A fight between him and Jackie Dee would be something to see,
Kane thought.

Jeffords let the phone ring while he made a show of studying
Kane.

"I didn't think working with Giuseppe DiSanto would be good for
you, Nik," he said at last. "It certainly doesn't seem to have increased
your respect for your superiors."

Kane laughed at that.

"We've had this conversation before, Sergeant," he said. "You have
a higher rank than I do, but that doesn't make you my superior. And
I don't care about all the rank and chain-of-command stuff. I've got
a job to do here. Considering that it was someone under your command who was killed, you don't seem to be particularly anxious to
help me, us, do that job."

Jeffords opened his mouth but seemed to think better of speaking.
Instead, he got up, walked around his desk, and closed the door to his
office. He returned, sat back down, and folded his big hands on the
desk in front of him.

"It would be extremely unwise of you to repeat that statement,
Nik," he said. "It's perilously close to insubordination."

"Then write me up," Kane said, smiling. There was no humor in
the smile. "But we both know what will happen. You and Jackie Dee
got some sort of mutual hard-on going, and everybody knows that.
You and I, on the other hand, have a record of working together suc-
cessfully. In fact, my jacket contains more than one good evaluation
that you wrote. So if you suddenly decide I'm not such a good cop,
it'll have a completely different impact in the department. You may
win in the end—probably will—but you won't be unmarked. It's
your choice."

For all the emotion Jeffords showed, they could have been talking about the weather.

"I thought you didn't like office politics, Nik," Jeffords said.

"I don't," Kane said, "but that doesn't mean I won't use them if that's what it takes to get my job done."

Jeffords nodded at that, then sat looking at Kane for a long time. Finally, he said, "We have examined Officer Shirtleff's case files. The open ones are all minor, street-level affairs. If people involved in cases like those start shooting police officers, we'll all have to drive armored cars. He's only been with us four years, not enough time for anyone to finish serving major time and come looking for him. Even with the ridiculous parole rules we have. So the chances he was killed for something he had done or is doing for this department are slim."

Kane waited for Jeffords to continue, and, when he didn't, said, "So you don't know of anything that would be a motive for his murder?"

"Nothing to do with his work for this department," Jeffords said.

"Anything *not* to do with his work for this department?" Kane asked.

Jeffords shrugged.

"I didn't know Officer Shirtleff very well personally," Jeffords said. "You know how it is with undercovers. After they've been at it for a while, they're not sure if they're cops or criminals anymore. They don't make very... useful... friends."

Kane recognized a nonanswer when he heard one. He thought about pressing Jeffords but knew him well enough to know that wasn't likely to get him anywhere. Jeffords had probably game-planned this whole encounter. He could say he'd been cooperative now and still refuse to give Kane anything useful.

"What can you tell me about this case he was working in Kodiak?" he asked. "Anything strange about it?"

Jeffords shook his head.

"Not much," he said. "The commander of the state trooper post there is an old friend from my days with that agency. He needed a fresh face to break up a drug ring that was selling to fishermen. Officer Shirtleff was the natural choice. He was fairly new to the state, had never been to Kodiak, in fact. So we loaned him out. The arrests were made before his return here, so it's unlikely that his death was related to his work there. But they might have missed someone. You never know."

Kane took his notebook out of his pocket.

"We'll have to talk with whoever ran that operation," he said. "Can you give me his name and telephone number?"

Jeffords frowned.

"We've already interviewed him, and I'm satisfied that we know all he can tell us," he said.

"If you were the head of homicide, that would be fine," Kane said. "But you're not. So if you could just give me the information?"

Jeffords was glaring now, and his neck was mottled with red.

"I don't see..." he began.

"Fine," Kane barked. He shoved the notebook back into his pocket and stood. "I'll tell my sergeant, who will tell his lieutenant, and everyone can get involved in this song and dance, wasting time and energy on something that probably isn't related to Danny's death. But you know perfectly well that 'probably isn't related' isn't good enough. So we'll do this the hard way."

"Nik..." Jeffords began, but he was talking to Kane's back.

"How'd you do?" Jackie Dee asked when Kane sat down at his desk.

"So-so," Kane said, and recounted his conversation with Jeffords.

"What do you think?" Jackie Dee asked.

"I think there's something going on," Kane said. "I think the stuff he told me about Danny's work here is straight enough, but there's something fishy about the Kodiak deal. You know anybody over there?"

Jackie Dee nodded.

"I got a guy I could reach out to there," he said. "Town cop, but he might know something. I'll give him a call." He handed a piece of paper across to Nick. "That's the name and telephone number of his last boss at Seattle PD. Maybe you could call him and see if there's any ghosts from Danny's time there that might have come back."

Kane nodded. Like a lot of police work, this would probably be a dead end. But it had to be done. So did a thousand other things.

As he reached for his telephone, it rang. The caller was his friend with the FBI.

"You guys getting anywhere with the Shirtleff killing?" his friend asked after they'd exchanged pleasantries.

"We're not planning to make an arrest anytime soon," Kane said.

"How about the buy money?" his friend asked. "That turn up?"

Buy money? Kane thought. What buy money?

"Yeah, the buy money," he said. "How much was it again?"

The sound of his friend's edgy laughter came over the wire.

"Jesus, Kane, you don't know about the buy money?" he said. "What kind of police department you got there, anyway?"

"The usual kind," Kane said. "All fucked-up. Tell me about the buy money."

There was silence at the other end of the phone. Nik waited. Finally, his friend said, "Okay. I don't like cop killers much, either. But you didn't hear this from me. At the request of your drug guy there—Jeffords—the agency provided twenty thousand dollars in buy money for this case in Kodiak. Your man—Shirtleff—was supposed to bring it back with him."

The moments stretched out as Kane listened to the crackling of the telephone line.

"You didn't find it, did you?" his friend asked at last. "There's twenty K of Uncle Sam's money gone missing. I got to tell my boss."

"You do that," Kane said. "Just don't tell him where you got the information, or my ass is grass."

Kane put the phone down, staring at Jackie Dee.

Well, at least we've got a motive now, he thought, and opened his mouth to relay the information to his partner.

eleven

To live is so startling it leaves little time for anything else.

—EMILY DICKINSON

## MARCH 2007

Kane was alone when he woke again. He could hear the beeping and humming of machines and see the multicolored lights they cast across the sheet that covered him.

Hospital, he thought. Something's happened, and I'm in the hospital. Why?

But when he tried to remember, his thoughts sailed away like eiderdown on the wind. Hunting accident? He could remember hunting ducks on the flats as a boy, watching the feathers fly as the shot hit them, each shot the difference between food on the table and hunger.

Maybe somebody shot me by mistake, he thought. Everything is so hazy. A woman was here before. Is she my nurse? Is somebody else supposed to be here?

Thinking is hard. Too many questions. I'm too tired.

Something reached up out of the darkness and grabbed him, and he let himself be pulled under.

The sunlight was trying to get through his eyelids. It turned them red, blood red, shot through with dark fault lines. His mouth tasted like metal, and a drum seemed to be throbbing beneath the wool in his brain.

This is some hangover, he thought. Worst ever. No, the worst was the time I drank that bottle of Jägermeister. That one felt like someone was trying to carve my brain out with a rusty spoon.

He realized he was thinking then.

I can think. I can remember. I'm Nik Kane. I'm in the hospital. Something happened.

He managed to get one eye open, but the blurs he could see were those of an empty room.

How did I get here? What happened? Somebody shot me, didn't they?

He could remember, if he made himself. But that would be so hard. Maybe he should rest first.


THERE WAS SOMEONE in his room. A woman was humming. Nik got an eye open. The lights were on, and the cheerful, round, mahogany-colored face of a woman was looking down at him.

I've seen her before, Nik thought. Where? When?

"Ah, so you're awake at last, you lazybones," the woman said. Her voice sounded like children playing, with just a touch of calypso beneath their shouts and laughter. "I am Nurse Yolanda. The sister who visits you—the religious—said you would come back to us. 'He is too stubborn to die,' she said. You were lucky, very lucky, and your doctor was very good, and now you are back with us."

Yes, I've heard that voice before, Kane thought. He opened his mouth to say so, but again his lips were stuck shut. Yolanda held a damp washcloth to his lips until he could open them.

"Where, where am I?" he croaked.

"People always want to know where they are," Yolanda said, the music in her voice even louder. "You are on the planet Earth, and lucky to be here, as I said. That should be enough for you. But if it is not, you are in Bartlett Regional Hospital, in Juneau, Alaska."

He opened his mouth again, but Yolanda held a finger to his lips.

"Enough questions," she said. "You are Mr. Nikiski Kane. You were shot. That's all I shall tell you right now. It is all you need to know. Now you must rest. I know that you are hungry, or will be soon, but right now we are feeding you through a tube until your doctor says you may have real food. So close your eyes, Mr. Nikiski Kane. Thank God you are alive, and then go to sleep."

And, like a child, Kane did just as he was told.

twelve

There are lots of people who mistake their
imagination for their memory.

—JOSH BILLINGS

## MARCH 1964

Crusty snow crunched under Nik's feet as he walked to work. Winter was gradually loosening its dark, frigid grip on the city. Another Friday night coming up, four to midnight and on his feet the whole time. Once the night would have been run-run-run, but the economy had slowed, and the waitstaff and back-of-the-house crew were all worried about falling tips and rumors of layoffs. The economy was making everybody jumpy. The manager was worried. The owner was worried. The whole town was worried. The city—the whole state— was limping along on defense spending, freight forwarding, this and that. Without a boom soon, the shrinking economy would squeeze more and more people out of Alaska. At least, that was the fear. The state's history was all boom-and-bust, and this smelled like a bust.

Nik was worried about other things. Finishing his last year in junior high was at the top of the list. Instead of giving the ninth graders an easy send-off, his teachers were piling on the work. Between that and his job at the restaurant, he was as busy—as he'd heard one of the chefs say during a nightly rush—as a one-legged man in an ass-kicking contest.

To top it off, Kevin had gotten himself arrested the weekend before, putting his graduation from high school in jeopardy. He and some of his hoodlum friends had broken into a liquor warehouse, and he'd been caught carrying a couple of cases of Jim Beam out of the place. His friends had scattered, and the cops were sweating Kevin to give them names.

Their mother had retreated to her bedroom, emerging only to shed mortified tears and curse Kevin for holding her up to public shame. Her reaction underlined for Nik the importance she put on appearances. He found himself wondering how that jibed with being married to Teddy Kane.

Nik hadn't really found out much more about his father. People who knew him would smile at the mention of Teddy's name; the men derisively, the women fondly. But everybody said pretty much the same: good dresser, good manners, a sponge. It was like Nik was asking about some two-dimensional character. The information he got had no depth. And he just didn't have the time to conduct a real investigation, like the Continental Op or Philip Marlowe.

If only I could get somebody to pay me to find him, Nik thought as he signed himself into work that night. Then I might be able to get somewhere.

Nik hung his coat in the little room tacked onto the back of the kitchen, opposite the owner's office. That office was dark, the owner on vacation in his native Germany. The little room held canned goods and linens and a row of hooks for coats. There was also a long mirror, so Nik checked himself over. He wore a white shirt, black tie, and black pants. The owner had declared that the proper attire for his busboys a few months before, and Nik had had to buy the clothes with his own money. His outfit was already starting to look a little ratty, and he didn't look forward to telling Oregon that he'd need new clothes soon.

Maybe if she'd give me the money to buy better clothes, they'd last longer, he thought.

When Cee Cee left, Oregon had taken over the family finances, but she refused to be stand-in mother, too. Not that any of the remaining Kane kids except Deidre needed mothering. Dee Dee would have to make do with Cecelia Kane as mother, and good luck to her, Nik thought.

He looked over the menu. Since it was Good Friday, there was lots of fish on the menu. He put in an order for halibut cheeks, picked up his plastic tub, and went through the swinging doors into the dining area. Aside from two old ladies having either a late lunch or an early dinner—or just getting quietly blotto—the place was empty. Carrie and Norma were standing next to the bar, chatting with the bartender. Nik walked over to where the old ladies sat to check their water glasses and noted the two empty wine bottles on their table.

Guess it's blotto, he thought.

He stopped at the bar to say hello, earning a smile from Carrie. Then he went back into the kitchen and shot the bull with the kitchen staff until his meal was ready. He stood at a side counter to eat. The halibut cheeks were stringy from having been frozen, but the mashed potatoes had been made with evaporated milk, and the canned corn was drenched in butter. Fine dining, Alaska style.

When he finished, he scraped his plate and carried the dirty dishes to the washing station. The Hacker wasn't there yet—had been showing up less and less, in fact—and Nik reckoned the manager would have to call in a replacement. Then he stuck his head into the restaurant again. Only a few more people sat at the tables.

Gonna be a slow night, he thought. Gonna be dull.

He went out to dispense water and fetch butter and rolls. As he finished the last table, Carrie came up and asked, "Ready to order?"

"Can you tell me..." the woman of the family began.

The floor beneath Nik's feet began to roll.

"Earthquake!" somebody yelled.

An earthquake was nothing new to Nik. But not like this. The woman's water glass stuttered its way to the edge of the table and jumped into her lap.

"Under the table!" the man said to his family. "Now!"

The building groaned, then gave three sharp cracks. Carrie screamed, her order pad and pencil forgotten in her hand. Nik dropped the big basket of bread and tried to walk the few steps to her. The floor rolled up to meet him, then dropped away like it had turned to water. The best he could manage was a stagger. It seemed to take a long time to reach Carrie. He took her hand, and they staggered to an empty table. Bottles crashed from the back bar one after another. Carrie screamed again and hit Nik in the chest with one fist, then the other. The big window on the front of the building shattered. The building moaned and groaned like a large, wounded creature. A section of the ceiling crashed to the floor, barely missing the two of them. Dust rose. Nik wrapped his arms around Carrie, kicked her feet out from under her, and lowered her to the floor. He went with her, then rolled the two of them under the table. They stopped, side by side, the table shielding them. The rolling got stronger. Carrie's screams were painful in Nik's ears. He couldn't think of what to do, so he kissed her. She stopped screaming and kissed him back, her tongue darting into his mouth like a peppermint-flavored knife. The rolling went on and on. So did the kiss. The building cracked and popped and groaned like it was being torn apart by a giant hand. Finally, the rolling slowed, then stopped as suddenly as it had begun. Nik tried to pull away, but Carrie put a hand on the back of his head. The kiss went on and on. Carrie's body moved in a way his body understood but his brain didn't recognize. Nik reached up and gently pulled Carrie's hand away, then lifted his head.

"The kitchen," he said. "Gas. Fire."

He rolled from under the table, stood, grabbed Carrie's hands, and jerked her to her feet.

"Get out of here," he said.

The restaurant was a mass of overturned furniture, broken glass, and pieces of ceiling. Norma was leading the bartender toward the front door. The rag he held to his head was speckled with red. Nik threaded his way through the wreckage of the dining room. As he reached the door to the kitchen, the head cook came through, followed by the rest of his staff.

"You can't get out this way," the head cook said. "It's blocked."

"The gas," Nik said. "How do I turn off the gas?"

The head cook pushed him out of the way and hurried past. Nik grabbed the next person in line, another cook named Emilio, who'd been there forever.

"The gas?" Nik said.

"In the pantry," Emilio said. "By the door."

He tore himself from Nik's grasp and was gone. Nik fought past the rest of the back-of-the-house crew and into the kitchen. The floor was littered with broken dishes and dented pots. The rotten-egg smell of escaping gas grew stronger as he moved through the kitchen to the back room. Nik went into the little room, found the shut-off valve, and dogged it down tight. He felt sleepy and seemed to move in slow motion.

Must be the gas, he thought. Gotta get out of here.

He looked around for his coat, but it had disappeared. He wobbled back through the kitchen and dining room. As he reached the door, an aftershock rippled beneath his feet. Fear shot through him. He scrambled through the door into the street.

"Over here, Nik," Carrie called.

The people from the restaurant clustered in the middle of the street. When Nik reached them, Carrie threw her arms around his neck.

"Thank God, you're safe," she said, pressing her body to his.

"That was very dangerous," the manager said.

Nik found he was grinning. He was afraid, but he was also having...fun. There was no other way to describe it.

I can't tell anyone that, he thought. They'll think I'm nuts.

So "I turned off the gas" was all he said.

Everyone stood around for a while. Nik, to his amazement, had his arm around Carrie's shoulders. She was warm against him.

"I guess that's it for now," one of the men said to the woman with him. "We'd better get home and see if there's anything left of the house."

The two of them left. A family followed.

"I suppose I'd better lock the place up," the manager said.

Won't do much good with the window lying in the street, Nik thought, but he didn't say anything. What could he say? He had no idea what you should do after a disaster like this.

"I'd better go and see if my apartment is still there," Carrie said.

Nik took his arm from her shoulders.

"Yeah, I'd better go, too," he said. "Check on my family."

He turned to go, but Carrie put a hand on his arm.

"Thank you, Nik," she said.

Nik suddenly had so much to say that the words banged into each other and stuck in his throat. So he nodded and walked away.

The walk home was an adventure, a matter of winding around obstacles: a car on the sidewalk, a fallen telephone pole, the limb from a tree that had shaken itself to pieces, cracks in the street and sidewalks. Little tremors ran beneath his feet as he walked. The house looked untouched. He scrambled through the door, happy to be in out of the cold. His mother, Dee Dee, and Aurora were in the kitchen, listening to a voice from a transistor radio.

"Nik," his mother said. "Why were you out without a coat?"

"Did you turn off the gas, Mom?" Nik asked.

"The gas?" Aurora said. "Why would we turn off the gas?"

Nik just shook his head.

Million-dollar face, ten-cent brain, he thought, and went down the stairs to the basement. He didn't smell gas, and the pilot light still burned in the stove, so he decided to leave things alone. He went into his room. He was supposed to be rooming upstairs with Kevin, but his brother's temper made that unwise. So he'd gradually moved down into the basement, into what had been some sort of storage room, sandwiched between the utility room and the furnace. There wasn't much to the room, but for someone who's spent most of his life sharing too little space with too many people it was paradise. His few clothes hung from a wooden dowel he'd installed, and the room was lit by a droplight plugged into an extension cord he'd run in from the utility room. The light didn't work, but he knew where everything was. He changed into warmer clothing and went back upstairs.

"If everything's okay here," he said, "I'm heading back downtown."

"You can't leave me, Nik," his mother said. "What if there's another earthquake? What if robbers come?"

Dee Dee, not yet two, heard the fear in her mother's voice and began to cry.

"I can't do anything about another earthquake," Nik said. "And why would robbers come here when there are so many nicer houses to rob? Besides, I might be able to get somebody to pay me to help them clean up."

Nik figured the mention of money would change his mother's mind, and it did.

"Well, okay," she said. "But don't be gone too long."

She turned to her youngest daughter.

"Hush, Dee Dee," she said. "Everything will be all right."

Nik put on an old coat that had belonged to his father. He was surprised to find that it fit him. As he reached for the doorknob, Aurora said from behind him, "Is it terrible, Nik? Are many people dead?"

He could tell from her tone that she was as excited as he was. He turned to look at her, marveling at her beauty, enhanced by the color in her cheeks and the brightness of her eyes.

"I don't know, Aurora," he said. "You stay here with Mom, and I'll be back."

He left the house and headed downtown. Parts of it looked untouched. Others didn't. The front of the J.C. Penney store had fallen into the street. Men worried the edges of the rubble, searching to see if anyone was trapped there. Small groups, mostly women and children, stood and watched, talking in low voices. Nik kept walking. A block over, the ground had opened beneath a theater and dropped it straight down. Its second-story marquee rested at ground level. To his left, a woman stood in front of a shop, wringing her hands. The shop's window lay in the street, and part of its ceiling had collapsed

"Can I help you, ma'am?" Nik asked.

The woman turned to Nik. She was pretty but old. Forty, maybe, dressed elegantly in a long coat and a hat with flowers on it. She wore a lot of makeup. She seemed to be looking not at Nik but at something behind him.

"This is my shop, my dress shop," she said. Her voice was calm and even, like she was talking about some everyday topic; the weather, maybe, or a child's report card. "I was doing some rearranging and I'd just closed up when the ground started shaking. I don't know what to do. I don't know where my husband is. I was supposed to meet him here for dinner. I don't know where he is. I don't know how to get home or if my home will even be there. I don't know what you could do about any of that."

Nik didn't know what he could do about it, either. Even if he could salvage some of the clothes, he had no safe place to put them. He turned to go.

"Oh, please don't leave," the woman said, and began to cry. Instinctively, Nik put his arms around her. Her breath was warm on his neck and her tears hot on his skin. She sobbed for a while, then stopped and stepped away, patting her head as if to make sure her hat was still there.

"Oh, I'm so sorry, young man," she said. "I'm letting all this turn me into a silly goose. I must pull myself together. Please, go on your way. I'll be fine."

Nik nodded and left, her perfume clinging to him like a half-forgotten promise. The sun was just a rumor on the horizon now, shadows obscuring much of the scene. Nik doubted the streetlights would be coming on. The next block didn't show much damage, and he walked along, peering through windows, hoping to find someone in need of cleaning help.

"You there," a voice called from across the street. "Stay right where you are. And keep your hands in sight."

A small man stepped out of the shadows, right hand on a gun that hung from his belt, left on the handle of a billy club. As he approached, Nik could see light glint from a badge on his chest. A cop. He stopped short of Nik.

"What are you doing creeping around down here?" he asked.

"I'm not 'creeping around,'" Nik said. "I'm looking to see if there's people who need help."

"Looking to see if there's an open door or a broken window, more likely," the cop said. "Let me see some ID."

"All I've got is a library card," Nik said.

The cop snapped his fingers impatiently.

"Hand it over," he said.

Nik fished out his wallet, extracted the library card, and handed it over.

"Kane, huh?" the cop said. "You any relation to that Kevin Kane kid?"

Nik sighed.

"I'm his brother," he said.

The cop stepped closer to Nik and peered into his face. Close up, Nik could see that the hair that leaked out from under his cap was fiery red.

"I should probably run you in just for that," the cop said. He stepped back again and gave Nik a hard stare. "I heard your brother got caught stealing booze the other night. I've had encounters with him, too. What's his problem?"

Nik shrugged. He had his ideas about Kevin, but he wasn't going to share them with a cop.

"Well, your old man should take him to the woodshed," the cop said. "Maybe beat some sense into him." He paused. "But I don't guess Teddy Kane would do that."

Nik had wanted the encounter to end, quickly and without any trouble. But the mention of his father changed that.

"You know my father, Officer...?" he said.

"Roberts," the cop said. "James Roberts. Yeah, I know Teddy. But I can't talk to you right now. I'm the only one patrolling all of downtown."

"It doesn't look like there's all that much going on down here," Nik said.

The cop, Roberts, nodded.

"Yeah," he said. "Even the criminal element has to be pretty shaken up. I expect they'll pull me out of here soon enough."

He turned to go.

"Can I walk with you?" Nik asked. "Just long enough to talk about my father? He disappeared, you know."

Roberts shrugged.

"Sure," he said. "Just stay clear of my gun hand."

The two of them walked west, both peering through windows, and Roberts rattling doorknobs to make sure they were locked.

"I'd heard that Teddy was gone," Roberts said. "Any idea where?"

Nik shook his head.

"No," he said. "I don't know where. Or why. What can you tell me about him?"

Roberts reached for a doorknob. It turned in his hand. He took the flashlight off his belt and held it in his left hand. He drew his revolver with his right.

"Step back, kid," he said softly.

Nik did as he was told. Roberts pushed the door open with his foot. He clicked the flashlight on and held it high, away from his body.

"Anchorage Police!" he called "Anybody here?"

There was no answer. Roberts walked slowly through the doorway.

The minutes Nik waited seemed like an hour. Then Roberts emerged.

"Come in here, kid," he said.

Nik followed him into the store. His feet crunched on glass.

"Watch it," Roberts said. "There's a lot of broken glass around. Try to walk in my footsteps."

Nik did his best to do that until they reached the counter.

"Whoever was here must have just run out," Roberts said. "They left the cash register with the money in it."

Roberts shined the flashlight on the cash register as he said that, and Nik could see the bills and change. Roberts walked around and lifted the cash tray out of the register.

"Good," he said. "There's a deposit envelope. Here's what we're going to do. You hold the flashlight, and I'll count the money. We'll put it into the deposit envelope and seal it. I'll write the amount across the flap, and we'll both sign across the flap, too. I'll take the envelope with me until we can find the owners."

Doing that took about five minutes. When they were finished, Roberts led the way out of the store, and they resumed their walk.

Roberts wasn't a particularly big man but he walked fast. Nik had to take long strides to keep up.

"My father?" he prompted.

Roberts nodded.

"Yeah," he said. "Teddy Kane. I haven't been on the force that long. Newcomers get the crap jobs, and downtown patrol on the swing shift is one of the crappiest. Drunks. Bar fights. Robberies. You name it. If you do it for any length of time, you get to know the regulars. Teddy was a regular."

Another shock rippled through the earth. Roberts grabbed Nik by the arm and stepped quickly into the middle of the street. Power lines swayed above them, and the buildings along the street gave a low hum. They stood for a moment, knees flexed to absorb the shocks, as the disturbance subsided.

"Damn," Roberts said. "That never gets old, does it?"

Somewhere, a dog began to howl, and its cries were taken up by other dogs. The whole scene seemed weird to Nik: the empty streets, the gathering darkness, the howling dogs, he and Roberts walking along the street as if it were the most normal thing in the world. Nik thought that he'd never forget the experience for as long as he lived.

They started walking again.

"What do you mean by 'a regular'?" Nik asked.

Roberts gave Nik a searching look.

"You don't give up, do you?" he said. "If you're a regular down here, usually you're a drinker. Teddy was a drinker. And, by all accounts, a mooch, too. But he was never any trouble, except for once that I saw. He was often in the company of ladies, but he never took it past being polite. He was just too—I don't know—vague to be a real drunk or a real ladies' man, or a real anything."

They hadn't gotten ten steps when Roberts crinkled his nose.

"Do you smell that?" he asked.

Nik took a breath.

"Gas," he said.

"They're supposed to have shut off the gas to this part of town," Roberts said. He pulled a walkie-talkie off his belt and spoke into it.

"This is Fireball. I'm down at the corner of Fourth and I, and there's gas in the air."

A garbled voice came back through the walkie-talkie's earpiece. Nik couldn't tell what the voice said, but Roberts replied, "Copy that, 'kay. Ten-four."

He put the walkie-talkie back on his belt.

"They've shut the gas off," he said. "Some of it must have just settled into a pocket of some sort."

They set out again, quickly reaching a bluff. Earth shaken loose by the quake slumped down to the edge of Cook Inlet. They walked along the edge of the bluff to Fifth Avenue, then began walking east.

"Tell me about the time he caused trouble," Nik said.

Roberts continued in silence for half a block.

"You sure you want to hear about this?" he asked. "Maybe you should just try to remember whatever good things there were about your dad."

Nik shook his head.

"No," he said. "I want to know everything I can. If I never find him again, I've got to understand why he left."

Roberts walked along in silence some more.

"So that you can be sure it wasn't because of you, you mean?" he asked.

The question was like a physical blow. It stopped Nik in his tracks. Roberts stopped, too, and waited. But Nik didn't know what to say.

"I had some problems with my father, too," Roberts said quietly. "Every son does. Don't let those problems control you."

Nik shook himself all over, like a dog just out of the water.

"I'm not," he said. "At least, I think I'm not. I just have to know."

Roberts set off again, Nik following.

"This was maybe two years ago, maybe a little longer," Roberts said. "I was brand-new on the force and on the beat. It was outside the Silver Dollar. Your dad was yelling at a woman out on the sidewalk. 'Anyone can tell they're not mine by looking at them, you whore,' he was yelling. 'Go talk to that goddamn gambler about money.' The woman said something I couldn't hear, and he slapped her. She slapped him back. Then I stepped in. The woman didn't want to show me any ID. She just kept saying, 'I'm so embarrassed. Don't tell anyone. Please.' But I made her show me her driver's license. It was Teddy's wife. Your mom. They both apologized, said it wouldn't happen again, and I let them go. Never saw your mother again. Not too long after that, I guess, I stopped seeing Teddy down here. That's all I know."

They were passing the restaurant where Nik worked. Nik could see the manager inside, working by flashlight, picking things up from the floor and dropping them into a large garbage can.

"This is where I work," Nik said. "I guess I'll stop and see if my boss needs any help."

"You do that, kid," Roberts said. "And stay out of trouble. You don't want to end up like your brother."

Or my father, Nik thought. He won't say that, but that's what he's thinking.

Roberts gave a sketchy wave and walked off down the street. Ignoring the opening left by the broken window, Nik tried the door and, when he found it locked, knocked. The manager looked up. Nik waved and stood there, waiting.

thirteen

Nothing is as far away as one minute ago.

—JIM BISHOP

## MARCH–APRIL 2007

Kane felt very small when he awoke. He looked out from his bed at
the big man sitting across the room. It was his father. It must be his
father.

"Da—" he said, but the rest of what he was going to say stuck in
his throat.

"Nik, are you awake?" the man said. The sound of his voice made
Kane swell up into an adult. That wasn't his father. He wasn't a small
boy anymore.

"Are you okay, Nik?" Tom Jeffords asked. "Do you need the
nurse?"

Kane didn't answer. His voice wasn't working, and, even if it had
been, he wouldn't have been able to get any words past the lump in
his throat.

"I'll get the nurse," Jeffords said, and left the room.

This nurse was small and white, dark-haired, young-looking, and quite pretty. She stuck a thermometer in his mouth and stood holding his wrist in a warm hand, looking at her watch. She took his pulse in the light from the readout of the machine that was already counting his heartbeats. Hands-on nursing. When she was satisfied, she removed the thermometer, checked the numbers, popped the covering from it into the wastebasket, and made some notes on a clipboard she'd taken from a hook at the end of his bed.

"Everything's fine," she said crisply. "You're doing well. Would you like some water? The doctor says you can have liquids."

Kane nodded, and she held a straw to his lips. Trying to lift his head sent a lance of pain shooting through his left side. He groaned. The nurse reached down and lifted his head. He sucked at the straw and managed to swallow a couple of mouthfuls. The nurse lowered his head gently to the pillow. Her finger traced the scar that ran down the right side of Nik's face, from temple to chin.

"If you'd had better medical help then, you wouldn't have this scar now," she said. "How did this happen?"

"Cut myself shaving," Kane said, his voice sounding like a frog croaking. Why go into it?

"Hmmph," the nurse said. "Well, there's surgery now that will reduce that scar. You'd be quite handsome without it."

Kane rocked his head from side to side.

"I'm used to it now," he said.

The nurse gave him a disapproving look.

"Well, then, maybe you could let your beard grow to cover it," she said. "You're giving the orderlies fits trying to shave you."

I'm too weak to argue, Kane thought.

"Okay," he said, "let's do that. Let the beard grow. Less of my face to offend the world."

The nurse gave him a smile and wrote something on her chart, then turned to Jeffords.

"You're not family, so you shouldn't really be in here," she said.

"But the hospital administrator had a word with me, so I'll leave you two together, as long as you promise not to tire him out."

Jeffords nodded as if he were used to taking orders. He wasn't. Anchorage's chief of police was used to giving orders, and having them obeyed. Kane had worked for Jeffords for a long time, until he got drunk, shot somebody, and ended up in prison. He'd spent seven years behind the walls, acquiring, among other things, the scar. Since he'd gotten out, Kane had worked for a private security firm that he was sure the chief quietly owned. And when Kane decided to go out on his own, it was Jeffords who gave him the lead to the job that had put him here in the hospital. Most of Kane's adult life had Tom Jeffords in it, but he couldn't really say the two of them were friends.

"Why are you here, Tom?" Kane asked, his voice soft and weak.

Jeffords's form shifted.

"These hospital chairs," he said. "I wonder if they are designed specifically to be uncomfortable."

Kane didn't say anything. He didn't have the energy. Besides, he knew Jeffords would get to the point only when he was good and ready.

"I had some meetings down here," Jeffords said, "so I thought I'd stop in and check on the patient."

He squirmed some more and, apparently giving up on the chair, got to his feet.

Kane waited. His eyes tried to close, but he fought them back open. He wanted to be awake when Jeffords finally got around to the point. If he ever did. The chief took a step forward, which, in the confines of the hospital room, was all it took to get to the bed. He stood there looking down at Kane. To Kane, lying flat on his back, the chief looked as big as King Kong.

"Jesus, Nik," he said, "I've seen better-looking corpses."

Kane tried to smile, but he couldn't really feel his face so he didn't know what expression he made. Whatever it was made Jeffords's eyes open wider.

"Tom, you sentimental fool," Kane said.

A wisp of a smile danced across Jeffords's lips. Kane fought his eyelids to a standstill again and said, "Tom, if you've got anything to say, you'd better say it before I fall asleep again."

Jeffords stood looking down at Kane, shrugged, and said, "I hear you've been talking in your sleep, or whatever. About Danny Shirtleff."

I have? Kane thought. I sort of remember dreaming. But talking about it?

"Is that a problem?" he asked.

"It might be," Jeffords said. "Do you know something about the case I should know?"

Kane felt his eyelids going again, and this time he didn't try to stop them.

"I'm sorry, Tom," he said, "I can't..."


THE ROOM was dark again, and the figure in the chair was smaller.

"Are you awake, Nikky?" Cee Cee asked.

Kane nodded and groped around for his plastic drinking glass. Cee Cee got to her feet to help him, but he managed to get control of the plastic cup, raise his head, and take a drink without spilling too much water. By the time he set the cup back down, his hand and arm were shaking.

"Jeez, I'm weak," he said.

"That's normal," Cee Cee said crisply. "You've had a lot of trauma, and the drugs they've been giving you interfere with muscle control."

She'd know, Kane thought. She's a nurse herself.

"It's good to see you, Cee Cee," he said.

He meant it. Something about having his oldest sister, the woman who was the closest thing he'd had to a mother, around made him feel better. Safer, somehow. Although it was odd to see her in civilian clothes. In her blouse, sweater, and long skirt, she could have been anything. A wife. A mother—grandmother now, he supposed. A businesswoman. When he said that, she smiled and said, "I still have the penguin suit, Nik. We all do. I just don't wear it as often."

"Why are you here, Cee Cee?" Kane asked. "I mean, I'm glad you're here. But how did you find out what happened?"

"When you were shot, they called your next of kin," Cee Cee said. "Laurie wasn't interested, but she had somebody named Antonio call me."

Laurie. Soon to be his ex-wife. The divorce was her idea. She'd stuck with him through his drinking, his trial, and his years in prison, but not long after he'd been exonerated and returned home she told him she'd had enough. Kane still couldn't figure that out. Unless, as he suspected, it had something to do with Antonio. There was something going on with Laurie that he couldn't quite put his finger on, and another man made as much sense as anything. But what did it matter? Whatever her reasons for wanting a divorce, he couldn't keep her from it. And after what had just happened, she'd be even less likely to want to see him.

"The order agreed to let me come," Cee Cee went on. "The other sisters all thought you shouldn't have to go through this alone."

I guess that's right, Kane thought. I am alone. He and Laurie still had two daughters, but the girls were young and both had their own, very different, lives. Neither of them would want their father around even if he was healthy.

"How . . . how long have I been out?" he asked.

"Two weeks," Cee Cee said. "It'll be three weeks tomorrow."

"Three weeks!" Kane said. "Isn't that a long time?"

Cee Cee got to her feet and, with some effort, moved her chair to the side of the bed. She sat again and took Kane's hand.

"It is," she said, "but they kept you under for a while because they didn't want you moving around, pulling things loose. And then you just sort of stayed under on your own. The doctors say that's un-usual, but not completely unprecedented, in a situation where there's no head trauma."

She squeezed his hand.

"Anyway, we're all glad you're awake at last," she said.

Something bolted through his chest, some emotion he didn't rec-ognize. Relief? Gratitude?

"I'm glad you're here, Ceese," he said, feeling like a boy once again. "Something terrible has happened."

"I know, Nikky, I know," she said, stroking his hand. "Do you want to talk about it?"

Kane rolled his head from side to side on his pillow.

"No, I don't," he said. "I don't, I don't, I don't. I don't want to talk about it. I don't even want to think about it."

Cee Cee nodded.

"All right, Nik," she said. "Think about something else."

"I have been," Kane said. "At least, I've been remembering. I've been remembering how, when I was a boy, I really wanted to find out what happened to our father."

"I know you did, Nik," his sister said. "Maybe when you're feeling better we can talk about that."

"Talk about what, Ceese?" Kane asked. "Do you know some-thing?"

His sister looked steadily at him for what seemed to be a long time.

"They are going to want to move you out of here sometime soon," she said. "They need the bed. Do you have a place you want to go?"

Kane had an empty apartment in Anchorage, but that didn't appeal to him much. Besides, he didn't know how long it would be until he could take care of himself.

"I don't really, Cee Cee," he said. "I guess I'll have to find someplace to recuperate. I've got some money, so that's not a problem. Of course, I don't know how much all this hospital stuff is going to cost."

Cee Cee smiled at him.

"It's not going to cost you a cent, Nik," she said. "I talked with the hospital administrator, and she said a Mrs. Richard Foster was paying the bills. I talked with Mrs. Foster on the telephone. She seems like a lovely woman. Who is she, Nik?"

"She's the woman I was working for when I got shot," he said. "She feels some responsibility for this, apparently."

"Apparently," Cee Cee said, then, after some time, went on, "Well, the order has a home in Anchorage, up on the Hillside. I'll see if they'll let me take you there."

Nik thought about that. He had to go somewhere, but he didn't want to spend his time being preached at.

"You know I'm not religious, Ceese," he said.

Cee Cee laughed.

"Don't worry, Nik," she said. "I don't have designs on your immortal soul. You may not be religious, but you are my brother."

"Thank you, Cee Cee," he said. "Right now, I'm your tired brother. Would you mind asking the nurses to let me sleep for a while? And could you find Tom Jeffords? Do you know who he is?"

Cee Cee nodded.

"He was here last week," she said. "He left a telephone number where he can be reached."

"Could you get in touch with him and tell him I'd like to see him, if he's here?" Kane asked. "Tell him to come by at . . . Cee Cee, what time of day is it?"

"Early afternoon, Nik," she said.

Early afternoon, Kane thought. Early afternoon of a day I don't know. Oh, well.

"Could you ask him to come by this evening, please?" he said.

Cee Cee said she would, then turned down the lights. Kane closed his eyes and let his thoughts drift. When they drifted too close to the place he didn't want to go, he steered them toward his father or Danny Shirtleff. Soon, he drifted off behind them to the place where no thoughts could reach him.

YOLANDA WAS BUSTLING around the room when Kane awoke, straightening and arranging. She was singing softly to herself, a lilting tune Kane didn't recognize. The words of the song collided with the dread in Kane's chest, pushing it down and out through his back, replacing it with a joy so seductive that Kane let his guard down for an instant. An instant was all it took. The events that had put him in the hospital slammed into his mind with brutal force.

"Oh, God," he said. "Dylan. Dylan."

Yolanda came quickly to his bedside. Kane could see the concern in her face and he began to cry.

"My son is dead!" he cried. "My son is dead! I killed him!"

His son had gone to confront a killer—perhaps to prove something to Kane, he wasn't sure—and been overpowered. Later, during Kane's own struggles with the killer, his gun had gone off, and one of the bullets had found Dylan where he lay, bound and gagged, in a metal cabinet. Kane's last memory was putting his fingers to his son's neck and finding no pulse.

"Oh, Jesus, Jesus, Jesus," Kane said. "Why him? Why not me?"

Yolanda laid a cool hand on his forehead.

"It's all right," she said. "Yolanda is here. You just cry. Yolanda will take care of you."

Kane did cry then, giving himself up to tears completely and thoughtlessly. He tried to drown the jagged memory in tears. Each time he drew a shuddering breath, pain shot through his body. He welcomed the pain, and tried to use it to pry loose that memory. But when he could cry no more, the memory was still there, black and horrible.

"What can I do?" he asked. "I can't live with this. What can I do?"

He could feel the earth opening under his feet. He'd felt this feeling before, the first time when he realized his father was gone for good. Then, as now, he'd known he was responsible, somehow, for the tragedy. Maybe if he just quit fighting it, if he would just let go, he would be swallowed up and, at last, be at peace.

Yolanda petted his hair and crooned to him. His sobs abated. When he was quiet, she said, "No one knows what to do with a great sorrow. No one knows how to live with it. Everyone must find his own way. Yolanda locks it away with a promise to not look at it again for some time. Then, I pay attention to something else, to life, and, when I do look at it again, the sorrow has shrunk somehow, and I can go on. Perhaps you could try this. For now, I think I should give you something."

Kane watched her inject something into his IV.

I hope it's strong, he thought, strong enough to rob me of memory. And, if not, maybe I'll try Yolanda's way. I'll try again to find out what happened to my father. Or maybe who killed Danny Shirtleff.

Whatever Yolanda had given him wrapped itself around his mind and robbed him of feeling, then thought.

KANE WAS STARING into a plastic bowl on a plastic tray on the plastic top of the rollaway plastic platform when Jeffords came into the room.

"From the look on your face, that's not a cheeseburger in there," Jeffords said.

Kane could see him clearly this time. Jeffords was the same big, silver-haired, ruddy-faced, unstoppable force he'd become after years of police work and ladder climbing. Jeffords knew the state's wheeler-dealers by their first names, and was neck-deep in the politics of his city and state. If the talk was true, he was even becoming something of a player in national politics. Being Anchorage's police chief had made him rich, not from graft but from his business dealings with the other insiders. And from marrying a rich widow after he shed his first wife. Most people who knew him, ally and foe alike, thought Tom Jeffords was a cold, calculating son of a bitch, an indifferent friend and a dangerous enemy. Kane knew he was all that and more.

"It's custard of some sort, I think," Kane said. "And something else that looks for all the world like boiled Kleenex. Tastes sort of like it, too. I've got to eat it, though, because they're not going to let me out of here until they're sure all my plumbing works."

Jeffords nodded, looked at the chair, and remained standing. He was wearing a tan overcoat dotted with raindrops or melted snowflakes over a charcoal pin-striped suit, white shirt, and red power tie. His big hands held a gray hat with a feather in the brim that matched the coat. It had been a week since Kane had asked his sister to bring Jeffords to his hospital room.

As if he could read Kane's mind, Jeffords said, "Sorry I couldn't get here any sooner but I had a conference in New York City and then some lobbying to do in D.C. As it is, I had to rearrange my travel plans to stop here. What can I do for you, Nik?"

Kane sawed a corner off the square of custard with a plastic spoon and popped it into his mouth. It had the taste and consistency of vanilla-flavored mucus. He sucked on it for a moment and swallowed.

"They want their hospital room back, Tom," Kane said, "so I thought maybe I could come and stay with you and Gwendolyn until I'm better."

Kane could count on the fingers of one hand the times he'd seen

Tom Jeffords surprised. He could add one to that total now. Jeffords opened his mouth to speak, closed it, opened it again, closed it again.

"Nik..." he began at last.

Kane held up a hand.

"Don't worry, Tom," he said. "That was just a joke. What I really want are the files on the Danny Shirtleff murder."

The pale blue eyes that looked down at Kane turned steely.

"No," Jeffords said. "You know department policy, Nik. There's no statute of limitations on murder, so the Shirtleff case is still open. I can't give anything to an outsider, most certainly not the files on an open case."

Kane ate some more vanilla-flavored mucus.

"Still open, eh, Tom?" he said. "When was the last time anybody in the department even looked at those files?"

"That's not the point, Nik," Jeffords said. "Now, if there's nothing else, I'll be going."

Kane let him get to the door before he said, "I need those files, Tom. I need something to take my mind off of what happened. What you had a part in making happen."

Jeffords stopped, turned, and said, "Now, Nik..."

"Don't 'Now, Nik' me," Kane said. "I want those files. I wrote most of them, so what can it hurt? If I don't get anywhere, you're no worse off. And I might see something after all these years that will help solve the case. You do want the case solved, don't you, Tom?"

Jeffords's look was a glare now, and his ruddy face was even redder.

"Don't you start that, Nik," he said. "I know that clown DiSanto thought I was holding things back. His allegations probably cost me five years getting to the chief's job. I don't need any more of that unfounded talk going around the department."

Kane ate the last of the custard.

"We both know Jackie Dee was no clown," he said. "But I want those files, so I'll make you a deal. You give them to me, and, if I find anything, I'll bring it to you first. Don't give them to me, and, well, you know how people talk."

A smile crossed Jeffords's lips before he strangled it.

"Are you trying to blackmail me, Nik?" he asked.

"I am, Tom," Kane said with a grin. "How am I doing?"

"Badly," Jeffords said. Then he laughed. "Oh, well, what harm can it do to have you review some old files?" His voice hardened. "But if you do find anything, I'd better be the first and only one who hears about it. Where will you be?"

Kane told him about the residence in Anchorage he was going to. Jeffords pulled out a cell phone. It was big, one of those phones that did everything but shine your shoes. He punched some notes into it.

"Call the office when you get settled, and I'll have the files run out to you," he said. He put the cell phone away and turned to go. At the door, he stopped and turned.

"It was a long time ago, Nik," he said. "We were all much different. Don't let your need for distraction make you forget how we all were then."

Kane waved a hand weakly at the chief.

"Don't worry, Tom," he said. "I may not be much of anything else, but I'm still a good investigator."

The chief nodded and left the room. Kane picked up his spoon and shoved some of the damp toilet paper stuff into his mouth and chewed thoughtfully.

He didn't fight that very hard, did he? Kane thought. I wonder why.

Memory itself is an internal rumor.

—George Santayana

## SEPTEMBER 1985

"We need. A list. From you. Of everyone. Who knew. About the buy money. Right now."

Jackie Dee spat out the words the way the Army instructors had taught Kane to fire an automatic weapon. Short bursts, carefully aimed. But the words seemed to bounce off the rocklike calm Tom Jeffords projected into the chief's office. For all the concern he showed, Jeffords might have been planning how he'd decorate the place once he became chief.

If the missing twenty thousand dollars didn't become a permanent roadblock on his career path.

"Now, now," the room's current occupant said. "Now, now, now. We've got to pull together here. Show the feds a united front. And not a word to the press. Nothing to the press."

William Hickock was a small man in a big man's world. He was short, bald, and egg-shaped, but hard, in the way that small, ambitious men often are. What there was of him looked like so many bags of walnuts that had been sewn together, and, through the bonhomie he employed on official occasions, his dark eyes glittered like chips of polished stone. He often worked the patrol fallouts like a politician stumping for votes, slapping backs with a force that could bring tears to the eyes of young, fit men.

"Call me 'Wild Bill,'" he said, so of course no one did, even though that had once been his street name.

Wild Bill Hickock believed in bravery, loyalty, and accepting favors from a grateful public without a fuss. He'd come to the attention of his superiors in the mid-sixties by breaking up a brawl between a platoon of GIs and a group of construction workers, single-handedly quelling a potential riot and sending three of each group to the hospital, using nothing but his baton and a sap that had mysteriously appeared in his hand during the fight and just as mysteriously disappeared when the fun was over. He'd outlasted better cops by attending slavishly to the needs of his superiors and overlooking the small failings of the people who worked for him. But he'd ruthlessly crushed a handful of cops who made the mistake of shaking down some bar owners without the requisite connivance of higher-ups, making himself a hero to the local newspaper at just the right time to vault over a couple of less astute lieutenants and into the chief's office.

Kane didn't have anything against the chief. He wasn't bothered by the fact that Hickock lived in a big house built by a construction company that had also won the bid on a couple of police substations after the apparent low bidder was disqualified by the police review panel Hickock chaired. And the chief's appreciation for bravery was the reason that Kane was no longer working patrol. But Hickock could smell retirement and he didn't want any trouble in the eight months he had left. That made him pretty much useless in a situation like this.

Which left his three lieutenants: Barnes of admin, widely despised by the rank and file; Anders Hedberg of patrol, a big, humorless head-breaker who was well on his way to setting the department record for wives; and Willie Tolliver, the chief of detectives. Tolliver was another small man, but where the chief was bulky and bald, Tolliver was wiry and mop-headed. The standing joke on the force was that when Tolliver was growing up on the San Francisco waterfront, he could have become a cop or a crook, so he'd joined the APD and became both.

The six of them—the chief, his lieutenants, Jeffords, and Jackie Dee—were sprawled around the big room that served Hickock as an office. The room contained so many leather couches and armchairs that walking from one side to the other was a chore. The walls were hung with the usual photos. The only personal touches in the whole place were a couple of sad-eyed clowns painted on velvet that flanked the chief's chair. His new, much younger wife, a former artiste, was said to fancy herself an artist now.

The only other people in the room were Kane and Jeffords's second-in-command, Charlie Simms. Simms looked like he would rather have been almost anywhere else. Kane knew how he felt, so when Simms looked at him, Kane dropped him a wink and was rewarded with a hint of a smile.

After looking carefully at the chief and the other lieutenants, Tolliver took control of the meeting.

"I know you two don't like each other," he said to Jackie Dee and Jeffords. His voice was mild, almost friendly, but that didn't fool anyone. "Hell, everyone in the department knows you two don't like each other. But brawling in the station house is simply not acceptable. Do I make myself clear?"

Jeffords nodded, Jackie Dee muttered, and Tolliver decided to take that as agreement.

They're getting off easy, Kane thought. When he'd told Jackie Dee about the missing money, his partner had stormed into Jeffords's office and said some things you just couldn't say to a fellow cop without punches being thrown. It had taken Kane, Simms, the rest of the antidrug squad, and the department's hand-to-hand combat instructor, who had just happened to be passing, to pull the two men apart.

"Now, the chief understands that feelings are running high over Officer Shirtleff's murder," Tolliver went on. "So there will be nothing entered in anyone's personnel file over this incident. But we've got a dead cop and a pile of missing federal money. Both big problems. So you will work together to solve these problems or I'll make sure you wish you had."

Jeffords crossed one leg over his knee, flicking at an invisible speck of lint.

"Of course we will, Lieutenant," he said. "I'm certain that Sergeant DiSanto and I both have only the best interests of the department at heart. And justice, of course. The best interests of justice. But there's no certain connection between the disappearance of the money and Officer Shirtleff's death,"

Jackie Dee snorted, but before he could say anything Tolliver raised a hand. He looked around the room until his gaze settled on Kane.

"You're Kane, aren't you?" he asked. "New from patrol?"

Kane nodded but said nothing. Tolliver had been standing right next to Wild Bill when the chief handed Nik his gold shield. He probably knew Kane's personnel file by heart, not to mention his shirt size and bank balance. Not much got past Willie Tolliver.

"Maybe you'd be able to offer a different point of view," Tolliver said. "Do you have a theory of the crime? Or"—here he nodded toward Jeffords—"crimes?"

Great, Kane thought. A chance for the new guy to make an asshole of himself in a room full of brass. He really wanted to light a cigarette, just to stall a little, but nobody else was smoking so he figured it would be bad form. Nothing to do but plunge in, then.

"Not really," he said, "no real theory, anyway. We haven't come up with any reason for someone to shoot Officer Shirtleff except to take the money. We know he brought the money back with him from Kodiak. At least, that's what the paperwork says."

"Do you have any reason to doubt that?" Tolliver asked, sounding hopeful. It would solve a lot of problems if the money had never left the island.

"None," Kane said. "But paperwork has been wrong before."

Everyone nodded at that. Records were notoriously inaccurate, especially with something as powerful as twenty thousand dollars in cash as an inducement for a little creative writing.

"Go on," Tolliver said.

"Assuming, then, that Officer Shirtleff brought the money back with him, he had several hours to dispose of it," Kane said. "So it could be anywhere in Anchorage. Anywhere, apparently, except the police property office, since there is no record of it here. Or at the FBI office."

Tolliver looked like he wanted to say something, but when Kane opened his mouth to continue he nodded instead.

"If Officer Shirtleff had the money with him, the killer could have taken it," Kane said. "If he didn't, then..."

He let his voice trail off. Everyone understood what might have happened if the first officers to respond had been confronted with the cash. And if Fireball hadn't taken it, the money might still have been there when the next officers, the newbie Adams and the vet who was giving him OJT, arrived. If they hadn't found it, then someone at the impound garage might have.

"So what you're saying," Tolliver said, "is that there are six ways the money could have vanished and five of them involve dirty cops. Or police employees."

"Seven and six," Kane said, and ticked them off on his fingers. "The Kodiak cops still have it, Officer Shirtleff stashed it, he brought it to property here and it vanished, he took it to the FBI and it disappeared there, the killer got it, the responding officers got it, somebody at impound got it."

Tolliver gave him a look when he finished.

"That's right, seven and six," he said. "That's very good. I forgot about the FBI. Somehow I just don't think of the Fibbies going rogue. Too straight."

He looked at Kane again.

"I don't suppose there's any way the investigating officers could have gotten their hands on the money?" he asked with a smile.

Kane smiled back.

"Actually, I suppose there is," he said. "We were alone with the car for a couple of hours. But we didn't know there was any money. Darn it."

His response got a bigger laugh than it deserved, the men in the room using it as an outlet for the tension they were all feeling.

"Well, we'll have to put more shoulders to the wheel on this," Tolliver said. "Sergeant DiSanto, you'll continue to be in day-to-day charge of the murder investigation. When we're done here, we'll go back to my office and see who we can free up to help. We don't have to call this a task force, but, by God, we're going to put some more manpower into it."

He looked at Jackie Dee, who nodded, then at Jeffords.

"And, for the time being at least, the missing money will be part of the murder investigation," Tolliver said. "Which means, Sergeant Jeffords, that you will give every scrap of paper pertaining to Officer Shirtleff's work for you, the Kodiak investigation and the buy money, over to Sergeant DiSanto. And then you will go back to your job, fighting the scourge of drugs."

Jeffords opened his mouth, closed it, opened it again, and said, "Of course, Lieutenant."

The chief looked around the room, nodded once, and stood up. He wasn't much taller than he'd been sitting.

"Thank you, gentlemen," he said. "I'm confident you'll find the killer and the money. Lieutenant Barnes, if you could stay behind, we have some invoices to review."

The rest of the cops filed out of the office, dispersing as they went. Kane went back to his desk, sat, lit a cigarette, and began making a checklist for the investigation. He'd finished filling two pages of a steno pad and was starting on a third when Jackie Dee returned.

"Christ," the older detective said. "Every deadbeat and idiot in the department is now a part of this investigation. I don't know what I'm going to do with them. Throw me a smoke."

Kane did. Jackie Dee lit up. Kane passed over the two pages he'd finished.

"There's plenty for them to do," he said. "Spend a few minutes sorting this into order of importance, and we'll let them start with the least important." He grinned. "By then, I'll be finished, and we can re-sort the list if necessary. And see if you can't add a thing or two that doesn't include trying to tear Tom Jeffords's head off."

Jackie Dee looked up from the papers Kane had handed him.

"You on my ass, too?" he asked.

"Aw, fuck no, Jackie Dee," Kane said. "Why would I be on your ass? Every brand-new detective wants a violent hothead as his partner to get him into the shit with the brass. Hell, it's what I asked for for Christmas."

Jackie Dee put the palms of his hands on his desk and leaned forward.

"Fuck you, rook," he said. "I been catching bad guys since before you learned to jack off. For two cents, I'd come over this desk and teach you a lesson."

"Jackie Dee," Kane said, his voice flat, "sit down. My ribs still hurt from that elbow you gave me, so I'm not inclined to mess around. You come after me and I swear to God I'll shoot you in the knee."

Jackie Dee looked at Kane for what seemed like a long time, then let his arms relax.

"I'm sorry about the elbow," he said, "but you had ahold of my hair."

"I had ahold of what I could get ahold of," Kane said. "You weren't being very cooperative."

Jackie Dee nodded.

"You're right, I'm a dickhead. Let's finish up this list and get some of these sad sacks moving," he said. "Then maybe we can go out and do some detecting ourselves. What's at the top of your list?"

"Danny's apartment," Kane said. "We should have been through it before now."

Jackie Dee nodded. He ground out what was left of his cigarette in a desktop ashtray.

"That's the thing about these investigations," he said. "You need to do everything first."

They put their reinforcements—Harry and Larry, of course; a sad sack named Don Young, who wasn't smart enough to get out of his own way; and the newest of the department's three female officers—on various tasks: canvassing the neighborhood of the shooting again, chatting up drug dealers to see if there was any word on the street, checking the parking attendants at the airport to see if any of them remembered Danny's Corvette passing through the lot. Nothing that would be fatal if it got screwed up. Jackie Dee and Kane didn't expect much from their new helpers, except maybe the woman cop. Her name was Kim Lewis, and she wasn't just a woman; she was black.

"Jesus, a twofer," Jackie Dee said when she walked into their cubicle. "What the hell are you doing here?"

"Here on the force?" she asked. "I got kids that like to eat. Here in this office? I'm here because my sergeant said you two were in the process of completely screwing up the Danny Shirtleff shooting and could use my help."

Kane and Jackie Dee looked at each other.

"She's got attitude," Jackie Dee said. "I like her."

"I'm standing right here," Lewis said, "so don't you be talking about me like I'm not."

"You sure you're not related to Jackie Dee?" Kane said, unable to hide a grin. "Like maybe a cousin or something? You got the same personality."

"Shee-it," Lewis said, laughing. "No way I'm related to that big ofay oaf."

"'Oaf'?" Jackie Dee said. "'Oaf'? I've been called a lot of things in my time, but 'oaf'? That really hurts."

The banter went out of his voice when he continued, "But, anyway, I'm Sergeant Oaf, so why don't you tell me what you're good at, and we'll see if we can't arrange for you to do some of that?"

So Lewis was on her way to see what Jamie Roberts might be able to tell them about the off-duty Danny Shirtleff, and Jackie Dee and Kane were on their way to Danny's home.

"I guess you won that round with Jeffords," Kane said as Jackie Dee wheeled the Trans Am through the afternoon traffic. He flicked cigarette ash out the window into a cold rain.

"How do you figure?" Jackie Dee asked.

"Well, the brass sided with you in the investigation, and now Jeffords is on the sidelines," Kane said.

Jackie Dee nodded. He whipped the Trans Am out into the oncoming traffic and zipped around a station wagon. The woman driving the wagon was applying lipstick with one hand and, with the other, trying to keep two small boys from hitting each other. The car seemed to be steering itself.

"Jesus," Jackie Dee said as he pulled back into the proper lane, "these civilians will be the death of me."

The two men were quiet for several moments. Kane flipped his cigarette out the window. The Trans Am left the main drag and wound along a street lined with small houses built very close to one another. Except for their paint jobs, they appeared to be identical.

"That's one way to look at it, that I won," Jackie Dee said. "Here's another. This is a high-profile investigation that's going nowhere, and now Tolliver has moved his protégé, Jeffords, out of the line of fire. He's not even responsible for finding the money his man lost, or whatever. So if we solve the murder and find the money, Jeffords wins, because he doesn't have the missing money on his jacket. If we don't, then we lose and he skates, because it wasn't his investigation."

Jackie Dee shook his head.

"There's a lesson here for you, free of charge," he said as he laid the Trans Am against the curb in front of a light blue house with beige trim. "Police politics at its finest. Jeffords, Tolliver, and our illustrious chief all dodge responsibility, at least direct responsibility, no matter what happens. And, most likely, us working stiffs get fucked."

There were no trees in the neighborhood, no plantings of any sort. Nothing but tightly packed houses with attached carports reached by short asphalt driveways and separated by patches of indifferent grass.

"Jesus, I'd hate to come home drunk to one of these places," Jackie Dee said as he climbed out of the Trans Am. "You could end up in bed with anybody."

He looked at the sheet of paper in his hand, then at the numbers on the side of the house. The curtains were drawn tightly across the windows that faced the street and orange-wrapped newspapers had built a nest on the front porch.

"This is the place, all right," he said. "I wonder who the pickup belongs to."

The pickup, a newish Ford, was parked in the carport.

"One dead cop's enough," Jackie Dee said, drawing his weapon and holding it down along his leg. "Better do this by the book. You take the back."

Kane trotted across the postage-stamp front yard and along the side of the house. When he reached the corner, he took a quick peek along the back. There was a door reached by a pair of concrete steps. He moved quickly to stand beside it, crouching as he passed under windows. He drew his .38 and waited, listening to his heart beat.

This was the first time he'd drawn his weapon in earnest since the shooting and he wasn't sure he liked the feeling very much.

The sound of Jackie Dee pounding on the front door was like thunder, and Kane thought he could feel the whole house shake.

"Anchorage Police," Jackie Dee bellowed. "Open up, and keep your hands in plain sight."

Kane heard footsteps, then a creak that he took to be the front door opening.

"Hey," a voice said. "What's...?"

The words turned to a gurgle. Kane reached up and tried the doorknob. Locked. He swung up the two steps and lifted his leg to kick the door in. As he started forward, the door swung open. Jackie Dee stood in the opening, holding the photographer, Murphy, by the throat with one big hand. Kane stumbled but managed to stay upright.

"Don't hurt yourself, Nik," Jackie Dee said around a big smile.

Kane scowled and took two steps into the house. He was in a short hallway. He followed Jackie Dee and the photographer into the living room, passing a bedroom to one side and a bathroom to the other. The living room had a tiny kitchen attached to it on one side, and on the other was a closed door. Kane walked to the door and turned the knob, standing to one side to let the door swing open. The room was tiny and full of equipment of some sort. Kane looked at Jackie Dee and the photographer and shrugged.

"It's a darkroom," Murphy gasped. Jackie Dee let go of the photographer, and Murphy stood there massaging his throat.

"What the fuck?" he said at last, croaking like a raven with a head cold. "What'd I do?"

Jackie Dee stood looking at the photographer with his head cocked, like he'd never seen anything quite like him before.

"Besides almost getting your sorry ass blown away?" Jackie Dee said. "Try interfering with an officer in the performance of his duties and tampering with evidence."

"'Tampering'?" Murphy croaked. "What tampering? I'm here on behalf of the family. And I've got permission from the department."

He slid his hand under his coat.

"Uh-uh," Jackie Dee said. The gun that had been forgotten at Kane's side was now pointed between the photographer's eyes.

"Oops," Murphy said.

"It's okay, kid," Jackie Dee said gently. "I've got him."

Kane slid his finger off the trigger. Had he been going to shoot the photographer? Moving slowly, he holstered his weapon. Jackie Dee slid his hand under Murphy's coat and came up with a folded sheet of paper. He opened it and read.

"Goddamn stupid desk-jockey cocksucker," he said, handing the paper to Kane. It was handwritten, giving Richard Murphy permission to dispose of the belongings of Danny Shirtleff. The signature was indecipherable, as were most of the handwritten notes stapled to the letter. Kane could make out the words "aunt," "telephone," and "Bank of Oregon," with some numbers after it.

"It's Lassiter's handwriting," Jackie Dee said. Lassiter was a corporal known for his laziness and dishonesty. He held down the front desk at police headquarters. "What the fuck is he doing giving this pinhead permission to mess with Danny's stuff before we even had a chance to search the place?"

Kane looked at the photographer.

"How much did you pay him?" he said.

"Pay?" Murphy croaked. "Pay who?"

Kane and Jackie Dee looked at each other and shook their heads.

"Don't fuck with us," Jackie Dee said, "you sleazy..."

Kane held up his hand to stem the storm of invective.

"One more chance," Kane said to the photographer. "Wrong answer and you go directly to jail. You do not pass Go. You do not collect two hundred dollars."

Murphy looked from Kane to Jackie Dee and back again.

"I gave him a hundred bucks," he said, "against ten percent of the gross value of what I sell."

Jackie Dee took the photographer by the shoulder, marched him to the couch, and forced him to sit. He sat, too, close enough to reach Murphy. Kane took a seat in the cheap leather recliner and took the notebook from his pocket.

"Give," he said.

"It's just a straightforward business deal," Murphy said. "We've done it a couple times before, when there's camera gear involved. I sell the stuff, kick back ten percent to Lassiter, and send the rest of the money to the family. It's not tricky, and it sure as shit isn't supposed to happen until after you guys are done with the stuff. I guess Lassiter just got sloppy."

"Uh-huh," Jackie Dee said. "I notice that you didn't say anything about what you get out of this. You just doing it out of the goodness of your heart?"

"No," Murphy said. "I get my expenses; my time, gas, ads, if I have to."

"But you don't get a dime of profit?" Kane said, looking up from his notebook. "Nothing but expenses?"

The two detectives let the silence lengthen until Murphy blurted, "I get images. I get my pick of the images."

Jackie Dee and Kane looked at each other again. Kane shrugged.

"'Images'?" Jackie Dee said. "What's this 'images' bullshit?"

"It's not bullshit," Murphy said. Kane could hear his enthusiasm through the rasp. "Images are what photography's all about. Capturing moments in time. Storing up people and places and activities. It's why photographers record images. Real photographers, anyway. I get first crack at images no one else has."

Jackie Dee scratched his head.

"That's it?" he said. "You get images. They aren't worth nothin'?"

Murphy tried to clear his throat. Kane got up from the recliner and went into the kitchen, returning with a glass of water. Murphy drank it down and set the empty glass on a small, cheap-looking end table.

"Some of the images are worth something," he admitted. "In Alaska it's mostly scenery and animals. I hustle the good ones around to the ad agencies and magazines, see who might want to pay for using them, then list them with a stock agency. I make a few bucks. But that's not really why I do it."

Kane believed him. When he talked about images, Murphy sounded like a true believer talking about religion. When Jackie Dee looked at him, Kane nodded.

"Okay," Jackie Dee said. "Officer Kane and I are now going to search the premises. You're going to sit here while we do that, keeping perfectly still unless one of us calls you."

Jackie Dee went out to the Trans Am and brought back the evidence kit. The search went quickly. The kitchen looked unused, the only item in the refrigerator a cardboard box of orange juice. There weren't even the fixings for coffee. The garbage can under the sink held an empty bottle of cheap champagne. Two clean wineglasses sat in the dish drainer. Kane wrapped each in a separate evidence bag. Not much chance of prints, but you never could tell.

The bedroom held regular clothes and a selection of flashier garments in the closet and chest of drawers. A snub-nosed .38 was tucked up in a holster behind the headboard. Jackie Dee found a bunch of thumbtack holes along one wall near the bed but no clue as to what might have been there or when. Kane took a spare pillowcase from the closet and bagged the bedclothes.

The bathroom contained what you'd expect to find in a bachelor's bathroom, right down to a towel that looked like it should be burned rather than washed. Jackie Dee got down on his knees and used a pair of tweezers to pick hair out of the tub's drain, putting his take into another bag.

The living room yielded nothing but some photography magazines. There were no messages on the answering machine and no confession neatly folded and left waiting in an end-table drawer.

"Okay," Jackie Dee said to the photographer, "you and me are going into the darkroom. You are not touching anything. You are telling me if you see anything strange."

The two of them went into the darkroom. The room was so small they couldn't have closed the door.

"The cameras and lenses were in that cabinet," Murphy said. "I put them on that counter to make notes on what's here. The other cabinets hold chemicals used to make prints. Nothing unusual there, all stuff for black-and-white. He must have his color prints made at a commercial house. And I suspect that filing cabinet contains prints and negatives, but I haven't looked."

Jackie Dee let Murphy out of the room. The filing cabinet was metal, three-drawer, and green. Jackie Dee opened the top drawer. It was full of dark green hanging folders, each containing a manila folder. The tab on the first folder read "Avalanche," and when Jackie Dee removed it he found black-and-white prints of a cloud of snow rolling down a mountainside. He put the folder back and ran his finger along the rest. He closed the drawer and opened the second, then the third. They were all alike, with extra folders taking up the back of the bottom drawer.

"Lot of images here," Jackie Dee said. "Probably a gold mine, for a guy like you."

He opened the second drawer again and pointed to an empty green hanging folder, the only one in the whole cabinet.

"Got any idea of what might have been in there?" he asked. "It's between 'Mountains' and 'Ocean.'"

Murphy shook his head.

"No way to tell," he said. "Most of the labels seem to be for outdoor images, and some of them, like 'Puma' there, aren't even Alaskan. So it could be anything."

Jackie Dee nodded, closed the drawer, and stepped out of the darkroom, pulling the door shut behind him.

"Here's what we're going to do," he said. "We're going to close this place up and hang crime scene tape all over it. "You"—he pointed at Murphy—"aren't going to say boo to Lassiter about what happened. If he asks, you didn't make it over here until after we sealed the place. We'll take this stuff to the forensics people and see what turns up. We'll probably search the place more thoroughly, too. If there's nothing interesting, we'll open the place up, and you can come back for your camera gear and images. Not a word to anyone in the meantime. Got it?"

The photographer nodded. Jackie Dee opened the door and shooed him out. The two detectives put their evidence in the backseat of the Trans Am, took yellow tape from the trunk, and sealed the doors and windows.

"You went pretty easy on that photographer," Kane said as they drove back to the police station. "You have him on bribery as well as that other stuff."

Jackie Dee nodded.

"So I do," he said, squinting against the smoke from his cigarette. "That's why he's not going to squawk when I tell him that we'll be sitting on him when he pays off that crooked fuck Lassiter. We may not be getting anywhere on this killing at the moment, but we can help weed the crooks out of the department. Even if we have to do it one weed at a time."

**fifteen**

Time is more valuable than money. You can get
more money, but you cannot get more time.

—JIM ROHN

## APRIL 2007

Kane made the trip to the Juneau airport strapped to a gurney in an
ambulance. He bitched and moaned, but both the doctor and Cee
Cee insisted.

"I don't think you should be flying at all," the doctor said, "but
Sister Angelica is determined."

She must be, Kane thought, if she's throwing her nun name
around.

A doctor he could have ignored, but he was in no shape to test wills
with his sister. Especially since she was wearing her complete nun
outfit, which made her even more imposing. So he let them shift him
to a gurney, grunting with the pain from his knitting rib and various
other wounds. They wheeled him to the ambulance, slid him in, and
drove him out the Egan Expressway to the airport. A light rain mixed
with snow was falling, and the hissing of the tires on the wet pave-

ment almost put Kane under but he fought sleep off. He was happy to be leaving Juneau and he wanted to do it conscious.

Came to town in a cab and leaving in an ambulance, Kane thought. That's not progress.

At the airport, Cee Cee had the ambulance drive out onto the tarmac to a private jet. As the ambulance attendants unloaded him, a pickup sporting a Transportation Safety Administration logo pulled up and disgorged a fat guy in a puffy blue coat. Cee Cee headed him off.

"What's this?" he asked, his muttonchops quivering. "I don't have any record of anyone being loaded on a private aircraft."

Cee Cee thrust some papers at him.

"I'm sure your agency received the proper notification," she said sweetly. "These are the approvals and this is my patient, who should not be lying here in the rain."

She turned to the ambulance attendants.

"Please proceed, gentlemen."

"Now, wait..." the TSA guy blustered.

"Officer," Cee Cee said, not so sweetly, "do you know what kind of liability you are incurring, both for yourself and your agency, by trying to keep a very sick man waiting in the rain and cold despite the fact he has the proper authorization?"

"Now, Sister," the man began. Kane could hear the defeat in his voice. So could the ambulance attendants, who rolled Kane to the stairway and carried him into the airplane. Working smoothly, they transferred him to a bed. A teenager in a white coat checked him over while a nurse plugged him into various pieces of equipment. As they worked, Cee Cee came through the airplane door.

"TSA," she said, her voice thick with scorn. "Talk about locking the barn door... Good morning, Doctor. How is the patient?"

The kid looked up from his examination of Kane's stitches.

"He seems to be doing as well as can be expected, Sister," the teen-ager said.

"This kid's a doctor?" Kane asked. "Where'd he get his degree? The University of Sesame Street?"

The nurse giggled and turned so Kane could see her face. It was Yolanda.

"Fancy meeting you here," Kane said, ignoring his sister's defense of the doctor.

"I have a few days off from the hospital," Yolanda said. "And, this way, I get a free trip to Anchorage to shop and see my sister."

She leaned in so her lips were close to his ear.

"Besides," she said softly, "I already know what a handful you are. I am fully prepared."

She reached over and picked up a needle big enough to inject horses with. The needle, and the look on her face, made Kane laugh, an activity he quickly regretted.

"Nurse," the doctor said as sternly as his high tenor could man-age, "we don't want to have to stitch the patient up all over again, do we?"

"No, we certainly don't, Doctor," she replied in her musical voice.

The doctor finished his examination and Yolanda tucked Kane in and raised the railings around the bed.

"We can't belt you in because of the nature of your injuries," the doctor said, explaining the obvious.

The door to the cockpit opened and a tall woman with close-cropped, graying blond hair emerged. She was wearing a gray uni-form with four stripes on the sleeve of the jacket.

"I've already done the preflight," she said, "so we're ready to go anytime you are."

"We're ready now," the doctor said.

"Actually," the woman said, "I believe the sister is the client for this charter."

Even Kane could read the look that passed between Cee Cee and the woman.

"If the doctor is satisfied," Cee Cee said politely, "so am I."

"Thank you, Sister," the woman said even more politely. She stuck her head out the door and beckoned. Someone clambered up the stairs and helped the woman close the door. She dogged it shut and said, "You all need to take your seats now and buckle up. Turn off your cell phones. No two-way communication devices of any kind. I'm sure you've all heard the flight attendant's instructions often enough to know it by heart." She turned and reentered the cockpit, closing the door behind her.

Yolanda took a seat where she could keep an eye on Kane's monitors. The doctor buckled himself in, reached into his overnight bag, pulled out a copy of *Thrasher* magazine, and began to read. Cee Cee rummaged in her pockets and came out with what looked suspiciously like a breviary.

"On the wings of prayer, eh?" Kane called.

Cee Cee smiled and opened her mouth to reply, but the winding up of the aircraft's engines made conversation difficult. Kane wanted to feel the wheels leave the runway, but sleep overcame him before the aircraft even started moving. His last coherent thought was to wonder if Yolanda had pumped a sedative into him with something less obvious than the horse needle.

When he awoke, a couple of burly guys dressed in white were carrying him out of the airplane. At the bottom of the stairs they shook the gurney's wheels down and locked them. Cee Cee, Yolanda, and the doctor stood in a semicircle near the bottom of the stairs. Pale yellow light from the sun bounced off the snow that lay all around.

That's what I get for coming north, Kane thought. More winter.

"He's all yours now," the doctor said to Cee Cee. "Good luck."

Yolanda walked over to where Kane lay.

"You behave yourself now," she trilled. "And remember, somebody could have snatched you off the planet anytime after you got yourself all shot up. And he did not. That must mean something."

She gave him a critical look.

"I suppose that beard will look like something eventually," she said.

Kane tried to think of something to say to that but couldn't. So he gave her a weak smile and said, "Don't spend too much money shopping."

Yolanda laughed at that.

"What else is money for?" she asked, and followed the doctor across the tarmac.

The burly guys pushed Kane to a waiting ambulance and stuck him in the back. Cee Cee, carrying a small suitcase, got into the back with Kane.

"You can ride in front," she said to the attendant. "I'm a trained nurse. I'd like to talk with my brother."

"Yes, Sister," the attendant said, and climbed out of the ambulance, pushing the back door shut with a bang. A moment later, the ambulance shifted as he got into the front and thumped the door closed. The ambulance began to move.

"How are you feeling, Nik?" Cee Cee asked.

"Thirsty," Kane said.

Cee Cee found a water bottle and poured some into a plastic cup. Then she held Kane's head up so he could drink.

"Is that better?" she asked.

"Much," Kane said. If he told her how tired he felt, she'd either fret or stick him back in the hospital, and he didn't want either of those things to happen.

"I need to know how you are feeling, Nikky," Cee Cee said, "both physically and, well, spiritually."

"Spiritually?" Kane said.

"Well, mentally, whatever," Cee Cee said.

Kane spent some time in silent thought.

"Well, physically, I feel like I've been shot. I'm weak, I tire easily, and there's some pretty bad pain. I've been wounded before, though, so I think I'll recover. Not as fast as when I was younger, maybe, but eventually."

He paused to think some more.

"Mentally? I don't know how to answer that question. I'm too woozy from the pain meds part of the time and asleep most of the rest. I have been dreaming, though, Ceese. Or remembering, maybe. I can't really tell which. Why do you ask?"

Cee Cee reached out and laid a hand on Kane's forehead.

"I've seen a lot of people hurt, Nik," she said. "Sick, too. And what those who recover have in common is a positive attitude."

"Ceese," Kane said, "I already said I thought I'd recover."

"Yes, you did, Nik," she said. "From your bullet wounds. But there are other issues."

Kane lay there, looking at his sister, seeing both years and weariness in her face. He could feel some combination of panic and anger moving through his body and he forced himself to relax and breathe. When he thought he had himself under control, he said, "I've been dreaming about Dad, Ceese. Or about us, really, after he left us. About the family after you left us, too."

Cee Cee sighed.

"I had to go, Nik," she said softly. "I had a calling."

"I know that, Ceese," Kane said. "I'm not blaming anybody. I'm just telling you about my dreams. Or my memories. Whatever they are. I'm dreaming about when Dad disappeared. And about an old case, too. It's weird. I don't know why I'm having these dreams."

"Don't you, Nik?" Cee Cee asked, her voice still soft.

Kane let the silence stretch out until Cee Cee shrugged and said, "Tell me about your dreams, Nik."

So Kane recounted what he remembered about his father's disappearance and how the family adapted. The story took them through arrival at the nuns' residence, Kane's installation in a big room with south-facing windows, and a parade of aging nuns come to look at the patient. He had another nap then, and a dinner of broth and custard, and, with the help of a nun on each side, a trip to the bathroom. When he finished his halting account, Cee Cee went off to evening prayers, promising to return later. He must have dozed off again, because she seemed to have returned almost immediately. One minute she was gone and the next she was sitting in an easy chair, sipping something from a thick glass.

"Is that what I think it is?" Kane asked with a smile.

"Scotch," Cee Cee said. "Pretty good scotch, too. I understand one of the local liquor distributors is a devout Catholic."

Kane watched her sipping and said, "It's all I can do not to drool."

"Alcohol is absolutely contraindicated," Cee Cee said sternly, then smiled. "It's not time to tie one on yet, Nikky."

Kane wondered if that was some sort of commentary on his drinking. If Cee Cee had talked to Laurie, there was no telling what had been said. The two had always been as friendly as his mother and his wife had been distant.

"Do you want to tell me what these memories mean now?" Cee Cee asked. "Or why you're remembering them?"

Kane knew the real question she was asking but chose to ignore it.

"I'm not really remembering them," Kane said. "They're more like dreams. They're not really under my control."

"Hmmm," Cee Cee said.

"What does that mean?" Kane asked.

"Well, we don't really know much about dreams, do we?" his sister said. "About where they come from or why we have them? There's speculation that dreams are our subconscious minds attempting to communicate with our conscious ones. There's also a theory that we will our dreams even if we don't know it. Or that they're some sort of problem solving, a way we sort out the problems that baffle us when we're awake. No one really knows, of course, even with all the new techniques for mapping our brains and observing brain function. What we do know is that dreams and symbols are important. Maybe not as important as Carl Jung thought but important nonetheless."

Kane looked at his sister in surprise. He had always respected her common sense and courage in dealing with everyday problems big and small, but he'd never known her to be particularly intellectual. She saw his expression and laughed.

"Didn't know your sister knew all this psychobabble, did you?" she said. "Well, nursing involves more and more psychology these days. Plus dreams have been important in my calling. Dreams or visions."

"I can see that," Kane said, "but I'm not really very interested in examining my motives, conscious or unconscious, right now. What I want is information. I want you to tell me what you remember about our father vanishing."

"Why do you think that is, Nikky?" his sister asked.

"Cee Cee," he said. He could hear the strain in his voice. "Please."

His sister was quiet for what seemed like a long time to Nik. Then she took a long pull on her drink and sat up.

"Okay, Nikky," she said. "I don't think it makes much sense to go raking up the past, especially the painful parts, but I'll tell you what I know."

Again she was silent for a long time, so long Kane began to think she'd forgotten what they were talking about. How old is Cee Cee now? Mid-sixties? Not too young to be having those kind of problems. Hell, I can't remember things half the time anymore.

"I was nineteen when our father left," Cee Cee said. "That would have made you thirteen, I think. Mom had a child a year for seven years, from me through you. So you would have been thirteen. That's a bad time in a boy's life to lose his father."

A thought shot across Kane's brain: That's about how old Dylan was when I went to prison. He strangled the thought and said, "Is there a good time for a son to lose his father, Ceese?"

His sister shook her head.

"Of course not, Nik," she said. "That was just a particularly bad time. Anyway, he was prone to wandering off. He'd been doing it more and more frequently, so it was nearly a month before we thought it was something more than one of what our mother called his 'wanderings.' Benders is more like it. Anyway, I wanted to notify the police because, well, something might have happened to him. Mother refused. She said he was enough of an embarrassment without dragging the police into it."

Cee Cee was silent for a moment, then continued, "It's odd, but when I think about it I don't remember thinking his departure was anything very important. Actually, it was a relief of sorts to me. One less person to manage. And I had other things on my mind. I was growing more and more certain that God wanted me for his own, and that meant leaving home, and that meant trouble with Mother."

"Trouble with Mother?" Kane asked. "What sort of trouble?"

Cee Cee looked at Kane and smiled.

"Nik, have you ever really thought about your parents—as people, I mean?" she asked. "Particularly Mother?"

The question confused Kane. Damn drugs, he thought. He concentrated hard on his answer.

"I guess not, Cee Cee," he said. "They were our parents. Who can be objective about their parents?"

"Fair enough," Cee Cee said, then went on, choosing her words carefully: "I never pretended to understand our father. It was like he never grew up, like he was a teenager in a man's body. He had all these dreams, and Mother said that when one went bust he'd drag everybody off after the next. That's how we ended up here, in Alaska. Maybe he just had a dream that didn't have the rest of us in it and that's why he left."

She sat letting the silence grow, then continued, "I understand our mother, though. At least, I thought I did back then. She just wanted someone else to handle all the responsibilities so she could do what she liked. And that someone else was me. So when I told her I wanted to go into the convent, she pitched a fit. 'Your father left me and now you want to,' she screamed. I'll never forget it, how angry and wounded she was. Or pretended to be. That kept me at home for another year, almost, until I just had to leave. Part of it was that there were just too many things about our family that I couldn't handle, that no young woman should be expected to handle. And part of it was, well, I just heard this voice in my head, telling me that my life lay with the church. So, one day, I just packed a bag and left. I felt terrible about that for a long time."

Cee Cee drank the last drops from her glass and sat rattling the ice around.

"If you had to go, Ceese, you had to go," Kane said quietly. "None of us ever blamed you for it. Not even Mother."

What Kane didn't say was that, once one of her children left, Cecelia Kane never mentioned that child again. Just as she had quit talking about her husband soon after he left.

"But what you say doesn't make a lot of sense, Ceese," he went on. "If Mother wanted someone to take care of her, why on earth did she marry Teddy Kane?"

Cee Cee shook her head.

"I don't know," she said. "Maybe it was the difference in their ages. You knew she was several years older than he was, didn't you? He was barely twenty when I was born. If I had to guess, I'd guess that she let him get her pregnant and she used that to hang on to him."

Kane didn't say anything. He'd always thought of his parents as being about the same age. In fact, his mother always said they were. When he said that to Cee Cee, she laughed.

"Lying about her age," she said. "Certainly not the first woman to do that."

Again, Kane didn't say anything. Despite all of his experience as a detective, the idea of his mother lying was a surprise. He'd seen her lie for a reason, to put off a bill collector or something like that. But lie out of vanity? He'd have to think about that more later.

"And she was religious, Ceese," he said. "Having a daughter become a nun would have pleased her."

His sister smiled but said nothing.

"Ceese?" he said. When she didn't reply, he tried to put a little more iron in his voice. *"Ceese?"*

"Okay, Nikky, okay," his sister said. "Our mother certainly behaved more religiously as time went on. But to say she was religious at that time would be stretching the point. Oh, she had her upbringing as a Catholic, and she always said and did the right things, particularly when she was trying to get something from the clergy. But her life wasn't particularly religious. Not then."

Kane was really confused now. When he thought of his mother, he thought of the woman who said the rosary every night, who criticized him for leaving the church and not bringing his children up Catholic. But was that the Cecelia Kane of his youth or an older Cecelea Kane? He already had some memories that suggested that there was a more complex woman there, and now this from Cee Cee. He wasn't sure what to think.

Cee Cee got slowly to her feet and crossed to the bed to look down at her brother.

"That's enough for today, Nik," she said. "You need your rest, and so do I. Do you need anything before I leave?"

"I don't think so, Cee Cee," he said. He wanted the conversation to continue, wanted to question his sister the way he would a suspect, to get at all the hidden nooks and crannies of her memory, to ferret out her motives and desires as well as her memories. But he didn't have it in him right then.

"Then I'll see you in the morning, Nik," she said. "Good night."

She turned to go.

"Wait, Ceese," Kane said. She turned toward him. "I...I just want to thank you. I don't know where I would have gone if you hadn't taken me in, and I really appreciate it."

Cee Cee's smile lit up the room.

"That wasn't easy for you, was it, Nik?" she said. "I remember you as a child not wanting to owe anybody anything, so it must be hard for you to acknowledge kindness. But you're my brother. And remember, this is several corporal works of mercy all rolled into one. It's worth big points with the man upstairs."

She reached down and tousled his hair.

"I think you should let all of this go, Nikky," she said. "You can't change anything, and you might learn some things you don't want to know. Now sleep—perchance to not dream, in your case."

With that she left the room. Kane lay there, wondering if she was right. But when sleep finally came, it brought dreams with it. Anyone passing by the room would have heard cries and whispers from within.

sixteen

When I was younger I could remember anything,
whether it happened or not.

—MARK TWAIN

## OCTOBER 1964

"You're coming over to help me, aren't you?" Carrie said. Her eyes seemed larger than normal, dark and liquid and outlined with just a touch of mascara. She batted them at Nik, and gave him a smile that seemed to hold wonderful secrets.

Nik nodded. He still had trouble talking around Carrie, but he forced himself to.

"I am," he said, striving to sound normal. "Tomorrow, about noon?"

Carrie laid a hand on his bicep.

"That will be great," she said. "I really want to rearrange the furniture, but I can't manage it on my own. And you're so strong."

Nik heard Norma snort and felt himself blush. He knew he should say something to Carrie, but his throat seemed to be closed. Concentrating, he said, "I'llseeyouthen," and fled the restaurant.

The air seemed particularly cold after the heat of the restaurant. Nik's breath escaped in puffs, white in the light from the building's windows. He looked farther into the shadows and was rewarded with the orange glow of a burning cigarette. As had become his habit, he stopped to talk with the Hacker. His health was obviously deteriorating, and Nik never knew if the conversation would be their last.

"That woman likes you," the old man said.

"What do you mean? What woman?" Nik asked.

"Nobody's that dense," the Hacker said. "That Carrie woman, the waitress. I see the way she looks at you. You know what to do if you're put to the test, don't you?"

Nik drew himself up to his full height.

"Of course I do," he said, wondering: What test?

Nik thought he could hear humor in the Hacker's voice when he replied, "'Course you do. Well, people been doing it for a million years, so it can't be that tough to learn."

The ash on his cigarette grew brighter as he took another drag. That was followed by a series of painful-sounding coughs.

"Can't say I'm surprised," the Hacker said after his breathing returned to normal. "The ladies all liked your dad. You don't look that much like him. You favor your mother, I guess. But you got the same shy manners. Women like that."

Nik didn't know how to respond. Relations between men and women were mostly a mystery to him, and so was his father.

"So my dad liked women?" he asked at last.

The Hacker laughed, which led to coughing and spitting. When the fit subsided, he said, "Any real man likes women. But I don't think your dad was really interested in any woman but your mom. Oh, he could talk to 'em, all right, and I never seen anybody as good at getting around an angry woman with soft words, but I always figured him for a one-woman man. Friendly, sure, and polite, but a little distant, for all that."

Nik didn't know what to make of the Hacker's description.

"You remember any more about the last time you saw him?" he asked the Hacker.

The tip of the cigarette moved back and forth as the old man shook his head.

"Nope," he said. "Like I told you several times before, he'd come into some money and he bought me a couple drinks. That's all I remember."

The cold was settling in through Nik's clothes, so he simply said, "Thanks," and set out for home. He was carrying a steak dinner, which he knew would make his mother particularly happy.

"I like the finer things in life," she always said, "more than a religious woman ought to."

New snow covered the ground, making the footing a little dicey in his Keds with the threadbare soles. He needed new shoes. These weren't just worn; they were too tight. Nik seemed to be growing in every direction, and his feet were leading the way. He thought there was a pair of oxfords Kevin had outgrown and he'd have to ask his older brother about them even though talking to him was like juggling dynamite. Kevin was awaiting his court date for grand theft, out on bail put up by some benefactor their mother refused to name. He had a lawyer, too—a private lawyer—who was said to be negotiating on his behalf.

Nik got all that from Oregon. He and Kevin rarely spoke. The only time Kevin ever started a conversation was to tell Nik to steer clear of the priest who ran the Catholic Youth Organization or to tell Nik what a "feeb" he was. Nik didn't even go to church when he could skip it, let alone attend CYO. And as for being a feeb, well, how many feebs had older women interested in them?

The house was dark when Nik reached it. He let himself in the front door with his key, took off his shoes in the arctic entryway, and crossed the worn rug in his socks. He entered the kitchen, put the dinner in the refrigerator, and padded down the stairs into the basement.

He hung up his clothes carefully, put on a raggedy bathrobe his father had left behind, and padded out to the big, galvanized sink in the utility room, where he washed his face and brushed his teeth. He'd have to fight his way into the house's lone bathroom at some point tomorrow to shower before going to Carrie's, but this would have to do for now. He returned to his room, set his alarm clock, stripped off the bathrobe and the rest of his clothing, and crawled into the sleeping bag that served him for bedding. He lay his head on the pillow he'd had as long as he could remember, intending to think some more about his father. The next thing he knew, his Big Ben alarm clock was clanging. It was four-fifteen a.m. and time to get up.

He was still groggy when he reached the Silver Dollar Bar on Fourth Avenue right at five a.m. Dapper Dan, the bartender, and Tully Ames, who owned the joint, were ushering the late, late drinkers out of the bar. Some of them went straggling off in various directions, but maybe half a dozen sat down on the curb to wait. The law required Anchorage's bars to close at five a.m. but allowed them to open again at five-thirty a.m. Except on the coldest nights, there were people who decided to wait out the half hour on the sidewalk, hoping that they wouldn't sober up too much before the doors opened again.

Nik passed them with a nod and walked through the door Tully Ames held open for him.

"Not too bad this morning, kid," he said, his voice sounding, as always, like a machine with stripped gears. "Hardly anybody puked."

The Silver Dollar was a big, dimly lit rectangle. A wooden bar lined with stools ran along one wall. A jukebox and cigarette machine occupied a side wall, while the opposite wall was pierced by doors for the restrooms and a janitor's closet. A couple of dozen tables were scattered around. The only decorations were neon signs advertising Miller High Life, Budweiser, Olympia, and Pabst. The Silver Dollar catered to people who were there to drink, not to be entertained.

Nik started in the bathrooms. By the time he'd finished cleaning the toilets and sinks, washing the mirrors, emptying the trash containers, sweeping and mopping the floors, and refilling the handtowel dispensers, the drinkers were settled in at the bar again. Dapper Dan had gone home, and Tully Ames was behind the stick, sitting on a high chair, drinking coffee and reading the morning newspaper. Nik moved through the room, emptying ashtrays and wiping tables. When he reached the bar, Ames looked up from his paper and said, "Don't bother, kid. Dapper Dan cleaned up here."

That left the floors, which Nik swept and mopped, working around the drinkers. He took the mop pail into the alley and dumped it, put the mop and bucket away in the janitor's closet, and pulled out a bottle of Windex and a rag. He washed the insides of the two small windows that would have looked out on Fourth Avenue if they hadn't been covered with blackout-style curtains. The denizens of the Silver Dollar didn't want daylight to remind them they had other places to be and neither did Ames.

When he finished, Nik went back to the bar. One old guy was asleep, his head pillowed on arms folded on the bar. As Nik watched, another drinker reached for his glass and succeeded only in knocking it over. He looked at the beer running across the top of the bar and slid off his stool onto the floor.

"That Eddie really knows how to pass out," Ames said to no one in particular. "He's been passing out in this place for—what?—twenty years? And he's never hit the floor hard once."

"All done, Mr. Ames," Nik said.

Ames nodded and looked at Nik.

"You look tired, kid," he said. "Siddown and let me buy you a Co-Cola."

Nik sat on a stool away from the other drinkers. Ames picked up a glass, inspected it, polished it, sprayed dark liquid into it from a nozzle, and set it in front of Nik.

"Drink up, kid," he said, and resumed his seat behind the bar. "You doing okay in school?"

Nik nodded. He had a B average. He could do better if there were more hours in the day, but working two jobs and doing chores at home didn't leave him as much time to study as he would have liked.

"Tha's good," Ames said. "Tha school's important. If I'da stayed in school, I wouldn't be sittin' in a broke-down bar this time of the mornin'."

Nik nodded again. Ames told him the same thing every time they talked. Other people said Ames was doing more than all right with the Silver Dollar, and a tavern he owned on the east side of town, but he always made it sound like he was just scraping by. Nik wasn't sure what to believe, except that he had no intention of spending his life tending to a bar.

He sat nursing his Coke and getting up his nerve. He'd been swamping out the bar for Ames for three months now, ever since it had reopened after the Good Friday earthquake. The hours were rugged, but the work wasn't hard and the money wasn't bad, so he didn't want to irritate the bar owner. But he had questions he thought Ames might be able to answer. Once again, he'd let his determination to find out about his father flag in his efforts to meet the demands of daily life: work, school, a growing interest in the opposite sex. Again, he vowed to work harder to solve the riddle. He took a deep breath and began.

"Mr. Ames, you knew my father, right?" he said.

Ames looked up from his newspaper and scowled. The scowl made his battered face look fearsome. Tully Ames would not be a good man to piss off.

"I already said I did, kid," he said. "So what?"

"Nothing," Nik said. "I was just wondering about him. He took off a couple years ago, and I'd like to find him, or at least find out if he's okay."

Ames slid off his chair and walked over to freshen up a couple of drinks. The drinkers were young, hairy guys, construction workers or fishermen, maybe, come to the big city to have a toot. Ames took some money from the pile in front of the two men and put it into the cash register drawer, depositing some change on the pile. Then he resumed his seat.

"I unnerstand what you're sayin', kid," he said. "My own dad died about the time I was your age. I missed him terrible. But I got over it. So will you."

He held the paper in front of his face again.

Nik put his hands around the glass of Coke. It felt cool and damp, and, suddenly, he wished it held something more powerful than Coke, something that would help him forget his father and his family and the cold, dark place he lived in. He sat up straight and stretched his back muscles, trying to will away the feeling.

"It's just the not knowing," he said softly. "I think I could live with it better if I knew where he was. Even if I knew he was dead."

Ames shook the newspaper, sighed, and lowered it.

"I can respec' that," he said in his gravelly voice. "So I'll tell you what I know. But you gotta quit bothern' me about it after. Agreed?"

Nik nodded, then sat very still, as if the slightest movement would make Ames change his mind.

"I first seen your dad maybe seventeen, eighteen years ago," he said. "Around the end o' the war, anyway. He was a likely lookin' young fella, with a pretty wife. They come into a place I own then, have a few drinks, do some dancin'—the place had a little band played on weekends. I put 'em down as social drinkers, and that was what they was for a while. Then, years later, I ain't sure when, your dad started stoppin' in by himself. I was surprised. Your folks seemed t'enjoy each other's company. Not like some married people I know. I didn't say nothin'. Not my business. Anyway, your dad always had real nice manners an' was never any trouble. He fooled me, kinda, 'cause I let him start drinkin' on a tab. He'd settle up, all right, but the settlin's got to be further and further apart."

Ames looked up and down the bar to see if anyone was listening, but the few remaining drinkers seemed to be minding their own business.

"Truth is, kid, there's no nice way t'put this: Your dad become a barfly," he said. "I never threw him out, which I shoulda, 'cause the other patrons all liked him. Hell, I liked him, too. I just tried to keep him from drinkin' me out o' house an' home."

Ames shook his head and stared across the room, as if he could conjure Teddy Kane, sitting at one of the tables.

"I dunno, kid," he said. "You spend as much time as me in joints an' you see all kinds. I always figgered your dad for a guy who got disappointed in life, somehow. Didn't get the breaks, maybe. Somethin'. But I never figgered him for a guy'd run off from his family. Anyway, the last time I seen him, he come in here an' he's wearin' new clothes. He always dressed nice, but his clothes was getting kinda worn. He's got on a brand-new blue blazer an' gray slacks an' one-a them ascot things. Musta been summer, 'cause he wasn't wearin' no galoshes, just shiny new shoes. I say he's lookin' sharp, an' he says to me, 'Tully, my friend. Get out my tab. I'm payin' it off.' An' he flashes a big roll. I tell him to put it away, these ain't the kind of people to be showin' your money to. But he just laughs, pays me cash for what he owes, has a quick one on the house, an' leaves. Tha's a coupla three years ago, an' tha's the last I seen of him."

Ames sat without speaking for a minute, then went on, "Later, I hear he's paying off his tabs all over town. An' in the middle-a that, he just isn't here anymore. So there's barmen in this town bless his name an' others spit when they hear it, dependin' on if he made it to their place to pay off before goin' wherever he went. Odd, that, 'cause he had plenty to pay off them debts, an' more besides, last time I seen him."

When Nik was sure Ames was finished, he said, "So you think he just ran off?"

Ames shrugged.

"Maybe," he said. "An' maybe some bad person seen that roll an' took it offa him, kinda violent like, you know."

Ames paused, then continued, "Tha's adult stuff. Nothin' for a kid to be messin' around in. If you was thinkin' about doin' that."

Nik nodded.

"Did my dad say where he got the money?" he asked.

Ames nodded.

"Said he won it in one o' Pat McCanta's card games," Ames said. "I never knew your dad to gamble before then, but even a blind pig finds a acorn oncet in a while."

And that was it. Ames didn't have anything to add, and Nik couldn't think of anything to ask. He finished his Coke and slid off the stool.

"Thank you, Mr. Ames," he said.

"Don't forget your money, kid," Ames said. He punched the cash register, took a ten-dollar bill from the drawer, and handed it across the bar. "See you tomorrow mornin'?"

Nik nodded and left the bar. Sunrise was still some time off, and the dark, empty streets were like Nik's own private town. He settled his neck down in his collar and walked along, thinking about what Ames had said. Would it be better if someone had done something to his father? At least that would mean he hadn't simply abandoned Nik and everyone else.

The house still looked dark when he reached it. But when he went inside, he found his mother sitting in the kitchen in a housecoat, drinking a mug of tea. A cigarette smoldered in an ashtray at her elbow. Nik wanted nothing more than to sit down and somehow force her to tell him what she knew about his father's leaving. But they'd butted heads about that often enough to convince Nik that she would tell him only when she was darn good and ready. If ever. Besides, in the hard light from overhead, she looked old and tired.

"Tough night, Mom?" he asked.

"It's your sister," she said. "She's been crying half the night."

His mother had been a long time bouncing back from the birth of his youngest sister. The child was nearly two years old now but often didn't sleep through the night. With Cee Cee gone, all the mothering chores fell on Cecelia Kane and she didn't seem to like that very much.

"I guess I'll have to take her to the doctor again," Cecelia Kane said, "if we can afford it."

Nik said nothing to that. Such decisions weren't his. He turned in his money, got a small allowance, and left the decision making to others. That's about as much responsibility as he wanted, at least until he got older. He headed for the basement door.

"I've gotta get some sleep, Mom," he said.

His hand was on the doorknob when his mother asked, "You haven't seen your brother, have you?"

Nik turned and smiled at his mother.

"Kevin?" he said.

She nodded.

"I stay as far away from Kevin as I can get," he said.

His mother nodded again.

"He didn't come home last night," she said. "I'm worried something's happened to him."

"He'll be all right," Nik said. "Kevin can take care of himself."

He walked downstairs to the basement, wondering if what he'd just said was true.

The Big Ben read eleven a.m. when it dragged Nik from a deep, dreamless sleep. He wrapped the bathrobe around himself, climbed the stairs, and discovered a minor miracle: The bathroom was empty. He could hear Dee Dee crying, but otherwise the house seemed deserted. Since it was Saturday, they were probably all at work. If Kevin had a job these days.

Nik managed to shower without being disturbed, the warm water feeling good in the chill of the poorly insulated room. When he finished, he spent some time looking at himself in the foggy mirror. Even features, lots of dark hair, a strong chin. A "black Irishman," his mother called him. Did he look like his father? He thought he saw a resemblance, but it had been so long since he'd seen the man he wasn't really sure. Did he need to shave? He did. He went back to his room for his safety razor. Personal items left in public areas tended to vanish. He managed to shave without cutting himself.

Maybe I really am getting to be a man, he thought.

Nik went back to his room and spent some time trying to decide what to wear. He didn't have many choices.

"Jeez," he finally said aloud, "you're just going to move some furniture."

Carrie lived a few blocks away, in a nice-looking white house with green shutters. In a place like Anchorage, with no real zoning to speak of, nice houses like hers and piles of junk like Nik's house could stand side by side. Those that had survived the earthquake, anyway. The city was bouncing back nicely from the big quake, but not every building had survived. Parts of Fourth Avenue had fallen into the ground and parts of the city's nicest residential area had fallen into Cook Inlet. But people had simply gotten to work putting things right, and federal disaster-relief money was starting to flow to finance the reconstruction. And as the earthquake receded into the past, it became more exciting and less frightening, more of a challenge and less of a disaster.

Carrie lived in a top-floor apartment reached by a long flight of exterior stairs that ran up one side of the house. As he passed a second-floor window, Nik could see children playing. They were clean, well-dressed, well-fed children, in a bright room full of toys. It was like getting a glimpse of another planet.

Carrie opened the door with a big smile on her face. She was wearing blue denim coveralls over a blue work shirt that didn't seem to have many buttons.

"Right on time," she said, stepping aside to give Nik just enough room to enter. As he passed close to her, he smelled a spicy scent and, beneath it, something that smelled more like musk.

"Let me take your coat," she said.

Nik handed it to her obediently, then looked around as she hung it on a wooden coatrack. The apartment was a series of brightly painted rooms: a fair-sized living room; a narrow, galley-style kitchen; a smallish bathroom; and, through an open door, what looked like a bedroom. Except for the tile in the bathroom, the floors were all wood and well polished. Nik knelt and removed his shoes, and, when he stood up, Carrie was standing close to him.

"It's this darn living room," she said, taking Nik by the hand and leading him to the center of the room. "I just can't seem to get the furniture right."

There didn't seem to be that much furniture to Nik, but they tried each piece here, there, and everywhere: couch, armchair, floor lamp, bookshelf, wooden-box end tables, rug. The room was warm, and Nik was sweating, partly from the effort of moving the furniture, partly from the effort to not look down the front of Carrie's shirt every time she bent over. He lost that battle, and, when she looked up and caught him staring, she just smiled and bent over again to shift whatever she was moving. They chatted as they moved things; or, rather, Carrie chatted, mostly about how she'd come to move out of a friend's place into this place of her own. Nik couldn't tell from what she said if the friend was male or female.

They'd been at it for an hour—moving, considering, moving again—when Carrie pronounced herself satisfied. Nik wasn't positive but he thought they had the furniture right back where it had been.

"Boy, it's warm, isn't it?" Carrie said, walking over to stand next to Nik. "I think I'll take a shower. Would you like to join me?"

Nik heard the question but didn't really understand it. It was like Carrie was speaking some foreign language he was supposed to know but had failed to study. So he just stood there.

"Have you ever been with a woman, Nik?" Carrie asked, taking his hand.

Carrie's words were like bands across his chest, cutting off his breathing, so he just shook his head.

"I didn't think so," Carrie said. "Would you like to be?"

The bands squeezed Nik tighter. He was afraid he would pass out. He nodded.

"Dealing with men is hard for me, Nik," she said. "I'm just a woman who wants what she wants when she wants it. I don't like having to accommodate people. People will say there's something wrong with me taking up with someone so young, but I think right now you're just what I want. I'm sure there will be lots of times I'll want you. But there will be times I won't. Can you live with that?"

Nik had no real idea what she was talking about. All he could think about was right now, this moment. And for this moment to become the next moment he was sure he wanted, he had to agree. So he nodded.

"Good," Carrie said. She dropped his hand and stepped away, raised her hand to the straps of her overalls, undid the clasps, and let the overalls fall to the floor to puddle at her feet. She stepped out of them, turned, and walked to the bathroom. As she crossed the sill, her shirt dropped to the floor. She bent and turned on the faucets. Steam began to rise from the tub. Carrie hooked her thumbs in her panties and skinned them off and stepped into the tub. She pulled the shower curtain closed, and, a moment later, needles of water hissed from the showerhead.

"Nik?" she called.

Goddamn, he thought. But no other thoughts followed. He walked to the bathroom, stepped in, and closed the door. Moving quickly, he took off his clothes, folded them, and laid them on the toilet tank. Then he pulled aside the shower curtain and stepped in.

"I thought you'd never get here," Carrie said, turning to meet him.

She wrapped her arms around his neck and pulled him to her, her soap-slick body sliding along his, first one way, then the other. The touch of her body was like an electrical current on his skin. She lifted her face and he kissed her, the hot water beating down on them like all the blessings of Heaven.

seventeen

Time is the justice that examines all offenders.

—WILLIAM SHAKESPEARE

## APRIL 2007

The room was big, maybe twenty by twenty, big enough that the bed in which Kane lay didn't take up an appreciable part. It was painted white on white. The only decorations were a large crucifix that hung above Kane's head and, on the opposite wall, a large color print of a painting of the Sacred Heart of Jesus.

To Kane's right was the door to the hallway; on the wall behind him, the door to a private bathroom. The wall to his left was pierced by two large windows. White draperies hung from valances above the windows. They were gathered and secured by strips of cloth. A low, round table sat between the windows, with an armchair on either side. A third armchair sat near the head of Kane's bed. All in all, the room looked like a place to house a convalescent of religious persuasion.

Which is just what it is, Kane thought, if you leave out the religious-persuasion part.

The remains of a meal lay on the hospital table that stretched across the bed. Nothing too taxing for his GI tract: soup, scrambled eggs, tea. The day before, the idea of a bacon cheeseburger had taken up residence in a corner of his mind, making the soft food seem even more bland and unsatisfying than usual. Only the fact that he was surrounded by aging but still-tough nursing nuns kept him from trying to bust out and head to the nearest greasy spoon. That, and the fact that he had about as much strength as a baby.

The White Spot, he thought. I need a White Spot burger and fries. Their fries are particularly tasty. I don't think they've changed the grease in the deep fryer in forty years.

He remembered the White Spot from the time he was a kid, the same thin, vigorously permed woman behind the counter, a cigarette screwed into the corner of her mouth, dishing up diner food to all comers: businessmen, fishermen, hookers, guys who worked with their hands, cops, drunks, kids—anybody with a couple of bucks for a burger, fries, and a Coke. That place had been behind the old Hunter Bar, one of the town's toughest. When that whole block burned down, the White Spot began migrating here and there, until it lit in a tiny nook on the edge of downtown. Run by a nice young couple now, who'd taken over from—Lorene? Lorena? Whatever her name was.

Kane remembered going there once, the old place behind the bar, with his father. Or did he? He was beginning not to trust his memory. Were the details it had been serving up to him in his drug-addled sleep really memories? Or was his brain, prompted by hints and suppositions and sedatives and painkillers, on the run from the near past and its horrors, writing some new story?

He was trying to learn to think of nothing at all. Thinking of nothing was hard. Thoughts kept drifting into his head. Only chemicals or death could keep him from thinking, and the chemicals were temporary.

Kane reached out and picked up his teacup. His hand shook as he brought the cup to his lips. He took a sip and grimaced. Cold. He set the cup back down, his hand shaking even more on the return trip.

Am I ever going to recover? he thought. Or has all this made me an old man?

People think of aging as an incremental process; you age a little each day until, after enough days have stacked up, you are old. But, in Kane's experience, aging didn't really work like that. You did fine until something happened and, all at once, you were old. An illness. A fall. A disappointment. Something. Anything. That's what had happened to Kane's mother. He'd never been clear what it was that turned her into an old woman overnight. Maybe Cee Cee knew.

The room was warm and the bed surprisingly comfortable. Kane hadn't expected nuns to have comfortable furniture. He thought their lives would be austere, full of sacrifice and privation. But the mattress was like a cloud...

A knock on the door roused him from a doze. The nuns who cared for him were a baffling mixture of diffidence and assertiveness, careful to knock but unfazed by discussing bodily functions in detail. Just another of the contradictions that made life such a mystery.

"Come in," he called, turning his head slowly.

The woman who opened the door was definitely not a nun. Emily Lee was fifty, maybe older, but genes and cosmetics combined to make her look like a teenager. Her long black hair was shot through with gray now but still moved in graceful counterpoint to the turning of her head. She was, as she had been as long as Kane had known her, a babe.

"Hello, Nik," she said, sending him a smile that could have killed a man in Kane's condition. "May I come in?"

Kane nodded and watched her flow into the room, lissome as a young girl. She wore a plain black business suit over a white blouse with a high, starched collar. Her shoes were black and practical. Under her arm was a bundle of fat manila envelopes held together by an industrial-strength rubber band. Nik tried to raise himself in the bed, but she glided over and put a hand on his shoulder.

"Please, stay still," she said. "I've heard what you've been through."

She set the envelopes on the hospital table and stepped back.

"The chief asked me to drop these off," she said, "and to remind you of the agreement the two of you have."

Emily Lee had been Jeffords's secretary for a long time. When they were all younger, the whole force had believed that their relationship was more than professional, but Kane had never heard of any proof. Of course, the ideas that she put into men's heads just walking down a hallway were all the proof anyone had needed.

"It's good to see you, Emily," he said. "And thanks for delivering this. You can tell the chief I haven't forgotten."

She gave him another smile and moved to the door. There, she paused and turned.

"I . . . I'm sorry to hear of your troubles, Nik," she said. It sounded like more than a pro forma statement. "If I can be of any help, please let me know. You know how to reach me at the department."

She was out of the room before Nik could reply. He lay for several minutes lost in thought, then moved slowly and carefully into a sitting position, pulled the rubber band off the envelopes, picked up the top one, and undid the clasp. He slid the contents out far enough to see what they were. A brand-new beige file folder held copies of forms and handwritten notes and, in a separate folder, black-and-white prints.

Jeffords kept the originals, Kane thought. I wonder if he held anything back?

He slid the contents all the way out of the envelope and picked up the top document.

The crime scene sketch was as he remembered it, the contents of each grid detailed in the small block printing he'd started using after a succession of supervisors had complained about his handwriting. The list and sketch added nothing to his knowledge, and when he compared the crime scene photos to the sketch everything seemed to match. The only new information they seemed to add was a handwritten note that said someone had set a jelly doughnut on the original sketch, burying grids C-5 and C-6 under a coating of sticky red.

The sketch and the notes brought the scene back again: the cold rain; the gathering of cops behaving just like civilians at the crime scene, searching for a jolt of the electricity that always surrounded violent crime; the faces somehow distorted by memory, more garish, less human; the body—Danny's body—lying there, somehow shrunken in death, less than human now that the animating spirit had departed, another inanimate object for the list Kane made in the neat progression of capital letters that marched across the page. Kane felt a fresh stab of the disorientation that comes when you're alive and somebody you know isn't, and, unbidden, Dylan's face rose up in his memory to replace Danny's, the face of his son drawn tight in the rictus of death. Kane drew deep breaths and bit his lip until it bled, using the pain to drive the memory from his mind.

No, he thought. No. No. No. Not now. Later. After I'm finished with this.

He set the papers aside and picked up the next form.

The notes on the victim's vehicle—here, Kane shook his head and thought, Danny's Corvette, not the victim's vehicle, goddamn it. The patterns of language and thought that protected police officers from the sometimes-horrifying realities of their jobs also got in the way of understanding the humanity of everyone involved: the victim, the criminal, themselves. This was not about a victim; it was about Danny Shirtleff, and Kane had thought from time to time over the years that his inability to solve the case lay in the difference between the two.

The keys were in the Corvette's ignition, but there was no indication that the car had been running when Danny was shot. Bullets had punched holes in the left front fender, the left door, and the left rear fender.

Again, the words sparked memory. He was standing with a thick, bullet-headed man named Bledsoe, the department's mechanic.

"Car's in great shape except for them bullet holes," Bledsoe said, running a thick-fingered hand over his graying crew cut, "and maybe a little water damage from the rain. Shirtleff kept it up a lot better than the rest of you do your department cars. You coulda learned somethin' from him."

Maybe I could have, Kane thought then. But I'll never know what now.

"Find the bullets?" Kane asked.

Bledsoe nodded.

"Two of 'em, anyway," he said. "One inside the door, t'other in the rear wheel well. Sent 'em over to ballistics. The weapon, whatever it was, didn't have a lot of punch to get stopped by the bodywork."

Something about Bledsoe's attitude bothered Kane. Or maybe it was the case. Something made him want to put the big mechanic in his place.

"Had enough punch to do the job," Kane said, and, when Bledsoe didn't reply, he turned and left the auto shop.

Nothing else about the car was remarkable: the glove compartment contained an owner's manual, an ice scraper, and a tire pressure gauge; the trunk held a jack, a spinner wrench, a spare tire, and a suitcase. The suitcase was full of flashy clothes, all in need of washing. It also contained a shaving kit, holding the usual male toiletries, and the August 1985 issue of *Modern Photography*.

We never found the other two slugs, Kane thought. I wonder if that means anything?

The autopsy form contained no surprises, either. In dry medical language, the coroner confirmed what he'd said at the scene: Cause of death was gunshot wounds, a nice, tight, triangular pattern in the left breast. Any of the shots could have been fatal. The bullets had been extracted and sent to ballistics.

Time of death was between eight p.m. and eleven p.m. In other words, between the time he got off the airplane and when the kids found him, so the TOD was no help at all.

His last meal had been a not-very-big steak, a small portion of scalloped potatoes, and a Coke. Airline meal, Kane thought, as he had when he'd originally seen the report. If he'd eaten the meal on the airplane, what had he done between the time it landed and he got shot?

The next paragraph might explain that. Signs of recent sexual activity, including some stray pubic hairs mixed in with his own. Struck it lucky with a stewardess maybe? Kane remembered that they'd tried to follow that up but couldn't find anyone who would admit to having had sex with Danny that night. His notes would have more to say about that.

Danny was an otherwise healthy, fit fellow in his late twenties with an appendectomy scar and a "Semper Fi" tattoo on his left shoulder.

Nothing in there about the sight of Danny laid open like a fish that had been gutted, Kane thought. Nothing about the disinfectant that stung the nose or the soft whirr of the fans or the smell of human mortality that, every time, made him want to run from the room and vomit up his breakfast, his memories, his thoughts.

Kane set the autopsy report aside and picked up the ballistics report. The bullets that had killed Danny were .380 ACP. They matched the shell casings found at the scene, and both the bullets and casings matched the weapon found there, a Beretta M1934. A test firing of that semiautomatic confirmed it was the murder weapon. The Beretta had been stamped with two manufacturing dates, a standard date and one from the Fascist calendar. That had led the firearms inspector to speculate that the weapon had been brought to the U.S. as a souvenir of World War II.

Affixed to the ballistics report was a fact sheet, explaining the Fascist calendar markings and providing additional information on the weapon, which was still being made at the time of Danny's shooting. The fact sheet said the M1934 had been a standard sidearm of the Italian army, and that because of its size—about six inches long—and weight—a little less than two pounds—it had been a popular souvenir for GIs who fought in North Africa and Europe.

Even then, Kane had known not to read too much into that. Guns migrated. They got stolen. They got pawned. They were sold at gun stores and gun shows. Alaska was saturated with firearms, everything from hunting rifles to belly-guns, and people got shot with alarming frequency. They shot themselves or other people, accidentally or on purpose. New guns, old guns, homemade guns, ten-thousand-dollar-a-pop presentation models. And war souvenirs. At one time or another, Kane stood over bodies killed with every one of those. Ban guns, grab them all up somehow, and that would leave only the bodies killed with knives and clubs and fists. And cars.

Yeah, cars. For Kane's money, the automobile was the most effective weapon of all.

He remembered the first fatal automobile accident he'd responded to as a cop. Late November, probably; cold, dark, and icy. He was still riding with Fireball, and they'd caught the call. First on scene. A kid alone in a GTO, running on the ice with racing slicks—God knows why except kids that age think they'll never die—going way too fast, lost it and jumped into the oncoming lane in front of a ten-yard dump truck hauling sand and gravel to be spread on the streets. The truck hit the Goat broadside and sent it cartwheeling into the side of a small office building that was, at that time of night, empty—and a damn good thing, because windows had exploded as the car scraped all along the ground floor, sending glass through the offices there like shrapnel.

The rear of the car was still burning when he and Fireball got there. The trucker had gotten his rig off to the side of the street. He sat behind it in the snow, where his legs had given out after he'd seen what happened to the car.

"I couldn't stop," he said when he saw Fireball and Kane. "The car just slid in front of me and I couldn't stop."

"Where's the other driver?" Fireball asked.

The trucker just shrugged.

"Shit," Fireball said. "Let's go see."

He took his flashlight from his belt and switched it on. Kane did the same.

"You take the part that's burning," Fireball said.

Kane did, finding nothing but bits of glass and metal and rubber, smelling nothing but chemicals in the smoke that seeped from the wreckage.

"Over here," Fireball called, something terrible in his voice.

Kane turned and walked toward the other officer. As he got close, his foot hit something and sent it skidding along the icy street.

"What's that?" Fireball asked.

"Don't know," Kane said. "Tree branch?"

He walked to where the thing lay, reached down, and picked it up.

"What the fuck?" he said.

Fireball played the beam of his flashlight along the thing Kane held. It was a human arm, a left arm, torn from its shoulder, still wearing a black leather sleeve with metal studs at the cuff. Kane wanted to drop it and run howling into the night. Instead, he forced himself to look at it, to understand it and what it meant.

This is what I do now, he thought. I clean up other people's messes.

"I found the head," Fireball said. "Torn clean off. There's other pieces around, too. You hang on to that, kid, and I'll get some bags from the unit."

Kane sat there on the bed, his arm outstretched as if he were still holding that grisly object, wondering at the things people did to themselves and why he'd spent a good piece of his life dealing with their wreckage. He and Fireball had scoured the scene, picking up pieces of human body and putting them in bags, noting their locations, working with the industry and lack of emotion of a couple of ants, ignoring the paramedics and firemen, who stood aside and left them to their chore. They couldn't find the left foot and kept circling around and around looking for it until the shift sergeant, called to the scene by the paramedics, made them stop. They'd never found that left foot, a failure that Kane had never forgotten.

They'd stayed until the impound crew got what was left of the GTO loaded and carried off. Kane took the truck driver's statement, which amounted to little more than what he'd said when they first arrived. Fireball drove them back to the station, where, with two hours left to go in their shift and with the duty sergeant's blessing, they'd clocked out and showered and changed and taken a table in a dark corner in the Polar Bar. Not a cop bar; they didn't want a cop bar that night.

The waitress came up to the table and asked them what they wanted.

"Bottle of Jameson, two glasses," Fireball said.

"Hey, I can't do that," the waitress said, but something in Fireball's face sent her off to confer with the bartender. She returned with the bottle and two shot glasses and set them on the table. Kane reached for his wallet, but the waitress said, "Harvey says it's on the house," then left them strictly alone for the rest of the night.

Fireball uncapped the whisky and poured some into each glass.

"You did good tonight, kid," Fireball said.

"When I picked up that arm, I wasn't sure I could do it," Kane said.

"You did what you had to do," Fireball said. "People do what they have to do. Always."

He raised his glass and downed the whisky. Kane did the same.

Sitting there on the bed, Kane could feel that shot burning its way down his throat to light a fire in his stomach, feel the shot and the one after and the one after slowly melt the memory of what he'd seen and done that night.

Too many things seen and done, Kane thought, running his finger along the scar on his face, now all but invisible beneath his beard. Too many whisky nights.

He set aside the ballistics report and picked up the next set of papers. It looked like the notes and list from the search he and Jackie Dee had done of Danny's apartment. He began to read, but a knock on the door interrupted him. A nun poked her head around the door.

"Time for your medication, Mr. Kane," she said, her body following her head into the room. She handed Kane a paper cup containing four pills and a glass of water. Two painkillers, an antibiotic, and—what? Kane thought. But he didn't really care. He popped the pills into his mouth and washed them down with water.

"That was a very beautiful woman who visited you earlier," the nun said. "Is she a friend of yours?"

The forced nonchalance of the question made Kane smile.

"Isn't gossiping some sort of sin, Sister?" he asked.

The nun answered his smile with one of her own.

"If it is, it's not a very big sin, Mr. Kane," she said.

Kane could feel the painkillers start to kick in.

Funny, he thought. Didn't really notice the pain until it started to go away.

"She's just an old coworker," Kane said. "More's the pity."

"Where there's life, there's hope," the nun said.

She lifted Kane's head with one arm and, with the other, pulled the pillows out from behind him until he could lie down flat.

She's stronger than she looks, Kane thought. Wish I was stronger than I look.

As the painkillers took control, all the memories he'd been holding down burst forth. But they were too late. He wrapped the drugs around himself and leaped into the dark hole of sleep, where nothing could follow.

eighteen

We cannot change our memories, but we can change their
meaning and the power they have over us.

—DAVID SEAMANDS

## SEPTEMBER 1985

Kane and Kim Lewis were sitting in a booth at Leroy's, waiting for
Jackie Dee. Lewis looked around at the scene, took a sip of coffee,
and said, "Nasty."

"The coffee or the restaurant?" Kane asked. He took a drag on his
cigarette and set it back down in a small glass ashtray.

"Both," she said. "Either."

Kane nodded. The two of them sat in silence for a while, Kane smoking, Lewis crinkling up her nose. They were waiting for Jackie Dee.

"So, how did you get to be a detective, anyway?" Lewis said.

Kane looked at her. She was young, bright-eyed, and attractive.
The ideal audience for a tale of derring-do. He just didn't want to tell
this one.

"Nope," he said, putting out his cigarette and making a mental
note not to light another one. "You first. Tell me what you're doing on
the force. It's a low-percentage play for you."

"Why?" Lewis said. "Because I'm a woman? Because I'm black?"

"Both," Kane said. "Either."

Lewis laughed.

"Well, it's clear I'm just here for the witty repartee," she said.

Kane waited, and when Lewis began speaking again she had a serious look on her face.

"Some of this you can tell other cops, some you can't," she said. "Okay?"

Kane nodded.

"When I was a girl, my mama preached to me about education and self-reliance," Lewis said, "and about not messing around with no no-good piano-playin' man. She didn't mean just piano players. It was her code. Whenever I got all enthusiastic about some boy, she'd say, 'I hear piano music,' to remind me."

A couple of booths over, a thin white man with a ratty goatee reached across the table and slapped a young Asian woman wearing too much makeup.

"Excuse me," Lewis said.

She slid out of the booth and walked back to where the slapper sat. Kane stepped out of the booth and stood, letting his eyes walk around the room until they fell on a table where another man, this one stocky and black, sat with three tired-looking women. The black man smiled at Kane and put both hands flat on the tabletop.

"Stand up, please," Lewis said to the slapper.

"Wha?" the slapper said. "You talkin' to me, bitch?"

Bad move, Kane thought. The black man obviously thought the same, because he winked at Kane. It was all Kane could do to keep from smiling.

"I ain't your bitch, you ofay motherfucker," Lewis said. "Now, you rise up out of that booth before I snatch you out of there by those scraggly-ass chin whiskers."

The slapper threw his coffee cup at Lewis and stood up fast. Lewis flicked her head aside to let the coffee cup pass, formed her right hand into a blade, and stabbed him in the throat. The guy gasped, wrapped his hands around his throat, and fell to his knees. Kane saw Lewis's foot rise from the floor, hesitate, and descend again.

"Whatchu do that for?" the Asian woman said. "Now he beat me."

"Shut up," Lewis said. "You're a disgrace to women everywhere."

Kane walked around Lewis and jerked the slapper to his feet.

"You come with me, baby," the black man crooned to the Asian woman. "I won't beat you."

Lewis looked at him and he made his smile disappear like it was some kind of magic trick.

Kane leaned in close to the slapper. He could hear the air whistling in and out of his throat.

All she had to do was hit him a little harder, Kane thought, and I'd be traching him with a pocketknife and a ballpoint pen. Well, serves the dumb bastard right.

"That woman you threw the coffee cup at is a police officer, idiot," he said. "You want an assaulting-an-officer beef?"

The slapper shook his head.

"Good," Kane said. "That's the first smart thing you've done since you came into this place. Now, listen. You lay a finger on that woman and I'll find you and give you a beating you'll never forget." He paused. "No, I'll find you and let this woman behind me have you. Understand?"

The slapper nodded. His breathing seemed to be easing. Kane shoved him back down into the booth.

"Show's over," he said loudly. He turned, took Lewis's arm, and guided her to their booth. He sat, slid in, took his .38 from its holster, and laid it on the seat beside him.

"What's that for?" Lewis asked.

"If that piece of shit sits there long enough, he might have some feeling he mistakes for courage," Kane said.

"I can take care of him," Lewis said.

"I know," Kane said. "I watched you. But if he comes for us, it won't be bare-handed."

Lewis nodded. The waitress came over and flipped plates onto the table like a dealer setting out a hand of stud.

"Thanks for the floor show," she said out of the corner of her mouth as she served them.

Kane buttered a piece of toast, took a bite, and washed it down with orange juice that tasted of the can.

"You were telling me why you're on the force," he said. "Something about piano music."

Lewis drew a breath and popped a piece of bacon into her mouth. She chewed, swallowed, and smiled.

"Guys like that piss me off," she said.

"I noticed," Kane said. "The whole place noticed. That was a nice knife strike, by the way. Where'd you learn it?"

Lewis ate for a while.

"My mama's eagle eye kept me on the straight and narrow," she said. "I graduated high school and went off to college, got a degree. This was in California, southern California. It wasn't a week after I got my degree that I met my mama's worst fear, my piano-playin' man. Only he wasn't a piano player; he was an upright member of the United States armed forces, a captain in the Air Force. Even Mama liked him. We courted, got engaged, got married, made babies. I followed him to Germany, then Ohio, then up here."

She shook her head.

"Everything was fine," she said. "Then one day I said something to him and he hit me. When he was done hitting me, I could barely walk. I peed blood for a week."

She took a deep breath.

"When I could move again okay, I took the kids and went to a friend's house," she said. "He found us there. My friend called the cops. He was still beating on me when they got there, would probably have killed me if they hadn't gotten there in time."

They ate in silence for a while.

"It seemed odd to me at the time," she said, "but the cops were surprised when they came to ask me in the hospital if I'd press charges and I said, 'Hell, yes.' Now I know better, that a lot of women are like the woman over there in that booth. They think they deserve it, or that their man can change or something. Anyway, we put his sorry ass in jail, and I figured I'd better either run or toughen up before he got out. So when I was feeling better I signed up for martial arts classes at the university and a firearms training class that the department was offering then. I got used to being around the place and, when I saw a job listing for a clerk on the bulletin board in the shooting range, I applied and got it. I watched what went on and decided I could do that, so I applied and made it through the academy down in Sitka, and here I am."

Kane mopped up some egg yolk with a piece of toast.

"That's some story," he said when he'd finished chewing. "I can understand why you went after the guy with the goatee."

Lewis sat straight up in the booth.

"I would have gone after that asshole, anyway," she said. "No woman deserves to be hit."

"Hey," Kane said, putting his hands up in front of his chest. "Don't you be kung-fuing me. I didn't mean anything by it."

Kane watched Lewis force herself to relax.

"Sorry," she said. "Maybe my experiences do have something to do with how I reacted."

"Everybody's do," Kane said softly. "Any idea why your husband started beating you?"

Lewis shook her head.

"Nope," she said. "And he never explained. He actually got on the stand and denied the whole thing."

Kane leaned back in the booth.

"Makes as much sense as most things, I guess," he said. "What parts of the story do you want me to keep private? The beatings?"

Lewis laughed.

"Shit, no," she said. "My marriage wasn't any better or worse than lots in the department. It's the college degree."

"What's it in?" Kane asked with a grin.

"Social work," Lewis said, matching his grin with hers.

Kane nodded.

"Yeah," he said, "you'd never live that down. Mum's the word."

"Mum's the word about what?" Jackie Dee asked as he slid into the booth next to Lewis. "And why's your weapon sitting there?"

Kane gave him a quick account of what had happened.

"Damn," Jackie Dee said. "I miss all the fun. You can put your weapon away. I know that pimp and he ain't got the sand to try anything. Particularly not with Jackie Dee sitting here."

Kane slid his .38 into its holster. He and Lewis waited while Jackie Dee ordered. When he finished, Lewis said, "You aren't worried about your weight, are you?"

Jackie Dee snorted.

"The Jackie Dee machine is in perfect working order," he said. "Why would I worry? Now, tell me about your conversation with Jamie Roberts."

Lewis dug a notebook out of her purse.

"Mrs. Roberts said she and her husband have known Officer Shirtleff since he arrived, about four years ago. They saw him socially for a while. Had him over for dinner—he really liked her meat loaf—and they went to the movies, dancing, things like that, but when he went undercover for the first time that pretty much stopped. She said she tried to fix him up with some of her single girlfriends, but nothing came of that. Said one of her friends said Officer Shirtleff was sweet, but, after the first date, he just seemed to lose interest."

"Huh," Jackie Dee said. "He wasn't trying to get her in the sack?"

He said it like it was the most amazing thing he'd ever heard.

"Apparently not," Lewis said. "And that jibes with my experience."

The looks of surprise she got from the two men made Lewis laugh.

"You were involved with the victim?" Jackie Dee said. "And you didn't say anything about it?"

"I wasn't involved with the victim," Lewis said. "We went on one date. And it wasn't even a date, really. He was working some scumbags that were selling uppers by the bucket load out of one of those strip clubs down on Third. This was just about six months ago. He asked me to dress up trashy and go with him. 'Undercovers who always show up solo cause suspicion,' he said. 'Besides, I'd like to get to know you a little better.' So I put on a short skirt and some fuck-me pumps and went with him. Hung all over him. Stuck my tongue in his ear. It was a lot of fun, playacting. Coming and going, we talked a little about our lives. I told him about my busted marriage and all that. When we were done, I wrote it up and waited. But he never called again."

"That's it?" Jackie Dee asked.

"That's it," Lewis said.

"What did he tell you about himself?" Kane asked.

Lewis thought for a moment.

"Not much, now that I think about it," she said. "How much he liked his job. His photography. Some about growing up in Washington and his family back home. Nothing remarkable."

"Or very revealing," Kane said.

"Or very revealing," Lewis agreed. She closed her notebook and put it back in her purse.

"Anyway, that was that for the interview," she said. "If I didn't mention it, Mrs. Roberts's husband was sitting right next to her the whole time, holding her hand. So I didn't get any real girl talk out of her. Not that I would have anyway. Mrs. Roberts seems like a pretty polished person to me, not the type to show you anything she didn't want you to see."

I suppose if you're a whore at fourteen, you get good at hiding your real self, Kane thought, but he didn't say anything.

"Well, her story matches Fireball's," Jackie Dee said. "I don't suppose you noticed any signs of sudden wealth in the Robertses' household?"

Lewis grinned.

"Sports car in the driveway? Gold dinner plates? That kind of thing?" she said. "No, I didn't."

"Yeah, I know it was a dumb question," Jackie Dee said. "But I had to ask. At the rate we're going nowhere on this investigation, we're going to need a miracle of some kind."

"So none of the other detectives found out anything?" Kane asked.

"No, the other detectives didn't," Jackie Dee said, putting more emphasis on the word "detectives" than it warranted. "Nobody at the airport lot remembers Danny's Corvette coming through. None of his neighbors reported anything unusual, except for one old bag who said that Danny had a suspicious number of female visitors. Callaghan or Campbell—you know, I'm having a harder and harder time telling them apart—said that when he asked her how many, she mumbled something about how Jesus wanted us all to be monogamous. So he figures two would have been one too many for the old bag, and he's probably right. Still nothing on the blood they took from Danny, but that'll be weeks, and it's a long shot, anyway. Nobody on the street flashing suspicious wads of cash around or bragging about killing somebody."

The waitress brought Jackie Dee's food, and while he ate Kane thought about the case. There just wasn't much to go on. The missing money was the only concrete lead they had, and if whoever took it was smart he'd let that money cool off for a long time before doing anything with it. And there didn't seem to be any reason for anybody to shoot Danny except for the money.

When he said as much, Lewis agreed and Jackie Dee nodded. He swallowed the last of his breakfast, washed it down with coffee, and said, "You're right. That's why we're going to start interviewing anybody who knew about the money. When we leave here, I'm going down to FBI headquarters to butt heads with the special agent in charge about talking to his people. I'll probably have to haul the chief into it before I get anywhere there. You two are going to the shop, setting up in one of the interview rooms and interviewing the drug unit one at a time. Start with Jeffords. When his guys see him cooperating, they'll go along. They won't be nice about it, but they'll do it. Any questions?"

Jackie Dee looked from Kane to Lewis and back. Neither of them said anything. "I know interviewing cops is a pain in the ass," he said, "not to mention a great way to make enemies in the department. But it's got to be done. Just stay professional and do everything by the book and it'll be okay."

"Yeah, everything will be just peachy," Lewis said when they'd finished setting up the tape machine in the interview room. "Narcing other cops is great for the police career."

Kane looked at his watch. Jeffords was in a meeting with a couple of visiting Drug Enforcement Administration honchos from Washington, D.C., so it would be a while before they could interview him. Kane thought about going to his desk and knocking out some paperwork but didn't really feel like it.

"We got time now," Lewis said. "You were going to tell me how you got to be a detective."

Kane shrugged.

"Surely you've heard the story," he said.

"Not from anybody who was there," Lewis said.

"It's not really something I like to talk about," Kane said.

Lewis just sat there. Kane could tell by the look on her face that she expected him to talk. So he did.

"It was stupid, really," he said. "I was off shift, still in uniform, driving my unit home. You know, they like the uniforms to drive their cars home. Think having a police car in the neighborhood will encourage the citizens and discourage the criminals. Just as I was leaving the station, Laurie called and said we needed bread, so I stopped at a convenience store, the one in that strip mall on Arctic. I was working days, so it was like five-thirty. Who expects trouble in a strip mall at five-thirty in the evening? Anyway, I get out of my car and all hell breaks loose."

The first gunshots didn't really register as gunshots, just muffled noises from inside the store. Then, after a couple of beats, something shattered the window in the driver's door of Kane's car. Without thinking, Kane dove back into the unit, punched open the offside door, and swam out onto the pavement. While he was doing that, he could hear bullet strikes in the unit's bodywork. He rolled into a crouch and peered over the hood of his car. He'd drawn his weapon without thinking and he sighted along its barrel. He thought he could see someone standing to the side of the store's door, but he couldn't make out who it was.

Procedure was that, while he was in uniform, he was supposed to be carrying his portable radio. But the goddamn thing weighed a ton, so it was locked in the trunk. He could crawl back in and get to the radio in the unit, but he wouldn't be able to watch the store while he was doing that. He was about to do it anyway when a figure burst from the door of the store. The figure raised its arm, and the air around Kane was full of metal, whistling past his ears, thumping into the bodywork, spalling off the pavement.

The figure dropped its weapon, and, still running toward Kane, reached into its belt for another. Kane braced his elbow on the hood of the car and began shooting. The figure jerked once, twice, three times and went down, the weapon flying from its hand and skidding along the asphalt. The figure twitched like a landed fish, a little longer between each twitch, until it lay still.

Kane reloaded his .38 and waited. The silence was loud after the gunshots. It might have been raining. He couldn't really remember. Kane could see people peeking from the dry cleaner next to the convenience store. He waved at them to get back out of sight, but they stayed there like spectators unwilling to give up good seats.

"Herbie," a voice called from inside the store. "You okay, Herbie?"

Herbie isn't ever going to be okay again, Kane thought. There seemed to be movement inside the store. A face peeking out? Then a shriek, a shot, and a scream. Kane thought again about trying to use the radio.

Surely someone must have called the police by now, he thought, but he heard no sirens.

Another figure came out of the grocery store. This one moved slowly. It stumbled, and Kane could see that it was really two figures, one behind the other. The shielded figure held a handgun pressed to the temple of the figure in front.

"Anchorage Police," he called, trying to put authority into his voice. "Drop your weapon and put your hands in the air."

"You drop your weapon, cop," the shielded figure called in a high-pitched voice, "or one more gook gets greased."

The figure in front looked like a Korean woman, She was bleeding from her left arm and limping on her right leg.

She's been shot, Kane thought.

All Kane could see of the second figure was a spiky head of yellow hair and a skinny arm.

Just a kid, Kane thought. He's just a kid.

"I mean it, cop," the second figure called. "I'll waste her."

Procedure was to stay where he was until the shielded figure gave him a decent shot. Kane stood up, letting the .38 drop along his leg.

"Just put the weapon down," he said, moving out from behind the unit. "Everything will be all right."

The two figures kept moving. Kane walked toward them. They weren't far apart at all, maybe thirty feet.

"All right?" the figure screamed. "All right? You gonna make all those people alive again? Are you, cop? Are you?"

The figure pushed the Korean woman forward. The woman's right leg collapsed, and, moaning, she fell to the asphalt. The figure pointed its weapon at her.

"Hey," Kane called. "Over here. It's me you want, right?"

The figure brought its weapon up and started shooting. Bullets whistled past Kane, one tugging at his left sleeve. No choice now, he thought. Kane raised his .38 and put three bullets into the chest of a fifteen-year-old girl named Betty Blaisedale.

"She was dead before she hit the ground," Kane said, looking again at Lewis instead of the scene in his mind. "They were just kids. They were two kids who should have been in high school. Instead, they were dusted to the eyeballs. The boy was sixteen. His name was Herbert Wayne. 'Herbie,' he was called. They'd found a stash of guns his father had, killed her father—he'd been abusing her; they found pictures later—and took off in her father's car. Nobody knows where they got the PCP or when they took it. Nobody knows if they were planning to rob the convenience store or just freaked out. We found the woman's husband, their two small children, and a Serbian cab driver in the store, all shot dead. It was all just a stupid, stupid waste."

Lewis reached over and put a hand on Kane's.

"That must have been terrible," she said. "To have to shoot those kids."

"The shooting wasn't so bad," he said. "It was just training. A couple of people, a couple of civilians, said, 'Well, why didn't you shoot her in the shoulder?' But when the shit starts to fly, your training takes over. Aim for the body mass. Keep shooting until the other shooter goes down. But afterward, finding out that they were so young, that was pretty tough. And then being made a hero was toughest of all. All the witnesses said how brave I was, how I didn't shoot until I didn't have any choice. The woman, her name is Elizabeth Ahn, said in her statement that I saved her life, that it was the girl who had done most of the shooting in the store and that Ahn would certainly have been killed if I hadn't intervened."

Kane stopped talking and gave Lewis a twisted smile.

"What I didn't tell anybody is that the reason I stood up wasn't that I'm a hero," he said. "It wasn't to save Elizabeth Ahn's life. The reason I stood up was that I was still hungover from the night before. Bernie Kelly's bachelor party; I had a kitchen pass from Laurie. My head hurt, and I didn't have the patience to wait. Maybe if I'd waited, the girl might be alive."

"Yeah," Lewis said. "Maybe. And maybe the Korean woman would be dead."

"I know that," Kane said, "but the whole thing just should have gone down better. The girl should have somebody to send her to her room, to revoke her phone privileges—something—and instead I kill her in a parking lot. The bullets pushed her over backward, and when I went over to kick her weapon away and check on her, her blue eyes were wide open, looking at me with a sort of 'What did you do to me?' look. Or, at least, that's what I saw."

The silence lasted for a while.

"So two kids are dead, and I get made a detective," he said. "For being a hero. Isn't that perfect?"

"I'm sorry," Lewis said. "I'm sorry I made you tell that story."

"It's okay," Kane said. "It actually gets easier every time I tell it. That may be the worst thing of all."

# nineteen

Time is the reef upon which all our frail
mystic ships are wrecked.

—Noël Coward

## APRIL 2007

"You'll ruin your eyes, reading in this light," Cee Cee said.

Kane looked up from the accounts of their interviews with the members of the drug unit. The interviews were models of proper police procedure: logical, straightforward, precise. One question followed another in perfect order; each answer was just what it needed to be and no more. The teachers at the police academy could use these interviews as perfect examples of how to ask questions. And, of course, they had not yielded one iota of information useful to the investigation.

"What's all the paperwork?" Cee Cee asked, gesturing to the forms and reports spread across the table.

"An old case," Kane said. "My first as an investigator. A murder. Unsolved."

"You don't give up on things easily, do you, Nikky?" Cee Cee asked.

The sun had moved, leaving him with dim, diffuse light striped with the shadows of the barren limbs of birch trees that lined the big yard.

Cee Cee sat in the chair across from Kane. She set down the garbage bag she was carrying and crossed one leg over the other. She was wearing khaki pants, a bright red Hawaiian shirt covered with parrots, and leather sandals.

"Is that nail polish you've got on your toenails?" Kane asked. "What kind of nun are you?"

Cee Cee laughed.

"Sister Mary Magdalene asked me a question much like that just this morning," she replied. " 'One who is more like her mother every day,' I told her."

Cee Cee sat looking out the window for a while.

"This was always my least favorite time of the year," she said. "Winter goes on for so long, and it's like you're hanging on by your fingernails for spring to arrive. That's why I'm wearing these clothes, to cheer myself up."

She's got a point, Kane thought. Let her get to it.

"You know, Nikky, the experts say that the darkness can cause real psychological problems for people," Cee Cee said. " 'Seasonal affective disorder,' they call it. Have you ever thought that you might be happier if you lived someplace that had more light? Less cold? More warmth?"

Kane laughed.

"Like the Big Rock Candy Mountains, Ceese?" he asked. "Where the hens lay soft-boiled eggs?"

Cee Cee smiled.

"I take it you're not likely to be moving south soon, then?" she asked.

"No, I'm not," Kane said. "I'll be sixty years old soon enough. A little old to be making a new life, aren't I?"

Cee Cee shrugged,

"Only if you think you are, Nikky," she said.

Kane set the reports down on the table.

"You were going to tell me about our parents," he said. "Have you been avoiding me?"

Cee Cee nodded.

"I have," she said. "I'm not certain how to talk about this."

Kane smiled at that.

"Why not just try English?" he said.

Cee Cee blew air through her lips. Kane remembered the mannerism from his youth. It meant she was exasperated, and she'd done it often.

At least she did when I was around, he thought. Was I the cause of her exasperation?

"It's not that simple, Nikky," she said. "You and I see the world differently. We always have."

"What's wrong with my view of the world?" Kane asked.

"I'm not criticizing the way you see the world," she said. "I'm just saying it has always been very cause and effect. It's like you think everything that happens has just one cause, and that somehow you will understand what happened if you can just find that cause."

Kane thought about that. He had to admit that what Cee Cee said seemed accurate.

He said as much, adding, "That's probably what makes me a good investigator. I look at what's happened until I discover a reason that makes sense to me, and I go from there. I've solved a lot of cases that way."

Cee Cee got to her feet.

"I didn't come here to argue, Nikky," she said. "I came to take you for a walk. Your doctor says you need exercise."

Kane looked around the room.

"Do I even have shoes?" he asked.

"I brought some of your belongings over from that sea of despond you call an apartment," Cee Cee said. "Including some slip-on boots. Do you need help getting dressed?"

Kane shook his head.

"I'll be back in a few minutes, then," she said, setting the garbage bag on the bed, where he could get at it more easily.

Kane got to his feet and, moving very carefully, took clothes from the garbage bag and put them on. They hung from him. Fortunately, Cee Cee had included a pair of suspenders, so his pants would stay up. He tried putting on a pair of socks, but when he bent over the pain was too much. Cee Cee found him sitting on the bed with the socks in his hand.

"Oh, yeah," she said. "I should have thought about the socks."

She took them from Kane and, kneeling, whisked them onto his feet.

"There," she said, getting to her feet. "Your boots are by the front door. Let's go."

They walked out of the room and down the hall, Kane shuffling along, hanging on to Cee Cee's arm. When they stepped out the front door, the chill air surprised Kane.

"We'll just walk to the end of the sidewalk and back," Cee Cee said. "We wouldn't want to overdo."

They walked slowly along the concrete strip. Blue ice melt had been scattered along the ice that covered the sidewalk, giving good traction. Kane was surprised at how much effort it took just to get to the end of the sidewalk.

"The problem is that reality is not that simple," Cee Cee said. "Life is more complicated than you give it credit for."

"So what?" Kane asked. "What difference does that make?"

"It makes you judgmental, Nikky," she said. "If you think that X happened because person Y did something, and X is bad, then what Y did was bad and that makes Y a bad person."

They reached the end of the walk and stood there for a while. Kane's legs felt like rubber bands.

"Jesus, Cee Cee," he said, "I'm not looking for a lesson in moral philosophy here. I just want to find out what happened to our father."

They shuffled through a turn and started back toward the residence.

"Your attitude makes you hard on people, Nikky," Cee Cee said. "Yourself as well as others. And it makes you think you can know things you just can't know. Like what happened to our father. Even if you could look him in the eye right now and make him tell you his story, you still wouldn't know what happened. People forget. They lie. They misunderstand their own motives. They mix things up. You want simple answers, and the only things simple answers are good for are simple questions. Life doesn't ask many simple questions, Nikky. 'God moves in a mysterious way His wonders to perform.' Or, if you prefer, 'There are more things in heaven and earth, Horatio, than are dreamt of in your philosophy.' That's the truth about life."

Kane thought about what Cee Cee had said as he lay in his bed. The walk had tired him out, and he'd immediately fallen into a dreamless sleep. It was one of those naps that seems to be over right after it starts, and her words were fresh in his mind when he awoke.

Is she right? he thought. Probably. Life, his life anyway, seemed pretty complicated. He supposed everyone else's life was, too. But that didn't mean he couldn't figure out who did something or why he did it. If it did, they'd have to open up the prisons and let everybody out, because every investigator—every judge and jury, for that matter— thought that such things weren't just knowable but provable.

No, to his way of thinking, life was just as complicated as you made it. And if that meant holding people responsible for the bad things they did, so be it.

A vision of Dylan dashed across his mind. He closed his eyes tightly and willed it away.

I'll deal with that responsibility later, he thought.

Kane got to his feet, put on his robe, and went looking for his sister. He found her sitting in an easy chair in a big, book-lined room. She had a large book propped open in her lap, but her eyes were closed, and she seemed to be asleep. Kane realized that he had no idea what time it was, and, quietly, he started to withdraw.

"Where do you think you're going, Mr. Nikiski Kane?" Cee Cee said in her best big-sister voice. Then she laughed. "You never could sneak past me, could you, Nikky? Come in and sit down."

Kane moved slowly to a matching easy chair and sank down, wincing as he did so.

"Are you okay, Nikky?" his sister asked.

"I think so," he said. "I'm just awfully weak, much weaker than I expected. Even that little walk we took seems to have brought my pain back."

Cee Cee shook her head.

"It's not just the exercise," she said. "We've been cutting back on your pain medication. The doctor suggested it. Didn't want you getting hooked, I guess. But we'll kick it back up after you exercise for a while."

Kane nodded. With each breath, he could feel a stitch in his wounded side, followed by a pain that traveled up his ribs toward his heart.

"It worries me, Cee Cee," he said. "I should be getting better faster."

His sister got to her feet and laid a hand on his forehead. Her hand felt cool and dry.

"I think it's just age," she said. "We heal slower as we get older. And maybe part of it is that positive mental attitude we talked about earlier."

"Goddamn it, Ceese," Kane barked. "There's nothing wrong with my mental attitude that not feeling like a ninety-eight-year-old invalid wouldn't cure. That, and getting some answers instead of lectures about the unknowability of the known, or whatever the hell."

His sister laughed.

"That's more like the Nikky I remember," she said. "Stubborn and impatient. And not happy being sick. I remember once, when you were six or seven, you got the measles, and I thought keeping you in bed would be the death of us all."

Kane leaned back in his chair and closed his eyes.

"I'm too tired to fight," he said when he opened them again. "I want to know what you know, but I can't force you to tell me. So you do what you want."

He could hear the defeat in his voice, and he felt as he had sometimes as a child, when the world seemed too big and too complicated for a small boy to deal with. Cee Cee must have sensed his condition, for her answering words were soft, her tone reassuring.

"Don't worry, Nikky," she said. "I'll tell you what I know. I just don't want you to blunder into something that will hurt you more."

Kane could feel the smile twist on his face.

"I'm hiding from one truth by searching for other truths, Cee Cee," he said. "Does that seem like a successful long-term strategy to you? It doesn't to me. But I seem to be hooked and, for the moment anyway, I have to just keep going forward. So if you could just tell me what you know, please, I'd really appreciate it."

They sat in silence for some time then, long enough that Kane thought Cee Cee might have fallen asleep again. But, finally, her voice came, as if from a great distance.

"Mom and Dad met in southern California, in a defense plant, in 1942. Mom and her sister, Aunt Kate, had moved from Stockton to work there, assembling aircraft of some sort, when he showed up from somewhere. He was seventeen and should have been in the armed forces. I don't know why he wasn't. According to Kate, who told me this story, Mom 'went for him in the most shameless way.' She said, 'Your mother always knew what she wanted, and what she wanted was him, skinny little thing that he was, and her several years older, too.'

"Apparently, he didn't fight very hard. Who knows what the effects of ready sex would be on a teenage boy?"

She paused, as if expecting Kane to say something. So he did.

"I'd say they'd be pretty powerful," he said.

"Speaking from experience, Nikky?" Cee Cee asked, her grin wicked.

"Cee Cee, please," Kane said, answering her grin with one of his own. "We're not talking about my sexual experiences. You're not just my sister; you're a nun."

"Maybe we should, Nik," his sister said. "Wasn't there an older woman in your life when you were a teenager? Orrie told me once that Mom tried everything she could think of to break that up. Didn't you ever wonder why? Don't you suppose she saw—Carrie, wasn't it?—as trying to do just what she'd done? Trap a younger man?"

Nik shrugged, and pain shot along his ribs again. He did his best to keep any expression off his face.

"She didn't need to worry," he said. "Carrie had a very clear idea of what she wanted, and a poor, young husband wasn't any part of her plans."

Cee Cee nodded.

"That's what Orrie thought," she said. "I guess the phrase they use these days is 'boy toy.' Anyway, Mom apparently was interested in a poor, young husband. Or maybe God took a hand. Whatever the reason, she was soon pregnant. There were some tearful scenes, again according to Aunt Kate. 'He wanted to run away, like any sensible young man would,' she said. 'But your mother was determined to have him, and when Cecelia set her mind on something she always got her way.' "

Cee Cee shifted in her chair.

"My old bones don't like staying in one position very long," she said. "Anyway, they got married, but not in the church. 'By the time your mother had him bent around her little finger enough,' Aunt Kate said, 'she was showing too much. She tried stomping her foot and pouting at the local parish priest, a tough old bird out of a hard school in Ireland, and got nowhere.'

"So it was off to the justice of the peace," Cee Cee continued. "For all of their tough start, they seemed to get along well enough. Even Aunt Kate had to admit that they seemed happy. Dad kept working, and, after I was born, Mom babysat the children of other women who wanted to work in the plant.

" 'I don't know if he started to get restless and she wanted to keep him tied down, or if Cecelia just forgot how babies are made, or if she enjoyed making them so much she just didn't care,' Aunt Kate said, 'but they just kept having babies. I tried to talk to her about it—right after Barry was born, I think it was—and she gave me the strangest look and said, "Proper women don't talk about sex, Kate." And her with her knees tucked behind her ears every night. Proper women, indeed.' "

Cee Cee laughed. Kane, joining her, was rewarded with another bolt of pain.

"Our aunt Kate had some tongue on her, didn't she?" he said as the pain subsided.

"Still does," Cee Cee said. "Eighty-seven years old and sound as a dollar. She's living in a condo down in Cabo San Lucas, drinking a fifth of Irish a week, and still making the beach boys nervous."

She laughed again and fell silent.

"You've developed a pretty . . . earthy sense of humor, haven't you?"

Kane asked, as much to break the silence as to get an answer. But Cee Cee replied promptly.

"People think that those with a vocation become more spiritual as they get older," she said, "and maybe some of them do. But the religious I've admired, nuns and priests alike, got more human as they went, not less. I'm trying to do that, too.

"And in aid of that," she said, getting to her feet, "I think I'll have a drink."

One of the rows of books proved to be a false front that slid back to reveal an impressive array of bottles and a row of highball glasses. Cee Cee poured a couple of fingers of something dark into one of the glasses and recapped the bottle.

"No ice?" Kane asked.

"Aunt Kate would say that only a Protestant would pollute good Irish whisky with ice," she replied, sliding the false front back into place. Resuming her seat, she took a sip and gave a little sigh.

"You know, it's not polite to drink in front of somebody who can't," Kane said.

"Offer it up, Nikky, offer it up," Cee Cee said, and took another sip.

When the level in the glass was appreciably lower, she said, "Anyway, the war ended and the plants all cut production and laid off the women in favor of returning veterans. Kate took up with an unsuitable man around then, the first of five husbands, I think it was, and the sisters lost track of each other for several years. So I don't know why our family moved from California to Oregon or from Oregon to Alaska. Some combination of Dad not being able to find just the right job and Mom wanting a better life, I guess."

The room was silent for a while.

"So that's what Aunt Kate told you," Kane said. "But what do you know yourself?"

"Not very much, I'm afraid," Cee Cee said. "Children understand so little and remember even less."

She was silent again for a while.

"What I do remember is feelings," she said. "Children are particularly attuned to feelings, I think, because they understand so little of the adult world. What I remember from being very young are generally good feelings. The first concrete memory, I guess you'd call it, I have is how happy everyone was when Aurora was born. Amazed and happy. Everyone remarked on how beautiful she was, and I can remember tracing her features with a finger while Mom held her.

"Everything was fine then for a long time. I remember Dad coming home from work, tired and dirty. I remember you being born. Everybody was happy about that, too, even though you weren't beautiful."

Kane smiled at that.

"You've got that right," he said.

But Cee Cee continued as if he hadn't spoken.

"I remember disappointments, too, things I wanted that I couldn't have because there were too many mouths to feed. I remember Mom and Dad getting dressed up to go out and coming back, laughing and smelling of something strong. Like this."

She held up her glass and smiled.

"Then, some time after you were born, things changed. Mom and Dad quit talking to each other; stopped spending time together, in fact. Not long after, Mom started shifting the responsibility for the household to me." She paused. "No, that's not fair. She quit doing things, or at least quit doing them well, and I started doing them because they had to be done and they had to be done right. Little things at first, and, as I got older, bigger and bigger things."

"That was a lot of responsibility for a young girl," Kane said.

"I know," Cee Cee said. "I felt sorry for myself for a while. But I found I was actually quite good at running the household. The rest of you cooperated—I couldn't have done it without you—and I thought of it as preparation for having a family of my own. But, then, I started hearing God's voice more and more and realized a family wasn't in my future."

Kane didn't know how to phrase the next question, so he just asked it.

"Did you—do you—really hear God's voice, Cee Cee?" he asked. "You know, I've always expected to hear an answer when I pray but I never have."

His sister gave him a smile he remembered from his childhood, one she reserved for when one of the children said something particularly endearing.

"No, Nikky, I've never heard his voice, either," she said. "It's more like I saw his hand in the world's design more and more often, that the world stopped making sense without him in it."

Kane nodded. He could understand that explanation. Not experience it or agree with it but understand it.

"What is it that you think happened, Cee Cee?" he asked. "What caused Mom and Dad to split apart like that?"

"I'm not sure, Nikky," she said. "I've thought about it a lot and I'm not sure. I do know that it wasn't just Dad who started staying away. After the little kids were in bed, Mom would get dressed up and go out herself. I don't know where she went or what she did. I do know that she often didn't get home until quite late. And sometimes she'd be coming in the door when I got up to start breakfast."

Kane thought about what his sister had said.

"Do you think she was seeing somebody else, another man?" Kane asked.

Cee Cee didn't reply. The teachings of the Catholic Church aside, it wouldn't have been so bad if Cecelia Kane had taken up with another man after her husband left. But what if she'd taken up with another man *before* her husband left?

"I've been having these memories, like I told you," Kane said. "Or maybe they're dreams that I think are memories now. I'll tell you one of them."

He told her the story of his earthquake walk with Fireball Roberts and what Roberts had said about his encounter with their parents.

"What do you think of that, Cee Cee?" he asked when he finished.

"I think it's time I make sure the patient gets safely back to his bed," she said. "And don't think I haven't noticed all the wincing you've been doing. I'm giving you something for the pain tonight."

Kane let her put him to bed and dutifully swallowed the pill she gave him. As she turned to go, he said, "But, Cee Cee, what if what Mom was doing had something to do with Dad's disappearance?"

She turned back and looked down at him.

"Nik, I don't know what to do with you," she said. "I really don't. Whatever happened happened a long time ago. What possible difference could it make now?"

Nik started to reply but his sister raised a hand.

"I've already told you that I think you should forget this," she said, "but I guess I can understand why you can't do that right now. So I want you to make me a promise. Whatever you find out, I want you to promise not to tell me. I have enough trouble being God's servant every day without dredging up the sins of the past."

The room was starting to recede, and all Kane could do was nod. Apparently satisfied, Cee Cee walked to the door, opened it, turned off the light, and pulled the door closed behind her. Kane lay there, thinking about what she'd said, until thinking made no sense at all.

twenty

The palest ink is better than the best memory.

—CHINESE PROVERB

## JULY 1965

Nik slammed out of the house, cursing under his breath. He'd have to hurry to not be late for work. Why did his mother insist on starting these arguments in the morning, when he had to get up, shower, put on his work clothes, make himself a breakfast, and pack himself a lunch? If she wasn't going to help him, she could at least not get in his way.

She didn't like Carrie, didn't like what she suspected they were doing together. So what? It was his life, not hers. She thought she could get her way with him like she had his father. Well, he'd show her.

These thoughts and others like them occupied Nik's mind as he walked through town and down into the port area. The need to rebuild what the earthquake had destroyed was causing the economy to boom again, and every stick of building materials came through the port. As soon as school ended for the year, Nik quit his busboy's job and the job cleaning the Silver Dollar and got one as a laborer at a big lumberyard on the docks. The pay was spectacular for a boy who'd just turned sixteen—$5.65 an hour, with time and a half for overtime, and there was plenty of overtime.

He got to the yard just in time. He walked through the big warehouse, where the interior-grade lumber was kept, to the foreman's office, where he punched in at exactly seven a.m. Then he put his lunch in the refrigerator there.

"Hey, Nik," the foreman, a slow-moving, patient man with the unfortunate name of Pugmire, said. "I'll need you to work with Charlie this afternoon, breaking down that flatcar that came in last night."

"Okay," Nik said, his voice not happy. Charlie was the old fellow who ran the yard's big forklift, the Towmotor. Sober, he was an artist with the thing. Hungover, he was so-so. And if he started drinking at lunch, watch out.

Nik poured himself a cup of coffee and walked back out into the warehouse. He set his cup on one of the blades of the little forklift and checked the gas and oil. Satisfied, he picked up his cup, sat down in the forklift, fired up the engine, and drove it slowly to where the orders awaiting pickup sat. The little forklift sounded like an out-of-tune jalopy, the clanking of its pistons echoing loud in the warehouse. When he got to the orders, he climbed off the forklift and checked each pile of wood and hardware against its order form. He'd filled those orders last thing before he left the night before, but you couldn't be too careful.

Out in the yard, he could hear the voices of Pugmire, Charlie, and Herc Sanders as they got ready to load the big flatbed with deliveries. Charlie sounded pretty good, so he'd probably get the work done okay. He'd better, or Herc, who drove the deliveries, would pinch his head off. Nik was filling out, and the physical labor was building muscle, but he'd no more take on Herc Sanders than he'd try to outrun a hot rod on foot. Herc made Charles Atlas look like a pansy.

An International Harvester crew cab pickup pulled in. A guy with a crew cut rolled down his window and leaned out. He had forearms like Popeye.

"Order for Eagan Construction," he said.

Nik nodded.

"All ready," he said.

"You need help?" the crew cut asked.

Nik shook his head, jumped on the forklift, snaked it into a row of orders, plucked the one he wanted, and dropped it into the back of the pickup as nice as you please. He hopped off the forklift and gave the guy the order form, which he eyeballed against the contents of his truck.

"Thanks, kid," he said, signing the form and handing it back to Nik.

Nik tore off the green page and handed it to the guy, clipping the white original and the yellow copy to the bottom of the pile on his clipboard. Another truck, this one a small flatbed, was already waiting in line.

The last of the orders was filled a little after nine, so Nik drove the forklift out into the yard. The sun was out and the temperature must have been near seventy, hot for Anchorage. Nik picked up a pallet and drove across the yard to a boxcar that sat on a railroad siding. The boxcar was loaded with bags of sawdust insulation. His job, Pugmire had explained the other day, was to load the bags onto pallets and tuck them away in the warehouse until their buyer came for them.

"No more than four rows of bags a pallet," Pugmire said. "This pony lift'll tip right over if you try to carry more."

Nik lined up the bottom of the pallet with the bottom of the boxcar door, set the brake, and killed the engine. He climbed like a monkey out of the seat and onto the pallet. He unclipped the door and slid it open.

Christ, there are a lot of bags in here, he thought. He grabbed the nearest one, pivoted, and set it down on the back of the pallet, in the middle.

"These bags're fifty pounds each," Pugmire had said. "You let the load get outta balance and they'll dump you on your ass, then fall on top of you, likely as not."

Nik counted as he worked. Four rows of bags, eight bags to the row. The bags were made of heavy-duty paper. Strong enough, but not something you could just toss around or they'd rip. Thirty-two bags a pallet at fifty pounds each. Sixteen hundred pounds. The rated capacity of the forklift was eighteen hundred. He'd have to be careful. When he finished loading the pallet, he climbed over the bags and down onto the seat. He dropped the forks until they were just off the ground. He didn't want the load up high if he tipped over. He started the lift, backed in a tight circle, and drove slowly to the warehouse. Every pothole set the forklift rocking, and there were plenty of potholes. He drove into the warehouse and slid the pallet into position. He dropped the forks and backed away, picked up an empty pallet, and drove back to the boxcar.

Great, he thought. I've got a system. I can do this.

Nik was entitled to a midmorning coffee break, but he worked through it as he usually did. By the time he knocked off for lunch, his ass was dragging. He did the math on the bags he'd handled and came up with 19,200 pounds. Almost ten tons. No wonder he was tired.

Or maybe, as his mother kept telling him, it was because he was "burning the candle at both ends." It wasn't unusual for Nik to work until seven p.m., go home, shower, grab something to eat on his way out the door, and go right over to Carrie's. And not to sleep, either.

So he wasn't surprised to have Pugmire shake him awake.

"Lunchtime's over, kid," he said. "Go help Charlie take that flatcar load apart."

The flatcar was piled high with bundles of lumber, each bundle held in place by long metal bands. The entire load was secured with chains and braced by a series of four-by-four stakes. Nik grabbed a pry bar and a hand sledge and trotted over to where the Towmotor sat next to the flatcar. The big forklift looked like a prehistoric creature of some kind, its idling engine giving off a series of deep bass notes. Charlie gave him a cheery wave.

Uh-oh, Nik thought.

He stood on one of the forks and let Charlie raise him until he was level with the top of the pile. Then Charlie tilted the forks forward, and Nik stepped off onto the load. He walked to the first come-along, pried it upright, tapped the locking pin with the sledge, and backed off the chain. He did that all along that section of the load, then set the pry bar and sledge on top of the next section. Then he walked along the load, separating the come-alongs from the chain and piling them next to the pry bar and sledge. Finally, he walked along the load once more and, after looking to be sure no one was below, dropped the ends of the chains over the side.

When he was finished, he gave Charlie a thumbs-up. He walked back to get onto the forks, but Charlie already had the big machine in motion. Nik was supposed to ride the forks, helping line them up with the breaks in the load that allowed it to be removed a section at a time. Charlie obviously had other ideas. That didn't strike Nik as a good thing.

I should get off of this load now, he thought. But how? I've gotta be thirty feet in the air. No way I'm jumping from here without getting hurt.

Charlie jockeyed the forks up and down until he had them where he thought they ought to go. The forklift bellowed and surged forward, like a dinosaur attacking. The blades slammed into the load, and the machine ground forward. Over the racket of the engine Nik could hear the soprano *thwing* of a band parting.

Shit, he thought. Charlie missed the break. He yelled at Charlie to stop, but his voice was drowned by the engine noise. He saw Herc Sanders look up from checking the tie-downs on his truck, then start running toward the flatcar. Nik saw the chains that controlled the forks turn and felt the load shift under his feet.

Oh, Christ, he thought. His instinct was to move away from the forklift, but there was no escape in that. He'd never get to the part of the load that was still chained down in time. Instead, Nik danced forward toward the forklift. Charlie had the forks up high, trying to clear the four-by-four posts. Pieces of lumber dangled from the pile on the forklift like so many pick-up sticks. The forklift bellowed as Charlie tried to back away. The bottom of the load caught one of the four-by-fours. The forklift screamed as Charlie gave it more gas, and the four-by-four shattered. A foot-long shard of wood shot past Nik, hit the top of the pile on the flatcar, and exploded. Pieces of lumber rained down from the pile on the forklift, striking the load on the flatcar and rebounding at crazy angles.

Nik was past thought now. He took two more steps and launched himself for the forklift. At some level, he knew that if he grabbed the wrong thing he could lose a hand. But he was out of options. He focused on the crossbeam of the metal plate that raised and lowered the forks. He grabbed that and let his momentum carry him in an arc. A twenty-foot-long two-by-six fell like a spear, close enough that Nik could feel the air move as it whistled past him. It hit the ground and bounded wildly away.

Nik flipped himself around to the side of the forklift, then the back, grabbing one of the channels that the forks ran along. He let himself slide, the metal gouging at his palms. He looked up and saw the forks coming at him fast. Charlie must be panicking, trying to get the load to the ground before something came through the cab for him. If the fork rollers got to him, they'd cut his fingers off like shears cutting so many threads. Nik stopped himself, trying not to scream as the metal cut into his palms. He braced a foot and flipped himself backward, landing on the roof of the forklift's cab. He could see the forks rush past out of the corner of his eye. He let his momentum carry him to the edge of the roof and slid down onto the engine housing, jumping to the ground from there. He hit the ground awkwardly, turned his fall into a roll, and came up on his feet.

Herc Sanders came running up to him.

"Jesus, kid, are you all right?" he asked. Nik was alive. Alive was all right.

"What the fuck happened here?" Pugmire said as he arrived on the run. He was panting. "What happened, Nik? I told you to watch out for the old man."

"Hey," Sanders said. "This ain't the kid's fault. I warned you about letting the old alky work here."

Pugmire spluttered, but Charlie walked up on shaky legs and said, "He's right, Pug. I got no business here. I'm through."

The three of them watched the old man wobble away, then turned to face one another.

"Hey, what's that?" Sanders said, pointing to the blood that dripped from Nik's clenched fists.

"I, I guess I got cut," Nik said, opening his hands. The pads just under his fingers were deeply scored, and, as he watched, the blood welled up and began to overflow his palms.

"Christ," Sanders said. He pulled a bandanna out of his pocket, thrust it into Nik's left hand, and said, "Make a fist." Pugmire did the same with Nik's right hand.

"Wait here, kid," Sanders said. "I'll get my truck." Turning to Pugmire, he said, "I'll take the kid over to Providence and get him stitched up. I'll be back."

The nurse on duty at the emergency room took a look at Nik's hands and started barking orders. The next thing he knew, they'd given him shots to deaden the pain and cleaned out the wounds with something, and a thin, white-haired guy was sewing up his palms, peering at the cuts through a big magnifying rig as he sewed. He seemed to use a lot of thread.

"There'll be no nerve damage, if you're lucky," the doctor said when he was finished. "You've had your tetanus shot, right?"

Nik nodded.

"Okay, then," he said. "You sit here until you feel fit to move. The nurse here will give you some pills. Take two now, and two more when the pain gets to be too much. Make an appointment to see me in a week."

Nik walked out into the waiting room. Sanders was sitting there.

"I stuck around to give you a lift home," he said.

"I think I gotta talk to somebody about paying," Nik said.

"The company'll take care of that," Sanders said. "Pugmire knew better than to keep that old alky on. I think he was just cutting corners, using him 'cause he was cheap."

When they pulled up in front of his house, a guy in a suit and bow tie was getting into a Cadillac in the driveway.

"That was some scurrying you did there, kid, getting out of the way of all that lumber," Sanders said. "Hope your hands are okay."

The Cadillac backed out of the driveway, straightened, and drove away. Nik thanked Sanders and went into his house.

"Nik," his mother said, coming out of the back of the house, brushing her hair vigorously. "What are you doing here?"

Nik held up his hands to show the bandages.

"I had a little accident at work," he said. "What was that guy doing here?"

Cecelia Kane walked to the coffee table, picked up her purse, and rummaged in it. She removed a compact, opened it, and began applying lipstick.

"Are you hurt badly?" she asked in the tone of a woman asking the time.

"I'll be fine," Nik said. "Who was that man?"

Cecelia regarded herself in the compact's mirror. Apparently satisfied, she put the compact and lipstick away, and gave her hair several more strokes with the brush.

"I don't know what man you're talking about, Nik," she said. "And I don't like your tone."

"Big guy, curly black hair, mustache, fancy suit, bow tie," Nik said. "Driving a Caddy. Pulled out just as I got here. That guy. I've seen him before. Who is he?"

Cecelia dropped the brush into her purse and looked at Nik. He could see that she was struggling with her temper.

"You're not too big to punish," she said.

Nik grinned at that.

"Actually, I am," he said. "I've got six inches and sixty pounds on you. Who was that man?"

Cecelia seemed to be considering trying it anyway, but instead just waved a hand at Nik and slumped into an easy chair.

"Nobody important," she said. "A friend of your father's. He stops by from time to time to see how we're doing."

Nik nodded. The answer was about what he'd expected.

"He got a name, this friend of my father's?" he asked.

Cecelia flushed.

"Watch your tone," she said. "I'll not be given the third degree by one of my children."

"Answer the question, Mother," Nik said. "Please."

Cecelia peered at Nik as if seeing him for the first time.

"If you must know," Cecelia said, "his name is Pat McCanta."

"Uh-huh," Nik said. "I knew I'd seen him before. Pat McCanta, the gambler."

"Oh, he's much more than a gambler," Cecelia said. "He's an investor. He owns land and buildings. He's very well-to-do."

Her tone made Nik smile.

"Why, Mother," he said, "you sound impressed. Do you know this investor well?"

"Nik," Cecelia said, her voice sharp. "What are you implying?"

Nik's smile grew.

"Why, nothing, Mother," he said. "I just thought that if you knew him at all well, you might be able to tell me where to find him."

Cecelia got to her feet, walked to Nik, and grabbed him by the shoulders.

"You stay away from Pat McCanta," she said. "He can be a very dangerous man."

Nik raised his arms, put the outside of his wrists against the inside of Cecelia's, and pushed, forcing her hands off his shoulders.

"I'm no threat to this guy," he said. "I'm just a kid."

He turned and left the house, walking toward downtown. He wasn't sure what he was going to do, but what he wanted to do was talk to McCanta. Maybe he could find out more about his father, and he was certain he could find out more about his mother. If the gambler would talk to him. And, considering the accident he'd just survived, Nik figured this must be his lucky day.

Nik walked to the Silver Dollar. He found Tully Ames sitting behind the stick, reading the newspaper.

"Hey, kid," Ames said when he saw Nik. "You can't be n'here less you working. Cops'll close me down."

"Hi, Tully," Nik said. "I'm not staying. I just thought you might be able to tell me where to find Pat McCanta."

Ames's eyes narrowed.

"The gambler?" he said. "Why you want to find him? You don't owe him money, do you? Owing McCanta money c'n be dangerous to your health."

Nik shook his head.

"I don't gamble," he said. "It's personal. C'mon, Tully, what harm can it do to tell me where to find him?"

Ames seemed to think about that.

"He owns a motel over east," he said. "Got a little restaurant-bar. He's usually in it afternoons. Some evenings. Called the 'Red Rooster.' Don' tell him I tole you. Now, leave."

Nik did as he was told. Walking east, he thought about his mother and McCanta. Was there something going on there? Thinking about his mother and sex made him feel funny. Not that he thought she'd had all those kids without it, but sex between a husband and wife was different, wasn't it? More of an obligation than a pleasure? Something the law, even the church, said was okay?

He thought about himself and Carrie and laughed out loud. Whatever that was, it wasn't more of an obligation than a pleasure. No siree. What would the law and the church say about that?

The Red Rooster wasn't much to look at. It crouched at the corner of a couple of busy streets, a long, low-slung, U-shaped building with a paved parking lot in the center. The walls of the U were pierced with doors at short, regular intervals. The building was freshly painted and the parking lot had been carefully swept.

The main entrance was a pair of glass doors. Over it was a big neon sign that showed a rooster with its head on a giant pillow. A series of Z's rose from the rooster's mouth, each Z lighting up in turn. A smaller neon sign in a window near the main door said "Rooster's Nest."

Nik walked through the glass doors, turned left, and went through a single glass door into the restaurant. It was small, a counter and a half dozen tables, an appendage to a larger bar. A waitress stood at the restaurant counter, looking bored.

"Pat McCanta?" Nik asked.

The waitress jerked her head toward the bar. In addition to the bar itself and a collection of small, round cocktail tables, the room held a row of booths with high backs. Pat McCanta sat in one of them, bent forward, talking to a thin, slick-looking guy with a pencil mustache.

Nik walked over to the booth.

"Mr. McCanta?" he said.

"Beat it, kid," McCanta said. "I'm busy."

"What I want won't take long," Nik said.

The sleek man looked at Nik. He had no expression on his face. He made a stiletto appear from nowhere, clicked it open, and began to clean his nails.

"This kid bothering you, Pat?" he asked. "You want I should make him leave?"

McCanta shook his head.

"Don't bother, Rudy," he said. "Just go get yourself something to drink and give us a minute."

"You know I don't drink, Pat," the sleek man said. "Booze is bad for the reflexes."

McCanta sighed.

"There's soft drinks, too, Rudy," he said. "Go get yourself one. Now. Please."

It didn't sound like a request. The sleek man shrugged, closed the knife, and made it disappear. Taking his time, he slid out of the booth and stood very close to Nik, staring at him.

"Rudy," McCanta said, a note of warning in his voice. The sleek man smiled a smile with no mirth in it and walked to the bar.

"Sit, kid," McCanta said.

Nik sat in the booth opposite him.

"Tell me what you want," McCanta said, "and make it quick."

"My name is Nik Kane," Nik said. "I want to know what you know about my father's disappearance. His name is Teddy, Teddy Kane."

McCanta looked at him with no expression. His eyes were small and hard and cold, like the marbles Nik played with as a kid.

"I don't know what's wrong with me these days," McCanta said in a tone that made Nik think he was talking as much to himself as to Nik. "A cheap piece of goods like Rudy there thinks he can argue with me, and now some kid thinks he can ask me about my business and I'll tell him anything he wants to know. What is it, kid? Do I look like a softie to you, is that it? I'd really like you to answer that question, because in my business a guy who gets a reputation for being soft is a guy who is in deep trouble."

He tried to smile at Nik, but it came off as more of a snarl.

"You seem hard enough to me," Nik said, "but I'm not asking for much, and I don't mean to be impolite. I'm told that the day my father disappeared he was flashing a lot of money around, and that he was telling people he'd won it in one of your card games. So I was wondering what you could tell me about that."

McCanta was shaking his head by the time Nik finished.

"That's just it, kid," he said. "If I start telling people about my business because they're curious, pretty soon I'll be out of business."

"The gambling business, you mean?" Nik said. "Not an hour ago my mother was telling me that you're an investor, not a gambler."

McCanta shrugged.

"Women," he said. "What can you do?"

The two of them sat there looking at each other. The waitress from the restaurant walked through the bar and, when she was passing the booth, she stopped and said, "Hello, Pat."

"Hello, Flo," McCanta said. "Do something for you?"

"Nah," the waitress said. "Just on my way to the ladies'. I was just struck by how much the two of you look alike. Just sitting there, you could be father and son."

She gave them both a smile that wasn't particularly friendly and walked on.

"Flo there doesn't like me very much," McCanta said. "She had a boyfriend once who lost a lot of money to me and couldn't pay. He fell down a couple of times, got banged up something awful. He still didn't pay, and then, one day, he just disappeared. Probably ran away.

Anyway, Flo was saying the most awful things about me. Then she fell down, too. And when she healed up, I gave her this job."

He looked at Nik again.

"I guess I must be a softie," he said. "I gave a woman who said bad things about me a job. And you're still here."

The last sentence had the snap of a cracking whip behind it. Nik felt fear deep down, but above it was excitement, and, above that, determination.

"You could have told me what I want to know in about half the time you've taken to tell me a bunch of stuff I don't want to know," he said.

McCanta reached over and grabbed one of Nik's hands.

"Hurt yourself, kid?" he asked.

Nik tried to pull his hand from the man's grip but couldn't. He was too strong.

"Gotta be careful in this life, kid," McCanta said. "It's too easy to get hurt."

He put his thumb on the bandage and pressed. Nik could feel the stitches in his palm move. Pain shot along the cut. Nik's right foot snapped up under the table and the toe of his work boot hit the outside of McCanta's knee with a satisfying *thunk*.

"Shit!" the gambler yelled, and let go of Nik's hand.

Rudy was off his bar stool and flowing toward the booth, the knife back in his hand. McCanta's voice stopped him in his tracks, and a pointing finger sent him back to his stool, where he sat, looking like a guard dog deprived of its prey.

McCanta rubbed his knee and looked at Nik. The flatness in his gaze had been replaced with appraisal.

"Well," he said at last, "you're no sissy. That's worth something."

Nik sat in silence. The next move was the gambler's. He could feel blood running down his palm but ignored it. The moments stretched out, until McCanta said, "Okay, kid. I'll tell you what I know about your old man. He used to kibitz at some of my games, but he never played himself, until one night a coupla three years ago he sits in on a game at... Well, never mind where. He'd had some drinks."

The gambler reached down to rub his knee again.

"Steel toes in those boots?" he asked.

Nik nodded.

"I should have thought of that. Anyway, it's a funny thing about drunks. They can be great card players or lousy ones, and there's no telling which. You don't know if they've got the cards, if they're bluffing, or if they're too far gone to know the difference. Ask any real gambler, and what he'll tell you is that what he hates the most is playing against somebody who's been drinking.

"Your old man was all of that and more that night. He played damn near every hand and he couldn't lose. I tried to ease him out of there, but he made some crack about me not wanting to pay off, so I got mad and let him play. He played for four hours, never left the table once, and won more than ten thousand dollars."

McCanta shook his head, and when he looked at Nik again he was smiling.

"Never seen anything like it, before or since," he said. "Lady Luck was sitting on his shoulder that night. And the only reason he quit was nobody would play against him anymore. He cashed out his winnings, and that's the last I saw of him."

Nik sat there thinking. If McCanta was lying, he was too good for Nik. There was no way to tell what, if anything, he'd said was true.

"So, you weren't a particular friend of my father's?" he asked, striving to keep his voice even.

"No," McCanta said. "I saw him around town, but that's about it. Why?"

"No reason," Nik said. "How about my mother?"

Nik could see the gambler's face shut down.

"My relationship with your mother is none of your business, kid," he said. "Now, I think your time is up."

Nik slid out of the booth and onto his feet. As he turned to go, McCanta said, "Normally, a guy hits me wakes up wishing he hadn't. But I'm giving you a free pass on this; I guess because you remind me a little bit of me at your age. But it's only one free pass, and you've used it up. Don't come back, kid."

Nik couldn't think of anything to say to that, so he turned and walked to the door. Rudy was standing there.

"He means it, kid," Rudy said, making the knife appear in his hand. "Don't come back or you'll be dealing with me. And I ain't the friendly type."

Nik walked out of the Red Rooster and along the street. He sensed that something important had happened, but he couldn't put his finger on just what.

Maybe I became an adult in there, he thought. Maybe that's it.

He walked along, deep in thought, and his feet carried him to Carrie's apartment. He didn't know if she'd be home, but she answered his knock and, when she saw him, a big smile lit up her face.

"Nik," she said, grabbing him by the front of the shirt and pulling him into the apartment, "how nice. I was just thinking of you, and some things we could do together."

Her smile was wicked. Nik answered it with one of his own.

"I'm not sure how this will affect your plans," he said, holding up his hands to show her the bandages.

"Oh, don't worry," she said, reaching for the top button of his shirt. "I'm sure we'll figure something out."

# twenty-one

O, call back yesterday, bid time return.

—WILLIAM SHAKESPEARE

## APRIL 2007

Cee Cee stood in the doorway to Kane's room, an iffy smile on her lips. Her knock had awakened him. She was dressed, as she almost always was around the house, in what Kane thought of as civilian clothes.

Except for the small cross that hung from a chain around her neck and the prayer book she clutched in her left hand, Kane thought, she might just be any aging spinster.

"Are you awake, Nik?" she asked.

Kane nodded.

"Sort of," he said, his voice still thick with sleep and the residue of painkillers.

"Emily and Amy are here," Cee Cee said.

Time seemed to stand still for Kane.

It's funny, he thought. I've been dreading a lot of things, but I never thought I'd be afraid to see my own daughters.

"Nik?" Cee Cee said. "Did you hear me? Emily and Amy are here."

"I heard you, Ceese," Kane said. "What time is it?"

"It's early—early for you, anyway," she said. "A little after eight in the morning. Are you getting up?"

Kane was still half trapped in his dream or memory, or whatever it was.

"Do you think, Cee Cee," he said, "that maybe we, all of us kids, don't have the same father?"

The surprise that flitted across his sister's face was quickly replaced by the smooth deadpan that Cee Cee sometimes called her "nun face." She was silent for so long that he thought she wasn't going to answer.

"I think our mother is dead these ten years now," she said, "and only she knew for sure. But I also think it's not very important. What's important is that we, the children, were a family when we needed one, and still are when one of us needs it."

She paused as if thinking, then said, "Concentrate now, Nikky. Your own family is here. You should see them."

Kane threw the blankets back, gently swiveled his legs over the side of the bed, sat up, and walked into the bathroom.

"Give me a few minutes to make myself presentable, will you?" he said.

His sister nodded and faded back through the doorway, closing the door softly behind her.

Kane washed his face and combed his hair. He looked at his image in the mirror. The lines around his eyes were etched more deeply, and there was more gray in his hair. His beard had filled in nicely, though, covering a lot of his face from the nose down. It needed trimming, but he didn't have the time, and didn't trust his fine-motor skills enough even if he had. He walked slowly back into the big room, put on the bathrobe that the nuns had provided, and sat in one of the armchairs near the window.

What am I going to say to these girls? he thought.

He had seen Emily a couple of times in the year and a half since he'd gotten out of prison. He'd watched as her initial enthusiasm was worn away by the awkwardness of those encounters. He could see the effort it took for her to master her true feelings, the shame and anger she must have felt the public humiliation of his trial and imprisonment and the family's struggles while he was inside. She'd managed to mask all that with the placid, kind face that she presented to the world. He'd met her children, small, alien creatures to whom he felt no connection, and her husband, a proper, wary fellow a dozen years older than Emily, who looked at Kane the way he might at a particularly forward panhandler.

Of Amy, he'd not seen a trace.

The girls came into the room, Emily a bit timidly, Amy with the assertiveness Kane always associated with her. Emily was taller and slimmer, but they were clearly sisters, and as Kane watched them cross the room he could see a mixture of their mother and himself in them, in their coloring, in the way they moved, in the concern on Emily's face and the anger on Amy's.

They were dressed as anyone who knew them might expect. Emily wore a long skirt and matching blouse, polished black leather shoes with a moderate heel, earrings and a necklace. Her hair was carefully arranged, her makeup carefully applied. She carried a large, black leather purse, and a big diamond sparkled on her left hand.

Amy wore a sweatshirt with a hood, jeans, and hiking boots. Her hair was cut short and looked like she'd just stepped in out of a high wind. She wore no jewelry, and if she wore any makeup Kane couldn't see it.

Matron and tough chick, Kane thought. My daughters.

"You look thin, Dad," Emily said when the girls reached him. She leaned down and brushed his forehead with her lips. "Are you feeling okay?"

"I hope not," Amy blurted before Kane could reply. Her older sister looked at her. Kane watched his younger daughter set her jaw and heard defiance in her voice when she went on, "Well, why should he feel okay? After what happened?"

"We talked about this, Amy," her sister said, her voice low but firm. "If you can't control yourself, you can wait in the car."

The girls lived very different lives now, and thousands of miles apart, but it didn't take them long to assume the roles they'd had when they were growing up: Emily, patient and controlling; Amy, snappish and defiant. Kane wondered if they liked those roles or just couldn't help themselves.

So much of what we do, who we are, is programmed into us so early that we don't even know it's happening, Kane thought. Even if, later in life, you realize that programming is there, it's damn hard to change it. Look at me. Nearly sixty and still grappling with my childhood. What was it the old Native guy had said to him in prison one time? "Too soon old, too late smart." He got that right.

"Don't worry about it, Emily," Kane said. "There's nothing your sister can say that can make me feel any worse about what happened than I already do."

When neither young woman said anything, he went on, "Are you going to sit down?"

The girls looked around then. Emily sat in the armchair, and Amy walked to the bed, picked up the chair that sat there, and carried it to the table. When she was settled, Emily began.

"How are you feeling, Dad?" Emily asked.

"Physically?" Kane said. "I'll survive. Emotionally? It's a struggle."

He saw the surprise on the faces of his daughters. They expected to find the father they'd grown up with, closed up and stoic, a man who didn't even admit he had emotions, let alone talk about them. Their expressions said they were afraid of hearing him talk like that, so he navigated away from it.

"And how about you?" he asked. "How are you coping?"

"How do you think?" his younger daughter said. "Our brother is dead."

*"Amy,"* her sister said, a warning tone in her voice.

Kane waved a hand.

"I said it's okay, Emily," he said. He looked at his younger daughter, who dropped her eyes.

"Look at me," he said.

Amy didn't move.

"I said, look at me," Kane said. "What's the matter? Are you afraid?"

She lifted her head and shot Kane a look full of venom.

So easy to push those old buttons, he thought.

"I know you're upset," he said. "It is your brother who was killed. But it's my son, too."

"I know," Amy said, her voice hard. "Maybe you should have done a better job protecting him."

"That's enough, Amy," Emily said. "It's not like you were in the running for Sister of the Year, is it?"

Amy opened her mouth to reply, but something in her sister's look made her close it again without saying anything.

"Dad," Emily said, her voice edgy. "We're here for several reasons. One of them is not to place blame, no matter how childishly Amy chooses to behave."

The sisters exchanged another glance. Emily was usually the placid one, but everybody in the family knew that when she finally lost her temper you'd better watch out. Nobody knew that better than her younger sister.

"Okay," Kane said. "The floor is yours."

Emily nodded and paused, as if arranging her thoughts.

"First, we want to make sure that you're okay," she said. "We've been in touch with Sister Angelica, but we wanted to see for ourselves."

Kane wasn't surprised to hear his daughter use her aunt's nun name. Emily had embraced the conventional life much more fully than anyone else in the family. Kane thought she found refuge from her childhood in the rituals such a life demanded. She was a wife, a mother, and a faithful, devout, conservative member of the church. In short, she acted like she was thirty years older than she actually was, and seemed to get something from doing that.

"Second, we wanted to say that we don't blame you for what happened." The sisters exchanged another look. "At least, I don't. I talked with the Juneau Police, with a policeman named Harry Crawford, and with a very nice woman named Mrs. Richard Foster, who explained what happened. We all know how impetuous Dylan is—was—and apparently the person who did this is insane, or close to it."

Emily paused, as if expecting Kane to say something. He looked at Amy.

"And what do you think?" he asked.

His younger daughter opened her mouth, closed it, and sat, trying visibly to get herself under control. Finally, she said, "What Emily says is right. Dylan shouldn't have done what he did. The killer is crazy. But, still..." Her voice trailed off into silence.

"But, still, what?" Kane asked.

"But, still, he was your son," she said. "And it was your job to protect him."

Amy had always seen things in black and white. She was her father's daughter in that. Kane thought of his conversation with Cee Cee, about her argument that the world was more complicated than he gave it credit for. Well, Amy had his attitude, in spades. And considering where she'd gotten it, he couldn't really complain.

"Fair enough," he said. He looked at Emily. "What does your mother think about this?"

The sisters looked at each other, and, surprisingly, it was Amy who answered.

"We're not here to talk about that," she said.

Kane nodded.

"That bad, huh?" he said. "Okay. When I'm feeling up to it, I'll try to talk to her directly. What else?"

"Third," Emily said, as if she were reciting something learned by heart, "we wanted to say we're sorry that you couldn't be there for the funeral. We were told you would be a long time recuperating from your wounds, and Mother needed—we all needed—the chance to grieve, to find some sort of closure."

Closure. Kane heard that word a lot lately but didn't know what it really meant. He knew what it had meant in his life. Caught the bad guy, case closed. But now? I had a son, now he's dead, case closed? That seemed a little...abrupt to him. He hadn't really sorted out his feelings about Dylan's death—had been avoiding it, actually—but, when he did, he expected to find something more complicated than his son was dead and life goes on.

"And did you?" he asked. "Find closure?"

The girls looked at him as if he'd asked them to solve some sort of riddle. Nothing more confusing than having someone challenge a cliché, he thought.

"Never mind," he said. "I suppose that's a worthy goal, closure. And I suppose that wasn't the only reason to hold the service before I could attend."

Neither of the girls said anything, but Kane could read the answer in their faces. Laurie hadn't wanted to see Kane. Still didn't or she'd be here.

"What else?" he asked, hearing in his voice a sudden anger he was having trouble keeping under control.

The girls could hear it, too. Amy laid a hand on her older sister's arm.

A gesture of support, Kane thought. You're not wrestling this bear alone, or something like that. Can't help but approve of that.

"Finally," Emily said, "we'd like you to sign the divorce papers. I have them here." She reached into her purse, extracted a fat envelope, and laid it on the table. Then the girls sat there, waiting for Kane's reaction.

I should do something dramatic, Kane thought. But I don't have the energy. "The divorce is between your mother and me," he said, trying to keep his voice calm and even. "I don't think you two want to get involved in it."

"See?" Amy said. "I told you he'd say that."

"Amy," her sister said, exasperation in her voice, "does everything have to be about you?"

"Listen, Emily—" Amy began, but Kane talked over her.

"That's enough," he said. "If you two want to continue your life-long debate, you can do it without me. Tell me, Emily, why should I sign these papers now?"

With a glare at her sister, his older daughter gathered herself and said, "Mom is really hurting, Dad. I don't think it's any secret that she was very fond of Dylan."

"He was her favorite, you mean," Amy said.

Ignoring her sister, Emily continued, "He was such a sweet person, and so devoted to her. You were . . . away . . . for a lot of the time he was growing up, so you didn't see that much of the two of them together. But we did. She really misses him. And I'm afraid—we're afraid—that having to see you again, having to struggle over the terms of the divorce, will just remind her of what happened."

When she stopped, her sister spoke again.

" 'Away,' " she said. "That's a nice way to put being in prison."

The sisters were silent, and Kane thought for a while before he said, "Amy, I know I was in prison and I know you're angry about it. Maybe there's something we can do about that and maybe there's not. We may never be close because of it. But you have to find some way to deal with your anger, not for me but for yourself."

His younger daughter glared at him.

"What do you know about it?" she said. "You weren't the one who was left."

"In fact, I was," Kane said gently. "But that's another story."

He shifted his gaze to his older daughter.

"I don't know what's going on with you, Emily," he said. "You've always been good at hiding your real feelings. That may not be good for you, either, but you're an adult, so that's up to you now. Anyway, I appreciate the fact that you and your sister are concerned about your mother. But you weren't there when we started this marriage, and you're not going to be there when we end it. Now, is there anything else?"

The sisters looked at each other and got to their feet. Neither made an attempt to approach their father.

"We'll just leave the papers," Emily said, "in case you change your mind."

"You don't give up, do you?" Kane said with a smile. "Thanks for visiting."

The sisters got to the door before Amy exploded.

"I just wish it had been you that got killed instead of Dylan," she screamed, and stormed through the door. Her sister followed.

"So do I," Kane said softly. "So do I."

Kane wasn't sure what to do next. What he wanted to do was crawl into bed, pull the covers over his head, and stay there forever. But despite all that had happened, he just couldn't let himself give up. Instead, he opened the Shirtleff file and began reading the next in the series of reports on police officers and FBI agents he and the other investigators had compiled. But when he found that he'd read whole paragraphs without really knowing what was in them, he set the report down and stared out the window.

That's how his sister found him a half hour later. She walked through the door without knocking and sat in the other armchair.

"That can't have been very pleasant," she said.

"It wasn't," Kane said. "But you reap what you sow, I guess."

Cee Cee reached over and put a hand over his.

"Your daughters are upset," she said. "I'm sure that once they have put this tragedy behind them, their feelings toward you will be different."

Cee Cee's hand felt warm on his. He could remember her comforting him just this way when he was a child.

"I'm not sure what their feelings will be," he said. "I'd like to be closer to them, but that's not really within my control, is it? I suppose it was at one time, but I did what I did, and there's no way to go back and undo it."

He stopped talking and looked out the window for a while.

"You know, Ceese," he said, "I never meant for any of this to happen. Sure, there are ways I can explain it to myself, absolve myself from blame. Looked at one way, I could say I never had a chance. Being poor. Dad disappearing. Vietnam. Being an alcoholic. None of those things are my fault, really.

"But looked at another way, I should have been more prudent in living my life. Instead, I was heedless. I didn't mean for anything bad to happen, but I was willful. I just kept going straight ahead, and, if that meant walking into walls, that was what I did. As I sit here now, I can't tell you what I was thinking. I knew that when I did that, the wall was going to win. But, somehow, it was important to me, to my image of myself, to walk into them anyway."

He quit talking.

"Nikky..." his sister began.

"Looked at still another way," Kane went on as if his sister hadn't spoken, "maybe this was never in my control. Maybe nature or life or God or chance or whoever or whatever is actually in control just picks certain people out and says, I'm going to fuck with you just because I can."

"Nikky..." his sister began again.

"What I really need is a chance to start over," he said, "to start from scratch. I'd be much smarter this time, more thoughtful. I really would."

This time, his sister just waited. Kane shook his head and sighed.

"I'm sorry for whining, Cee Cee," he said. "I'm just feeling sorry for myself at the moment. I'll get over it."

He straightened himself in his chair, wincing as he did so.

"I take it you talked with the girls," he said. "Anything you want to tell me?"

His sister removed her hand and settled back in her chair.

"Probably nothing you don't already know," she said. "They're upset over what happened to their brother. And about what's going on between you and Laurie. Emily seemed to be particularly bothered by the fact you wouldn't sign the divorce papers."

"Why's that?" Kane asked.

"She just thinks that the less the two of you see of each other, the better," Cee Cee said. "I asked Emily if that meant her mother really blames you for Dylan's death. She said yes, but that there seemed to be more to it than that. 'It's like she coped for so long,' Emily said, 'and now she's decided to blame Dad for everything.'"

Kane nodded. He'd seen it before. A husband did something stupid and got himself arrested, and suddenly the wife was bringing up things that had happened years before.

"It's a way for her to distance herself from me," Kane said, "to feel justified in hating me and divorcing me." He paused. "Not that she doesn't have justification enough. Did Amy have anything to add?"

Cee Cee shook her head.

"No," she said. "She started the conversation by unloading on you, and I told her that I wouldn't listen to that. So she barely said another word."

"That's my girl," Kane said. "Was there anything else?"

"Not really," Cee Cee said, then paused. "Well, there was one more thing. When she was talking about how angry Laurie is at you, Emily told a story. She said that some woman called for Laurie a couple of days ago, and when Laurie got off the phone she started raving about some old case she thinks you're working on. Emily said her mother said that was just like you, trying to hide in your work instead of facing your problems. She said Laurie has been in a blue funk ever since."

Cee Cee smiled.

"I have to say, that's the first time in a long time I've heard somebody say blue funk," she said.

"Hiding in my work, eh?" Kane said. "Well, I suppose that's just what I'm doing. Although it's a puzzle why that should irritate a woman who doesn't want to have anything to do with me ever again."

Cee Cee got to her feet.

"I have chores to attend to," she said, and left the room.

Kane sat looking out the window, but not seeing anything. He thought about the disappearance of his father, his failure to find Danny Shirtleff's killer, all the mistakes he'd made, including the last, biggest, one.

I'm going to have to find a way to cope with this, he thought. Or escape it.

He picked up the Shirtleff folder and set it down again. He got slowly to his feet and paced off the room, walking from one wall to the other, turning and walking back. He should have stopped to take some painkillers, but the pain was reassuring somehow, proof that he was alive. He decided to wean himself off the pills, taking them only when he needed them to sleep.

"The damage'll do you good," he sang softly to himself.

He was interrupted by a knock at his door. It was the little nun who seemed to be one of his main nurses.

"Sister Angelica says you need to walk," she said.

"I am walking," Kane said.

The nun just looked at him. After she'd done that for a while, he went into the bathroom and changed his clothes. The two of them walked through the melting snow on the ground for what seemed like a year to Kane.

"Fifteen minutes," the nun said when they were back in his room. "You're improving. Would you like some pain medication?"

Kane shook his head.

"No thank you, Sister," he said. "I'm trying to control an addictive personality, and those pills, whatever they are, are just too good."

"Oxycodone," the nun said. "Very popular. Someone will be in this afternoon to take you out again."

Kane spent the rest of the morning trying not to think about his daughters and how little they seemed to like him. He tried thinking about the Shirtleff case, picking up the paperwork and laying it down again without accomplishing anything. At lunchtime, he pushed his food around his plate, then returned to the armchair and looked out the window. The sun shone. Birds flew. Squirrels scampered around. Time passed. A different nun came, and they walked. Later, still another nun brought his dinner. He gave up on the reports and tried a book one of the nuns had left about an African woman who ran a detective agency. Nothing very serious seemed to happen there, and most everyone was cheerful and polite.

Couldn't be less like real life, Kane thought. At least, my real life. Maybe I should move to Africa.

After a while, Cee Cee returned.

"How are you doing, Nikky?" she asked.

"One day at a time," Kane said.

"You want your pain medication?" she asked.

Kane nodded. She gave him a pair of pills and some water to swallow them with.

"I'm sorry your life is so difficult at the moment, Nikky," Cee

Cee said as he was taking the pills. "I'll pray that things get better for you."

Nik shrugged, and pain shot along his side. He sucked in a breath and expelled it slowly, then walked to the bed and lay down.

"I don't think I'll find the solution to my problems in God," he said. "I don't think I even believe in God anymore."

But the world was going away so fast, he wasn't sure he said it aloud.

twenty-two

Do not trust your memory; it is a net full of holes;
the most beautiful prizes slip through it.

—ROBERTSON DAVIES

## SEPTEMBER 1986

"Happy anniversary," Jackie Dee said as Kane slid into the booth at Leroy's.

"Anniversary?" Kane said.

"One year," Jackie Dee said. "Just a few days ago, it was one year since you became a detective. Today, it's one year since somebody murdered Danny Shirtleff."

He slid a small envelope across the distressed Formica.

"You shouldn't have," Kane said.

"I didn't," Jackie Dee said. "The brass did."

Kane opened the envelope and shook out a single sheet of paper. In best bureaucratese, it transferred Detective Sergeant Giuseppe DiSanto to patrol, where he was to be the swing shift supervisor.

"Aw, Christ, Jackie Dee," Kane said. "This bites the big one."

Jackie Dee nodded.

"It does, indeed," he said. "But it's not unexpected. A guy with an attitude like mine has to make cases. If he doesn't, he's got no protection from the politicians in uniform."

The waitress came over. Jackie Dee ordered breakfast: one English muffin, toasted; one black coffee.

"What the hell is that, Jackie Dee?" Kane said, his voice breaking like a schoolboy's.

When Jackie Dee was done laughing, he said, "Yeah. That's the other surprise in Jackie Dee Land this week. My doctor says I've got to cut back on all the garbage I've been eating and get regular exercise. No more booze, either. Apparently, the Jackie Dee machine isn't running as well as I thought it was. I set some sort of record for blood pressure during my last checkup."

The waitress looked Jackie Dee up and down.

"So you're going to be one of those skinny runts who lives forever?" she said. "I'll believe that when I see it." Turning to look at Kane, she asked, "You eating?"

"Just coffee," Kane said.

"Jeez," the waitress said, "what's the police force coming to?"

When she was gone, Kane said, "So what's going to happen?"

"With the diet?" Jackie Dee said. "If it was just me, I'd tell the doctor to go whistle. But Jackie DeeTwo is on my ass about it, so I'm going to have do something. She'll be able to tell if I'm sticking to the diet or not. She sees me naked, you know."

"There's a thought makes me glad I'm not eating," Kane said. "But I wasn't talking about the diet, although I bet the Reese's Peanut Butter Cup people are looking at layoffs."

Jackie Dee gave Kane a grin for that.

"I know you're not, kid," he said. "But what can we do? We've been at a dead end on the Shirtleff case for some time, and we've got nowhere to go, really. The brass has actually been okay about letting us play this out, but there's nothing left to play."

Kane nodded. Jackie Dee was right.

After the interviews with everyone who'd known—or could have known—about the buy money, Jackie Dee had sent Harry, Larry, and Don Young off to talk to every ticket agent, rental-car employee, and janitor at the airport. Then he, Kane, and Kim Lewis spent three days going through Danny's apartment very carefully. They knocked on walls and took apart the shower curtain rod, crawled around in the attic and stuck a hand in every nook, cranny, and crevice in the place, all without finding anything. They looked at every print of every picture in every file, handing them one to the next to the next. They saw some fine photographs but nothing that looked like it had anything to do with Danny's death. Nothing personal at all, as they commented to one another. No snapshots of family. No pictures of Danny himself. Nothing.

"That's a little odd, don't you think?" Kim Lewis asked the first time they noticed it.

Kane and Jackie Dee looked at each other.

"Never been a bachelor, have you?" Jackie Dee said.

"Nope," Lewis said with a grin. "Couldn't pass the physical. So?"

"So, Shirtleff was a bachelor, in his twenties," Jackie Dee said. "He's barely got enough plates and utensils and whatnot to have a bowl of cereal for breakfast. Guy like that isn't going to have a big stash of memorabilia anywhere."

"Men," Lewis said, and went back to looking at photographs.

When they finished the prints, they started on the negatives but soon gave up.

"I just can't make anything out," Jackie Dee said. "They all just look like blobs of gray and black to me."

"We're going to let that photographer have these when we're done, right?" Lewis said. "He's going to look at them and, unlike us, he'll know what he's seeing. So why don't we just ask him to tell us if he finds anything unusual?"

That made sense to Kane, who was getting a headache from trying to interpret the negatives. They put all the photo files back the way they found them. When they looked around the apartment, they realized that they had nothing else to do there.

"Ends don't come any deader than this," Lewis said, and the two men had to agree.

It was late in the day, so they drove to a bar called the Irish Setter. Jackie Dee bought a round, and they sat at a little, round table, staring morosely into their glasses without drinking. Kane offered cigarettes around and, ignoring Lewis's look, lit one for himself. He drew smoke deep into his lungs and let it seep back out through his nose.

"We're nowhere," he said. "Absolutely nowhere."

He took a pull on his drink, which sent a pleasant warmth through his body. Maybe I'll just sit here, he thought, and drink until I can't think anymore.

"Okay," Jackie Dee said, straightening in his chair. "Let's review. We agree that we haven't come up with any motive for Shirtleff's killing except the money, right?"

Heads nodded.

"And any one of the cops or Fibbies we talked to could have taken the money, right?"

Heads nodded again.

"But we don't think any of them would have killed a cop for a lousy twenty grand, right?"

Again, nods.

"So for one of them to have done it, he'd either have to have a real need for the money or he'd have to have had some other reason to kill Shirtleff and just taken the money as a bonus, right?"

This time, the nods were more tentative. Kane and Lewis could see where Jackie Dee was headed and they didn't like it.

"So we need to know more about the cops and Fibbies. Who needed money or who might have had a hard-on for Shirtleff, right?"

No nods now.

*"Right?"*

Reluctantly, Kane and Lewis nodded.

"This'll make us nothing but shooflies," Lewis said. "If the brass will let us do it."

Kane didn't say anything. He disagreed with where Jackie Dee wanted to take the investigation but couldn't exactly explain why. And, given the difference in their experience, he didn't see any sense in challenging the big man.

Besides, he thought, maybe he just wants to keep prying into the drug unit to get something on Jeffords.

Then, to his surprise, Lewis said what he'd been thinking.

"Maybe we're looking in the wrong place," she said. "Maybe we should be looking closer at Shirtleff."

Jackie Dee didn't take well to being questioned, but he seemed to be considering what Lewis said.

"Yeah, I thought of that," he said. "But what's there to look into? He worked. He took pictures. He went to cop parties and cookouts. Otherwise, socially, he seems to have been the King of the First Date. So just what do we investigate?"

"Well," Lewis said. "Maybe he had some sort of partner we don't know about and they stole the money together, and the partner killed him."

"Some dame, you mean?" Jackie Dee asked.

"It wouldn't have to be a woman," Lewis said. "Do you think, maybe, he might have been a homosexual?"

Jackie Dee looked like he'd been hit in the head with a two-by-four. Kane must have looked about the same, because all Lewis could do was look back and forth at them and laugh.

"Queer?" Jackie Dee said in a voice that made him sound like he was being strangled. "Danny Shirtleff queer? Christ, Lewis, you take some wild swings at the ball."

Kane looked at Lewis. He didn't really want any part of the conversation, but he could see she was right.

"There's no evidence that Danny was homosexual," he said, "but there's no evidence he wasn't, either. There's the stray pubic hair we found on him and the 'evidence of sexual intercourse,' whatever the hell that means, but there's nothing in any of that to show the sex he had was with a woman. In fact, we can't turn up a woman who'll admit to it. So what Lewis is saying isn't crazy. It might not be right, but it isn't crazy."

Kane couldn't remember having seen Jackie Dee uncomfortable before, but the big man was squirming like he was sitting on an anthill.

"I'm not buying it," he said. "Jeez, Shirtleff was a hell of an athlete. Ever see him play softball or pickup basketball?"

That made Lewis start laughing again, and, against both his will and his better judgment, Kane joined in.

"Goddamn it, it's not funny," Jackie Dee said. "I mean, I been naked with the guy, in the showers down at the station. And I never saw any evidence he was a fag."

That just set both of them to laughing harder.

"Jeez, Jackie Dee," Kane gasped, "you got... you got your own version of the peter meter going?"

Lewis was laughing so hard now, Kane was afraid she might break something.

"Maybe," she said, "you just"—gasp—"you just ain't"—gasp—"his type, Jackie Dee."

That made even Jackie Dee smile. The smile turned to a laugh, and the three of them went on for several minutes, hooting and honking and gasping for breath. Every time they calmed down, one of them would start again and the others couldn't keep from joining in. Finally, the waitress came over and said, "Stop. You're freaking out the customers."

"Remember that night in the Irish Setter?" Kane said as Jackie Dee slid his reassignment letter back into the envelope. "You and me and Lewis, laughing so hard I thought we'd cry? Because she thought Danny might be queer?"

Jackie Dee nodded.

"Yeah," he said. "There was a lot of tension in the investigation even then. Laughing it off was better than letting it make us cry, I guess."

Kane remembered something else about that night. After Jackie Dee had agreed that they should look more into Danny, too, Kane had finished his drink and, leaving Jackie Dee and Lewis at the bar, walked back to his car and driven home. He got home that night in time to give the girls their baths and put them to bed. He found Laurie sitting on the couch, staring at nothing.

"Can I get you anything, a drink, maybe?" Kane asked.

Laurie shook her head.

"The doctor says pregnant women shouldn't drink," she said. "It's not good for the baby. But get yourself one, if you want."

Kane shook his head. He rarely drank at home, and never alone.

"Tough day?" Laurie asked.

"They're all tough right now," Kane said. "We're working as hard as we can, but we're not getting anywhere."

"So you didn't find anything at Officer Shirtleff's house?" Laurie asked.

"Lots of photos, none of which is of the slightest use to us," Kane said, "and not much else. Danny Shirtleff was a young bachelor and he lived like one."

"And nothing else is helping?" she asked.

"Nope," he said. "It's been two weeks now and we don't know any more than we did that night."

Laurie didn't reply and the silence stretched out. Kane realized that this was the first time since he'd gotten the telephone call about

Danny that they'd spent any time together. He'd been busy, and it was almost like Laurie had been avoiding him.

"Are you mad at me because you're pregnant?" he asked.

The question seemed to take Laurie completely by surprise.

"No, of course not," she said. "I...it's just that this pregnancy seems different than the other two. Harder, somehow. And you've got this new job, and so much of my time is spent being a mother that sometimes I find myself talking to the girls like I'm their age."

They'd been silent again for a few moments when Laurie started talking again.

"Sometimes I think it would be better if something happened to this baby," she said. "That it was never born."

"Laurie..." Kane began, but she simply kept talking.

"We don't seem to be doing that well together, Nik," she said. "Even though you seem to have gotten your drinking under some kind of control, you're spending too much time at work. And me...I...about half the time I feel overwhelmed and the other half I'm restless. I was really looking forward to being able to go back to work, at least part-time, soon. We could use the money, and, frankly, I could use the freedom. But now this, and I don't know what will happen to us once this baby is born."

She started crying. Kane moved over to the couch and put his arm around her. He didn't understand half of what she'd said, but her condition worried him. She soon stopped crying, but he stayed where he was and held her, trying to think of something to take her mind off whatever was bothering her.

"Lewis thinks maybe Danny Shirtleff was a homosexual," he said. He felt Laurie stiffen when he said that.

"What?" she said. "Lewis thinks what?"

"That maybe Danny was queer," Kane said.

"Why?" Laurie asked. "Because he wasn't married and he had good manners? You cops."

"Hey, wait," Kane said. "There might be something to it."

He told her about the conversation they'd had. Somehow, their conversation didn't sound as intelligent or their laughter as funny.

"Look, just because Danny didn't jump into the sack with every woman he met doesn't mean he was a homosexual," Laurie said. "But even if he was, so what? That didn't give somebody the right to kill him. And"—here her voice rose—"why are we talking about your goddamn case when I'm trying to talk about us?"

She shook off his arm, rose awkwardly to her feet, and left the room. She might have been crying again.

Well, that worked well, Kane thought. I think I'll quit talking to Laurie about this investigation and hope that her mood improves.

The lab report on Danny's sheets came back a week later, saying that among the fluids the lab found there were vaginal secretions. Jackie Dee rode both Kane and Lewis pretty hard about that for a couple of days, and nobody involved in the investigation said the word "homosexual" again.

At about the same time, the brass reassigned Harry, Larry, and Don Young. Not much of a loss, really, since among the three of them they hadn't turned up a single useful fact.

"It's like getting rid of the Three Stooges," Jackie Dee said, "although none of them has Curly's skill with a seltzer bottle."

The reassignments did spread the smell of a failing investigation around the department and, eventually, Alaska law enforcement circles. As Kane, Lewis, and Jackie Dee combed through the private lives of five FBI agents and ten Anchorage cops, they heard more and more cracks about "Judases" and "fuckups." They learned a lot about their targets but nothing that made any one of them stand out as a suspect. When they finished with one of the men, they closed a folder and checked off a name.

They had just three folders left when Kane got the phone call and rushed home to take Laurie to the hospital. Dylan was born the next day, a month ahead of schedule, Kane standing there uselessly in the delivery room, wishing that they were still in the era when a father paced the waiting room, smoking cigarettes.

"Doesn't he look like his father?" Laurie said when they handed her the newborn, fresh from tests and cleanup.

Kane couldn't say, really. With his scrunched-up features and unruly black mop, the baby looked most like a hairy raisin, although it would have been impolitic to say so. As he had with the births of his daughters, Kane was paying the most attention to the fact that he wished he felt more on these occasions.

He got Laurie and the baby home a few days later and went back to work. Day followed day, and, nearly four months to the day after Danny Shirtleff was killed, they had fifteen closed folders and no more names.

About the only good thing that happened to the team during that time was busting Corporal Leo Lassiter. Murphy finished his inventory of the equipment, sold it, and set up a meet to pay Lassiter off. Jackie Dee used Murphy's statement to get a warrant, wired the meet, and busted in as Lassiter was counting the money.

"Gotcha, ya crooked prick," Jackie Dee crowed as he put handcuffs on the corporal.

Turned out, Jackie Dee got more than one crooked cop. Lassiter had been running the same game with a half dozen other people on various kinds of estate property and, according to his meticulously kept records, was splitting the take with Jerry Barnes, the admin lieutenant. When the smoke cleared, both Lassiter and Barnes were civilians without pensions, and the quickly promoted Lieutenant Thomas Jeffords was in charge of police department administration.

Jackie Dee was jubilant.

"It's the curse of admin," he said while sucking down a cold one at the Irish Setter, which had somehow become their bar. "That uppity cocksucker'll never be chief now."

The Shirtleff investigation continued its long, slow slide into complete failure. Once the team had finished "giving cops rectal exams," as Jackie Dee put it, the brass tried to reassign Lewis. But Jackie Dee dug in, claiming he still needed her. Somehow, he'd managed to get the money together to send two investigators to Kodiak.

"He must be cashing in every chit he's got," Lewis said when she and Kane found out about the coup.

Jackie Dee wanted Kane to go along, but he was still walking on eggshells around Laurie. She cried at the drop of a hat, and didn't seem interested in caring for her daughters at all. Kane thought about asking his mother for help but quickly rejected that idea. Instead, he found a woman to come in and keep house and care for the girls temporarily. That took care of the physical part of the problem, but whatever was going on with Laurie left a big emotional hole in the house that only he could try to fill. So when Jackie Dee told him about Kodiak, he begged off.

Jackie Dee and Lewis made the trip, and, when they returned at the end of ten days they weren't speaking to each other. Kane asked each of them separately what had happened and got nothing but a pair of mind-your-own-fucking-business looks in return. A week later, Lewis was back in uniform and behind the wheel of a patrol cruiser. A week after that, Kane learned she'd asked for reassignment but decided it was better not to ask her why.

Maybe it didn't have anything to do with Jackie Dee and Kodiak. Maybe it was just frustration. Even Kane couldn't deny they were headed for failure now. He started spending more and more time on the other cases they were assigned.

Not that he didn't do his part. He did that and more. When he drew the short straw and had to pick up a prisoner for transport in Seattle, he took leave time at the front end of the trip, even though Laurie still seemed to be fighting the blues. She was coming around, but about all that made her smile was holding the baby, which made it tough on the girls. But Kane had to go, so he used the leave time to talk to Danny's parents, his superiors in the Seattle PD, and a couple of guys Danny'd worked with there.

His parents were nice, kind people, still in shock over the death of their son. They'd already started to draw the golden veil that early death conferred over their son's life, and couldn't think of anyone who disliked Danny or, really, any reason anyone would.

The brass, while making a big show of being helpful to a brother department, were equally unhelpful. The only higher-up who remembered Danny said he was a likeable fellow and a good-enough cop. The personnel file he let Kane read, but not copy, said pretty much the same thing.

Over drinks with one of Danny's fellow officers, Kane learned that Danny had very nearly gotten himself caught in a pregnancy trap with a young woman who had been making the rounds of single cops. But he'd stood his ground, arranged and paid for a trip across the border to a Canadian abortion doctor, and, by all accounts, stopped dating. The experience seemed to explain his wariness with women.

Danny had lasted another eight months before quitting and heading north. Nobody knew, or would say, why he'd left. The guy Kane drank with thought Danny had had some sort of beef with a sergeant, but when Kane tried to ask the sergeant about it he'd been told to go fuck his hat.

With the lack of progress in the investigation and his problems at home, Kane decided to put the Shirtleff investigation on the back burner. Without saying a word about it, Jackie Dee did, too. They handled their other cases with alacrity, but the failure of the Shirtleff investigation clung to them like a bad smell.

Still, it was a surprise to hear Jackie Dee attribute his transfer to their failure to find Danny's killer, or the twenty thousand dollars. He would have expected his partner to blame Tom Jeffords, who, against all odds, seemed to be thriving in administration. Tolliver, who was chief by then, had gotten a very public pat on the head from the mayor for actually asking for a smaller budget, and everyone in the department knew that was only possible because of the efficiencies Jeffords was wringing from operations.

"So, why don't you think this transfer is the revenge of Tom Jeffords?" Kane asked after his coffee arrived.

"Oh, I do think it's Jeffords's revenge," Jackie Dee said. "But he wouldn't be able to take it if we hadn't botched the investigation."

He held up his hand before Kane could say anything.

"I know, I know," he said, "we did everything we could. And we did it by the book. But a failure's a failure, and when you're a—what was it you called me once, 'a loudmouthed asshole'?—you can't afford to fail in a high-profile case."

Kane couldn't think of anything to say to that, so he said, "What am I going to do for a partner now? Think they'll give me somebody who actually pulls his weight?"

"As opposed to me?" Jackie Dee asked, smiling. "I don't know. I guess the fact that I'm the one being reassigned means that I'm taking the fall, so maybe your career will escape."

Kane shook his head.

"We both know better than that," he said.

"Yeah, we do," Jackie Dee said. "Give me a cigarette, would you?"

"No can do, Jackie Dee," Kane said. "Your doctor says you're not supposed to smoke, and I quit."

"You did?" Jackie Dee said. "Since when?"

"Since my son was born," Kane said. "You didn't notice? Some detective."

"Why'd you do it?" Jackie Dee asked.

"I don't know," Kane said. "It just made sense to me."

Jackie Dee nodded, then looked at his watch.

"Time to get going," he said. "I'm told I'm to take over my new duties immediately, so this is probably our last breakfast as partners."

He looked at the two coffee cups and the small plate covered with English-muffin crumbs.

"We really did ourselves proud, didn't we?" he said.

They walked out into the parking lot, where Jackie Dee folded his big hand around Kane's.

"It's been real, partner," he said. "Still, I wish we'd caught the cocksucker who killed Danny Shirtleff."

"We will," Kane said. "Sooner or later, one of us will."

twenty-three

Time does not change us. It just unfolds us.

—MAX FRISCH

## MAY 2007

The rabbit peeked from behind a bush, its nose twitching like it was about to sneeze. It was gray and white, fat and fluffy, a domestic rabbit gone wild. Unknown numbers of them lived along the hillside above Anchorage, the legacy of a crazy German restaurateur who had installed four pairs outside his place for the amusement of his guests in the 1950s. They'd gotten loose, somehow, and only owls and lynx and coyotes and bad winters kept them from taking over.

The Shirtleff file sat on the table at Kane's elbow, untouched. The morning was fine, full of sunshine and birdsong, scampering squirrels, and now this improbable rabbit. Kane could feel the current of spring running strong through the landscape, strong enough to make him almost happy.

The rabbit took a tentative hop from behind the bush, then another, headed for the bed of flowers that ran along the edge of the big house which served as a retreat for the nuns.

"Pull out your pocket watch," Kane murmured. "Say you're late."

"What was that, Mr. Kane?" a voice said from behind him. He turned his head and saw Yolanda standing in the doorway. She was dressed casually, a yellow blouse over tan pants of some billowy material, brown leather shoes, earrings that glittered against her dark skin, nearly as bright as her smile.

She's like some sort of life force, Kane thought.

"How good to see you, Yolanda," Kane said. "Please, come in and sit."

He rose slowly to his feet as she entered and took a seat in the armchair that matched his.

"Would you like some coffee?" he asked. But when he poured some into the tiny china cups the nuns used, it was cold.

"I guess I've been sitting here longer than I thought," he said.

Yolanda made a small, dismissive gesture and sat looking at him in a way that made him wonder if she was examining his soul. It made him uncomfortable, and his discomfort drove him to speak.

"To what do I owe the pleasure of this visit?" he asked.

Yolanda greeted his question with a laugh that ran from her lips like water over a falls.

"My, how formal," she said. "I am here to see my former patient and to visit my friend."

Kane's confusion must have shown in his face, for she continued, "You are, of course, both."

Friend? Kane thought. We're friends? What do we have as the basis for friendship?

When he asked the question aloud, Yolanda laughed again and said, "We have shared experiences, shared hardships, shared the joy of life. What else makes people friends?"

What else, indeed? Kane thought.

"So you're here to check up on me," he said.

Yolanda's smile didn't waver.

"Are you a child, that you need checking up on?" she said. "The sisters invited me to visit, and so I have come. We have much in common, the sisters and I. Our profession, and a certain way of looking at the world. Their technical information is, of course, out of date, but they have much practical experience to impart. Why, just this morning, I have learned two possible amelioratives for colic in newborns and a remedy for constipation, using plants that grow wild along the Yukon River."

Laughter rippled through her and spilled out into the room.

"One never knows when one will need a remedy for constipation on the Yukon River," she said.

"And the way of looking at the world?" Kane asked.

Yolanda's smile vanished.

"We see order, the sisters and I," she said. "They are of the belief that the order is their god's. But the reason for order is not as important as believing in it."

"And what do you think brings order to the world, if not a god?" Kane asked.

Yolanda's smile returned.

"Why, humans bring order to the world," she said. "Why else would we be here?"

Kane sat, pondering her answer. In his experience, humans brought disorder to the world. But maybe that was a difference in their experiences, the difference between being a cop and being a nurse. Between shooting people and patching them up.

The thought made him look at Yolanda in a new way. Until then, he had simply taken her as she was. It was the cop's habit. You encountered people, you dealt with them, you moved on. You didn't try to engage them, to figure out their histories, ask about their hobbies, their triumphs and disappointments. Unless they were suspects. Then you tried to suck out every piece of information they possessed.

You answered a call, and you fit the civilians you met into a convenient category—victim, witness, whatever. You dealt with whatever unhappy situation required your presence, and then you went on to the next thing. If the situation was particularly funny or dangerous, if a woman was particularly beautiful or a man a particular asshole, you might remember what happened well enough to tell the story in a bar after work. But you never, ever attempted to engage people as human beings. Much, much too dangerous.

"It's not my life and it's not my wife," was the rubric that Fireball had taught him in that first week on the job.

Kane knew that the new breed of cops was taught a new way of thinking, a more humanistic approach to policing that fit better with their college degrees. He also knew that a year on the street brought them around to the more traditional view.

Well, he wasn't a cop anymore. And he'd met few people in his life who seemed less dangerous than his visitor.

"Tell me about yourself, Yolanda," he said. "Where are you from? How did you come to be here?"

The woman gave Kane a shrewd look.

"So we are to talk of me?" she asked. She thought for a moment. "Very good. First me, then you."

The look gave way to a smile, and as she spoke her words gained lilt.

"We are island people, my people. From Saint John in the Virgin Islands. We are first from Africa, of course, but our history there is lost to us. My gramma was born near Hawksnest Bay, during the great hurricane of 1899. She told me that all of the Bonair women were 'hurricane ladies' in the islands. It is well known that hurricane ladies can read palms and tell the future."

Here, Yolanda stopped to laugh, then continued.

"When she was a very young woman, my gramma ran off with an island boy, and, after many adventures I will not recount although she claimed to have told me every one, they settled in New Orleans.

My grandfather was a musician and my gramma opened a speak-easy and, I think, a sporting house. They prospered and had many children, one of whom was my mother. She was born during a mere tropical storm and so could not tell the future very well." Another laugh. "Good for me, since she said many times when I was a child that I would come to no good. How fortunate for me that she was not really predicting the future.

"My gramma sent my mama to college at Jackson State, and, when she returned, she was an educated lady. In New Orleans, she met a gentleman who was a doctor, and, in the fullness of a formal courtship, they married. They still tell stories of that wedding throughout all of Louisiana, I am told, because by then my gramma had become the most proper and wealthy former owner of a sporting house that great city had ever seen. There was not a black family or a white family or a Cajun family, not an orphan quadroon or octoroon, who was not invited to the wedding and the reception. They say everything in the city stopped that day, and that many people did not sober up until the following week. This made my mama and daddy famous, and, of course, helped my daddy's medical practice so that he grew very rich.

"My mama and daddy had children, too, one of whom was me. I myself was born during Hurricane Camille, so I am a powerful teller of the future. Be careful."

Here, she stopped, and something extra entered her voice, a wistfulness that was hard for Kane to listen to.

"I had the most wonderful childhood," she said. "We spent the winters in the city and the summers on the bayou. I could pilot a pirogue before I could walk. My only real regret in life is having to grow up. Private school. Finishing school. A debutante ball that was the talk of the parish. Me, a debutante. Imagine. College. Nursing school. Graduate school. I am a most educated lady myself."

The last sentence was so suffused with sadness that Kane felt he had to speak.

"Was it so bad, growing up?" he asked.

Yolanda shook herself like someone waking from unexpected sleep.

"Oh, no," she said. "I have had my rewards for growing up. Caring for people is very nice."

She gave him a smile.

"Now it is your turn to speak of yourself," she said.

"But you haven't finished your story," Kane said.

Yolanda laughed.

"If I tell you everything, I shall not maintain my mystery," she said. "A lady is nothing without her mystery. Or so I was taught at Madame Yvette's finishing school."

Kane saw the set of her jaw and tried another route.

"Perhaps, then, you can tell me what's happening in the outside world," he said. "The nuns aren't much for newspapers."

Yolanda shook her head.

"Asking questions is, of course, simply a way to avoid answering questions," Yolanda said, "but you shall not escape that easily."

She spent the next handful of minutes peppering him with questions, about how his ribs felt, about any fevers, and his appetite and his bowel movements. The questions were so quick and prying yet professional that, by the time she was finished, he was laughing hard enough to make both of them worry about him hurting himself.

"These sisters seem to know their business," Yolanda said when the interrogation ended. "I shall be able to visit my own sister without worrying about you. Except, perhaps, your mental state. How is that?"

Kane wanted to respond angrily to the prying, but Yolanda seemed to radiate something that caused anger to dissipate, like sudden sunshine driving the fog away.

"I, I'm okay," Kane said. "I'm taking your advice and thinking about other things for the time being. Other mysteries, I guess you could say."

Yolanda nodded.

"That is wise," she said. "Life will take you up in its own time, and you will have to face what you now avoid. But there's no need to hurry. It was hurry that brought me here, in a way."

"How's that?" Kane asked.

Yolanda answered with a story: An older man with a new, young wife, both of them off one of the first cruise ships of the season to reach Juneau.

"A man eager to show his vigor," she said, shaking her head slightly. "In a hurry to demonstrate his manhood."

So the two of them set off up the trail to the top of Mount Roberts. Halfway up, he fell.

"The trail is well posted, its dangers set out in plain English," Yolanda said, "but apparently this man was blinded by the woman's youth and beauty and his worry about keeping her in a world full of younger men. Perhaps he was showing off. Perhaps it was just a moment's inattention. Perhaps she pushed him." This said with a giggle. "She is young and he is well insured. But surely not, for she raced down the trail, forgetting entirely her cell phone, and set off a scramble of rescue workers and paramedics. A helicopter, even, although the terrain was so difficult all it could do was hover like some giant insect. They went down ropes, these young men of the very sort he was afraid would entice his young wife, and strapped him to a board, hoisted him, stabilized him, and carried him down the rest of the mountainside to the ambulance, which took him to my hospital. The doctors there saved his life and put him on a medevac to Anchorage. I attended him on the airplane all the way to the much finer hospital here, although I doubt there is much to be done. He will spend the rest of his life in a wheelchair, being the very aging and damaged object of pity that he had hoped so much to show he would never be."

"And the young wife?" Kane asked after a moment's silence.

Yolanda shrugged.

"The ways of the human heart are a mystery," she said. "She may be Penelope. She may be Helen. Only the fullness of time will reveal which."

What a remarkable woman Yolanda is, Kane thought, and when he said as much she laughed and replied, "All women are remarkable. Surely you are old enough to know that. We are, each of us, remarkable in our own way. We are always shaping the world and the men in it to our own liking, making you better than you would otherwise be. Or worse, as the whim takes us."

Maybe the idea that each of us is the hero of his own story is simply fiction, Kane thought. Perhaps all men are simply characters in tales composed by women.

"Will you marry me?" he asked.

"Of course," Yolanda said. "Or, rather, I would if it didn't mean abandoning my children. And what would become of my current husband, Mr. James Posey? I have been shaping him now for more than twenty years, and I am confident that, in another forty years or so, he will be a finished product. So"—here, she sighed—"I am afraid that we can only be friends."

"Story of my life," Kane said, and the wistfulness in his voice made them both laugh.

"Now, perhaps you will tell me a story," Yolanda said. "What is it you have been thinking about?"

And, to his surprise, Kane found himself telling Yolanda about the disappearance of his father, and his life with his family.

"You think you are telling me a story about others," Yolanda said, her words echoing in the big, sunny room long after she had left, "but you are really telling me a story about yourself."

"But—" Kane began in protest.

"Don't worry," Yolanda said. "All of our stories are, one way or another, about ourselves. Even the sisters, who are taught to love God and live quietly and not put themselves forward, find themselves at the center of events. I have heard some stories from them that, believe me, would surprise you. Including stories told by your own sister here. Perhaps she has told them to you?"

Kane shrugged.

"She's told me some stories," he said. "But how do I know if they're the same ones she's told you?"

"So skeptical," she said. "You might think that this is a lesson that life taught you, but people learn only what they will. And thinking in this way cannot help you as a detective, for it prevents you from seeing people as people, subject to the same human desires and limitations we all have."

She got to her feet and walked to the table beside Kane's bed. She looked at the bottles there, picked one up, shook a couple of pills out, picked up a glass of water, and brought glass and pills to Nik.

"Hold out you hand," she said, and, when he did, put the pills in it. "Your sister asked me to be sure you took your pain medication. She thinks sometimes you do not."

Nik looked at the pills in his hand.

"This stuff makes me foggy and gives me weird dreams," he said.

"Perhaps you are supposed to have these dreams," Yolanda said. "Now, take your pills."

Nik shook his head and set the pills down. Yolanda sighed and said, "Give me your hand."

She took his hand between hers, turned it palm up, and looked at it.

"There are scars there, very faint," she said. "You were hurt?"

"Both hands. An accident, at work, when I was younger," Nik said.

"The doctor who repaired your hands was very good," Yolanda said.

She looked down at his palm and studied it for so long that Kane began to feel uncomfortable. Finally, with a sigh, she placed his hand in his lap and stood.

"Your beard needs trimming," she said, "and you could use a haircut. With some care, you might look quite distinguished one day."

She looked at him again with an expression he couldn't quite identify.

"And you should gain weight," she said. "I shall speak to the sisters about that on my way out. You will need your strength."

Kane looked into her eyes and held them with his own.

"You're not going to tell me?" he asked. "What you read in my palm?"

Yolanda shook her head.

"The future is not certain," she said. "Even what I read plainly there might be wrong."

She turned and walked to the door.

"Yolanda," Kane said to her back. "Please."

He could see her shoulders slump for a moment. Then she squared them and opened the door. Without turning around, she said, "Pain and suffering. The human condition. And then, in the future, dimly, perhaps the beginnings of joy."

With that, she was gone, the door closing silently behind her. Kane took the pain pills and looked back out into the yard. A coyote was trotting into the underbrush, the gray-and-white rabbit lying limply in its jaws.

twenty-four

We do not remember days, we remember moments.

—CESARE PAVESE

## APRIL 1998

"She's your mother, Nik, and she's dying," Cee Cee said. "Can't you bring yourself to spend a final moment with her?"

His sister was in full nun costume. With the long, full black tunic and scapular, the wimple and the white coif framing her face, she looked every bit the head nun she'd been in hospitals all over the north. But she still looked like his older sister, and that would have been authority figure enough.

They were all there, all the surviving children of Cecelia Kelly Kane, gathered in a knot outside the hospital room she wasn't going to come out of alive: Cee Cee, still the boss after all these years; Michael, the oldest boy, working as an engineer for Boeing; Barry, a concierge at some fancy hotel in Thailand, as well groomed as Michael was messy; Aurora, a year older than Nik, and still the beautiful one; and Dee Dee, the baby of the family, born seven months after their father left, never to be heard from again. Six of the eight Kane kids. Their sister Oregon had died of breast cancer a dozen years before. Their brother Kevin was still officially MIA in Southeast Asia after thirty years.

"Yeah, c'mon, Nik," Michael said. "Say your good-byes to her."

Kane had come straight to the hospital after his shift, which had included a tense session with a man who had, finally, confessed to shooting a cabbie for a little more than twenty dollars. Nik didn't need pressure from his siblings; he needed a drink. But he knew that even if he'd managed to stop at just one, the alcohol on his breath would have brought a sad look from Cee Cee. After all these years, he still hated to make Cee Cee sad.

He looked at his other sisters. Aurora's face wore the slightly empty look that a lot of truly beautiful women had. It was like they learned early that their beauty would get them through most things, so they never bothered to develop their minds. Or maybe nature compensated for great beauty with lack of intelligence to keep the cosmos balanced. Whatever the reason, Aurora had always been beautiful—still was beautiful at, what, fifty—and simply floated through life without offering a thought or expressing an opinion. Nothing seemed to faze her. She was on her fourth—or was it her fifth—husband and didn't have a line on her face. Amazing. Kane had never wondered why a man would marry Aurora. That face and body shouted to men. But he was curious why they left her. Conversation too boring? Upkeep too expensive? Too many lovers too obviously? He'd ask, but the best he would get in return was a giggle.

Dee Dee was good-looking, too, but in her usual devilish way. Her hair was cut short and bleached almost white, and, in her leather jacket, cropped top, and jeans, she looked like a dissolute pixie. She had been, no surprise, the last to arrive at their mother's bedside, and this was the first time Kane had seen her.

"Still a biker chick in Oakland?" he asked with a smile.

The smile Dee Dee gave him back was mostly leer.

"Boy, are you behind the times," she said. "I'm practicing massage therapy in Palm Springs now."

"Massage therapy, eh?" Kane said drily. "We've got our share of masseuses here, too."

Dee Dee gave a loud honk and punched Kane in the shoulder.

"Not that kind of massage, Nik," she said. "The real thing."

Kane rubbed his shoulder.

"Yeah," he said. "That's what they all say."

Dee Dee hooted and punched him again.

"Will you two please stop that?" Cee Cee said.

"Please," Michael said. "This hospital is still owned by the nuns."

His oldest sister and brother were standing practically shoulder to shoulder, and Kane was struck anew by how much alike they looked. Barry, too, although he was slimmer and had a much better tan. The rest of the Kane children bore some resemblance to one another— except Aurora, of course, who looked like she'd sprung fully formed from Hugh Hefner's brow—but these three were almost carbon copies.

Except that Michael looked like hell; overweight, unshaven, and in need of a haircut. He was the one of the children who had the most conventional life; a wife, five kids, a big house in the Seattle suburbs, an important job, a deacon in the church. But his body gave him away. Drink? Drugs? Midlife crisis? Whatever it was, Kane expected his older brother to break out with a red sports car and a twenty-something girlfriend, or maybe a full-blown heroin habit. There was something in there fighting to get out and it didn't look like it would be pretty when it emerged.

A nun, a volcano about to erupt, a gay guy, a beauty queen, and a lifestyle-a-minute drifter, Kane thought. Does that make me the normal one? God help us all.

He was the only one still in Alaska at any rate, he and the old woman dying in the hospital room. Like a lot of Alaska women who

took the cloth, Cee Cee was in a Canadian order, and had been transferred to the motherhouse in Victoria. Michael lived in Kent, or one
of those places; and Barry lived in Bangkok, with somebody named
Kongsangchai who everyone was careful not to ask about. Aurora
rattled around a big house in La Jolla. And Dee Dee? Palm Springs
at the moment, but next month? Anybody's guess. But not Alaska.
She'd left home at fifteen, and kept going until she was all the way
out of Alaska. Good thing, too, since she had been widely suspected
of making off with a lot of cash belonging to an upright, middle-
aged, and very married male citizen. Kane had just joined the force
and took a lot of crap about that.

"So you all have talked to Mom?" Kane asked his brothers and
sisters. They all nodded. "Really? You, too, Dee Dee?"

"Well, it wasn't much of a conversation," Dee Dee said with a grin.
"She called me a whore, and I called her a dried-up old bat, and that
seemed to satisfy her."

"Deidre Kathleen Serena Kane," Cee Cee said in a stern voice.

"You're in trouble now," Kane said. "She used your confirmation
name, too."

"Serena," Aurora said. "I'd forgotten that. You're not really very
serene, are you? But, then, which of us is?"

Everyone looked at Aurora in surprise.

Maybe there's something going on there after all, Kane thought.
She certainly pegged that one.

A nurse came out of the room.

"All done, Sister," she said to Cee Cee. "You can go back in now."

"Nik?" Cee Cee said.

Kane nodded and went through the door. The room was semi-
private, a concession, he suspected, to Cee Cee. There'd been a
woman in the other bed when they'd wheeled Cecelia Kane in four
days before, but, as if the intrusion of a stranger was just too much,
the woman had died that first night and the bed had stayed empty.

Everything in the room that wasn't white was beige or pale green or shiny stainless steel. There were two beds, four chairs, and, around his mother's bed, a bunch of machines and the tray-on-wheels contraption they maneuvered into place to serve bad hospital food. Not that Cecelia was eating. She was past that.

The air was slightly chilly, and bore the tart smell of antiseptic over the musty odor of humanity, with just a touch of despair. Hospital smell. Unmistakable.

Sunlight filtered through the gap in the curtains and fell across the bed, illuminating his mother's face. She lay flat on her back, a shrunken, wrinkled figure attached to tubes that delivered fluids and wires that sent signals to and from a series of humming, beeping, blinking machines. Her false teeth sat in a glass on a table next to the bed, and, without them, her face had collapsed into something more simian than human. They'd scraped the layers of makeup off of her, and she looked oddly naked without it. Her breathing was loud in the still room, all but obliterating the faint hospital sounds that penetrated the closed door.

Kane walked to the bed and looked down at his mother. He reached for a feeling—any feeling—and came up empty. Once he thought he'd loved his mother and later that he'd hated her, but the truth was that his love had been wistfulness and his hate irritation. He'd only recently figured out that the connection between them had always been too flimsy to carry strong emotion. Cecelia Kane had always lived in her own world. Everyone else was just a visitor.

He pulled one of the chairs up to the bed and sat, listening to his mother's labored breathing. As the only child still in Alaska, Kane had been the one called on to help out when she needed it: buying groceries, chasing mice away, that sort of thing. As she got older, he'd been the one to take away the keys to the car Aurora had bought her for reasons too vaguely explained for Kane to understand. And he'd closed up her apartment and moved her to assisted living when she had her first stroke.

But more than that, he'd been the one to cope with her five-year slide into childishness. She began living more and more in the past, acting like a much younger woman, and, for a while, calling Kane by his father's name.

His mother stirred and muttered something indecipherable. She'd thrown back the thin blanket and Kane pulled it over her again, smoothing it with his hands as he looked down at his mother's time-ravaged face.

He wondered if Laurie should be there, what his brothers and sisters thought of the fact that she was not. Nobody expected Michael to try to bring his wife, or Aurora whatever man was paying her bills at the moment. But Laurie was right there in town, a handful of miles away.

"I could go with you, I suppose," she'd said when Kane asked, "but I won't be very good at faking grief. Besides, Emily's got a concert tonight, and I think Dylan might be running a temp."

"You could bring the kids," Kane said.

"What, and scar them for life?" Laurie said. "I don't think so. I saw plenty of young children creeping into the hospital rooms of sick old people when I worked there and I didn't notice it did either the kids or the old people any good. No, thanks."

Laurie had been a nurse in training when they'd met. One of the things that had attracted him to her then was the friendliness she extended to everyone, and the kindness with which she'd dealt with even the most difficult patients.

She's changed a lot since then, he thought. I guess life toughens everybody up.

Kane wasn't sure why his wife and his mother didn't get along, but they didn't, and that, as far as Laurie was concerned, was that.

Of course, Cecelia returned the favor. Or, as far as Kane knew, had initiated the hostilities. Cecelia had made a lot of demands on her son but never once had asked to come to his home or to have his family to hers.

Why does everything have to be so difficult? he thought. Or is it only in my life that it's that way?

He could almost hear the minutes ticking away as he sat there. He wasn't a patient man, and wasting time waiting to go through some meaningless ritual with his mother irritated him. Nothing new there. In his emotional arsenal, the crate labeled "Love" might be empty, but the one labeled "Anger" overflowed. He really didn't want his last words with his mother to be angry ones, so he tried to breathe deeply and relax his knotted muscles.

He must have dozed off then because he snapped awake to the sound of rustling sheets.

"Hello?" his mother whispered hoarsely. "Is someone there?"

Kane got to his feet and stood over the bed.

"It's just me," he said.

His mother looked at him through eyes cloudy with memory.

"Teddy?" she whispered. "Is that you, Teddy?"

Kane picked up a plastic glass from the rollaway tray and, lifting his mother's head gently, put the straw into her mouth. She drank almost by reflex, like a baby whose lips happened to encounter a nipple. When she seemed finished, he lowered her head and replaced the glass.

"Oh, that tastes so good," his mother said. "I always did like the taste of champagne. I like to drink it when we go to the nightclubs, now that the war is almost over and anything seems possible."

We're back to that, Kane thought. I can't imagine why she thinks I'm my father. We don't look that much alike.

"Oh, we have so much fun, don't we, Teddy?" she said. "I'll get up

soon and bathe and put on my good dress, and we'll go out, shall we?
I wouldn't be lying here"—there was an earthiness in her voice now
that made Kane cringe—"if you weren't such a naughty boy. I don't
know what I'll say at confession, I'm sure. I can hardly tell Father
O'Toole how much I like it."

That's enough of that, Kane thought.

"Mother, it's me, Nik," he said loudly. "Nik. Your son Nik."

Something shifted in her eyes.

"Nik?" she said, a flirtatious note replacing the earthiness. "How
unusual. I have a son named Nik, but he's much younger than you
are, of course. I'm far too young to have a son your age. Are you
here to take me somewhere? Maybe we could go dancing. I love to
dance."

Kane was baffled by his mother's behavior. The woman he remembered was stern and devout and, above everything else, proper. This
woman talking about going out and drinking and carrying on was a
stranger to him. Her doctor had warned that the stroke might cause
a change in her personality, but he'd said nothing about it revealing a much different personality that had been there all along. Kane
thought about trying to draw this woman out but was afraid of what
he might learn. Besides, he couldn't know if this was a real person or
some neurons firing off the dialogue to some old movie.

"I am your son Nik," he said firmly. "We're all much older now."

The woman was shaking her head before he finished.

"No, no, no, no," she said. "I don't want to be older. I want to have
some fun."

Kane laid a hand on her forehead. Her skin was damp and hot to
the touch. Was something happening? Should he call someone?

"It's okay," he said, forcing calm into his voice. "Just relax. Everything is fine."

His words or his tone seemed to calm her.

"Oh, goody," she said, her voice young and flirty again. "I'll just put my old coat on over my dress and tell the children I'm going to church for the rosary. You can pick me up at the corner."

Goddamn, Kane thought. Maybe this is the real person. Maybe the mother I thought I knew was the phony.

His mother's eyes closed, leaving Kane alone with his confusion. He sat preoccupied for a long time, until his mother opened her eyes again.

"Nik?" she whispered. "Is that you, Nikky?"

He stood and leaned over the bed.

"It is, Mom," he said. "It's me."

Her eyes were clear and bright, the eyes of someone anchored firmly in the present.

"Oh, Nikky, I'm so sorry about your father," she said. "I know it hurt all of the children, but it seemed to hurt you the most. I wish things had been different. I wish I had been different."

Kane picked up her hand.

"It's okay, Mom," he said, stroking the collection of frail bones, veins, and wrinkled skin.

"He had to go that way, Nik," she whispered. "It was the only choice."

Again, Kane was baffled.

"What do you mean, Mom?" he asked.

But her eyes were losing focus again, and when she opened her mouth she seemed to be speaking from a great distance.

"Remember, Nik, people live for money, but they die for love," she said.

He wanted to ask her what she meant but she'd closed her eyes again. Her breathing was slower now, shallower and more ragged. Death seemed to be hovering in the room, and Kane turned to summon his brothers and sisters. But he was too late.

"Oh, God, Teddy," his mother yelled. She sat up in the bed and looked directly at Kane.

"I'm coming, Teddy," she said, her voice a mixture of hatred and love and fear and ecstasy. "I'm coming."

As she fell back in the bed, her children came flying through the door, Cee Cee in the lead, summoned by their mother's shouts, and arriving just a moment too late.

twenty-five

Life is all about timing.

—STACEY CHARTER

## MAY 2007

Tom Jeffords sat in the armchair, showing Kane a bland, friendly expression that revealed nothing. He was dressed in his police chief's uniform. Not the dress blues with all the braid but the black working uniform, no rank insignia, just "Chief Jeffords" in white stitching above the left breast pocket. His white hair was freshly barbered and his tanned face glowed with good health. He shifted in the chair slightly to let the fancy, well-used Glock .45 he wore on his right hip sit more comfortably.

"You're looking better, Nik," he said. His voice was deep, with a friendly lilt. "You may even have put on a little weight."

Careful, Kane thought. There's nothing more dangerous than Tom Jeffords acting friendly.

"The nuns have been stuffing me like a Christmas goose," Kane said, smiling. "It's enough to make you wonder if cannibalism has suddenly become part of the Catholic liturgy."

Jeffords's lips shaped themselves into the wisp of a smile.

"I don't think the good sisters would be happy to hear you talk like that," he said. "After all, they've taken good care of you."

"You'd be surprised," Kane said. "Some of these women have subversive senses of humor. But you're right. They have taken good care of me. I owe them."

Kane let the conversation lapse, waiting for Jeffords to get around to his reasons for visiting. Jeffords never did anything without a reason—or six.

"Do you think you'll be going back to work when you're feeling fit?" Jeffords asked. "To detective work, I mean? On your own?"

Kane shrugged, something he could do now without pain.

"I haven't really thought about it," he said. "I suppose I will. It's either that or retirement, because I don't really know how to do much else."

The answer brought a frown to Jeffords's face.

"You should think about that, Nik," he said. "You need a lot of inner strength to do this kind of work, especially without the support you get from an organization. And you've taken some pretty hard knocks lately."

Kane ignored that. If Jeffords was there to talk about Kane's troubles, it was going to have to be a monologue.

"Is that an invitation to come back to the department, Tom?" Kane asked.

"Now, Nik . . ." Jeffords began.

"Forget it, Tom," Kane said. "I know the speech. But it's like I said, I've got to do something. I can't afford to retire. And even if I could, I don't see myself just sitting on the beach somewhere. Or playing shuffleboard at a retirement home."

Jeffords nodded and shifted in his chair again. That was one of the problems with wearing a sidearm. No matter what you did, the damn thing found a way to dig into you when you sat.

Another, of course, is that you sometimes had to shoot people with it. Even when they deserved it, shooting people was not as much fun as movies and video games might lead people to think.

"I saw Laurie the other day," Jeffords said. "She is pretty unhappy with you, and unhappy with me, too, for what she called my role in making you what you are."

Again, a wispy smile flitted across his lips.

"I thought about trying to tell her that I didn't think I'd had much effect of any kind on you, but she didn't seem to be in a mood to listen," he said.

"Welcome to my world," Kane said. "We'll be getting a divorce soon. Maybe that will make her happy. Or at least give her someone else to be unhappy about."

Jeffords shifted in his seat again.

"Just take the damn thing off, Tom," Kane said, "unless you think you'll be shooting it out with the nuns soon."

Jeffords stood up, unbuckled the utility belt, and laid it on the table so that the gun would be within easy reach. He wasn't carrying the whole rig—no handheld, no baton, no pepper spray—but the reload pouch looked full and a cell phone peeked from one of the belt's compartments. Jeffords might not be equipped to subdue anyone, but he looked well prepared to shoot and then call it in.

"She was with a man when I saw her," Jeffords said as he resumed his seat. "A big, dark, good-looking fellow, well dressed, with the kind of hands that haven't held a shovel in a while."

"Name's Antonio Vega," Kane said. "Don't know where she first met him, but he was hanging around when I got back from prison. She claimed they were just friends. Antonio doesn't look like the kind of guy who has women who are just friends, but you never know. Don't know what he does for a living, but whatever it is seems to pay well."

Jeffords made a steeple of his fingers and tapped the ends against his chin.

"Is that all you know about him, Nik?" he asked.

The question was so casual that it set off alarm bells in Kane's head.

"It is, Tom," Kane said. "When I first got back, I was trying to make things work with Laurie, and challenging her friendships didn't seem to be a very good idea. And, later, after she'd decided she didn't want to be with me anymore, it didn't seem like it would make any difference. Besides, he seemed to be a pretty decent guy, always polite, always kind to Laurie, and not at all hostile to me."

The truth was that Kane had done some snooping around, learning that Vega ran some sort of investment company and did pretty well at it, by all accounts. He'd also learned that he was single and didn't have so much as a parking ticket, so he'd decided that more digging wasn't worth the risk of getting caught by Laurie.

When Jeffords didn't respond, Kane said, "Why do you ask, Tom? What's your interest?"

Jeffords studied his fingertips for a while.

"Oh, no interest, really," he said in the casual way that had alarmed Kane in the first place. "You know how it is. When somebody you know swaps mates, you're curious, that's all."

Kane's alarms were shrilling at full volume now. He couldn't think of anyone less interested in people's private lives than Jeffords. Unless it had something to do with work. But he knew that if Jeffords didn't want to tell him what was going on, asking the chief would get him nowhere.

He thought about whether he should warn Laurie. But what would he tell her? Tom Jeffords is asking questions about your boyfriend? Even if she believed him, he didn't have anything more to tell her than that. So that would get him nowhere. Besides, who was he kidding? She wouldn't talk to him in the first place. Maybe he should send her one of those notes like blackmailers do in the movies, with the letters cut out of newspapers and magazines. That'd work. He realized suddenly that Jeffords was talking again.

"I'm sorry, Tom, I didn't hear that," he said.

Jeffords offered him the wispy smile again.

"Not being able to focus is one of the signs of aging, Nik," he said. "Maybe you should rethink retirement."

Kane laughed.

"Who's older than who, Tom?" he asked.

"Oh, there's nothing wrong with my mental processes," Jeffords said, his smile changing to something more like mirth. "I take my ginkgo biloba religiously. And whatever else is in those pills Gwendolyn hands me."

Gwendolyn—never Gwen—was Jeffords's second wife, younger, much better looking, and much, much wealthier than the one he'd discarded. Her grandfather had made a fortune running saloons during various gold rushes. Her father had increased—was still increasing—the fortune in the liquor business. She was an only child and stood to inherit the whole pile.

People whispered that that was why he'd married her, but they were wrong. Jeffords was a rich man in his own right. No, Tom Jeffords had married Gwendolyn Brooks because she had, despite some well-publicized antics when she was younger, a secure position in what passed for respectable society in Anchorage. She knew instinctively the right parties to attend, the right charities to support, the right destinations for vacations.

Just what was in the marriage for her was a mystery to Kane. But he knew there was something. Gwendolyn was that kind of woman.

Jeffords cleared his throat, and, when he spoke again, it was in a serious tone.

"What I was saying is that there are a number of us who are concerned about you. About what you might do when you're back on your feet."

"I appreciate that, Tom," Kane said, resisting the urge to ask Jeffords to name the others who were concerned about him. "But I'm not thinking much ahead at this point. It gets too confusing."

Pretty quickly now, he thought. We'll get to the real point pretty quickly now.

"All right, Nik," Jeffords said. "Just remember that I'm here to help."

Yeah, Kane thought. As long as it doesn't affect any of your plans.

Jeffords cleared his throat again. Kane poured some water from the pitcher on the table and handed the glass to Jeffords. After he drank, he said, "Ms. Lee tells me that you've been asking her for a lot of information lately, Nik."

Bingo! Kane thought.

"So I was wondering if you'd discovered something new."

"No, I haven't, Tom," Kane said. "I'm just checking on a couple of things."

"Quite a few things, actually," Jeffords said.

He took the cell phone from his utility belt. He fiddled with it for a while and said, "The whereabouts of several people. The World War Two service records of some of their fathers. Bank records. The ownership history of the land around Skeleton Lake. And much more. What are you looking for, exactly?"

Kane had been expecting this visit from the moment he'd handed Emily Lee the list of information he needed. If his health had been better, he might have tried to dig up what he needed on his own. But it wasn't, and there were undeniable advantages to having the requests come from Tom Jeffords's secretary—"assistant," he supposed she was now called. He'd known there would be costs, too, like this conversation. Which is why he'd asked for so much information, most of which he didn't really need. The last thing he wanted was for Tom Jeffords to get anywhere ahead of him.

"I'm not looking for anything, exactly, Tom," Kane said. "I found a few loose ends, and, since the department's ability to get information is much better than it was twenty years ago, I thought I'd take advantage of it."

Jeffords put the cell phone back into its pocket.

"So you don't have anything specific in the way of leads?" he asked.

Kane let some irritation seep into his voice.

"Surely you haven't been sitting in that big office so long that you've forgotten how investigations go," he said. "You have lots of questions. You start with the big ones first. Sometimes the answers lead you to other questions. Sometimes they don't. So you try the next-biggest question. And so on. You do that within the limits of your manpower and the time you have, and usually you find out what you want to know.

"This time, we didn't. After going back over the records of the investigation, I have some questions that weren't big enough to ask back then, an angle or two we never thought of. For some of the questions, I need to talk to people who were involved, and, to do that, I need to know where they are. For others, like I said, I just need the answers, and I think that we've got better access to those answers now than we did then."

Jeffords seemed to roll that around in his head for a while.

"That's a lot of words, Nik, but they don't add up to much of an answer. Why are you being so cagey?"

"Why do you think, Tom? Where do you suppose I learned to keep my cards close to my chest? Especially with a case like this one?"

Jeffords's face got redder as he thought about Kane's answer, and when he spoke again there was anger in his voice.

"Goddamn it, Nik," he said. "It's the money, isn't it? Giuseppe DiSanto always thought I took that money. Do you, Nik? Is that what you think?"

"Jackie Dee is dead, Tom," Kane said softly. "That battle is over. You won."

Jeffords ran his hands along his hair, patting it to make sure it was in place. He took several deep breaths.

Well, what do you know? Kane thought. Maybe that wasn't an act. Maybe he really did lose his temper.

"There was never a battle, Nik," Jeffords said, his voice calm once more. "I know DiSanto thought there was, but I didn't. It was simply a question of the right way to go about things, of how to turn what was essentially a Wild West sheriff's office into a modern, functioning policing agency. DiSanto was a cowboy, and there was no room for a cowboy at the top."

"He might have been a cowboy," Kane said, "but he solved cases."

"He did," Jeffords said. "Except for the most important case of his career. If he had been better organized, more deliberate, he might have solved it. If he had solved it, things might have been very different. For him. For me. For the department. But he didn't."

There was nothing to say to that. Jeffords was right. Jackie Dee had been old-school, in the way he lived and the way he worked. He would never have succeeded in a department that was turning to cost management and meetings and paperwork. Of course, if he'd been in charge he might have delayed some of that, but would the department have been better off?

"Giuseppe DiSanto was a good cop," Jeffords said. "I've always regretted the fact that we didn't get along. Given who we were and what was happening in the department, I don't suppose it could have been any different. But I've always regretted it nonetheless."

"How did you survive the loss of the money, Tom?" Kane asked. "The feds must have been superpissed. Everybody thought that when they sent you to admin, your career was over."

"And so did I, for a while," Jeffords said, his smile grim, "but Willie

Tolliver was really a very smart man. He saw that administration had the potential to be a place where I could reshape the department and rehabilitate my career, and he was right. It was a lot of hard, boring detail work, and there was a lot of resistance to change in the rank and file. I was successful, but I wasn't popular. And I'm still not. But not everyone can be an action hero, like Giuseppe DiSanto. Or you, Nik."

He looked out the window for a while before continuing.

"But, because I'm not popular, I can't have a twenty-year-old case coming back to bite me. I've probably got enough friends in the right places to survive whatever might turn up, but several things I'm trying to do will suffer. And when I reach mandatory retirement age, they'll all be there holding the door for me. So you have to tell me what you're up to, Nik."

"You want to stay on as police chief past mandatory retirement age?" Kane said. "You want them to carry you out of that office feet first?"

"Don't be silly, Nik," Jeffords said. "Lots of people are recommending that people delay their retirements. We're living longer, and we're healthier than we've ever been. There's no reason to let the calendar dictate when we stop being productive.

"But that's really neither here nor there. What's important right now is what you think you know. And if you don't tell me, well, Ms. Lee still works for me."

"And she just might not get me the information I want, you mean?" Kane said. "Is that smart, Tom? Shutting down the investigation of the murder of an officer who was under your command when he died? For a second time? How do you think that would play with the guys who have their eyes on your office?"

"What do you mean 'for a second time'?" Jeffords said. "It wasn't my decision to shut that investigation down and transfer DiSanto. That was Chief Tolliver's call."

"C'mon, Tom," Kane said. He couldn't keep the scorn out of his voice and he didn't even try. "You expect me to believe you didn't have your fingers in that deal? Pull the other one. It's got bells on it."

Jeffords ran his hand along his hair again, pat-pat-patting at it. Is he wearing a hairpiece? Kane thought. Or is that just a new nervous habit?

"We put a lot of resources into that investigation with no result," Jeffords said, the patience he was exercising obvious in his voice. "A rational cost-benefit analysis said it was time to shut it down. It's true, my division did the analysis, but nobody had a thumb on the scale. The recommendation was made straight up. If you're looking for the reason nobody caught Danny Shirtleff's killer, go visit Giuseppe DiSanto's grave. Or try looking in the mirror."

Kane could feel his temper rising, and he sat there breathing until he began to calm down. No sense in getting mad about something that had happened twenty years before. Particularly since Jeffords had a lot of right on his side.

If it hadn't been my first investigation, maybe I would have done better, he thought. If I'd had more experience, I certainly would have approached the case differently.

"Besides, who said anything about shutting down your investigation?" Jeffords said. "I'm just asking to be brought up-to-date. We had an agreement."

"As far as I'm concerned, we still have an agreement," Kane said. "But I really don't have anything solid yet, Tom. Just some thoughts and hunches..."

When Jeffords realized Kane wasn't going to say any more, he said, "And?"

"And if this goes where it might go," Kane said, "it's going to be better for you, and for the department, to let me handle this my way."

"What does that mean, Nik?" Jeffords said. "Spell it out."

Kane shook his head.

"There's nothing to spell out, Tom," he said. "Really. I have an idea, a hunch, a theory—call it what you want—but I've got no evidence. Until I do, I'm not saying anything more."

While Jeffords sat in silence, Kane thought: This is a risk. If he shuts down my access to information, I'll have a hard time getting anywhere. But if I spin a theory to the chief of police, there's no way the department won't get involved, and that will just screw things up.

"Okay, Nik," Jeffords said. "I'll trust you know what you're doing on this. But don't get too far out in front. You're still a civilian, and you're not in such good shape, physically or mentally."

The expression on Jeffords's face was anything but bland and friendly as he got to his feet. He looked like a man who'd bitten into something sour. Kane stood and accompanied him to the front door of the residence.

"Nik, I want you to take care of yourself," Jeffords said as he opened the door. "You're not really in any shape to be chasing killers."

"I'll be okay, Tom," Kane said. "It's what happens after I catch the killer that worries me."

When the door closed behind Jeffords, Kane walked back to his room and resumed his seat. He felt restless, but, until he heard from Emily Lee, there wasn't anything for him to do. He picked up a book he'd found in a drawer in the library. The drawer seemed to contain all the books the nuns actually read, mostly cookbooks, popular history, Alaskana, and fiction. He'd been hoping to find a few bodice rippers, but anyone who read those kept them out of the collective book supply. This was a book called *The Long-Legged Fly*. It wasn't a conventional mystery story, but the writing was so good it sucked you right in, anyway. He needed something. When he left his mind idle, it went to thoughts he didn't want to have.

He was just finishing the book—it wasn't really very long—when Cee Cee knocked and entered.

"I hear we had a visit from the chief of police," she said. "You haven't been breaking any laws, have you, Nikky?"

She smiled to show him she was just kidding.

"No," he said. "Not yet, anyway. I think Tom Jeffords was trying to see how much he'd regret letting me look into an old case again."

"And will he?" Cee Cee asked. "Regret it?"

Kane gave her the smile back.

"I don't know yet," he said. "I've asked for some more information, which is why Jeffords showed up. We'll see what that brings."

Cee Cee walked over to ruffle his hair.

"And will I?" she asked. "Regret talking to you about our parents?"

"How could you, Ceese?" he said. "Like you said, Mom's dead. And if Dad isn't, he's not likely to be anyplace I can find him."

She nodded but pursed her lips, unconvinced.

"You really need a haircut," she said. "You're beginning to look like some crazy hermit. Or a street person."

"It's on my list," he said.

His sister walked to the door. Her steps seemed to drag. Was her age starting to catch up to her? Or was her history weighing her down, the way Nik's sometimes did?

"Did you find out something new?" she asked when she got to the door. "New information? New clues?"

"No, not really, Ceese," Kane said. "I just remembered something Mom told me once."

# twenty-six

A memory is what is left when something happens
and does not completely unhappen.

—EDWARD DE BONO

## JUNE 2007

"I think that's everything you asked for," Emily Lee said, closing an expensive-looking black leather briefcase. "At least, everything we could get. Do you know what you'll do next, Nik?"

She was dressed in black again, except for the crisp white shirt with the high collar. Her hair shone with health, and, in the warmth of the afternoon, she smelled like spice and woman.

I ought to ask for more information just to see her again, Kane thought.

"I don't, Emily," he said. "I'll look through this stuff and talk to a few people and see where that leads me."

Looking at her, he couldn't help but smile. She returned the smile, showing even white teeth.

"Then I'll leave you now," she said, getting to her feet and smoothing her long black skirt. "Good luck. And remember the chief's offer. If you should need help following up, something could be arranged."

Something could be arranged, Kane thought. That's probably the motto on the Jeffords family crest.

Kane got to his feet and walked Emily Lee to the front door. He offered his hand and she took it, her hand cool in his.

"Remember what I said before, Nik," she said. "I know things have been rough for you. If I can help..."

Kane thought of several responses, every one of them completely inappropriate.

Men are dogs, he thought, releasing Emily Lee's hand with a smile. He stood in the doorway just to watch her roll down the walk, her skirt twitching with promise at every step. At the end of the walk, she turned, saw him there, offered a sketchy wave, and headed toward a black Audi sports car.

" 'Don't you know that women are the only works of art,' " he said softly.

"Pardon me?" said a passing nun.

"Nothing, Sister," Kane said. "Just talking to myself."

He walked back to his room and sat at the table, picking up the folders Emily Lee had left. Now that he had the information he'd asked for, he was reluctant to take the next step.

Am I afraid that I'll find the answers here? he thought. Or am I afraid that I won't? Either way, this will all be finished, and I'll have to face up to life as it is now. Maybe that's what I'm afraid of.

He sat looking at the folders for a while, sighed, sat up straight and squared his shoulders.

"No time like the present," he said, and opened the first folder.

When Cee Cee found him an hour later, he was putting down the last piece of paper on the taller of two stacks he'd made.

"I've come to see if you'd like to walk," she said. "There's just time before the midday prayer."

Kane was so accustomed to the daily round of prayers in the residence that he hardly noticed them. The nuns gathered in the library in the morning, just before lunch, and in the evening, after dinner, to pray and meditate. He was sure that they would have explained the rituals if he'd shown the slightest interest, but they seemed perfectly happy to leave him to his ignorant heathenism when he didn't.

"How are you feeling, Nikky?" Cee Cee asked when they were along the edge of the big, impossibly green yard. Flowers bloomed in all the plots, and a sizeable vegetable garden was thick with plants. After a week of low-lying clouds and rain, the sun hung hot in a deep blue sky. Birds sang and bees buzzed. All in all, nature seemed happy, and Kane could feel his own spirits rising in response.

"I'm feeling much better, thanks," he said. "The pain seems to be gone and my strength is returning."

"That's good, Nikky," she said, and Kane heard in her voice an echo from his childhood, a slight something he heard when things went wrong.

"What is it, Ceese?" he asked. "What's the trouble?"

Cee Cee stopped to look at the flowers in one plot. Johnny-jump-ups and daisies were running riot, fighting with each other and trying to edge out some taller flowers Kane didn't recognize that had been planted along the back of the bed.

"They're so beautiful, aren't they?" Cee Cee said. "But they last only a season and are gone."

She started walking again, and Kane moved to keep up.

"They want me back in Victoria," Cee Cee said. "They say the motherhouse needs me. I've been more or less running the business of the chapter, and the Mother Superior tells me my replacement hasn't been keeping up."

Kane thought about what she'd said.

"You don't have to stay on my account," he said. "You and the rest of the sisters have been more than kind. I can take care of myself now."

Cee Cee smiled at him, and he was suddenly twelve years old

again, handing in his earnings from a particularly good day selling newspapers.

"Thank you, Nikky," she said. "You really are very sweet."

They walked along the garden plot. Kane could see the greens of carrots just poking up out of the earth. He'd loved carrots as a child, loved to eat them fresh from the garden, loved the crunch they made and the rasping of the dirt that stuck in the folds in the carrots, dirt you couldn't brush off no matter how hard you tried. Like anything he'd loved, carrots had gotten him into trouble more than once. Not every gardener saw his childhood depredations as youthful exuberance.

"It's not that I don't want to go back," Cee Cee said. "But I didn't realize how much I miss Alaska, and it's been so nice to be able to talk with you. It's helped me recover my youth, in a way. I had been thinking more and more only of the bad parts: the scrimping, the arguments with Mother, the pain of being pulled between my vocation and my responsibility to the family. But just seeing you and hearing your voice reminded me of the good parts: doing things well, shaping young lives, and, mostly, the sense of shared purpose we all had to keep our family together and make it work. That carried me through a lot of difficult patches, then and later. I'm glad I've recovered it."

They walked along for a while in silence.

"When would you be leaving?" Kane asked.

"I don't know," Cee Cee said. "Soon, I think. But I've talked with the other sisters, and they are agreed that you should stay on as long as you need to."

"Thanks," Kane said. He knew he should go on, promise to visit and keep in touch. But he knew those would be hollow promises, and Cee Cee would know that, too. So he said, "I'll miss you."

"I'll miss you, too, Nikky," Cee Cee said, then continued in a rush. "Will you be okay by yourself? I mean, will you be able to cope with, with what's happened, and what's going to happen, in your life?"

Kane picked up Cee Cee's arm and entwined it with his, then kissed her on the forehead.

"I'll always be your little brother, Ceese," he said, "but you can't protect me from life."

From inside the house came the soft ringing of the bells that called the nuns to prayer.

"C'mon," Kane said. "Time for you to go talk to your boss. Put in a good word for me, would you? And then, after lunch, I've got to go out for a while."

"Out?" Cee Cee said. "Are you well enough to drive?"

"I made a few telephone calls," Kane said. "That's all taken care of."

Kane was drowsing in his armchair when a knock came at the door.

"There's a...gentleman...here to see you," the nun who had door duty that day said.

"Send him in, please," Kane said.

The man who entered the room was big in every dimension, not fat but fit, his round brown face topped with close-cropped black hair. His blue eyes twinkled. He was dressed in a suit of subdued gray, a brilliant white shirt, and a multicolored tie, a garment bag slung over his shoulder, held by the crooks of hangers that jutted from it.

"Winthrop," Kane said, getting to his feet and offering his hand. "Long time, no see."

The man's hand swallowed Kane's and he pumped it gently, then released it.

"You look some better than when I saw you last," he said, handing the garment bag to Kane. "Hope they fit all right. Had to do some guessing on sizes."

Kane took the bag and went into the bathroom, emerging in a suit that fit like a glove.

"Good guessing," Kane said. "Who do I owe for the clothes?"

Winthrop smiled and shrugged. Kane looked at him and decided to drop the subject.

"Well, tell her I said thanks," he said. "Did she tell you what we're doing?"

Winthrop shook his head.

"Mrs. Foster just said that I was to drive you some places where you would talk to people," he said. "Are we expecting trouble?"

Kane chuckled.

"Why would you ask that?" he said.

"Well, you seem to have a nose for it," Winthrop said.

"Fair enough," Kane said, "but I'm not really expecting any difficulties. At least that you, being large and brown, couldn't handle."

"Then it's very convenient for you that I am," Winthrop said.

The two men left the house and got into a shining black Cadillac, Winthrop behind the wheel and Kane in the passenger's seat.

"Mrs. Foster always sits in the back," Winthrop said.

"Yeah, but she's got class," Kane said.

Winthrop nodded, started the engine, and drove through the streets of Anchorage, headed first downhill, then toward downtown. He slid the big car through the spotty afternoon traffic so smoothly that they hardly seemed to be moving.

Kane had no idea how Winthrop had come to work for a notorious Alaska adventurer named Richard Foster, but after the old man died the big Inupiat stayed to work for his young, now very wealthy, wife. It was taking a job for her that had led to Kane getting shot and his son getting killed.

He pulled his thoughts quickly away from that and looked out the car window. Anchorage was every bit as ugly as he remembered it, a collection of box stores and strip malls and housing that would have fit right in in California. Not the nice part of California, either.

Winthrop slid the car to a stop in a strip mall parking lot. The sign on the storefront read "Instant Images," and, below that, "Portraits, weddings, graduations, all occassions."

"Sign painter needs a remedial spelling course," Winthrop said as they got out of the car.

The inside of the store was surprisingly nice. Good carpet, comfortable-looking couches, and a very decorative young woman at a desk next to a set of floor-length curtains that were pulled shut. The walls were covered with photographs of people—individuals, families, entire school classes—with smiles so big that Kane's face hurt just looking at them.

Winthrop gave the photos a sweeping glance.

"Not many Natives," he said.

"Probably afraid the white man's black box would steal their souls," Kane said.

Winthrop smiled. The decorative young woman looked horrified.

"We're here to see Mr. Murphy," Kane said. "I'm Nik Kane."

"He's in back, making a portrait," the young woman said, nodding toward the curtains. "If you'd just take a seat."

Kane walked over and sat on one of the couches. Winthrop took a seat next to him.

"I guess we wait," Kane said.

"At least the scenery's good," Winthrop said, smiling at the young woman. To Kane's surprise, she smiled back.

"So much for big and scary," he said.

"You're just jealous," Winthrop said.

After fifteen minutes or so, a man came out, herding a large woman holding a very small dog.

"I'm certain one of that last set will be perfect," the man was saying. "Fifi certainly settled down, and the camera loves you."

The woman smiled at Murphy and whispered something to the dog. Kane could make out the words "nice mans."

"I'll leave you and Jennifer to work out the financial details," the man said, turning to Kane and Winthrop. "Were you here for a portrait? I'm afraid I have someone coming in quite soon. Perhaps you could make a date with Jennifer."

"Splendid idea," Winthrop murmured.

Kane got to his feet, put his arm around Murphy's shoulders, and began leading him back into the studio.

"We'd love to make an appointment," he said, "but one never knows how long these relationships will last, does one?"

Winthrop's guffaw drowned out Murphy's reply, and the three of them were in the studio, Winthrop pulling the curtains closed behind them. Kane stood there, studying Murphy. The photographer had a few more wrinkles, and his hair and beard were now all white, but he looked thinner and more relaxed than he'd remembered.

"I'm Nik Kane," he said. "Remember me? APD?"

Murphy looked carefully at Kane.

"Wow, it really is," he said. "The years have been hard on you. But it's the same ears and nose and eye color. You didn't have a beard then, and there was a lot more of you, but it's you all right. What can I do for you?"

"Danny Shirtleff," Kane said. "Remember him? Cop got shot in '85? I'm looking into the case again."

Murphy nodded a little too enthusiastically.

"Yeah, yeah, I remember," he said. "A terrible thing. Danny was a nice guy and a heck of a photographer. What can I do for you?"

Kane looked around the studio. Cords snaked this way and that across the floor, lights and scrims lay around, and a fancy-looking camera on a tripod pointed at a blue backdrop lit from the side. In front of the backdrop was a seat of some sort covered in what looked like a blue velvet curtain.

"This looks like a pretty nice setup," Kane said.

Again, Murphy nodded with too much enthusiasm.

"It is," he said. "I've worked hard for it."

"I'm sure you have," Kane said. "I was wondering, you had all of Danny's images, I think you called them. Did you ever find anything out of the ordinary in them?"

" 'Out of the ordinary'?" Murphy asked, giving Kane an expression that was supposed to have been as guileless as a puppy's. It would have been, too, if not for the worry in his eyes. "Out of the ordinary how?"

Kane smiled.

"Oh, I don't know," he said. "Maybe naked women?"

Murphy's face fell. He walked over and sat on a backless stool near the camera.

"How did you find out?" he asked.

Kane walked over and stood near the photographer.

"You just told me," he said. "All I had was a hunch."

"Damn," the photographer said.

"Don't beat yourself up," Kane said. "Basically honest people make piss-poor liars. Why don't you show me what you've got."

Murphy stood and looked around the studio.

"I'm, I'm not sure I can lay my hands on it right away," he said.

Kane looked at him. He could feel his face twisting into a not-very-pretty smile.

"Remember what I said about piss-poor liars," he said.

Murphy's shoulders slumped. He walked to the side of the studio, to a three-drawer filing cabinet. He pulled open the top drawer, reached in, and came out with a file folder.

"There's just the one," he said. "It was just one negative, in with a bunch of other stuff in a file labeled 'Working.' I guess he just forgot it was in there. I made a print."

Murphy stopped in front of Kane, making no effort to hand the folder to him.

"Why didn't you report it when you found it?" Kane asked, taking the file from the photographer.

"You'll see," Murphy said.

The folder contained an eight-by-ten print and a glassine envelope holding a negative. The print was a naked woman, facing the camera with her hands on her hips in a Wonder Woman pose, sweat dripping from her disheveled dark hair, smiling from ear to ear. It was Jackie DeeTwo.

"I found this a couple of months after I got the images," Murphy said. "I couldn't show it to you guys. Your partner had a lot of violence in him. He would have killed me."

"You knew who this is?" Kane asked.

"Sure, I'd seen them around," Murphy said. "And I saw the way he looked at her. I wasn't going to be the one to hand him proof his wife was doing some other guy."

Kane nodded.

"Yeah," he said, "but you could have given it to me."

It was Murphy's turn to smile a twisted smile.

"No offense," he said, "but you were the junior guy. Giving it to you—hell, giving it to anybody—would have been the same as giving it to that guy, that Jackie Dee. The least I would have gotten was a beating, and he had me still on the whole ripping-people-off thing. Uh-uh. The moment I saw that photograph, I made two decisions. One was I was never going to show it to another human being, at least not voluntarily. And the other was that my time hanging around cops and crime scenes was over."

Kane closed the folder and tucked it under his arm.

"I'll be very, very disappointed to find that there are more photographs you're withholding."

"Swear to God," Murphy said, putting his hand over his heart, "there aren't any."

"And I'll be equally disappointed to learn that you have, say, called this woman and told her about our conversation."

"No, no, no," Murphy said, shaking his head so that his white mane slapped from side to side. "Nope. Never going to happen. I've never spoken to this woman and I never will. I wouldn't even know where to find her."

The young woman stuck her head through the drapes.

"Your two o'clock is here," she said. She looked at Winthrop again and smiled.

"I'll be right there," Murphy said.

The young woman withdrew her head.

"Are we finished?" Murphy asked.

"For now, anyway," Kane said. "Maybe permanently. We'll see. If you don't have any more evidence, and you don't know anything more about Danny's murder, you've got nothing to worry about."

"I don't," Murphy said, his voice full of conviction.

He walked to the curtains and pulled them apart. Kane and Winthrop followed him into the waiting room. A family waited: mother, father, two daughters, and a young son clearly unhappy in his tight collar and tie. Murphy ushered them into the studio as Kane and Winthrop left the shop. Kane was getting into the Caddy when Winthrop said, "Be right back."

He returned to the shop and emerged a minute later, smiling. When he got behind the wheel, Kane said, "Telephone number?"

"This is the twenty-first century, you old fossil," he said as he started the car. "I got landline, cell, and e-mail address, all preprinted on a business card that smells real good."

Kane nodded.

"Like I said," he said, "big and scary."

Winthrop grinned as he started the car.

"You forgot handsome," he said. "You always forget handsome."

twenty-seven

Time discovers truth.

—SENECA

## JUNE 2007

"I'd say you're looking good, Nik," Jacqueline DiSanto said, "but that would be a goddamn lie."

Her smile said she didn't mean it but her eyes said she did. Somewhere in her sixties, Jackie looked like a million bucks. She sat behind a rosewood desk the size of a tennis court in a bright corner office on the top floor of a midtown high-rise. She wore a blazer that matched the desk, black pants, and a soft, cream-colored blouse. When she'd come around the desk to shake hands with Kane, she'd moved like a woman half her age. She was thinner now, and her hair was streaked with gray, but otherwise she looked as good as the woman in the photo Kane carried in a folder under his arm.

Expert makeup, he guessed. Good lighting, and his chair placed farther than normal from her desk. But so what? It worked.

"Getting shot can be hazardous to your health," Kane said, offering a smile of his own. "You, however, look wonderful."

Jackie cocked her head, held her thumbs in front of her face, and squinted.

"Charm from Nik Kane?" she said. "I'm having a hard time picturing this."

The minute he'd seen the photograph, Kane had wanted to talk to this woman. But a cell phone call from the car had established that was impossible, so he'd made an appointment for the following morning and had Winthrop drive him back to the residence. There, he'd packed his few belongings and sat in the armchair, thinking about how to manage this interview. He rejected various stratagems one by one. Jackie DeeTwo had been a cop's wife for forty years. He wasn't going to trick her.

Kane let the smile fade from his face and said, "I'm sorry I missed the funeral. I would like to have been there."

About halfway through Kane's prison sentence, Jackie Dee's heart had exploded, dropping him in the middle of the driveway he was shoveling. When Kane heard about it, he thought briefly of asking for permission to attend the funeral. But he never did. The prospect of standing among his former colleagues in handcuffs, a guard at his shoulder, just didn't appeal to him.

"It was a blessing, in a way," she said. "That's not the way I saw it then, but it seems like that to me now. He never was happy, really happy, after they made him stop being a detective. He hung in there, though. Jackie Dee was nothing if not stubborn. But when he hit mandatory retirement age and they forced him out, he didn't really know what to do with himself. He was drinking pretty heavy, and he was eating everything in sight. He weighed more than three hundred pounds when he died. You should have seen those pallbearers wrestle with his casket. I was sure he was there somewhere, watching and laughing."

The smile on her face faded quickly.

"It was like he was hoping for the heart attack," she said.

Kane shook his head.

"I doubt it," he said. "He would never have wanted to leave you."

"Charming twice," she said. "I must be in some kind of trouble."

Kane saw that as her offering an opening to talk about why he was there but he didn't want to hurry, to make this a cut-and-dried encounter. He knew that Jackie DeeTwo knew things he needed to know, and the longer they talked, the more likely she was to tell him. He could force her, he knew, but he had decided not to do that unless she made him.

"Tell me about yourself, Jackie," he said, sweeping an arm through the air. "About all this."

The woman leaned back in her chair.

"I go by 'Jacqueline' now," she said. "I always have, professionally." She seemed to think for a moment.

"There's not all that much to tell," she said. "Jackie Dee liked to have me at home, but after he got transferred back to patrol I wasn't sure how long he'd last in the job. And I was bored. So I promoted myself to a job in a real estate agency."

Here, the grin reappeared.

"In the heart of the real estate bust," she said. "Great timing. But I decided that if Jackie Dee could hang in there, so could I. By the time the market turned around, I knew pretty much everything there was to know about the real estate business in Anchorage. Turns out, I was good at sales and had a head for figures. I run this place now, and I really enjoy it."

"Not thinking about retiring soon?" Kane asked.

Jacqueline gave him a quizzical look.

"I'm training my replacement now," she said. "But it'll be a few years."

"And not remarried?" he asked.

The furrows in her brow deepened.

"Why pay for the cow when you can get the milk for free?" she said. "Or at least for a reasonable price that doesn't involve having somebody clutter up your private space."

She looked at her watch.

"Nik, I'd love to sit here answering impertinent personal questions all day," she said, "but I've got a big closing this morning that I've got to get ready for."

Kane nodded.

Here goes, he thought.

"I was wondering if you might know something about Danny Shirtleff, about what might have been behind his killing, that you haven't shared," he said.

Nothing in the woman's expression changed when he said that. She sat looking at him with a professional smile on her face.

"What do you mean, Nik?" she said after a few moments. "I hardly knew the man."

The answer neither angered Kane nor surprised him. In the years since the killing, Jacqueline DiSanto would have come to half believe the story she told the world.

"Are you sure, Jacqueline?" he said. "Anything you might remember could be important."

"I'm sure," she said quickly.

Too bad, Kane thought.

He got up from his chair, crossed the polished hardwood floor, and laid the folder in front of Jacqueline.

"Then maybe you could tell me about this," he said, returning to his chair.

The woman opened the folder and looked at the contents. Just the one print; the negative was in Kane's breast pocket. Jacqueline gave the photo a good look before her eyes returned to Kane's face.

"Goddamn it, it would have to be me," she said. Then she smiled. "I was a babe, though, wasn't I?"

Kane nodded.

"You were that," he said. "Still are, from where I sit."

Jacqueline looked steadily at Kane for a minute.

"You're not trying to get lucky here, are you, Nik?" she asked, smile still in place.

Kane laughed then, and, after a moment, Jacqueline joined in.

"I'm still healing, Jacqueline," he said. "I'm afraid I wouldn't be up to that."

The woman nodded, dropped her smile, and said, "Okay, suppose you tell me why I should answer some very personal questions for you. You're not with the department anymore."

"I am investigating Danny Shirtleff's murder," Kane said.

"I know," Jacqueline said. "I heard."

Kane cocked an eyebrow at her.

"We women still keep in touch. Some of us, anyway," she said. "We old-timers keep current with the gossip, and the younger wives get the benefit of our counsel. Being married to a cop—any cop— is no day at the beach. So many marriages end in divorce. I hear yours is."

Kane nodded.

"It is," he said, "although I think it's fair to say Laurie has had more provocation than most."

Kane looked down at his hands, and when he looked up he was wearing a smile of his own.

"I'm here out of respect, actually," he said, "for your husband and for you. You know there's no statute of limitations on murder, and if I hand this over to the department you'll be sitting in an interview room at the cop shop answering questions from strangers who lack the, shall we call it, discretion that I can exercise. So it's your choice, really."

The look Jacqueline gave him then was anything but friendly.

"You always were something of a bastard, Nik Kane," she said.

"True enough," Kane said. "But that doesn't give you the moral high ground here. You've withheld information that may be—probably is—material to the investigation of the murder of a police officer. Have you thought about how life would have been different, for Jackie Dee as well as everyone else, if you hadn't?"

Kane could see the woman turning pale as he spoke, but when he finished she said nothing. So he went on.

"I don't want to turn you over to Tom Jeffords's young, eager police officers, Jackie DeeTwo," he said, leaning hard on the nickname, "but I will if I have to."

Kane watched the woman's lips move. At first, he couldn't tell what she was saying. Then he realized she was cursing him.

"That's fucking low, Kane," she said, raising her voice. Kane could hear the steel in it. "Blaming me for what happened to Jackie Dee. I should throw your ass out of this office. I can't stand the sight of you, you bastard."

"If the shoe fits," he replied in a voice every bit as hard. "And if you throw me out, you'll be sitting in an interview room this very day. The safest way for you to deal with this is to talk to me."

She sat there staring at him, her lips moving but no sound coming out, her hands made into fists on her desk. Finally, her hands relaxed, and her shoulders slumped.

"How did you know?" she asked. "To look for the pictures, I mean?"

"I didn't," Kane said. "But when I started thinking about it, the idea of the photographs made sense. We knew Danny was seeing women in his place. There was a lot of forensic evidence of that. We knew he liked to take photographs. But we didn't find anything at his place, and the money threw us off. Jackie Dee was convinced that was the motive. So were all the brass. And I was, too. If I hadn't been so wet behind the ears, I might have known not to lock in on a motive so quick, but I didn't. I guess I needed to live more before I could understand what the evidence was trying to tell me all along."

Jacqueline DiSanto sat looking at him, nodded, and began speaking in the tone that Kane had heard a thousand times before, the tone people used to explain how they'd gotten to a place where they were talking to the police. Tired, resigned maybe, and soft, as if speaking softly would make whatever they'd done not as real, not as bad.

"You have to realize how it was," she said. "I knew that Danny was fooling around with some of the wives in the department and that there was a chance that one of the husbands killed him. But how could I tell anyone without everything coming out, I mean about Danny and me? I talked to some of the other wives about it, ones I knew Danny had been banging, but none of them wanted to talk, either. At one point, I decided to talk and damn the consequences, but Jackie Dee came home and told me about the money and how he thought that was why Danny was killed. And I thought, What if he's right and I'm wrong? Do I really want to break up my marriage, and lots of others, if I'm wrong about why he was killed?"

Kane waited for her to continue. When she didn't, he said, "How did the two of you get involved?"

Jacqueline gave a very unladylike snort.

"How do you think?" she said. "Danny was a cop. All you cops are hounds."

She was silent for a while, then began again.

"Danny wasn't interested in single women," she said. "He'd gotten into some kind of scrape with one down in Seattle and it scared him. He was, however, young and horny, so he settled on the idea of married women. He had to leave Seattle because he got caught doing the wife of one of his bosses there, but all that did was make him more careful."

She went silent again. Kane waited.

"You won't understand this," she said, shaking her head. "I don't think I do, really. We all knew Danny was a hound. But he was young, good-looking, polite, and persistent. And, somehow, he had a way of picking out a wife who was bored or restless or pissed off at her husband. Or all three. Then he'd cut you out of the herd some-how, and, the next thing you knew, you were looking at the ceiling of Danny's bedroom."

She shook her head and sighed.

"I loved Jackie Dee," she said. "Always. But sex for him was like storming a beach or something. All muscle and combat. That was nice a lot of the time, but a woman wants something different. Danny could do different. He could do anything you wanted him to do, without having to ask. The sex with him was great. Jeez, it makes me hot just thinking about it."

She stopped and cleared her throat.

"At my age," she said. "You'd think I'd know better. Anyway, his MO was to talk you into the sack, then give you a month or six weeks of pretty exclusive attention before dialing it back. I say 'pretty exclu-sive' because Danny was always ready to give a former lover a rematch when he could schedule it. But before you realized it, you weren't see-ing Danny so often and he was after someone else. I think he figured if he spread it around, got in and out quick, so to speak, no husband would get suspicious and no wife would get too clingy."

"Didn't that...calculated...an approach cause him problems?" Kane asked.

"You really don't know much about women, do you?" she asked. "Danny never lied about what he was doing and never made any promises. That was part of the appeal, actually. You knew Danny wasn't going to come knocking at your door some night, asking you to run off with him. He wasn't going to screw up your life."

"And what about the pictures?"

"Danny called them 'graduation photos.' He'd take them, and, the next time you were there, you'd lie in bed with him and pick the best one. He'd thumbtack it to the wall of his bedroom. After a while, he had quite a collection. He said it seemed to calm the new wives down, seeing the photos of the others. Made it seem less like infidelity and more like joining some girls' club."

"Didn't that worry you? That other women saw your photo there?"

"Not really. How could they tell anybody? I mean, what would they say? 'I just happened to be passing through Danny Shirtleff's bedroom and saw a naked picture of your wife on his wall'? No, actually, we *did* become kind of a club. It's like we all had this wonderful, dirty secret that only we shared."

Kane let the silence grow as he thought about his next question.

"Did you ever really graduate?" he asked. "I mean, did you stop having sex with Danny?"

Jacqueline shook her head.

"Some of us did, some didn't," she said. "Some of us were doing Danny until the day he died. Not very often, any of us, except for his new woman. But regular, if you know what I mean."

"Then you know who else he was seeing. I'm going to need names."

Jacqueline DiSanto looked down at her desk, and, when she looked up again, her jaw was set.

"I've been thinking about that since I saw your phone message," she said. "I'm not going to give you any names. I took a vow. We all did. I'm not breaking it."

"Jackie..." Kane began.

"No!" Jacqueline DiSanto said. "Here's the way it is. I've told you everything I know except the names. I don't know who killed Danny, and I don't have any information about who it might have been. I don't even know for sure it was somebody's husband. If you pass this along to that prick Tom Jeffords, I'll tell his people I don't know who else might have been involved with Danny. And I'll put the word out to the other wives to clam up, and they'll be safe."

"And if it was one of the wives?"

The question seemed to draw Jacqueline up short. She sat there looking at Kane, who could almost see the wheels turning in her head.

"No, it wasn't one of the wives," she said at last. "I'm not saying that there weren't women who would have dumped their husbands in a heartbeat to play house with him. Or who tried to talk him into just that. But he just wasn't interested, and, sooner or later, even the most persistent wife saw that. Danny was Danny."

She was quiet for a moment, then said, "And if he had gotten interested in one of the wives that way, then she would have had him all to herself. Not really a motive for her to kill him."

Kane let the conversation die, thinking about what he'd been told.

"Do you remember the last time you saw Danny?" he asked.

"I do," Jacqueline said. "It was about two weeks before his death. He was back in Anchorage for a visit and managed to squeeze me in."

"How did he seem?"

"Pretty much the same as always. Maybe a little preoccupied, but I thought that was just the job. He certainly concentrated when he needed to. We had fun."

Again, Kane was silent while he thought.

"The photos weren't on the wall when we got to Danny's place," he said. "Got any idea what happened to them?"

Jacqueline shook her head.

"Did I take them, do you mean?" she asked. "I did not. And I don't know what else might have happened to them. I was just grateful they weren't there. Very grateful. And you know what they say about looking a gift horse in the mouth."

Kane couldn't think of anything else to ask. He got to his feet, walked to the desk, and reached for the photo.

"Can I keep this?" Jacqueline asked.

"Sure," Kane said. "Why not? I've still got the negative."

"No chance you'd give that to me, is there?" she asked.

Kane just shook his head, turned, and walked toward the door of the office.

"You realize, don't you, Nik," Jacqueline said, "that if you men had just paid more attention to your wives, this might not have happened? And if it had anyway, you might have solved this case twenty years ago?"

There are no good answers to those questions, Kane thought, so he kept walking.

"What we did wasn't so wrong," she said as he opened the door.

He stopped then, turning to face her.

"What you did is your business," he said. "What the other wives did is their business. I don't think it was right to do it, or that doing it was just some little thing, but it's not my problem. I'm pretty sure now that somebody murdered Danny Shirtleff because of it, though, and that is my problem."

He had the door open when she said, "You know, it might be better for everybody if you just forgot about this, Nik."

Too late for that, he thought, and closed the door behind him.

twenty-eight

It's a poor sort of memory that only works backward.

—Lewis Carroll

## JUNE 2007

"Find out anything?" Winthrop asked as Kane got back into the car.

"Yes, I did," Kane said. "It confirms what I was beginning to suspect, twenty years too late."

"So we going to nab a killer now?" Winthrop said. "If we are, I want to stop off and put on my snap-brim hat."

"Been watching old movies?" Kane asked.

"You bet," Winthrop said. "Those things are great. Humphrey Bogart. Robert Mitchum. Fred MacMurray. Drinking. Smoking. Nailing loose women. If more of you white guys were like them, the world would be a lot more interesting."

Kane ran a hand over his face. Seeing Jackie DeeTwo had brought back a lot of memories and opened up some unsettling possibilities. He needed to think things through, but he had another errand first.

"We're taking a slight detour," he said, and gave Winthrop an address on the Hillside. The big man slid the Caddy into gear, and they glided away toward the mountains.

The address belonged to a sprawling McMansion on the eastern shore of Skeleton Lake. A tall, businesslike fence ran around the house and a sizeable chunk of property, starting and ending at the lake. Four other properties, each with a different style of big, fenced home, sat at intervals around the lake. A big Cape Cod occupied what looked to Kane like the spot where Danny Shirtleff's body had been found.

"Money," Winthrop said as he stopped the Caddy next to a speaker at the front gate of their destination.

"You know these places?" Kane asked.

"The old man did," Winthrop said. "I took him here more than once, usually when he was hatching some business scheme. He told me the people who live here weren't too picky about how they made their money."

"That's true of this one," Kane said. "Tell them it's Nik Kane. I called and made an appointment."

Winthrop palavered with the squawk box and the big gates swung open. He drove the Caddy along the circular drive. The lawn was even and green as far as the eye could see, rich with beds of dazzling flowers and small trees that were not quite fully leafed out. Winthrop stopped the Caddy in front of a tall section of the house with a slanting roof and two big doors that looked like they might be sheathed in copper. The doors were flanked by sheets of smoky glass and the glass by carved wooden panels. A pair of surveillance cameras that hung from the panels swung slowly back and forth.

"You going to need me in there?" Winthrop asked.

"I hope not," Kane said, "but come along, anyway."

Winthrop shut off the engine, and the two of them got out of the car and walked to the front door. As Winthrop raised a fist to knock, one of the copperish doors opened.

The guy standing at the door looked like your typical butler, if

your typical butler moonlighted in the World Wrestling Federa-
tion. His thick body was covered with designer gym clothes topped
with a checked sport coat that he didn't even bother to keep but-
toned over a big handgun, a .357 or .44. His features were clustered
in the middle of a big head topped with a mullet haircut: thick lips,
a nose that had been broken more than once, and a cauliflower left
ear. He looked like a Mr. Potato Head who'd come up the hard way.
The little smile he had on his face froze when he saw Winthrop, and
he took a quick step back. Winthrop brushed past him, followed by
Kane.

"Hey," the guy said.

A pair of floor-to-ceiling doors opened on either side of an entry
hall the size of a tennis court. An ornate staircase curled upward from
the far end of the hall. Kane started for the staircase. The door opener
hustled around to block his path.

"That way," he said, pointing to one of the set of doors.

It opened onto a room that contained half a dozen couches, twice
that many armchairs, a baker's dozen tables, a large globe, what
looked like an honest-to-God elephant's foot umbrella stand, and
several Persian carpets. A barrage of oil paintings in gilt frames hung
on the walls. Three men stood in front of a fireplace Winthrop could
easily have parked the Caddy in, thick tumblers of cut glass gripped in
their fists. One of them detached himself from the group and strode
over to Kane, juggling his glass so that he could thrust his right hand
at his visitor.

"Mr. Kane?" he said in a voice plenty big enough for the room.
"I'm James Waldo, Mr. McCanta's attorney."

Waldo was probably Kane's age, with central-casting white hair
and a face that looked like it had been pickled in very good scotch.

Kane stopped and looked at the man's hand until he let it drop to
his side.

"Attorney?" Kane said. "This is a social call."

"That's what I told them," said another of the men, a slight, sandy-haired young man of thirtysomething with a hairline in full retreat. "That you said my uncle and your mother were friends back in the day."

"Then that makes you a McCanta," Kane said. "Casey, right?"

He looked at the third man. Like the lawyer, he was dressed in a suit. Unlike the lawyer, he didn't look that comfortable in it. He was big but not fat, with the complexion and eyes of a man who slept in a coffin during daylight.

"And you are?" Kane said.

The man flicked a hand in front of his face like he was shooing away a fly.

"I am someone whose name doesn't matter," the man said. "I'm an associate of Mr. McCanta's."

"The senior Mr. McCanta?" Kane said.

The question seemed to stump the man for a moment.

"Yeah, yeah," he said. "The senior Mr. McCanta. Pat."

Kane looked at the three men. Out of the corner of his eye, he could see the guy who'd answered the door, loitering at the side of the room.

"This is quite a congregation to greet a guy who is just stopping by to pay his respects," Kane said. "What's the deal?"

The three men looked at one another, then at Kane.

"Mr. McCanta had for many years an active part in the business of Anchorage," the lawyer began, as if he were practicing a eulogy. "He did very well financially. He also led an active social life, a *very* active social life. Since word of his . . . illness . . . has gotten out, several people have attempted to meet with Mr. McCanta to press claims to some part of his estate. He is in no condition to deal with such claims, and since his nephew here found him trying to write rather a large check to a young woman who was almost certainly born in Russia, a place Mr. McCanta has never visited, we have found it wise to be present when he has social visitors. I represent the estate. Young Mr. McCanta here is, as far as we know, the heir. And Mr.... Well, this gentleman represents Mr. McCanta's business associates, who have a legitimate interest in who will take over Mr. McCanta's many and varied businesses."

Kane looked at the three men, then at Winthrop.

"What do you think of that?" he asked.

"I think if he had that printed on a card, it'd save his vocal cords," Winthrop said.

"True," Kane said. "But don't you think he likes to hear himself talk?"

"Please," the lawyer said, "there's no need to be insulting."

Kane sighed and shook his head.

"This could have been so simple," he said.

He looked at the nameless man and said, "How many guys do you have in the room on the other side of the entry?"

The nameless man said nothing.

Casey McCanta said, "How did...?"

The lawyer said, "What makes you think there are other people here?"

Kane laughed at that. A reckless feeling had come over him, even though he knew he wasn't in any physical condition to do much about it.

"A cheap piece of goods like that," he said, nodding at the nameless man, "doesn't travel without a bunch of guns to make him feel like a big man."

The nameless man took a step in Kane's direction. So did Mr. Potato Head. Winthrop cleared his throat, and they both stopped moving.

"In the normal course of events," Kane continued, "I'd just go up and see the old man and tell Winthrop here to shoot whoever tried to stop me. But if there are too many of you, all the bodies won't fit in the trunk of the car."

The lawyer started to say something, but Kane held up a hand.

"So we'll have to do this your way," he said. "You being a lawyer, I imagine you've got some complicated document that I have to sign saying I've got no claim on the estate, right?"

Casey McCanta said, "How did...?"

The lawyer just nodded.

"Well, trot it out," Kane said.

The lawyer left the room. Kane sat in one of the armchairs.

"So when you heard about your uncle and decided to try to get your hands on his money, did you imagine what you'd be getting into?" he asked the younger McCanta pleasantly.

Nobody said anything after that. The lawyer returned with a multipage document and set it on the table nearest Kane.

"Show me where to sign," Kane said.

"Aren't you going to read it first?" the lawyer asked.

"You mean, I can't trust you?" Kane asked.

He spent the next couple of minutes signing and initialing where the lawyer pointed. When Kane was finished, the lawyer picked up the document and left the room. When he returned, he said, "You can see Mr. McCanta now. I'll take you up."

Kane looked at Winthrop.

"Why don't you stay here and discuss interior decorating with these people?" he said.

"I will," Winthrop said. He swept an arm around the room. "I can learn a lot here."

Kane got to his feet. He patted his breast pocket and heard the muffled clink of the contents of the envelope he carried there.

"You know, we're only putting up with you 'cause you're connected

with the cops," the nameless man said. "If you wasn't, maybe you and
your pet Indian'd be in the trunk of a car."

Kane looked at Winthrop.

"Pet Indian," he said.

*"Gussiks,"* Winthrop said. "What can you do?"

Kane followed the lawyer out of the room and up the staircase.

"What's wrong with McCanta?" he asked as they climbed.

"What isn't?" the lawyer said. "He's lived ninety hard years."

"Is he rational?" Kane asked.

"Sometimes," the lawyer replied. "He'll go whole days where he
makes perfect sense. It's why his, ah, associates haven't replaced him
yet. He still knows things they need to know. Then there are the days
when he just speaks gibberish. And the days where he switches from
one to the other without warning."

"What kind of day is it today?" Kane asked as they walked along
a hall.

"I guess you'll find out," the lawyer said.

They entered a big, dark bedroom.

"I'll leave you alone," the lawyer said.

"Why not?" Kane replied. "I'm sure you've got the room bugged."

The lawyer left. Kane looked around the room. The contrast
between it and the room he'd just left couldn't have been starker. An
iron cot, a straight-backed wooden chair, a crude bedside table, and
a cheap reproduction of a painting of the Blessed Virgin. That was it
for furnishings. They looked like doll furniture in the big room.

Like walking out of a Persian bordello and into a monastery, Kane
thought.

He walked over and sat in the chair. The cot held an old man
barely recognizable as Pat McCanta. Age and disease had shrunken
him and robbed him of most of his hair, but the dark eyes he turned
to Kane were still bright.

"Do I know you?" he asked.

"We've met before," Kane said. "I'm Nik Kane."

"They think they're going to get my money, you know," the old man said. "But I'll show them. I'm taking it with me."

He cackled, then started coughing. Kane stood and walked around the cot, picked up a metal pitcher from the table and poured some water into a glass. He carried the glass to the bed, lifted the old man's head, and helped him take a drink.

"Thanks," the old man said.

Kane set the glass down and resumed his seat.

"Can you really take it with you?" he asked.

The old man cackled again, this time without coughing.

"No, of course not, you idiot," he said. "But I'm giving all my money to the church. They'll get it to me. They've got connections, you know. If you've got the right connections, you can do anything."

"Like make a harmless drunk disappear?" Kane said.

The old man peered at Kane's face.

"Hey, I know you," he said. "You're that Kane kid. Didn't recognize you at first because you look like shit. What happened?"

"Woman shot me," Kane said.

The old man nodded his head vigorously.

"I had that happen once," he said. "Hurt like hell. I got a scar somewhere I could show you. I got lots of scars. They been cutting off pieces of me for a long time now. Here's all the surgeries they've done."

He launched into a litany of words ending in "-ectomy" and "-scopy" that Kane didn't even try to keep track of. He'd been afraid he wouldn't be able to get the old man to talk. Clearly, that wasn't going to be a problem.

The old man ran out of medical terms, and said brightly, "Do I know you? You look like somebody I knew once. Did you work for me?"

"I'm Cecelia Kane's son," Kane said.

The name made the old man smile.

"Cecelia Kane," he said. "What a piece. I was in love with her once, you know. Might have married her, if it wasn't for the church. Damn priests anyway, with their rules."

He frowned.

"But then bad things happened, and we really couldn't be together anymore. She said people would talk. I had to go to Mars, and, well, that was that. I was a long time on that rocket ship, and when I got off the air and the sand and everything was red. People, too. Damnedest thing you ever saw."

He peered again at Kane.

"Do I know you?" he asked. "You an' me used to play sandlot in Stockton, didn't we?"

"I'm Cecelia Kane's son," Kane said again. "Did you know her in Stockton?"

"Know her?" the old man said. "I courted her there."

McCanta stopped and snorted.

"Listen to me," he said. " 'Courted.' Us poor white trash didn't court. I took her to the park and pumped her until she couldn't stand up. It was fun. But then I got sent away, and, when I come back, she was gone. I heard later she was in the space program or something."

"She was married, wasn't she?" Kane asked.

"Who?" the old man said. "Who was married? Not me. Nope. After they done the experiments, I couldn't marry. Know what they did to me? I'll tell you."

And he was off on his litany of surgeries again. When he finished, Kane said, "We were talking about Cecelia Kane."

"Cecelia Kane?" the old man said. "Who is that? I never knew any Cecelia Kane. I knew a Katie Kelly once, back in Stockton. What a sweet piece. I used to take her to the park and pump her until she couldn't stand up."

Kane looked around the room.

Any minute now, Alice is going to show up, looking for the way to get back to the other side of the looking glass.

"No," he said in a firm tone. "We're not taking about Kate. We're talking about Cecelia."

The old man nodded vigorously again.

"She told me once, she said, 'I decided you weren't going to amount to much, but I was wrong,'" the old man said. He lowered his voice. "Once you're an astronaut, the women are all over you."

"What about her husband, Teddy?" Kane asked.

The old man rolled his head around on his pillow.

"She didn't like Teddy anymore," he said. "She didn't want to have any more of his kids. She wanted to have my kids."

"Did she?" Kane asked.

"I just said so, didn't I?" the old man said.

"No. I mean, did she have your kids?" Kane said.

"Who?" the old man asked.

"Cecelia Kane," Kane said.

"Cecelia who?" the old man said. "I'm not talking about anybody named Cecelia. I'm talking about Champagne."

"Who is Champagne?" Kane asked.

"Champagne isn't a who," the old man said. "It's something you drink."

He rolled his head around on the pillow some more and his arms twitched under the thin wool blanket that covered him.

"Go away now," he said. "I need to pray."

"I'm asking you about Cecelia Kane," Kane said.

"Our Father, who art in heaven..." the old man said.

"About her husband, Teddy Kane."

"...hallowed be thy name, thy kingdom come..."

"About what happened to Teddy Kane."

"...thy will be done, on earth as it is in heaven..."

"I checked the ownership of this property," Kane said, speaking over the old man's droning. "You bought an old homestead in the mid-fifties. A hundred and forty acres, including the ground this house sits on and the lake. You developed some of it, held on to some, and sold some off to other people, developers and so on. Must have made some money off of it."

"Hail Mary, full of grace..." the old man said.

"I guess you didn't keep such good track of what you did up here, or where you did it, because sometime in the late seventies, a guy using a backhoe to dig a foundation found pieces of a skeleton," Kane said. "He didn't notice right away, so they never found parts of it. The skull, for instance. So they couldn't identify the body. They found enough of the pelvis to be able to tell it was a man's body, but that was it. The parts they did find had either been in the ground a long time or the body had been burned before being buried. They couldn't really tell which. With what they had, they couldn't establish a cause of death, either."

"Holy Mary, Mother of God..." the old man said.

Kane reached into his breast pocket and took out the envelope.

"They still have the remains they could find in the police evidence room," Kane said. "Not much to look at, and nothing of much help identifying the body, except maybe these."

He poured the contents into his palm and held them in front of the old man's eyes. They were blackened and misshapen, but a couple still showed some brass finish, and the one least changed by heat showed the outline of a ship's anchor and rope.

The old man stopped praying, stopped breathing even, and lay stalk still.

"They're buttons," Kane said. "The sort of buttons you'd find on a blazer."

The old man closed his eyes.

"Our Father," he said. "Our Father...Oh, Teddy, I let you win. Why couldn't you do the smart thing for once?"

Then he opened his eyes, peered at Kane, and said, "Do I know you?"

twenty-nine

Wish I didn't know now what I didn't know then.

—Bob Seger

## JUNE 2007

The sunlight that woke Kane was impossibly bright. He didn't know where he was for a moment, then remembered. He got out of bed, pulled on the khaki shorts he'd bought at the Honolulu airport, and walked across the hotel room to the big window.

Below him, people frolicked in a swimming pool shaped like a lagoon or lay in the chaise lounges that surrounded it. Farther out, the water they splashed and surfed in was the neon blue of the tropical ocean, and the chairs were folding canvas.

Behind Kane, the telephone rang.

"Mr. Kane? Nik?" Yolanda's voice said. "Are you awake? It is time for breakfast."

"Give me fifteen minutes," Kane said. He hung up and got into the shower.

Yolanda hadn't wanted to accompany him when he'd called her after his meeting with Jacqueline DiSanto.

"I would have to make arrangements," she said. "If you need a nurse, there are many in Anchorage."

"I don't need a nurse," Kane said. "I need a friend."

There was silence at her end of the line.

"If that is the case," she said, "let us discuss our travel plans."

A fourteen-hour day had carried Kane from Anchorage to Juneau, where Yolanda joined him, then to Seattle, Honolulu, and Kauai. Kane had picked up a rental car and driven them to the Hyatt on the southern shore of the island. He'd gone to sleep the minute his head hit the pillow and had no real idea what time it was.

He emerged from the shower, toweled off, and dressed in the shorts, a University of Hawaii T-shirt, and flip-flops. The clock beside his bed said it was just after eleven.

The knock at the door was both Yolanda and the room service she'd ordered, and, in a few minutes, they were sitting at the table, looking out at the scene below and eating breakfast.

"I'm sorry to make you wait so long for breakfast," Kane said.

"I did not wait," Yolanda said. "I had a wonderful swim in the ocean this morning, then some toast and fruit. The fruit here is wonderful."

Kane used his coffee cup to cover a smile.

Maybe this is why I brought her, he thought. She makes me smile.

"Why are we here, Mr. Kane?" Yolanda asked, as if reading his thoughts.

"I'm here to see a man," Kane said. "And you're here...I don't really know why you're here."

Yolanda laughed at his answer.

"I am certain the reason will emerge," she said. "And, in the meantime, I certainly cannot complain. It is so beautiful here. Will we be going to visit this man soon? The one you are here to see?"

"We won't be going at all," Kane said. "I will."

He handed her a pair of envelopes.

"If I am not back by dinnertime, put this envelope in the mail," he said. "And if anyone comes asking for me, tell them that you mailed something for me and that's all you know. In the other envelope are your airline ticket home and some money for the bills here."

Yolanda took the envelopes and set them on the table.

"I will not do this," she said. "If you are going to do something dangerous, I am sure you need the authorities to go with you."

"Please, Yolanda, don't fight me on this," Kane said. "This is something I have to do by myself, for reasons I can't tell you."

Yolanda smiled and got to her feet, leaving the envelopes on the table.

"We will talk of this again," she said. "No one does anything in the heat of the day in the tropics. I think I will go and lie by the pool with a book."

Kane sat looking out the window after she left.

This place is too beautiful, he thought. I don't see how anyone gets anything done here.

Watching the people below, he had no problem picking out Yolanda. She walked like a queen through the crowd, found a chaise in the shade, and opened her book. When Kane saw she was settled, he got to his feet, picked up the envelopes and his sunglasses, and left the room. He stopped at Yolanda's door and knelt to slide the envelopes under it. The one containing the money wouldn't fit, so he left it for her at the front desk instead.

He walked along a paved path to the parking lot, pausing to admire a black swan that swam in a small pool bright with koi. Then he got in his car, took his directions out of his pocket, and, following them, left the lot and drove down the road. A couple of turns, a few speed bumps, and a little up and down, and he was turning into a small condo development called Poipu Shores.

Kane parked his car outside the office and walked down the driveway toward the condos, which were housed in three off-white buildings along the shoreline. The building he was looking for looked like it might once have been a hotel, with doors on each floor opening onto a breezeway. He walked down a flight of stairs to the ground floor, then past a few doors until he found the one he wanted.

Should I do this? he thought. Will it do anyone any good after all these years? This place is so beautiful. Should I really be dragging this old trouble into it?

He stood there lost in thought for a while, then squared his shoulders and knocked. Sweat ran down his back, and he could hear the faint cries and splashing of children in a swimming pool.

The man who opened the door was thinner than Kane remembered. His face was lined and drawn, his once-red hair now white. His blue eyes had lost their sparkle, and the hand that rested on the door shook slightly. The clothes he wore looked like they'd been slept in more than once.

"Nik Kane," he said. "I thought when someone came it would be you."

"Hello, Fireball," Kane said. "Mind if I come in?"

The man stood aside to let Kane enter. A bedroom opened off a short hall, a small bathroom opposite. Then he was in a single room divided by a counter into a pocket-sized kitchen and a larger living room. He could see another bedroom through a door. One wall of the living room was covered in mirrored glass. The room ended in sliding-glass doors and louvered windows. Through the doors, he could see a small concrete patio, green lawn, a hedge of some sort, and the ocean. Ceiling fans stirred the warm air.

"I was just lying down for a bit, Nik," Fireball Roberts said. "The heat takes it out of me. Would you like something to drink?"

"Water would be fine, thanks," Kane said. He walked to the sliding doors and looked out at the ocean. A catamaran was sailing past, her decks jammed with people in swimsuits.

"Here you go," Roberts said, handing Kane a glass of water. "Would you like to sit on the lanai?"

"Sure," Kane said.

Roberts slid the glass door open, and the two of them sat at a glass-topped table that was shielded from the neighbors by plantings. Kane helped the other man put up a big umbrella over the table, and the two of them sat in the shade, sipping from their glasses. Roberts was drinking something more than water.

"Jamie loved the ocean," he said. "I rented a helicopter and scattered her ashes day before yesterday. I had him fly a ways out. I didn't want the currents to bring the ashes back to the island. I don't like the idea of people walking on her ashes."

They sat in silence for a while longer. Kane wondered what it would be like to be in the ocean with no land in sight, nothing but you and the fish. He wasn't much of a swimmer, and, despite the heat, the idea sent cold creeping along his spine.

"I guess you know why I'm here," Kane said.

"I do," Roberts said.

The door of a nearby condo slid open and a woman walked out onto the lawn. She was young and blond and wore a tiny bikini and high-heeled sandals. The two men sat in silence, watching her. She stood looking at the ocean, then turned, reaching down to adjust the bottom of her bikini. For a moment, a downy growth of pubic hair was clearly visible. Roberts looked at Kane and smiled. The woman caught sight of the two of them.

"Oh, I'm sorry," she said. "I didn't know anyone was here."

She walked quickly back into the building.

"Great scenery you've got here," Kane said.

"It's a rental, next door," Roberts said. "I've never seen that woman before, and, in a week, it'll be a couple of lesbians or a family of four."

"Do you want to tell me what happened?" Kane asked.

Roberts was silent for so long that Kane was beginning to think he hadn't heard the question.

"She died eleven days ago," Roberts said. "Cancer. It wasn't fast and it wasn't pretty."

"I'm sorry to hear that," Kane said.

"You shouldn't be," Roberts said. "If you'd come for me when she was still alive, I would have killed you. Just to have one more day with her."

He reached behind his back and came up with a small automatic that he pointed at Kane.

"If you shoot me, Fireball," Kane said, "you'll be doing me a favor. You're not the only one who's had it rough lately."

"Huh?" Roberts said, looking down at the automatic as if wondering how it had gotten there. "Oh, I'm not going to shoot you."

He set the automatic down on the table, picked up his glass and drank.

"It's just hard to sit in a chair with that thing in the small of my back," he said.

He pushed the weapon across to Kane.

"You can have this if you want," he said. "I've got no use for it now."

Kane picked up the automatic, examined it, and put it into the pocket of his shorts.

"Beretta model M1934," he said.

Roberts nodded.

"That's right," he said. "My dad brought back two of them from the war. Got one in North Africa and the other in Italy. He brought back some medals, too, but he was always prouder of the Berettas. 'They give you the medals,' he told me, 'but I took the guns the old-fashioned way.'"

"You used the other one to kill Danny Shirtleff," Kane said.

Roberts nodded again.

"Yeah," he said, "I really hated to do that. But I didn't have any other choice."

Kane sat and waited. A small gray-and-white bird with a vivid red head landed on the table and hopped up to him, cocking its head. Kane looked at the bird, then at Roberts.

"Jamie used to feed him," he said. "She said that, with the red head and all, it reminded her of me when we were younger. This bird got so bold, it would sit right in her hand and eat. He still comes around, hoping to see her, I guess. Sometimes, at night, I hear this really sad singing and I think it's him."

"Look, Fireball," Kane said, "if you don't want to talk about what happened..."

"Yes, I do," Roberts said. "It's just that Jamie's so fresh in my mind. I haven't changed the bed because I can still smell her on the sheets. I'm wearing these clothes because they're the last clothes I held her in. We had her all set up in the bedroom and hospice people would come. They were great, those women. A great help. She called my name, and I was wearing these clothes and I held her and she died."

Kane watched another, smaller boat pass. Its stern rail was lined with tanks.

Must be a dive boat, he thought.

When Roberts stopped crying, he said, "I'm sorry about that, Nik. I'll do better."

"Don't worry about it, Fireball," Kane said. "Take your time."

When Roberts had his breathing under control, he said, "I've written all this down, at least an official version of it. You can take it with you when you go. But I'd like to talk about it, if that's okay."

"Sure, Fireball," Kane said. "Sure."

"I didn't know what Danny was doing," Roberts began. "About the women, I mean. I just knew that Jamie started behaving in a peculiar way, and it made me suspicious. Maybe if I thought she loved me, I would have been more relaxed. I mean, she was grateful to me and could be pleasant, even fun, to be with. But I'd catch her looking at me sometimes and there'd be nothing in her eyes. Absolutely nothing. For a while I thought it was a reaction to, well, you know, the stuff that happened to her when she was younger. Maybe it was, I don't know. I do know that a lot of the time it was like she was going through the motions.

"Then, one day, maybe six weeks before I killed Danny, she just seemed happier. I thought maybe time was helping. She'd been out of that place for six or seven years, and I thought, well, time heals all wounds."

He stopped talking and shook his head.

"But you know how it is when you're a cop," he said. "You notice things, even when you don't know you're noticing them. I'd come home from a shift and she wouldn't be there. She'd come in a few minutes later, out of breath and apologizing for being late. Or I'd come home and find her in the shower. And, one day when she was out, I woke up early and decided to do the laundry, to help her out a little, and I found this very sexy underwear at the bottom of her laundry hamper.

"That told me something. I put it right back and started following her. I'd tell her some story about having to double-shift and I'd borrow somebody's car and I'd sit around the corner from my own house, watching."

Again he stopped talking, and they both sat staring at the sea. A slight wind had come up, and Kane could feel it cooling him through his sweat-soaked T-shirt.

"It didn't take long. She got into her car and drove over to this house on the eastside. I didn't know whose it was until Danny came to the door. I'd never been to his house. I'd known the guy—what?— three, four years, and he'd never invited me to his house. That should have told me something. They put their arms around each other and he kissed her, and they went inside and closed the door."

Again, Kane waited while Roberts pulled himself together.

"I didn't lose my temper. Amazing, isn't it? Me, I find out that my wife is screwing around and I don't lose my temper. What are the odds? If I had, maybe things would have gone better. Maybe I would have gone up to the door and punched Danny in the nose and yelled at Jamie and, somehow, things would have turned out okay. But I didn't. I drove back and dropped off the car and walked to a bar and sat there, drinking ginger ale and thinking.

"I didn't say anything about it to Jamie when I saw her again. And I quit following her. I staked out Danny instead. Jamie came to his house regularly, but other women, other wives, showed up, too, once in a while. That Danny was a busy boy. There were, I don't know, three or four women at his place in the two weeks I watched it.

"Then, once, when Jamie was there, I saw flashes in the house. I could see them leaking out around the curtains. I couldn't figure out what they were until I remembered that Danny was a shutterbug. So I figured he was taking pictures in there. I could imagine what kind.

"Those other women visiting made me feel better. If Danny was doing that, then he and Jamie weren't serious. When Danny went off on that job in Kodiak, I figured they'd cool down a little. I didn't know what to do, exactly, about Jamie still seeing him, even as occasionally as the other women. But my main concern was losing her."

He looked at Kane, who could see the tears lurking in his eyes, blurring but not hiding the pain there.

"Jamie was the best thing that ever happened to me," Roberts said. "I mean, what was I? A plain-looking guy, a mediocre cop who'd end up with a pension and a cheap gold watch. With Jamie, there were a lot more possibilities, a lot more reasons to be someone better than I really was. I couldn't lose her.

"So when Danny called me up that day and told me he was just back from Kodiak and wanted to meet and talk, it was like I already knew what I was going to do. I told him that I had to go on shift, that we'd have to meet later, during my dinner break. I suggested Skeleton Lake because I knew it would be pretty private, the kids wouldn't show up until later. And I took one of my father's guns with me. I didn't even think about it really. I just took it. I got there first, and, when Danny pulled in, I told him to get into the unit so I could monitor the radio.

"He told me the whole story. About his womanizing. About running into Jamie one day and having coffee with her. About how he'd always liked her but never did anything about it because she seemed so unapproachable. About how they hit it off that time and made another coffee date, and one thing led to another, and he was tired of all the running around and thought he should settle down, and it was a good thing because he figured out over in Kodiak that he was in love with Jamie. He was going to quit all the other women and ask her to live with him, to marry him."

Roberts was into the story now, staring straight ahead, his drink on the table untouched. Kane was afraid to move and maybe interrupt the flow of words.

"He just talked and talked, like a kid with a great new toy. By the time he finished, I could hardly hear him for the buzzing in my ears. I started asking questions, more like a reflex than anything else. Had he told Jamie? Had he told anyone else? Was he sure? What did he think Jamie would say?

"All the answers he gave were the right ones. He'd asked Jamie to come and live with him, but she'd said she needed to think about it. He hadn't told anyone else. He was sure. By the time he was finished, he was looking at me kind of funny. I figured he was wondering why I wasn't trying to talk him out of it, so I said some bullshit about how I wanted Jamie, too, and that I'd fight for her, and may the best man win. That seemed to satisfy him. He got out of the unit and walked toward that fancy car of his, and I realized right then that I knew she'd go with him and I knew I couldn't let that happen. So I got out of the car and walked toward him, and when he had one foot in the car I called his name, and when he turned I brought up my father's gun, which was right there in my hand somehow, and I shot him. Bang. Bang. Bang."

In the ocean in front of the condo, a dolphin leaped from the water, spun completely around, and fell back with a splash. Near it, Kane could see fins rising and falling in the water. Another dolphin leaped. Then another. Roberts seemed not to notice.

"I looked all around, but you know how that place was, pretty deserted. I figured nobody could hear the shots, so I walked closer and emptied the gun into the car, trying to make it seem like maybe the killer wasn't such a good shot. I wiped the gun down and dropped it, and checked Danny. He was dead. I backed out of there, messing up my footprints along the way. I was going to wait a few minutes and call it in, and make up some story about finding the body. Then I remembered the photographs. I was sure he had some of Jamie and I couldn't leave them there like a finger pointing at me. I hadn't just killed a fellow officer to get sent to prison. I'd killed him to keep Jamie. So I took Danny's keys and drove as fast as I could to his place, and searched and found the file of photos—they were labeled 'Nudes'—and grabbed it. I took the ones on the wall of his bedroom, too. I was going to head straight back to the scene but I decided it'd be better to wait, so I just resumed my patrol. It was my patrol area, so if someone found the body I'd be the first one to the scene.

"My nerve broke, finally. I thought I should go back to the scene and replace the keys. But my luck held, and those kids flagged me and we went back to the scene together, and, while I pretended to examine the scene, I put the keys back. Then I sent out an 'officer down' call because I knew it would bring everyone, and the messier the crime scene, the better."

Roberts stopped talking, and both men sat there. The dolphins had moved on, but out on the water Kane could see a guy who seemed to be standing on a surfboard and paddling with a long paddle. It didn't look like a very efficient way to travel.

"What about the money?" Kane asked.

Roberts looked at Kane, then dropped his eyes.

"The money was right there on the floorboards of Danny's car, in this blue gym bag," Roberts said. "I saw it when I was getting the keys. You know I'm no thief, Nik, but I figured if the money disappeared it'd confuse things some more. I guess it did that, didn't it?"

Kane nodded.

"It certainly did," he said. "It's one of the things that kept me from suspecting you in the first place. I'd seen the way you treated other people's money. I could imagine you getting pissed off and shooting Danny but not stealing the money. Where is it now?"

"I hid it in a tree near the lake there," Roberts said. "Retrieved it a couple of days later. I knew it was dangerous to have around, but it would have been more dangerous if it'd been found. You'd have started looking for another motive right away. So I hid it behind some boxes in my garage. Jamie never went out there. The next summer, I put in a little concrete patio in the back of my house. The money's under that concrete, if it hasn't rotted away."

"You never thought about spending it?"

Roberts shook his head.

"It wasn't mine," he said. "And it was blood money."

Kane thought about the money and decided he didn't really care if it still existed. He'd tell Jeffords about it and let it be the chief's problem. He had enough of his own.

"I didn't really expect to get away with it," Roberts said. "But there wasn't much evidence left intact by the time you and Jackie Dee got there, and then the money threw everybody off. It was mostly just luck."

"Did it work?" Kane asked. "Killing Danny, I mean? Did you get what you wanted?"

Roberts seemed to think about the question.

"Yes," he said. "I got to keep Jamie. I'm not sure what she thought about Danny's killing. For a while I think she suspected me, but she never said anything, so maybe not. We were happy enough, even though I was never sure she was really in love with me."

"Maybe you loved her enough for the both of you," Kane said.

"Does it work like that, Nik?" Roberts asked.

"How the hell would I know?" Kane said.

They were silent again. It was like neither of them wanted to do what came next. Finally, Roberts said, "Here's what I would like to have happen, Nik. I've got some things to give you, a handwritten confession and Danny's photos. I kept them all these years. I don't know why. I burned Jamie's last week, I thought it would be a violation of her memory to leave them. But the rest are there. In return, I'd like you to let me go for one last swim out there."

He waved an arm at the ocean.

"Is that what you really want to do, Fireball?" Kane asked.

"Instead of die in prison, you mean?" Roberts asked with a thin smile. "My life ended when Jamie died. The only reason I'm still breathing was trying to figure out how to wrap this up. You showing up helps with that. Just let me do the rest of it. Not having a trial will be good for everybody."

Kane nodded. He was right. Jeffords would be really happy if there was no trial. And he'd like having proof that it wasn't somebody under his command who had killed Danny Shirtleff.

"Okay, Fireball," Kane said, getting to his feet. He followed Roberts back into the condo, where Roberts handed him two envelopes.

"Confession in the small one," Roberts said. "Photos in the big one."

As they walked to the door, Roberts said, "The story I told in writing doesn't say anything about the photos, in case you want to just destroy them."

He opened the door and stuck out his hand.

"Thanks for letting me do this my way, Nik," he said.

Kane took his hand. He could feel it trembling in his grasp. He shook it gently and released it.

"Good luck, Fireball," he said.

Kane got into his rental car and went back to the hotel, threw the envelopes on the bed, and lay down to think. Instead, he fell asleep. When he awoke, the sunlight was softer, and the clock read five-thirty. He picked up the telephone and called Yolanda's room.

"Would you like to eat some dinner?" he asked.

"I am just back from the pool," she said. "I must get ready."

An hour later, they drove to a small shopping center and got a table at a place called Roy's. When their dinners arrived, Kane just picked at his.

"Are you not hungry?" Yolanda asked.

He shrugged.

"Is it the man you must see?" she asked. "Are you worried?"

"No," Kane said. "I've done what I came to do."

"Already?" Yolanda said. Then her face softened into a smile. "You are a naughty boy, and a bad patient."

Something about her tone and the smile on her face made Kane feel better.

They spent the next couple of days doing not much of anything. Kane put on a swimsuit and swam slowly around the lagoon, then slept next to the pool, ignoring the people who stared at his scars. He felt like he could have slept the clock around, except that Yolanda would wake him and make him eat.

Over breakfast on the third morning, he read about Fireball's death in *The Garden Island*. His body had washed up and been caught in the rocks on Makahuena Point, where it had been found by some local surf fishermen. The story said nothing about suicide but did say he was wearing his driver's license in a waterproof bag around his neck and that his wife had recently died.

"We can go home now," Kane said when he finished the article.

Yolanda put down her coffee cup and said, "It is so warm and beautiful here. Let us stay a few more days."

Kane nodded, picked up the phone, and made the travel arrangements. Then he went back to his room and put on his swim trunks, pausing as he did every day to look at the envelope that held the photographs. He left the room and went down to the pool, where he swam, then lay down on a chaise. But instead of sleeping, he thought about the pictures. He couldn't decide what to do with them. They were evidence in a murder, but that was all wrapped up now, or at least as wrapped up as it was going to get, and there would never be a trial. He should destroy them. All they'd do now is cause problems. So why didn't he? He knew why. He was wrestling with himself over whether he should look at them.

What good would it do? he asked himself. What difference would it make?

The next couple of days were more of the same. Kane spent a lot of the time asleep and the rest of it eating, swimming, and talking to Yolanda. On their last night in the islands, after getting ready for dinner, he sat on the bed and took the envelope in his hand.

"Who am I kidding?" he said aloud. "I have to know. I always have to know."

He undid the clasp and slid the photographs onto the bed. Laurie's was the third one in the pile. She stood, glistening with sweat, her short hair like a dark haystack. On her face was a grin that Kane had thought only he saw. Her right hand was pointing at the camera and her left down at the slight bulge in her abdomen.

Kane's stomach climbed up his throat. He barely made it to the bathroom before throwing up. When he was finished, he went back into the bedroom. He separated Laurie's pictures from the others. Then he pulled the wastebasket over and tore the other photos into small pieces without looking at them. He put Laurie's back in the envelope, took the plastic bag out of the wastebasket, and rode the elevator to the ground floor. He dropped the bag into a trash can and walked to the bar. It was a beautiful bar, all wooden walls and brass fixtures, and almost empty. He took a stool. The bartender put a bowl of snack mix in front of him and stood there expectantly.

"Jameson. Neat," Kane said. "Make it a double."

The bartender put the drink on a cloth coaster. Kane handed him some bills and waved off the change. The bartender went away. Kane sat looking at the soft amber liquid, imagining how it would feel going down, the first of many. He wasn't sure how long he sat there. He reached for the glass a couple of times but brought himself up short. He thought about himself and about Laurie and about Dylan.

"Are you going to drink that?" Yolanda asked.

He looked up and she was standing next to him in a floral outfit, a spiky white flower in her hair.

"A lady gave me this in the elevator," she said, patting the flower. "It is a Queen Emma lily. Is it not beautiful?"

She is so happy over such a small thing, he thought. That's why I brought her.

"I am not going to drink this," Kane said. "Shall we go?"

Yolanda turned and started walking out of the bar.

"Not yet," Kane said softly to himself as he got to his feet, leaving the drink where it sat. "Not yet."